"Jack Fuller's new novel, *The Best of Jackson Payne,* will become the standard against which jazz novels are measured. . . . Like a jazz soloist, Fuller knows just how long to hold a note or repeat a riff to create tension. When Fuller describes Payne's playing, the writing soars."
—Eric Miles Williamson, *San Francisco Chronicle*

"Quite simply, one of the best novels I've ever read. In an ensemble of voices as sweet and smooth as jazz, Jack Fuller reveals lasting truths about America, music, race, addiction, the process of art, and the oneness of things. Fuller has written an American classic."
—Robert Olen Butler

"There are so many themes within themes, contrapuntal echoes, and multiple voicings in this dizzyingly brilliant novel that the reader emerges from it, as from a John Coltrane solo, overwhelmed . . . ."
—Bill Ott, *Booklist*

"Syncopated, wily and attitudinal, Jack Fuller's new novel . . . is as jazzy as its subject matter."
—Diana Abu-Jaber, *The Oregonian*

"Full of wit and grit and sizzle, Jack Fuller's latest book is a thrilling blend of murder mystery, musicology, and Americana. *The Best of Jackson Payne* is a jazz chronicle of a death foretold."
—Henry Louis Gates, Jr.

"A tour de force. The subject is jazz music, but the ambience is equal parts Dostoyevsky and Nelson Algren. Everyone knows that the blues will break your heart; and that is what this novel does."
—Ward Just

"Charles Quinlan, the storyteller-within-the-story of Jack Fuller's new novel, is biographer whose quest makes him lose his grip on his life. Quinlan is a musicologist reconstructing the rise and fall of a rare jazz talent, Jackson Payne, a man whose meteoric crash ended in the wreckage of drugs. The saxophonist's odyssey is like a kaleidoscope of the music and the sometimes jagged edges of jazz life. . . ."
—Jason Berry, *The Chicago Tribune*

"Jack Fuller's writing about jazz is the most vivid and inspired that I've encountered in fiction. I was also deeply impressed by the book's own 'jazz'—its multitude of voices, and the seamless progression of the arguments and answers they exchange about the concerns that define Jackson Payne: music and passion and race. Slowly and fatefully this novel surrounds and, finally, beautifully captures an enigmatic life."
—Scott Turow

"Transposition, call and response. Music, and jazz in particular, Fuller is saying, give our tone-deaf, race-befuddled nation perfect metaphors for the peculiar relation of musician and listener, player and writer, user and used-up, black and white, Payne and Quinlan."
—Jonathan Levi, *Los Angeles Times*

the
best of
jackson
payne

also by jack fuller

NOVELS
Convergence
Fragments
Mass
Our Fathers' Shadows
Legends' End

NONFICTION
News Values

the best of jackson payne

a novel by jack fuller

the university of chicago press

Published by arrangement with Alfred A. Knopf, a division of Random House, Inc.

The University of Chicago Press, Chicago 60637
Copyright © 2000 by Jack Fuller
All rights reserved. Originally published as a Borzoi Book by Alfred A. Knopf in 2000
University of Chicago Press edition 2001
Grateful acknowledgment is made to Alfred A. Knopf, a division of Random House,
Inc., for permission to reprint an excerpt from "Dear Lovely Death" from Collected
Poems by Langston Hughes, copyright © 1994 by the Estate of Langston Hughes.

Printed in the United States of America
09 08 07 06 05 04 03 02 01   1 2 3 4 5

Library of Congress Cataloging-in-Publication Data

Fuller, Jack.
    The best of Jackson Payne : a novel / by Jack Fuller—University of Chicago
Press ed.
        p.   cm. — (Phoenix fiction)
    ISBN 0-226-26868-3 (alk. paper)
    1. African American musicians—Fiction.   2. African American men—Fiction.
3. Jazz musicians—Fiction.   4. Saxophonists—Fiction.   5. Chicago (Ill.)—
Fiction.   I. Title.   II. Series.

PS3556.U44 B47   2001
813'.54—dc21   2001027512

for Alyce

What one's imagination makes of other people is dictated, of course, by the laws of one's own personality, and it is one of the ironies of black-white relations that, by means of what the white man imagines the black man to be, the black man is enabled to know who the white man is.

—JAMES BALDWIN

". . . it's not your fault you couldn't write what I myself can't blow."

—JULIO CORTÁZAR

contents

one
taps

A toot
A toot
A toot diddle ah da toot

"BOOGIE WOOGIE BUGLE BOY,"
BY DON RICE AND HUGH PRINCE

1.

The first time I heard Jackson play, he was doing "Taps" on the E-flat alto saxophone. It wasn't his natural instrument, but the way he played it could have raised the dead.

Behind him the drummer didn't have but a pair of marching sticks and a raggedy old practice pad. And the piano in the colored Service Club was so funky you couldn't tell where in Hell the man at the keyboard was trying to take the chords. But Jackson was in a groove, and we were right there with him. The 11th Boogie Woogie Infantry, smack in the middle of redneck Georgia, getting ready for war.

Only a few minutes before I'd been lying up in my bunk, with Jackson sitting on his footlocker, a butt in his mouth, shining up some brass. Then all of a sudden I heard the sound of the blues coming across the company square.

"Ain't bad," I said.

He didn't say it was or wasn't, but he did go with me to have a look.

The Service Club was sorry, no matter how much crepe paper the ladies from the local AME hung from the rafters. I stopped at the punch bowl for a taste of something sweet, but the brothers had already killed the Kool Aid. All that was left was a little green pool in the bottom with some butts floating in it.

The tables were pushed back and the chairs were in a basic straggle formation around the piano. Next to it a guy on an alto saxophone was doing something real basic. It wasn't much of a tune, but I noticed Jackson's fingers moving along with it on the buttons of his fatigue blouse.

"You play?" I asked.

"A little," he said.

So, just to make things interesting, I called out: "Somebody here say he can blow that thing better'n you."

"He do, do he?" says the alto player. "Who?"

"It's Payne," I say. "Jackson Payne."

"I know this man?"

All I can think of to answer with is the truth: "Nobody do."

But sure enough, the alto nods Jackson up front and lends him the horn. Then Jackson turns to the piano player and asks do he know "Taps."

And the brothers say: "Man think he got a bugle."

And: "Wake us up come morning, hear?"

The piano player don't look any too sure, so Jackson goes over and picks out a couple of the chords for him. Then he turns back to the crowd, and suddenly he's on the note as sweet as nightfall when the air begins to cool.

Gone the sun. One day over, another to come. Until all your days are done and the tune rises over your flag-draped box and some sweet thing throws the dust then pockets the insurance check. That's what he said on that old horn.

"Well lookee here," say the brothers.

"Talk to me, Jackson Payne."

Then just when it seemed the sun was gone forever, all of a sudden it's Resurrection morning, Jack. You never heard so many notes. It was like he'd inhaled the saxophone and blown it out in a million pieces like stars in the sky.

You know, I always wondered why Jackson never played that tune after Korea, when he got big.

He did at least once.

Say what?

Played it.

How you know a thing like that?

They say somebody sneaked a recorder into the performance.

I'd've given my one good leg.

5

If I ever locate the tape, I'll make a copy for you.

Where'm I gone play it in this shithole here?

Wardell Flowers, so animated only a few moments ago, now slumped in his wheelchair in the VA room equipped with nothing but an auto parts calendar and an old AM radio. His face, which had darkened to health with the telling of his tale, now seemed as gray as ash.

There's another cut I'll send. It's from Art Pepper's album recorded live at the Village Vanguard years later. He quotes Payne at the end of a tune called "Goodbye." Payne was already dead by then and Pepper wasn't long for the world himself. Day is done. It was like he was telling Payne he'd see him somewhere soon.

Art Pepper was a fucking racist.

Not his music.

You a regular expert, ain't you, the man in the wheelchair said.

•

The expert had two Nakamichi decks for dubbing, plus a cheap portable cabled to a foot pedal to make it easier to do transcriptions. Quinlan touched his toe to the switch until the tape paused. Then he got out from behind his desk and cued up a pirated recording of Payne doing "Skylark." For a moment he regarded the silence around him, how rare and precious it had been when the kids were still with him. There was a precise color of sound for every emotion, but silence was invisible, was loss.

He hit the PLAY button and waited until the leader ran out and the first tones came over the speakers. Then he adjusted the volume and bass. He had worked hard to build his collection of Payne's oeuvre. In this he had been supported by a number of grants (and at the expense of countless trivialities his ex had wanted for herself and the kids). But discography was not his field, except as an adjunct to the biography, for which he had received, in addition to the Guggenheim, a decent advance.

Among his colleagues, of course, there was a raging debate over whether the music and the life had anything to say about one another. But by listening to Payne play, Quinlan felt sure he was able to divine things about the man that simply could not otherwise be known, because jazz gave the listener privileged and immediate access to the inner state of the man playing it. Perhaps the truths this revealed did not meet the standards of scholarly proof. But hearing the scratchy, raw-edged recording, he pushed beyond the epistemological borders of the aca-

demic form, opened himself to leaps of improvisation, turned his own
work into jazz.

•

The reed was soft with the alto player's spit, the brass at his
fingertips rough with corrosion patterned to another man's hands. The
mouthpiece between his teeth was tiny compared to the tenor's, more
sensitive to a burst of breath or the quick flick of the tongue. A tenor
was built, like a siren, to carry; an alto was for flight.

He showed the piano player the chords and gave instructions
about the break. As he blew the first line of the tune, Payne turned back
to the crowd, eyes open, gazing out at the men with whom it might fall
to him to die. *Day is done.* The second phrase repeated the first, but differently, the way you might live your life over again: better, not holding
anything back. *Gone the sun.* When he paused to breathe, it was as if
every man in the room breathed with him.

•

It would be good to say right here whose faces his eyes lighted
on. That was determinable, wasn't it? There were rosters somewhere.
Wardell Flowers, of course, had been right up front that night. His voice
on the tape was proof enough. But who else heard Jackson Payne sing
their future like a tribal bard?

•

Wardell Flowers's burnt orange face under the dusky overheads
caught Payne's eye as he gave each note a spirit as individual as the
men whose fate he mourned. *God is nigh.* Payne closed his eyes and
fought the reed, fought to make it speak of the bonds and burdens of
race, the squalor of barracks and city block, the loneliness of a man
among men.

Then as the last note of the chorus began to fade, the piano player
jumped the tempo. After a measure of groping, the drummer ticked off
a fast, steady four. The chord changes, which during the rubato had lain
there for the taking, now came at Payne like tracer rounds.

He glided over them. He swooped. It was maybe half what he
was able to do on the tenor, but the shouts from the audience told him it
was enough. He was preaching hellfire, and they gave it back to him
like the praise of the Lord.

The piano player was struggling, but suddenly Payne heard something from the out-of-tune upright—quarter-tone intervals no well-

tempered keyboard could reach. For a moment the chords were out there beyond Bud or Monk or anybody. Payne picked up on them, pulling his melody clear off the scale to the place where all music began in the *gliss* of the single human voice.

Then he tried to take it out a klick or two more and lost it. The sound went empty, and all he could do was grab onto some old, thoughtless riffs that offered themselves like barroom women to his hands.

•

No, that was what happened on "Skylark" on the tape machine, its final chorus fumbling back to basic bop. There was no way of knowing what had happened on "Taps" that night in the Service Club. The cassette ran out. Payne removed the reed from his mouth and licked the spit from his lips. Quinlan slipped the tape of Flowers into the other recorder and touched his toe to the switch to turn it on.

•

After "Taps" he played standards—"How High the Moon," "Bewitched," "Body and Soul"—you know, anything the piano could figure out. Some fool even asked did Jackson know "I'm Getting Sentimental over You," like it was some kind of ofay lounge. But Jackson didn't mind. He could make a circle of a square.

We kept him going until the Man came through and chased us out. Then, when everyone else was down and the lights were off, Jackson and me sat on the barracks steps and had us a smoke.

I told him he played righteous enough to blow himself right out of the infantry altogether.

"The band, Jackson," I said. "The Army band."

"The horn ain't even mine," he said.

"One thing Sam's got in abundance," I said, "is brass."

Jackson took a draw on his cigarette, snapped it away, then spit over the edge of the stairs.

"Would you go with me to talk to Top?" he said.

I don't know why, but I said I would.

Now in those days the Army provided certain opportunities to a Negro who had the brains to do what he was told. The officers, of course, were white, and they needed somebody to live in close to the troops, a man who wouldn't forget who he was and where. So when I took Jackson to the orderly room the next morning and started telling Top about his talent, I'm sure all Top could see was trouble.

"What is it, Payne?" he said. "You too damned good to carry a rifle?"

"It ain't what he's too good to do, Top," I said. "It's what he's too good *not* to."

At this point I noticed the company clerk at his desk hiding behind the morning reports and trying to stifle a laugh.

"Something funny?" said Top.

"Feeling a little sick today, Top," said the clerk, clearing his throat. "Got a catarrh."

"Come into my office," Top said, pointing Jackson and me to a little supply closet.

On the shelves were boxes of blank disposition forms, spare rations, miscellaneous scrounge, and a helmet liner with master sergeant stripes painted on it in yellow.

"In case you ladies didn't notice," he said, leaning up against the shelves as straight as a rifle barrel, "this here regiment ain't like the others. We're unique."

At this point Jackson was beginning to look pretty uncomfortable, squeezed into that little closet with Top and me.

"I'm right there with you, Top," I said.

"We're self-contained," he said.

He drew the word out then bit it off. It was pure color Top was talking. I swear if somebody white'd been there, they would've brought him up on charges.

"You're speaking about something else entirely now, Top," I said. "I want to stick with what Jackson Payne can do best. For the Army. Best for the Army, Top. You see my point?"

"What are you then, Flowers? His Jew?"

"I ain't a churchgoing man, Top," I said. We already had one too many colors going here without dealing in shades of white.

"I'll put it to you straight," said Top. "They don't take Jackson Paynes into military bands in Georgia."

If it wasn't religion, it was geography. Something was steady getting in the way of the music.

"How about just showing the Man what he can do?" I said. "You told us that was why we been busting ass—to prove we can give better than we get."

I was about ready to make Jackson into the Booker T. Washington of the saxophone when Top turned to him.

"You ready to have them laugh you right out of the practice barracks, son?" Top said.

"I guess I am," said Jackson.

"If you do manage to get over, you'll be all by your lonesome. They may take one, but you know they ain't gone take two."

"I know it, Top."

"If you're lucky, they'll polite you to death."

"Tell it, Top," I said, like Sunday morning.

"You gone be as alone as any man ever drew a breath." Then Top stood up tall and shook his head against what he said. "I'll set it up for you."

I let out a whoop.

"What you doing this for me for?" Jackson said.

Top went to the window at the back of the little room and lifted his chin toward the Service Club across the yard.

"Last night," he said, "I heard you play."

•

For the next few days Jackson really worked the horn. We had Sunday free, so he had plenty of time to run the scales and limber up his fingers on the keys. During breaks he worked on getting the borrowed alto in shape, softening the pads with linseed oil applied with a Q-tip, lubricating the tiny brass pivots, tightening little screws with the point of a fingernail file to get just the right tension.

It wasn't until the morning of the audition, after the company had gone out to the range and Jackson and I were lounging around the barracks, that it hit me what we'd forgotten.

"You know how to blow that horn while you're on the move?" I asked him.

In the club he just stood there dead center, all six-foot-whatever of him, his ax straight down his gig line like it was hooked to the buttons. Well, I sure God wasn't going to let some shit like marching keep him from getting over, so for the hour we had left, I put him through a drill on the dusty company street. Didn't take long before he got the hang of it. He even worked up a piece of business with the horn, flashing it back and forth against the beat as he marched, like a white idea of swing.

"You trying to look like them?" I asked.

"Maybe they trying to look like us," he said.

Even back in those days it wasn't easy to keep track.

The band HQ was in a piss-yellow building just like all the others. We had a hard time finding it at first because none of the rednecks we ran into seemed the kind you'd want to ask. Luckily, somebody was inside working scales on the trombone and we followed the sound.

I was nervous. And when I saw the band director, it didn't exactly settle me down. He was a big tech sergeant of a color more red than white, like he'd already built up a head of steam.

"This here is Jackson Payne," I said.

"The one and only," said the band sergeant. "I wasn't expecting two."

"I'm Wardell Flowers."

"What do you play?"

For a second the thought crossed my mind that maybe I could say triangle or cymbals or something and find a ticket out the infantry myself.

"I'm just along to keep him company," I said.

The back of the squad bay was set up with a half-moon of folding chairs and rickety music stands.

"Meet Jackson Payne and his bodyguard," the band sergeant told the trombone player.

The trombone player stuck out his hand.

"Billy Roderick," he said. "That your alto in the case?"

"Borrowed it," said Jackson. "Tenor's my natural horn."

"Double threat," said the trombone player, lifting his eyebrows to the band sergeant. "You do dance music?"

"A little," said Jackson, with the grin.

"We got a group," said the trombone player. "We're light on reeds."

"Not so fast, Billy," said the band sergeant. "He's got to show me something first. Why don't you direct his bodyguard to the PX while Private Payne and me go through the routine."

"Jackson don't mind me being here," I said.

"I do," said the band sergeant with more behind it than rank.

So I gave Jackson a thumbs-up and followed the trombone player out the door. Before we got very far we heard Jackson warming up on scales and then launching into "Cherokee."

"Your friend knows his way around the horn," said the trombone player.

"Pretty good duty playing in the band?" I asked.

"Has its moments," he said. "You're from the colored unit, right?"

"By the looks of it," I said.

"Be a little careful around here, OK?" he said when we reached the PX. "Lots of Georgia boys about."

I didn't wait around the PX to make the acquaintance of any. I just bought a candy bar and a Coca-Cola and walked back toward the band barracks so I could get a listen to how it was going. But before I got there, out came Jackson.

"That didn't take long," I said.

"I didn't make it," he said, brushing past me.

I grabbed at his fatigue blouse to slow him down.

"He knew your color going in," I said.

"That wasn't it," Jackson said.

"Hell it wasn't, fool."

I let him go and he took a couple steps more then stopped.

"He asked me did I read music."

"Good as you are, you could learn just like that."

"A man don't need to read, if he can hear."

2.

No matter how far out a player was willing to go, there were always limits. Without structure, his sound turned into noise; too much and it became the manacled march of slaves. Freedom and constraint. A man singing out in chains was the origin of jazz. Every player felt the weight of the changes that linked together beneath a song, felt them like keys under his fingers, as solid as ebony or ivory.

•

At first the men in Payne's unit lifted up when they heard that the all-black 24th Infantry Regiment had achieved what *Time* magazine called "the first sizable American ground victory in Korea." But then a black battalion broke and ran west of Sangju. And even though the American infantry all over the bloody peninsula was having difficulty holding the line, the 24th was singled out. The Army went so far as to court-martial one of the unit's few black officers for deserting his position. He would have been executed if Truman hadn't said no. As Payne's outfit marched among the Caucasians in the bitter dust of Fort Benning, preparing to do battle with Orientals, the men must have remembered the sad old song they first heard at their mothers' breasts: There are three races in this world, and none that loves you half enough.

But for Payne there were other songs. By 1950 a defiant new sound had made a triumphant march up the island of Manhattan and then spread out to the territories. Bebop. Cats would call a standard in F-sharp or some other unplayable key, just to see who was good enough. Many simply gave up, saying, "This music's too black for me." They were not speaking of skin color; they referred to the forbidding look of all those sixteenth notes and accidentals on the staff. Payne had first heard this music live at the Yes Yes Club on the South Side where you found cats like Gene Ammons, in town with the Eckstine band, sitting out the strippers to get a listen to some hot new trumpet playing in the pit. Eventually it forced its way onto the radio, which carried it everywhere, like windblown seed. Even at Fort Benning, Georgia, a person might have tuned in to Rudy Vallee and heard the call of Bird.

In order to escape the war a younger musician had to have come of age, like Miles, during the brief window of peace. Or else he had to hop himself up on coffee and Benzedrine inhalers before his physical until his heart leaped like Dizzy's "Oop Pop A Da." The only other alternative was to play the role and hope you'd seem, like Bud and Thelonious, just too dark for olive drab.

He'd also heard about older cats who had followed a different chart. John Lewis and Kenny Clarke had gone ashore at Normandy. Then there was Lester Young. Drafted in '44, he only served fifteen months before they busted him. His playing suffered during his time in the detention barracks, but at least he came out with one decent tune, "D. B. Blues."

So when the time came, Payne put his horn in hock, gave his records to the guys he'd played with, and got aboard the bus with nothing to his name but a small roll of bills and a change of clothes in a sack.

•

I would've taught Jackson how to read if he'd've let me.

Do you remember who else was there the first time you heard him play?

Where?

In the Service Club.

The guys. I don't know.

Names, Johnny. I'm looking for names.

All I remember is how he handed the alto back to me to take a solo after him. It was like being on a ledge a hundred stories in the air.

You played with him that night?

Marked me all the rest of my life as the guy who jammed with Jackson Payne, the guy who beat him out for the Army band.

Tell me about that.

One man gets lucky, another gets killed. How the hell do I know why. After the band sergeant heard Jackson, he called up Top and asked did he have any other colored boys with a gift.

I was able to sight-read, and I got around the horn as well as the men the band sergeant was used to. So I got the job. And the Army was good to me. Things were just beginning to loosen up about then. Put me through school. Gave me some rank and eventually my own band.

Ever feel guilty about it?

Somebody got trouble with my skin color, it's their problem, not mine.

I mean about Payne going to Korea in your place.

I did my time. And now I got me a wall of trophies from the contests my kids here at Attucks High have won. We always do one of Jackson's tunes at the jazz competitions. It's sort of a trademark with me, and the judges eat it up.

So you never looked back.

Whenever I try out a guy, if he has talent but can't read a chart, I teach him, just like I could've taught Jackson Payne.

•

Wardell Flowers. Johnny Dart. Jackson Payne. Sure, I remember them. You ask any man who ever served under me and he'll tell you a soldier's a soldier as far as old Top is concerned. Long as they got arms and legs that move and eyes that see. A dick is optional equipment. If I can't get 'em to move when I say, they gone lose it anyway. Stop fiddle-fucking around with that boom box of yours and listen up, son.

Now you take Payne. I'm not shy about telling a man what I want. But there's some things you can't force. For example, a man's either got leadership in him or he don't. You can see it right away. Payne had it. The way he carried himself. The way others gave ground.

So one day I took him aside and told him I saw potential.

"You been dealt a good hand, son," I said. "Play it right and you'll get some rank."

Now I don't care how little a man cares for the Army, usually anybody who hears that speech comes around to it. But not Payne. I've only known a few like him. There's a hard thing in them that even old Top can't bend. Only a fool would try. Best you can do is get some use of it. That's why, when Payne didn't make the band, I asked him could he sing.

"I been bothering somebody?"

"Bother me if you don't do what I tell you to," I said. "You don't want to bother me, do you, Private Payne?"

Payne, he was smiling now. Straight out of that hard thing.

"What kind of music you dig, Top?" he said.

"See this ear?" I said. "Made of solid brass. Any damn thing gone make it ring."

At this point the smile on his face took on a funny shine.

"My songs ain't got no words," he said.

"Then what the hell do they have?"

Before I knew it, he was off into this boop-be-doop shit like nothing you ever heard in your life.

Oh, I've heard it all right.

What's that, son?

Scat.

Who you telling to scat, boy?

Scat singing. That's what Payne was doing. Improvising with his voice. Just like he did on his horn. Making it up as he went.

Well, whatever it was, it had a lot of movement to it. So I told him I wanted him to be my company guidon.

Guidon?
The trooper who carries the unit flag and calls the cadence.

> I got a girl all dressed in red
> Hope she'll miss me when I'm dead.

You should've heard him. Joshua at Jericho. If I'd've wanted to, I could've marched my chocolate soldiers to the gates of Hell.

•

Top got that right. Everybody dug Jackson's rhythm. It was like an Afro-Cuban band, with ten different things going all at once, except this was just one man.

"Where do you go when you're not singing?" I asked him once.

"You see me, Wardell," he said. "I'm right there."

"Are and ain't."

"I'm just counting."

"Counting?"

"Three against four. Five against six. Different things."

"Why?"

"One. Two. One two three four," he said.

•

Staff Sergeant Ray Staggers had lived in a world totally separate from the men of the 3/11th—different NCO clubs, different hangouts in town, different family quarters, different promotion lists because of the restricted movement across the color line. Eventually Quinlan learned the name of an Arkansas trailer park where Staggers was supposed to be drawing his pension checks on the shores of what the proprietor called a scenic lake.

To get there Quinlan had to fly from Chicago to Little Rock then rent a car. As he drove down the dusty gravel path inside the park, he smelled the water before he came up over a rise and saw it surrounded by trailers that had to be chocked up on one end to keep them from sliding in. Staggers's was a silver Airflow. Through the screen door came a raspy radio tuned to country. Staggers's wife was much younger than she should have been. All the band sergeant was able to remember was Johnny Dart.

"Good player. Bad attitude. Went on to have a band of his own. Army always pushed the colored ahead."

As to Jackson Payne, Staggers came up blank, even when Quinlan told him how Payne had gone on to have a band of his own, too.

"Good for him. The colored got it in them natural. Have a beer?"

Payne was probably the first black player to be considered for the Benning band, Quinlan said. Surely there must have been a lot of discussion. Think.

"A little sour mash then?"

Quinlan pulled out the photographs. They did not refresh Staggers's memory, but they drew the woman away from the radio. Seeing Payne often had that kind of effect.

"The black one in trouble?" she said.

"Not at all, ma'am. He was a great musician and I'm writing his biography. He auditioned for your husband's band once."

"Keep tryin', honey," she said. "He recalls more than he lets on."

The band sergeant was pouring himself a couple of fingers in a striped, plastic glass.

"It was summer, Mr. Staggers," Quinlan said. "Sun beating down. You were in the band barracks with a trombone player. The top sergeant of Bravo Company 3/11th had called."

"The colored unit."

"That's right. He said he had a hot sax player he wanted you to hear."

"Were you there?"

"The sax came with a friend who did all the talking. You sent the friend away."

"It's a real personal thing, testing a man on a horn."

"First he played something he had picked."

"I always let them do that to give them a chance to show off. It relaxes them."

"It was 'Cherokee.' He played it very fast."

"The colored love to hot dog."

"Then you gave him something to read."

" 'El Capitán.' "

"You do remember."

"I always used the Sousa. Got sick of it, if you want to know."

"Payne couldn't read the part."

"That tells you something," Staggers said.

two
stormin'
at the
point

Warm as May wine,
Wild as the sea . . .

"ALL THE TIME,"
BY JAY LIVINGSTON
AND RAY EVANS

1.

You been had, dad. By Jackson's jungle genius jive.

Red Sloan put his hands on the piano keys and struck a simple seventh chord.

> Man never gave that shit to me.
> He knew he didn't dare.
> 'Cause I knew all about it.
> Old Red was always there.

The band sergeant was persuaded he couldn't read a note.

Jackson persuaded a lot of folks. Up on the stand he had a way that made you think he was feeling things real deep, when all he was thinking about was how to move from the key of F to the key of B. Maybe if I'd've picked up some of his attitude, I wouldn't't've been stuck in this dump doing three-chord blues all the days of my life.

> But I'm not moaning.
> He paid for what he got.
> I just don't like faking,
> Making him what he's not.

Maybe he couldn't read the alto part because he'd learned on the tenor.

Shit, I've seen him play off a piano chart, transposing it on the spot. I think he could have read a score backward if he had wanted to.

He used to practice all the time. Carried his music around in an old canvas satchel. Sometimes during breaks I'd find him out in the alley under a dim old lightbulb, his charts spread out on a garbage can lid, running through the scales in six sharps or seven flats like he was trying out for the symphony. Or we'd work 'til one or two in some blind pig then go out for another couple hours to jam. Next day I'd go looking for him, and they'd tell me he got up early to go down to the Loop and blow on the street corner. And when he picked up a few bucks, he'd walk to Carl Fischer and buy more things to practice on. Read music? Only whenever his eyes was open was all.

But he never did like to let on how hard he studied. I don't fault him. The white audience didn't want to think of us working through the permutations on an E-flat seventh with a flatted ninth. They wanted it straight from the soul, not the higher centers of math. Don't forget the real reason Miles turned his back on the audience: so they wouldn't see him thinking. He'd been to Juilliard. If he didn't show them an attitude, they'd have eaten him alive. Follow this primitive idea, motherfucker.

Look, I've got to get back to work. But let me give you one tip about Jackson Payne. Don't believe a word he said about himself. Just listen to what he tells you on his horn.

•

It did not take much detective work to start separating the reality of Jackson Payne's childhood in Chicago from the tales. Payne's father, for example, did not die in a gang war, as Jackson often told interviewers. He was shot in bed with another man's wife. Payne was only six months old at the time and his first memory was of the man Ella married afterward, Sam Payne.

By all accounts Sam Payne was a good, steady sort, a jitney driver who put in the hours and brought home what he earned. When he wasn't working and the weather was fair, you could find him out on the front stoop of the apartment in a snap-brim hat and sleeveless shirt, making Ella the envy of all her friends.

After they were married, he promptly went downtown and formally adopted Jackson. The papers are there in the circuit court files, complete with the tiny thumbprint of the baby and Sam's strong, simple signature on the line.

The family lived in a three-flat that had not yet been cut up by the slumlords. Payne used it on the cover of his album, *Third Floor Rear,* though by the time the picture was taken, the neighborhood had gone way down. Several of the titles on the album referred to things Payne grew up with. "Maxie" was the name of the grocer's spaniel, which Payne and his half sisters loved to play with. "Stormin' at the Point" referred to Payne's favorite place on the lakefront. And the lilting waltz called "The Mayor of Lake Park" took as its title the phrase folks used to describe Sam Payne.

In many respects Jackson's childhood was graced by fortune. His family was spared serious illness. Crime passed the household by. Sam and Ella were God-fearing folks who dressed their children all in white each Sunday and promenaded with them to Ebenezer Baptist, where Rev. Elijah Corn was so stirring that a squad of ladies with Red Cross armbands always stood by to minister to anyone overcome by the spirit. Jackson never wanted for food or a room to call his own. As his half-sister Charnette remembered it, he liked to keep his own company there. Wouldn't make a good jitney driver, Sam Payne said, because folks want a little palaver for their fare. Too bad driving wasn't work for the ladies, he said, 'cause those girls could talk a man right back to Africa. Um, um, um.

Ella was quick to recognize Payne's musical talent when she heard him playing along to Benny Goodman on an old Marine Band harmonica. She put aside money until she could buy him an instrument for his twelfth birthday, a tenor saxophone, because that was all the pawnshop had. It was so big that he had to rest the crook of it on a foot-stool when he sat down to play.

The first sounds he brought forth were nothing more than squawks. His mama covered her ears with her big, wash-hardened hands.

"God of mercy, boy. It's supposed to sound sweet."

"It will," he said. Then he lifted the mouthpiece to his lips, bit down on the dry reed, and let out another honk.

"Don't you be doing that when your daddy's home," Ella said, "or we both be in hot water sure."

"You won't be sorry for what you done," Jackson said.

He blew again and the buzzing of the reed reminded him of Dr. Hayes's foot-pedal dental drill.

"I been sorry before," Ella said.

He experimented all afternoon. After supper he left his mama in the kitchen trying to explain her purchase to her husband while he took the footstool and a chair out behind the apartment. The open air invited him to blow with all his breath. And by the time the rags and old iron man came calling in the alley at dusk, Jackson was able to answer him note for note.

Unfortunately, the purchase of the horn left nothing to pay for lessons. But Ella had already been talking to the pastor about taking on Jackson for instruction at church.

Rev. Elijah Corn was an accomplished piano player with a fondness for the Romantics and a manner that made you think his tastes came directly from God.

"Show him what you can do, Jackson," Ella said.

They stood at the front of the chapel near the choir loft, and the sound Payne got out of his horn was bigger than the most full-throated of the pastor's contraltos. Payne played the only thing in his repertoire that his mother thought was appropriate, "Wade in the Water." The way he did it was all mud and roil.

When he was finished, Rev. Corn said, "I'll expect him to give up this crude instrument."

"Mama!"

"Hush now, boy," Ella said.

"A child is like a plant," said the preacher. "To be straight he needs to rise to a single light."

"Then you'll help him," said Ella.

"I shall see whether he has the spirit," said the Rev. Elijah Corn.

At his first session Payne immediately made the connection between the spots on the lines on the page and the tones he played on the keyboard or in the alley under the waning sun. He went to church every day and practiced the piano for hours—scales, arpeggios, and canons to gain the independence of the fingers. The demands of music left little free time for play. He did not care whether the other boys in the neighborhood taunted him for not hanging around idle until mischief came his way. He preferred to be in the company of his horn.

This discipline impressed Sam Payne. But his basic beliefs were shaped by the things he saw every night through the windshield of his cab: the kind of people who went in and out of the nightclubs where they played the music Payne was drawn to, zoot-suit pimps and high-heeled women, all manner of dealers and their marks.

In return for his lessons, Payne had to sing in Rev. Corn's choir. Practice was one night a week, and then there were the two services Sunday morning, during which Rev. Corn's preaching seemed to pass judgment on everything that was going through Payne's head.

This reached its greatest pitch when the preacher delivered his once-a-year sermon, "The Song of Satan." Along with Good Friday, when he led the congregation in acting out the final sufferings of Christ, it was a high point on the congregation's calendar, and at least once it was even broadcast on the radio.

Rev. Corn would rise to the pulpit on waves of music. When the last chord faded and the final yelp of joy from the pews settled down, he would lift his hands to Heaven, his words booming out past the folding chairs in the overflow rows.

Ah, such mighty music, brothers and sisters. The majesty of voices joined in song.

Tell it, brother.

It knows the way to reach our deepest places and restore our souls.

Yes, Lord.

But the Devil knows, too.

Lord have mercy.

Oh, he is cunning, brothers and sisters. I have seen him in the lovely face of a woman. I have heard him in a man's sweet song.

Amen.

He lurks in the fruits of the soil, the work of human hands. Even the wine that is Christ's sweet blood goes sour on the drunken tongue.

Have mercy, Lord.

Do you believe that our songs can be pure enough to drive him away?

No, Lord. No.

He is in the instruments we raise up in exaltation. He is in our voices. Turn on the radio and you will hear him, for he is in the very air.

Save us, Lord.

But the Lord is there, too.

Hallelujah.

Listen.

At this point Deacon Turner at the piano struck a chord, nothing far out, a minor seventh, then skimmed a chromatic scale off the top, pulling his stool back as he did, as if the keyboard were aflame.

There are twelve tones in the good Lord's scale, brothers and sisters. Twelve apostles to show the way.

Hallelujah.

But before you sing it, there's something you got to know.

Tell us, brother.

Satan's scale is exactly the same.

Save us.

Have mercy.

Amen.

Close your ears to the Devil's melody, my friends. And open your hearts to the Lord.

Tell us how.

The first note of the scale is C, the Christ child come down to redeem us from our sin.

Hallelujah.

But C is also the cross where they nailed Him. There has never been an evil greater than C.

Save us, brother.

And next to it is D, which can be delightful, for it is the dawn of eternal life.

Hallelujah.

But it is also damnation, waiting with the Devil's hundred fires.

Lord, have mercy.

And E is everlasting peace, an eternity of glory in the good Lord's loving eye.

Amen.

But it is also the evil in man's lustful ways.

Save us, Lord. The women's voices dominated this time, for they knew about men's lust deeply, down where pleasure was taken but not returned.

Beware, my sisters. For evil spares not the woman. E is also Eve, mother of Jezebel and all the foul, painted whores of the night.

Thank you, Jesus. The testimony resonated again, well supported in the bass.

F is for frankincense and the other sweet gifts of His birth. But mind you, F is also the fire.

Save us.

And G is glory and the gruesome torments of sin.

Amen, brother.

A is adulation and adultery, the voice of praise and the fleeting glance of shame.

Show us, Lord.

And B completes the circle, brothers and sisters. B is the blood Christ shed. But don't be boasting. Don't be blind. For B is what befalls us when we fail Him. B is Beelzebub. B is to burn.

Praise the Lord.

Amen.

The sharps are the stars of Heaven, the points of the nails that fixed our Lord Jesus to the cross. And the flats are the wafers He makes His body, the silver pieces for which He was sold.

Tell it, brother.

The treble clef is the Trinity, the trident of Satan that pierces unholy flesh. And each note on the staff of life is also the staff of punishment. Each note is a wound.

Hallelujah, Lord.

Lift up your hearts!

We lifting, brother.

The Lord's voice is sweet. And the songs He sings are psalms.

Hallelujah.

They may inflame you.

We burning, Lord.

They may make you dance and wail.

Wail away, brother. You be wailing now.

But they will not drag you down.

Amen.

Raise up your voices!

Hallelujah!

Drown out Satan's music.

Praise the Lord.

For Heaven is the melody, and glory the words of His song.

The congregation was on its feet now. The preacher's face was glazed with sweat. He nodded to Deacon Turner, who began to play. The ladies in the front row of the choir lifted their tambourines and began to strike and shake. From behind, Payne watched the folds of their robes quiver like flesh.

Sing out to the Lord, my brothers and sisters!

The choir led and the congregation followed, swinging as hard as any tune that had ever flown up from the nearby strip of sin on the wings of night. Payne's voice soared out over the multitude as he filled the space inside the melody with plaintive blues turns. He felt for a moment as if he himself were the preacher, moving the congregation as he was moved, in the trinity of singer, audience, and song. He did not know whether it was exaltation or evil, the way the music touched his deepest and most unutterable centers of pleasure. But he did know this: when the music stopped, he wanted to be touched there more.

.

After Quinlan had finished transcribing the last of Rev. Corn's sermon, he started on the brief narrative of what followed. He was due at the faculty club, but he stayed at his computer, composing. Something came to him. He did not know where the next paragraphs would fit. Perhaps in a footnote. Perhaps interlarded in the text. But wherever he put them, they came in a rush that made him think of them as sound.

.

The first important structural principle of jazz is call and response. One can hear it in many different manifestations. The most obvious is when players "trade fours," that is, alternate four measure solos, each responding to the statement made by the previous player.

Jazz drew this pattern from many sources. The gospel tradition, of course. But field recordings of prison work gangs, drill sergeants marching their troops, and auctioneers selling horseflesh all show the structure in its most rudimentary form. It is not too much to imagine that when a slave was traded, it was to the voice of call and response.

.

Ebenezer Church, built when the neighborhood was white, had a spacious robing room in the rear with closets of dark wood and windows that deeply colored the sun. As Payne unsnapped his linen collar and hung up his gown, he felt his shirt sticking to his sweat-drenched flesh. The cool breath of the other singers' passing played across his shoulders like the brush of fingers. He was embarrassed that the mark of his enthusiasm was so much upon him, the more so when he noticed that the sweat stain on his khaki pants was spreading past his belt to his loins.

Down the way Sarah Evans was just lifting the robe off her shoulders. He often rested his eyes on her during the services, studying the soft, dark curve of her neck. Now she turned and stood facing him under the stained light, the whiteness of the elastic binding under her blouse burning against the moist black shadow of her skin.

She caught him watching and turned away, but slowly, giving him witness to all her emerging curves.

"Jackson!"

His mother called through the door without entering. Sarah caught him watching her once more as he made ready. He did not allow himself to test the plain meaning of her smile.

"Hurry up, Mister Man," his mother shouted. "Time for praying's done."

•

Payne did not reveal his spiritual side plainly in his music until the later years, when it took on an incantatory style that seemed to be trying to speak directly to or for some higher power. But there were signs even earlier, if you searched for them, and for Quinlan they were as exciting as they were occult.

It was this search that led him to the tape of Rev. Corn's annual sermon, which turned up in an archive of evangelical radio broadcasts preserved under the auspices of a local Bible institute. And the tape in turn revealed to Quinlan a whole new meaning of the title of Payne's funky masterpiece, "No Greater Evil Than C."

At the time Payne first released that tune on his third album, *Payne and Suffering*, the liner notes referred to it as a "pure Sunday romp." But even in those more innocent days, the cognoscenti agreed that the title had a bitter meaning. They guessed that it referred to cocaine, which reinforced the prevailing myth of life corrupting music.

But now Quinlan was in a position to give a better interpretation. Payne's reference to the sermon seemed to say that the music was not only the victim of corruption but also its means. Understood this way, even the jacket photo took on greater significance—dark and back-lighted to bring out the brooding shadows. Payne's profile dominates, but beside it is the silhouette of the horn, its curved neck and sharp mouthpiece poised, like a snake, to strike.

As he listened to the song, now knowing the context, Quinlan felt again the exhilaration of the privileged access that jazz can give to a creator's soul. The key of the song was B-flat, which put C a major 2nd from the tonic. In a way that prefigured the cabalistic significance with which he later invested such relationships, Payne must have seen the C as the awful duality of his soul. It was as if he were already leaving clues to his death by overdose two decades later. The evidence was there, submerged, in the deepest structure of a song.

2.

Jackson spent so much time at Ebenezer Baptist that some folks in the neighborhood thought he had heard the call. It's a long time ago, you understand. I was still young enough to have an eye, even though I didn't have much time to use it, what with trying to feed my poor, daddyless babies by cleaning the rectory like a common char. A lot of folks didn't think it was proper for an eighteen-year-old girl of high chest and low reputation to be spending so much time around an unmarried man, even if he was a man of the cloth. Men usually found me a looker—which was the first part of my trouble. The other was that I usually found them, too.

Where was the piano?

There was one in the chapel. That was where Rev. Corn usually gave lessons. But with special boys he sometimes also used the one in the rectory. It fit right into that big living room the white folks built. The woodwork was hand-carved, just like the pulpit, crosses and shields and all the bounty of the earth. It was hell to clean.

Did he and Payne play there often?

Mostly it was records. He had hundreds of them. Books, too, and shelves of music. Some of the music was bound in yellow covers, some loose in the files. Mornings after, I'd find it all strewn around, and he'd expect me to put it back right.

•

At first it was glory to do a lesson perfectly on the Reverend's private grand or be caught by him while practicing in the chapel, all dark except for the little lamp over the keys, and then be invited over to the house afterward as a reward. What riches Rev. Corn had, all the songs of the ages, row after row on shelves so high he had to use a ladder to reach the top.

"You have the gift, son," Rev. Corn would say. "We only need to build a channel to let it out."

But the channel that was most ready to hand was unacceptable.

"You know what the beat of that jungle music means?" he said. "It's how the white man thinks of us."

•

Sometimes I'd come past the church after stopping off in one of the clubs and find Jackson just coming out or either sitting blank-eyed on the curb. Now you might think I'm a vain, jealous old bitch, but if you're a char, there are certain things you can't help but see.

I'm talking about picture books, honey. Full of musclemen, bodies all greased up so's it looked like they'd slide right off you. He kept them in a desk drawer upstairs. They got me a little hot. The difference was, everybody knew *my* trouble was men.

•

At first the touch was innocent, no more than the kind of pat his daddy gave him to send him on his way. And at the piano they always kept the interval of master and student, Payne on the bench, Rev. Corn on a folding chair. Only afterward, when they were in the rectory listening to Caruso or Toscanini did the hand linger. And even then the feeling was too weightless to be the Devil's stroke.

•

Don't you believe a word of it. That bitter old whore's got a mouth on her. Jackson was just lucky he had Rev. Corn. He sure didn't get any help from Daddy, because Daddy didn't see music as a way for a black man to get ahead. It got so Charnette and I didn't even want to be around when they started in. Maybe if Daddy'd come right out and said it wasn't the music but the places they played it in. Maybe if he'd talked about what he'd seen happen in those clubs. But a black man has trouble expressing his true feelings. One day he'll rant and rave like a cheated pimp and the next want you to mama him like a child. That's why a black woman's got to be cold and steady as a stone.

•

I'm telling you, that preacher gone and poisoned this man. Once Corn got through with him, Jackson didn't think that anybody could ever do him right.

But there came a day when Jackson walked away from the Reverend and never came back. And that was the day he came to me.

•

Wrong, wrong, wrong. Jackson loved Rev. Corn like a second daddy. It wasn't until he stopped going to church that he started to be wild.

Here, let me show you an album Mama kept. That's me he's holding hands with there. He doesn't look any too happy about it, does he. I have a print of that picture in my book, too. Mama was real meticulous. And these are the measurements that show how much each of us had grown, year by year. Then in the middle here are the report cards, church programs with his name listed, everything.

He was good at math, wasn't he.

He always loved numbers. It was like they took him to an enchanted world.

Do you mind if I use this for a while?

Not at all. You can make any notes you want. I'm going to have to think about the photos. Leticia's got it into her head there will be some value to them down the road.

Back here at the end of the book Mama kept a list of the places Rev. Corn took Jackson. See. Here. The Historical Society. Field Museum. Art Institute. These are the souvenir books he brought home. She was good about recording the dates. She had such a strong, lovely hand.

This is the list of the Grant Park concerts. Mama used to make sandwiches and sweets so they could have a picnic on the lawn. The Reverend treated him like a son, no matter what trash that filthy Butler woman is trying to spread.

•

Quinlan mined the scrapbook for every detail: the grades and teachers' comments, the dates of all childhood diseases, the heights and weights his mother had progressively recorded as he grew into the body of a man.

It took some doing to dig up what he was looking for from the public library's microfilm collection of the *Tribune*. But eventually he found an article about a program at the Grant Park band shell in honor of American fighting men. The concert was the last listed in the scrapbook, the final outing with Rev. Corn. The program included a selection of Sousa marches. *"El Capitán"* had been played that day.

•

Say the first unmistakable sexual advance came in Grant Park that July afternoon. Say the hand crept where it had never gone before. Payne was confused, excited. The blood rose in him, and he did not know why this man should have such an effect on him. The orchestra played a march, and it etched itself into his memory, note by hateful note.

Say he accepted the touch. Was afraid not to. Or perhaps he wanted it, shamed by the thrill he could not separate from the fear.

He wanted to ask someone whether this was something that happened to everybody. But he knew that it was not. This was the thing boys joked about, accused each other of doing. Not the thing they wanted or bragged that they had done.

And so he remained silent and pretended that nothing had happened. Rev. Corn, too, reverted to a decent distance. For some time afterward, whenever they touched it was only so the teacher could guide the student's hands.

Then at some point it happened again. It might have been one of the nights Cassandra Butler found him sitting late on the curb outside the rectory. It was no wonder he became an object of her eye. She must have felt his heat.

•

They had finished at the piano a little later than usual after a particularly good session. Rev. Corn's behavior had been so unthreatening that Payne began to doubt his memory of what had happened. When the preacher suggested they repair to the rectory to listen to some new recordings he had acquired, Payne did not know how to tell him no.

"You seem to be climbing to a new level, Jackson," he said, placing a coffee cup before him and putting his own on the table next to his favorite listening chair.

"Been feeling pretty good about it," Payne said.

Rev. Corn went to the phonograph and threaded a stack of records onto the spindle.

"This is Wagner's *Tristan and Isolde*," he said. "It is about the yearnings and glories of love."

Payne did not recognize the chords, but he wanted to make up harmonies like that himself someday.

"You have deep feelings, don't you, Jackson," said Rev. Corn.

"Sometimes I do."

"Are there girls?" said the preacher. "Don't be ashamed."

"I think about them."

"When you're playing. I mean the music you play on the saxophone."

The question this time was not censorious. And yet still Payne felt that he was being backed into something.

"That don't make it bad," he said.

"Ear to heart and heart to ear," said the preacher. "You don't know what to do about those feelings, do you."

"Put them out of me, I guess."

"Put them through that horn of yours, you mean," said the preacher. Still his tone was indulgent. "I came by one day and stood at the corner of the alley where you were playing."

"All I ever promised was not to take time away from the piano," said Payne.

"There was an awful intensity to it, son," said the preacher.

The Reverend's back was to him now. His voice had gone strange at the end, like he was going to force Payne to choose between his piano lessons and his horn.

"Don't make me go," Payne said.

Rev. Corn abruptly raised the needle and then replaced the records of *Tristan* in their sleeves. Payne saw him take out some others, but he could not tell what they were.

"From time to time we all have strong feelings, son," Rev. Corn said without looking at him as he piled records on the stack.

When he turned around, the machine gave a whir, a record dropped onto the turntable, and the tone arm came down with a pop. Payne knew from the first few notes what it was.

"Coleman Hawkins," Payne said. " 'Body and Soul.' "

"Do you like it?" said the Reverend, moving next to him on the overstuffed couch.

Payne knew the phrasing of the solo by heart. He began to hum along.

"Listen to what he does here," Payne said, his voice grown tremulous, like Hawkins's horn.

Then he felt a hand on his thigh. The second chorus broke, the horns of the band coming in on sustained chords. He was not humming anymore.

"Don't stop, son," said Rev. Corn. "It's all right."

The tenor had come in again under the preacher's words, making a counterpoint, voice with music, hand with voice, rising as Payne rose, shaming him as the feeling grew impossible to deny.

"It captures you, doesn't it," said the preacher, his hand going to the center of all the young man's confusion. "It speaks of something pure."

As the music came to a close, Hawkins reached the edge of frenzy, then let it ebb away. The hand became insistent, and Payne could not resist the sensations it caused in him. He tried to shift away.

"I only want to do for you," Rev. Corn said.

The record changer whirred and clicked, and then the sound of Lester Young came on, faster, less languorous.

"Prez," said Payne.

"Don't leave me," said the preacher.

So Payne let himself lay back into the soft mounds of the couch, closing his eyes to the sounds he understood, the touches he did not. And when it was over, nothing was familiar anymore. Everything had changed.

The needle ticked at the end of the last record, and to Payne it was a metronome. One. Two. One two three four.

The preacher sat hunched over at the other end of the couch, not looking up from the carpet. Payne stood.

"Can I have these?" he asked, touching the records on the spindle.

"Take them," said Rev. Corn. "Take them all."

Payne wiped his hands on his shirt and then picked up the disks and put them in their jackets.

The air outside turned the moist afterspots on Payne's pants cold.

He could not go home yet. He sat down on the curb just out of the streetlight. A woman walked past, but he did not look up even when the musky sweetness of her perfume told him who it was. Otherwise the night street was empty, and Payne was alone.

•

He did return to the preacher. Not that night, but later and often, even after he had dropped out of the choir. The time they spent at the piano in the chapel declined. The time in the rectory increased. There were new jazz recordings each visit. Payne no longer asked whether he could have them. He simply took them when the preacher was finished, the measure of his worth.

3.

At times it seemed to Quinlan like trying to reconstruct a building from its wreckage. He became obsessed with protecting from disturbance the piles of material he had gathered—handwritten notes, transcripts, files of clippings, printouts—lest the whole shaky edifice topple to the ground. He did not let the cleaning ladies anywhere near his desk. During visitation days the room was locked up like a closet full of shameful paraphernalia. This made the kids especially curious, of course. The only time he relented was to show his older son some of the things he had gathered about Payne's war.

The boy was at the age of fascination with combat, and he was deeply disappointed that Quinlan had opted out. Of course, the joke that history played on young men was to prepare them for the last war. So as Quinlan had learned the pointless stalemate of Korea, his son learned the painless glory of the Persian Gulf.

The lesson of Payne's youth had been total victory. When men poured home from Europe, it was glory to behold. The old *Herald American* had even run a picture page of black GIs and their French girlfriends celebrating VE Day. In Bronzeville the implication was clear: the liberators had been liberated, even if the images were so controversial that the next day the paper had to apologize.

As the boy leafed through the photo books his father had collected, Quinlan put on a recording of Payne. It was bluesy and accessible, and he could see both children warming to it.

"Do you have a picture of him as a soldier?" the boy asked.

"The only picture I have," he said, "is the one in my head."

•

We got to Korea before Christmas, and it was colder than a whore's dream. The name of the place was Wonsan. Even sounds sorry, don't it? The hawk swept down from Siberia right into our face no matter what side of the hill you dug into. Didn't dare sleep. They said that men froze to death, dreaming of the sun.

Hill 622. Funny how you remember things. It just meant the hill was 622 feet high. Or meters. Either way, it measured how far you had to drag your sorry ass. We were all black on 622, but on the next hill over they weren't even Army. They were Marines, and we could see them through field glasses, their faces specks against the gray stone.

What did you think about the segregation?

One morning I looked over and saw two black Marines cooking something over a fire with the whites.

"Jackson, come over here," I said. "Is that what it looks like? Or do the cold make you color blind?"

Jackson took the glasses.

"Your eyes are OK, Wardell," he said. "The Marines take black in with white."

"They more fucked up than we are," I said.

•

The 3/11th took no serious casualties the first weeks in the field. The only ones killed were South Korean ROKs, whom the GIs thought were more trouble than the country was worth.

What was wrong with them?

One minute they'd be there, the next they'd bugged out and their northern brothers were pouring through the line. Hell, they didn't even learn the language, so when we'd try to rally them on the 356 radio, all we'd get back was a lot of sorry chop-chop.

But they weren't the only foreigners. One time when we relieved a Turkish unit I found Jackson with a group of them smoking something that smelled like buffalo chips. One guy was playing a wooden flute.

"Cat was in a groove," Jackson said afterward.

"Must've been the shit you were smoking," I said. "You probably like those Chinese bugles, too."

Sometimes when we were bogged down, the Reds would put out speakers and blast us with bugle calls and shit about the white man. Then they'd put on some race records, and Jackson would test himself to see how few notes it took him to name the artist, tune, and year it was made.

•

From bugle calls to the blues and beyond, the history of Western music has proceeded through the incorporation of higher and higher orders of overtones into the diatonic structure. This took it from the familiar steps of an open brass instrument to the most avid chromaticism of the late Romantics.

Overtones result from the complexity of waveforms. At the first order one can detect resonance with the familiar third, fifth, and seventh. Beyond that the second, fourth, and flatted seventh. Then eventually the flatted ninth, sharp fourth, flatted thirteenth, and so on.

One of the reasons the blues has become the backbone of the most popular music in the world is because its simple diatonics are fractured by chromatic "blue notes." This strikes sympathetically upon the human ear, perhaps suggesting the broken harmony of human life.

•

We were holding a ridgeline over one of the main roads south during the Marine bugout from the Chosin Reservoir. First day and night were some kind of awful. Cold to take your breath away. Down the road the column of Marines kept passing and passing. And they didn't look so good.

I'd just gone off watch the second night that we lay up over that road and was taking a leak out front of our hole before rolling up in my bag.

"That you, Robinson?" Jackson called.

I didn't answer. Not out there all exposed.

"Emmett?" he called again, way too loud.

I buttoned up and scrambled back to my hole.

"Keep it down," I said.

"You hear something?"

"Just you, fool."

"Listen," he said.

"Relax," I said. "It's the wind."

Five minutes later the bugle blew and Joe Chink launched his attack.

Do you mind talking to me about it?

Not half as much as I minded being there. A cloud passed and there they were in front of us in the moonlight. If you never saw that many men trying to kill you, you better pray you never do. I'll tell you this: If I hadn't done my business a few minutes before, I'd've let go of it then.

Our BARs was working out and the machine guns were raking nice and low. But that didn't stop Joe Chink. Each time they'd drop back, we'd figure it was over. Then the bugles would start up again, the sky light up with tracers.

Wasn't 'til dawn we saw what we'd done. The Reds finally pulled back for good at sunup and didn't even try to carry off their dead. They lay all over the slope in those quilted, yellow-gray jackets they wore, frozen in angles where they fell. A few of them were still on fire from the incendiaries. The flames burned strange and wispy, like genies rising up from stone. Jackson and I looked for any Chinese that were still moving and took turns sharpshooting them.

•

Don't tell me about the Negro soldier, not after what I saw Bravo Company do on Sumbitch Ridge. God, what a beautiful sight.

There were always some geniuses in the command who wanted to break up my regiment, saying separate wasn't equal or some such shit as that. Well, my only mission was to kick Chinese ass. And my black boys could do it as well as anybody in the AO. So forget the Sunday school shit. Just give a Negro the job and the ammunition to get it done.

That was why I gave Division holy hell for talking about pulling in another unit to chase the Chinese down. Sure the boys were bone weary and they'd taken some casualties. But they deserved a chance to finish what they started.

•

Motherfuckers weren't satisfied we beat hell out of Joe Chink. Dead Chinese heaped up all down the line, and Top says the Man wants us to haul ass after the ones we missed.

I told Top, I bet they wouldn't do this to a white unit.

"White man'd get more respect," I said.

"You'll never know, Robinson," Top said. "You gone be black your whole, sorry life."

We saddled up and started to move. Marched all morning with no sight of Joe Chink. Then, over the next ridgeline, we spotted a village. Not too big, but enough to hide somebody. Top told us to spread out so Joe Chink would have to use a separate bullet for each of us.

"That'll wear 'em down," I said.

•

My troopers did a simply outstanding job on the sweep. Outstanding. Pursuit, pursuit, pursuit. Bunch of hounds after game. Don't let anybody tell you the Chinese are a better military race.

•

That night, when we got to within five hundred yards of them, Top had us to fall out and put a cross on each other's back with medic's tape so we could see to stay in line.

"What you want to give the Chinks an aiming point for?" I said.

"Only way they be aiming at this cross, Robinson, is if you turn tail and run," Top said. "And I'll be there to shoot you first."

I taped up Jackson and Jackson taped Wardell and Wardell taped Leon and Leon taped Sam and Sam taped me. Wardell asked the medic did he have enough left to patch us if we fell. And the medic said not to worry, because if that happened, Top would put us out of our misery.

•

My first unit in contact was not Bravo Company, but Bravo ended up hitting the hardest part of the line. Pretty soon it had stalled out maybe seventy-five yards from its objective. The incoming was withering. It wasn't until the flanking positions fell and we were able to swallow the enemy up in enfilading fire that Bravo Company got moving again. I suppose that meant it was pinned down maybe forty-five minutes. Maybe an hour.

•

It was for-fucking-ever, friend. Don't be talking no forty-five minutes. Joe Chink was in holes and shit. We were so close we could smell their garlic.

I didn't even notice Jackson got hit until I had to roll over to reload. Then I saw his helmet was funny and his face flat to the ground. When I touched him, he didn't make a sound. I couldn't even see where he'd been shot.

I called for the medic. I would have stayed, but Top ordered an attack. Forget the wounded, he said. They ain't going anywhere.

•

By daybreak I was able to report to division headquarters that my Negroes were in complete control. The XO was from Mississippi. Pure Citadel. A regular Rebel yell. I got him on the field radio and reported overrunning the enemy.

"It's your worst nightmare, cracker," I said. "These black troopers can kick anybody's ass."

•

Fourteen had fallen, three of them dead. We couldn't get the wounded out except by carrying them. Bearers lost their footing in the bloody snow. Litters went down.

"Top, I'm hurting!" they'd call. "Make it stop!"

Payne's wound wasn't anywhere near the worst. It appeared to be a ricochet. By the time I got to him, the medic'd already gotten some morphine in him. I asked him how he was doing.

"That shit he stuck me with is all right," he said.

4.

Rev. Corn died while Payne was overseas. The police never arrested anyone and, apparently in deference to the victim's standing in the community, officially listed the matter as a homicide in the course of an armed robbery. This despite the fact that the police report showed

that the preacher still had $47.62 USC and a gold watch on his person at
the time police arrived at the Greyhound station men's room. The coroner called the cause of death a blunt injury, which may have occurred
when the victim struck his head on a washbowl in a fall. But there were
also numerous other injuries to the face and neck and a severe contu-
sion in the region of the groin. The site of the incident, the viciousness
of the beating, and the blows to the testicles suggested, even to persons
not expert in forensic pathology, a reason other than theft.

·

> Jackson was a swordsman
> From the first get-go.
> If you don't believe me
> I guess you just don't know.

You take the woman that did the cleaning at Ebenezer, the one we
called the Bitch in Blue.
I always wondered who that song was named after.
Man don't forget a color like that woman's, dad.

> Hips so smooth.
> Lips that soothe.
> And all the moves
> That make you groove.
> Oh, yes, the sweet,
> Hard Bitch in Blue.

·

Red Sloan been telling stories on me, has he? I suppose he told
you how good I was. Well, he ain't lying, honey. Somewhere along the
line I done everything he said and everything he made up, too. But the
best thing I ever done was make a man out of Jackson Payne.

That first night I went to see him in a club it didn't take much to
get his eye. Pretty soon he had it running all over me. Next thing I know
he's at the table asking me could I come outside. Honey, I could've
come right on the spot.

·

Don't get me started. She changed him into a common junkie. It
wasn't enough for that woman to parade around in her slinky blue
dresses until he was as wild as a rutting dog. It wasn't enough to pour

whiskey down his throat in those hootchy-kootchy clubs until he was half out of his mind. When she couldn't keep him any other way, she's the one started him on dope.

•

She's a piece of work, that Leticia is. I'd've stayed in Korea, too, if I had that one back home.

One thing she never understood: Jackson didn't play nothing unless he was ready. If it wasn't the Bitch in Blue, it'd've been some-body else.

And his sister's also dead wrong about when he got hooked. It wasn't until he came back from the service. I know what I'm talking about, because I did time in Hell myself and saw him from the vesti-bule. But back when he was fooling with the Bitch in Blue none of us did nothing harder than a little bit of reefer.

> Don't let sister jive you
> 'Bout who did what to who.
> You want to know the simple fact,
> Leticia don't have a clue.
>
> The one she blames got hurt herself.
> He walked without ado.
> And no one left for her but me,
> That's why the Bitch was Blue.

•

As good as his technical skills were becoming as he copied solos off the records Rev. Corn had given him, his music was derivative, and he knew it. Except perhaps when he escaped to the lakefront to tell the stars who he wanted to be.

His favorite spot was far enough out on the Point that nobody in the Hyde Park apartments on the other side of the Drive could hear. Some nights a storm would rise, and Payne would play to the gathering thunder, rim shots of lightning, his head thrown back, horn to horizon, blowing as defiantly as he knew how, as if he were vowing never, never to submit to another anymore. Not even cynically, to get what he wanted in return. One. Two. One two three four.

At the Point he played things no audience had ever demanded or would have understood. And in his room, ear to speaker, he immersed himself in a distant element—Monk's cosmic dissonances, John Lewis's laconic precision, Miles's ellipses like points in the void. He needed to see where they were, to see if there was anywhere they weren't.

He went to the Point whenever he could, telling no one. He did not want anything disturbing him as he sat on the huge breakwater slabs of stone, the humidity cushioning his sound, the smell of the water and the feeling that came when the weather changed, like one key modulating to another. On nights like this, when a quarter-moon shone flat across the calm expanse and the insects sang out behind him, he played ballads of unutterable longing and let them vanish into the dark.

Lost in his reflections, he did not hear the awkward wobble of spiked heels on gravel. As his last note faded in a breathy vibrato, a voice said, "So Mama finally found you."

He turned and saw her silhouette above him on the rocks, hands on hips, legs rising high into her skirt.

"You don't have to hide your light from me, baby," she said.

Payne lowered his horn between his knees and opened the case that lay next to him balanced on an angling slab.

"Don't be in such a hurry, baby," she said. "Mama came to make you happy."

"You followed me," he said, voice as flat as a tuning tone.

"It wasn't hard, baby," she said. "The way you was walking, you didn't see nobody in the world."

"Thinking about you, girl," he said.

"Don't say it if it ain't so."

He did not rise to help her as she leaned over to pluck off her heels and then picked her way down the rocks. When she was next to him he lifted his horn to his lips and let out a blat.

"Jackson," she said.

He blew another shapeless growl.

"That supposed to be funny?" she said.

"You don't like your song?" he said.

"Maybe you don't like girls."

She was ready for him to hit her. Any man would have. Every man had. But Payne just blew a single, bleating note at the top of his horn.

"Put that thing down and talk to me, baby," she pleaded.

He gave a mocking little cornball run like something from one of the Dorseys, white as the moon.

"Why you so mean to me?" she said. "I hate that preacher, too, you know."

This time he took a breath deep into his belly and then, as if weary of his horn, let out a sigh.

"I been jealous," she said. "That's all."

"Preacher don't mean shit," he said.

"Jealous of the saxophone."

She reached into her purse and pulled out a pint bottle, the kind you could find smashed on the rocks at the Point any morning you cared to look.

"That sweetass wine of yours," he said, "and not enough of it to do either of us any good."

He lifted the horn from his lap and laid it softly in the case, then he reached for the bottle. Teasing, she drew it away.

"That's for after, honey," she said, opening her purse. In the moonlight he could see a bedlam of female implements inside, among them a wax paper bag, which she took out. "This is first."

"I got my own brand," he said, touching the pack of Kools in his breast pocket.

"This ain't a cigarette, baby," she said. "This is a trip uptown."

Yes, Cassandra Butler later allowed, sister Leticia was right about one thing. The night she first offered it to him she was quite sure Payne had never smoked a reefer before.

He turned it in his fingers, feeling how loosely packed it was.

"Which end do you light?"

"It feels fine whichever way you put it in," she purred.

He reached into his pocket and pulled out a pack of matches from one of the nicer clubs.

"Here. Let me," she said.

Before she could, he snatched his hand back from hers, lighted up, and drew the smoke into his mouth then down. It was too harsh to enjoy the way he did the icy breath of Kools. The smell was sharp and slightly sour, like the fall when they burned the leaves.

"Here. Let me smoke off it," she said.

"You done this before."

"I done everything there is to do twice," she said.

She talked on and off while they shared the first reefer, then the second, but he didn't listen to the words. It was the pitch of her voice that he locked onto, the rhythms. He began to anticipate them the way he anticipated where Red Sloan was going to take the chords. Then at some point he noticed the silence which, as soon as he did, seemed to have gone on forever.

"You're easy, baby," she said. "I think you one of those that just leans in the direction of high."

"Don't feel nothing special," he said.

"You doing a mighty fine imitation."

He wondered how, if she felt the same way he did, she could possibly tell.

"How 'bout some of that wine now, woman," he said.

She passed him the bottle. As he unscrewed the top, he studied the motion of every finger. Sweetness rose to his nostrils and touched his lips. It was not cloying the way it usually was. The taste was of a summer garden, the flowers in Jackson Park.

"You ready for more of this weed, baby?"

She lighted it for him. Every good thing was outsized now, seen through a lens. He took the hot breath straight into his lungs and held it like she did, not wanting any to leak away. Then he lifted his horn to his lips and exhaled a riff.

"Blow for me, baby," she said.

It wasn't like being drunk. His fingers seemed distant, but not clumsy. It did not matter that the smoke had made an ember of the tip of his tongue. It had also reached the place where songs began.

The sound he made was intimate. His fingers were others, but they touched the truth, as the woman in blue touched his knee.

"All right, baby," she said. "Oh, yes."

But he was alone. And when he was finished, he had no idea how many choruses he had played. The sweat rolled down his forehead into his eyes, and he wiped it away like tears.

"Didn't I tell you, baby?" she said.

The woman had suddenly reappeared beside him, and now that the song had ended, it was all right that she had.

"Got any more of that shit on you?" he said.

"So you do like it," she said.

He liked it too much.

How much is too much, honey?

More than was good for him.
Everything he liked at all he liked that way.

•

The prime excuse all players had for their habit was the way they lived: out there where everything written came to an end. And at the average jazz joint any human appetite, no matter how lurid, could be satisfied within the time it took for a band to get in tune.

But there had to be more than risk and access. Lots of people from Quinlan's generation had tried grass, but only a few died with needles in their calves. The odds were much worse for somebody who blew jazz at mid-century. Dying was a riff too many of them played; you got tired of it after a while.

One explanation was in the music itself: The same compulsion that drove players to make it new led to a compulsion to repeat. And you had to remember the way they learned. All right. All right. The young woman in the back of the room reminds us that we are veering preciously close to stereotypes here. They did not all learn exactly the same way, and they weren't all men. That is a useful correction, and I thank you for it.

But listen. These men's . . . these players' primers were radio and 78 rpm records. They memorized the masters' solos, note for note, not only to get the cadences under their fingers, but also as if through repetition they might be able actually to become the men who made them. When Dizzy grew a goatee for fear of giving his precious lip a shaving nick, young aspirants all over the country let the stubble on their chins grow, too, even if they played the guitar. And it was not uncommon to hear pianists playing perfect copies of runs that Bud Powell, gone on drink or drugs or natural psychosis, had thoroughly muffed. Character lessons: they not only imitated their idols' genius, they imitated their deepest flaws.

•

I still ask myself why he left me, honey. Wasn't I good to him? Oh, but he was fine while he lasted. There just wasn't a moment of sameness in him. He did it different every time.

Then one day I hear he don't want me no more. I went straight off to find Red Sloan.

"What's this they're saying?" I asked, and Red gave me one of those fool poems of his.

"Hate to bust your day to Hell,
But I guess I got to tell.
Tonight he got him someone new.
I thought that you knew, too."

"Who is she, Red?"

"Why do I got to get into this with you, woman?"

"Come on baby," I said, all sweetness now, 'cause that'll work with any man. "Tell mama the tale."

"All right, all right," he said. "The preacher's niece. That Evans girl. The one in the choir."

"She's a child."

"He don't know a good thing," he said.

Red had a look on him that I wish just once I could've put on Jackson's face. And that gave me an idea.

"You gone stand there all night, baby?" I said.

"You want to go outside for some air?"

"Air's just fine right here," I said.

I was making it sassy as hell and still he didn't make a move. The man was such a fool I had to spell it out for him.

"Can't you see I need somebody now?"

"Got any in mind?" he said, all proud of himself, like he really done something past standing there like a cigar store Indian waiting for a dog to pee on his feet.

"Jackson ain't the only man in the band," I said.

But, of course, I knew he was.

•

At the beginning the family was thrilled. Jackson started appearing in church again, and you could hear his voice booming out from the back of the chapel, as Sarah Evans's sweet soprano rose over the congregation from the loft in front.

Mama was so excited she invited him to bring Sarah over to dinner. Daddy handed out cigars. Eventually even Leticia began a sampler, just in case things worked out.

But I was the blindest. I was the one who decided to share the joy with Rev. Corn.

He rose when I entered, turning to put some records on the

player, then sat down silently across from me for the longest time as the sweet music played, his fingers squeezing the bridge of his nose.

"So," he said at last, "what brings you here?"

"We're all so excited about Jackson coming back into the fold," I said.

"Your brother," said Rev. Corn, "is the Devil's seed."

I watched the record spinning. I began to cry. If he was bad seed, maybe I had it in me, too.

"Stop your whining, girl," he said.

A few days later Rev. Corn led the poor girl and her family up our front steps.

"She's three months gone already," he said. "Small as she is, pretty soon she's going to start to show."

She stood behind him, head slung down. Mama was acrying. Charnette just went and hid her face.

"A man is expected to control his kin," said Rev. Corn.

Daddy reared up.

"He wasn't never no kin of mine," he said.

When the time came, I helped get the poor girl settled into the Lying In. No way Jackson was going to do right by her. He didn't even go see her but once, and that was when the baby died.

Did Sarah say he showed any remorse?

Seemed like the only thing he was sorry about was that the thing he put inside her didn't take.

I ought to try to get in touch with her.

She moved away for shame. I got a letter from her mother some years later that said she had come down with polio and died.

•

Quinlan flicked the sweat from his eyes then wiped his fingers on his running shorts and switched off the Walkman. He slowed to a walk when he reached his block and fished the key out of his pocket as he mounted the steps. Inside, it was warm. Three flights up, each step a pull at old muscles. He had made a lot of progress since Donna left him. Before, with the kids' demands, there was no time to chase after retreating youth; now he had the time and no one to be youthful for.

He paused in the living room and let his breath return. On the shelves were the books he had inscribed to her, right where she had left them when she had gone.

He opened the first he had published. There on the dedication page were her name and the words, "The one who gives this its meaning." But she never actually read his books. They were not in her field.

Of course, it was wrong to project one's own experience onto your subject, especially across distances as great as race, but still he could not rid himself of the deep, empathic sense of a man torn between passion and obligation, one excluding the other.

Quinlan replaced the book next to the other two, whose inscriptions he could not bear to read. Then he went into his office and put a tape of Payne's ballads on the machine.

One question was whether the work was worth the suffering it caused. And whether he could have hoped to do otherwise than he had done? Could he have settled down into a decent, respectable marriage and avoided the awful darkness that shadowed him? She would have sensed the emptiness in him, felt his dissatisfaction galvanically in the touch of his flesh. She would have become jealous of the things into which he displaced his passion. Music. Drink. Drugs. They are all women, when women are not enough. Lord, it was silent in this apartment alone, except of course for the cry of Payne's big, concordant sound.

three
**the
shell
casing**

Somewhere there's music. How faint the tune.

"HOW HIGH THE MOON,"
BY NANCY HAMILTON
AND MORGAN LEWIS

1.

Some are brave. Born with it. I got him the Bronze Star with V Device, didn't I? Speaking of color, Bronze is harder for a black. And don't forget Purple. Getting the Heart does something to a man. Once you been hit, you know you can be hit again.

If it'd been up to me, I'd've given him the Silver just for returning to us. If that ain't what the manual of decorations means by conspicuous valor, they ought to burn that whole book of colors and let courage lie where it belongs, between a man and the other men at his side.

•

We called Jackson the Million Dollar Man. Fool had a going-home wound and he gone got himself healed. Sometimes when we fell out, I'd see him pull up his fatigues and rub at the bad places. The scars were so pink we said the doctor must've been trying to make Jackson white.

•

For understanding this period of Payne's life the music was no help. Many of Payne's compositions drew their titles from important experiences in his life, but none referred to the war.

As Quinlan pored over the material he had gathered, he canceled long-standing arrangements with friends, failed even by university standards to participate in the rituals of community, not to mention the neglect of his kids.

"Is anything wrong, Charles?"

"Damned book project."

"Why am I not surprised."

"Let's not start, Donna."

"The boys were upset not to hear from you Sunday."

"I was in the middle of something. Do you have plans for the weekend?"

"You don't need to make anything up to me, Charles."

"I was hoping to take a rain check on visitation."

"Use it or lose it, my friend."

He holed up in his study, reading every history and memoir of the war he could find, plotting the movements of the 3/11th on laminated, grid-square maps. He became so taken with these graphic representations that he consulted his editor about including them in the book.

"It's a story about music, Charles," the editor said.

•

Payne's leg bothered him the way they had warned him it would. His unit moved north again almost as soon as he drew his gear. The unfamiliar equipment, salvaged from casualties, settled uneasily on his shoulders and hips, as if they retained someone else's shape. The rifle, too, seemed to resist him; it was alive with eccentricities and tics. The magazine went in only with coaxing. The bolt was stiff; it needed just the proper English to snap it to. The trigger's torque made him unsure of the firing point.

The 3/11th was out in the open on the low ground. Eventually they had to dog it so as not to get too far ahead of the flanking units on the more protected but punishing hills. It was clear that this was a big, coordinated operation. Tanks drove out ahead as the vanguard. Planes flew recon overhead. The officers spent every smoke break talking on field radios.

That night, forty-two hours after Payne returned from the hospital, the Chinese mounted a furious attack.

•

Motherfuckers just kept coming. When Top threw up a flare, we could see gooks by the hundreds. Thousands. I said to myself, Wardell, your ass is grass.

The 3/11th held on for two full days and three nights. Nobody Quinlan talked to remembered it as other than an unrelieved horror. The men hid and fired and prayed and died in five-foot squares as wave upon wave of Chinese in mustard-colored jackets tried to pry them out.

Artillery came crashing in during the enemy barrages, the rounds digging for them in the dirt. Then the American batteries would respond. No wonder memories were addled. Did Percy Jones catch it on the first day or the second? This many years later nobody could remember. Daryl Jacobs was hurt right from the get go, but the others never knew he had made it until Quinlan told them.

How about Wilson Scott? He keep his leg or not?

I'm sorry. I don't know.

He alive though, ain't he?

I'm not sure.

You can't find out a simple thing like that, how you gone figure out a brother as much trouble as Jackson Payne?

•

Payne saw little more than the narrow, individual wedge of the mass spectacle that the strategists from their pinnacle disdained as a vivid, transitory distraction. But on the second night the Chinese made their final push, breaching the crossfire and getting inside the American lines.

•

All I can tell you is that when it was over there were four dead Chicoms, one dead American and one dead ROK in and around Payne's fighting hole. Ain't nobody can say who killed who.

Here's a fact, though, if that's what you're after: Payne got him a second Heart that day. It was just a cut on his arm, and after the medic dressed it, Payne fired into a corpse at 100 yards to show me it didn't affect his aim.

•

Once it reached the rear, the 3/11th soon forgot its victory. With safety came hassles: inspections and the snap of military courtesy, the empty rituals of obedience. There was KP duty, too, and make-work details that Top called the WPA, "We Punish your Ass." Periodically, the brass came calling, and this put everyone on edge. Then the visits became more frequent, and it looked like something was up.

For every restriction, of course, there was an evasion. To reach the women in the village beyond the wire, for example, you had to secure a pass. You could get one by staying on Top's good side. But you didn't need to if you got right with the redneck MPs. Some guys shined their boots. Then at the gate they'd present a sheet from one of the pocket Bibles the sodality women had sent in the mail, and the MPs would wave them right through.

There also was whiskey. The medics from the MASH unit were well-known for having the steadiest supply, a blend of 190-proof medicinal, water from the lister bag, and burnt sugar to give it body and a nice amber shade. Payne never did boots for the MPs, but he did not mind doing the job for the medics. It was steady work. Blood played hell with a shine.

"Why you want to do that nigger duty for?" Elroy Carter asked him one day.

"Ain't any particular color to me," Payne replied.

"My old man blacked white men's boots in the train station all his working days," Carter said. "Breathed in so much he was darker inside than out."

"Doctors don't treat me bad," Payne said.

"But you all on your knees to them and shit."

"They got the gift to heal."

He meant the cough medicine bottles full of hooch that he stuffed deep into the pockets of his utilities, wrapped in Army-issue handker-chiefs to keep them from ringing as he walked. He usually found a dark, untraveled spot behind the mess tent. In the moonlight he set out the night's ration of bottles, soldiers in a line.

As the numbness crept over his nose, the clench went out of his jaw. Then it was time to pour on a little more fuel. He measured it pre-cisely by the hash marks on the side of the bottle—one, two, one two three four.

•

Well, sonofabitch. So Pilgrim made something of himself. Maybe I shouldn't be surprised. He was always thinking. Maybe more than was good for him. I used to see him lying outside the tent in the sun like he was in a trance.

"What the hell are you thinking about, Pilgrim?" I asked.

"Just counting the tent pegs," he said.

"Why?"

"Makes certain feelings go away," he said. "Don't have to be tent pegs. Could be steps from here to there. Seconds as they pass. Is that normal, doc?"

"Whatever works," I told him.

•

All music is built on regular patterns, more often than not in multiples of two. Four beats to the bar, two or four chords. Four or eight bars to the phrase. The blues comes in twelve-, twenty-four-, and thirty-two-measure varieties. Every chord also has a mathematical pattern. The basic triad on the first note of a major scale includes the tonic, the third (which is two whole steps above), and the fifth (which is a step and a half above that). These intervals are constant whether the key is C or F-sharp, and musicians use this algorithm to transpose from one key to another. Chord patterns, too, show arithmetic regularity, with many tunes, for example, including phrases built on the pattern II-V7-I.

These cadences, which to the casual listener might be barely discernable, still have an effect, fall following summer, night following day.

•

Far as I was concerned, you gave a man as much slack as you could when you were in the rear. All old Top required of a trooper was that he be on deck when the time came, moderately sober, with his rifle clean. Payne never let me down.

Did he ever get in fights?

No more than anybody else.

He injured his embouchure during this period.

Sounds like something a man wouldn't want to hurt.

His embouchure. His mouth. The part of him that he used when he blew his horn.

•

One of them fancy white doctors did it, man. Got drunk and didn't like the shine he gave or something. That's the way I heard it.

From whom, Elroy?

I don't recall.

•

Kicked in the teeth you say? First I heard of it. I can't imagine it happening in our tent. I'm not saying we didn't get a little raucous at

times. But physical violence was not like us. Not after a day in the oper-
ating theater putting boys like Pilgrim back together again.

As I'm sure you're finding, the black soldiers had all sorts of
strange ideas. Pilgrim would tell us about them. They thought something was put in their food to make them less fertile so they wouldn't
leave too many dark babies with the whores. They thought the war was
being fought to carve out a piece of Korea where the United States
could ship its Negroes. They thought they had fought so well together
that somebody was going to realize how dangerous they had gotten and
break up their units.

You can see, Mr. Quinlan, they were all variations on a theme.
That's probably where the story about how Pilgrim got hurt came from.
An overheated imagination colored by race.

•

It was a white boy give him that busted tooth, all right. But Elroy
don't know shit. It was some fucking redneck at a USO show, that's
who it was.

Jackson, Emmett, Top, and me had scrounged a Jeep and lit out
for this show we heard about outside Seoul. They had set the stage up
against the wall of a wooden building so the sound would carry. When
we pulled up, there was already a little crowd, and Top led us straight
into the middle of it.

"I ain't seen so much white since mama hung out the wash," said
Emmett.

"You best get used to it, troop," said Top.

"Where I come from," I said, "they don't let you."

"They gone break up the 3/11th," said Top.

"What kind of shit you talking, Top?" said Emmett.

"That's why the brass has been all over us," said Top. "They've
been making plans to integrate us into other units."

"Nobody's gone integrate my ass," said Emmett.

"Then I guess," said Top, "you planning to leave your ass
behind."

Jackson disappeared into the crowd, trying to get a better view of
the dancing girls, I suppose. But apparently somebody didn't like to see
a black man that close to them, because when he returned, his lip was
bleeding and swelling up.

"What happened?" I asked.

"Feels like I busted a tooth," Jackson said, taking out a fresh bottle and downing it.

"That shit ain't gone sprout it back," said Top.

"But it do ease the loss," Jackson said.

•

Every day *Stars and Stripes* reported the two sides circling around the idea of a cease-fire. The lull dragged on until it seemed like the war would end of boredom. Then Top announced that the Chinese had launched an offensive and the ROKs were in trouble to the west.

The men saddled up and rolled out in trucks at dusk. The roads were a wreck. Every hole was spine-jarring. Start and stop. Hour after hour. The men could not get a fix on direction or distance. They could have been heading up to the Yalu again for all they knew.

Two hours after dawn the convoy halted and the men disembarked. When the trucks were gone, an awful quiet descended. They found themselves in a narrow draw between two high, impassable ridgelines. If the Chinese Army were heading this way, it would have to bunch up at the bottleneck. The 3/11th deployed itself, rifles forward, heavy weapons dug in slightly to the rear. Boulders strewn around the plain gave everyone cover. It was an ambush on a regimental scale.

Payne was fine-tuning the windage on his sight when he first spotted the dust. He poked Flowers awake.

Flowers looked up over the lip of the hole to where Payne was pointing.

"Jesus Christ," he whispered.

The Chinese were a squall line blowing toward them. A typhoon.

The Reds were arrayed with one company up for reconnaissance in force, the rest bunched behind. It was essential to keep fire discipline in order to take out as many as possible in the first volley and start to even out the appalling imbalance of force. They moved so close that Payne could hear their equipment clatter.

The Americans rose slightly, as a single man, and sighted in. Payne targeted first one Chinese soldier, then another, taking the slack out of the trigger, dropping them with imaginary rounds. The sun had come up over the cliffs behind the 3/11th, blinding the enemy and lighting them up for the American guns. Payne wiped a bead of sweat from the corner of his eye. He was ready to kill whoever fell under the blade of his sight when the order came. He counted the footfalls of the man he now had in his sights. One. Two. One two three four. One. Two. One two three four. A pain stabbed through his jaw from his broken tooth. He removed a shell casing from his pocket and slipped it into his mouth. The metal where it stuck out beyond his lips was corroded, but it was burnished where he had worried it with his tongue.

Then suddenly the heavy weapons opened up behind him with a rush of thunder. He pressed the trigger again and again. Men fell. One. Two. One two three four.

•

You ain't never heard a racket like it in all your life. Once a cop put a metal wastebasket on my head and beat on it with the butt of his pistol. This was worse. This noise could kill.

The Chinks just kept on coming. Walked right into our artillery, which was firing flat out like two-ton shotguns. Not to mention our rifles and BARs. They were falling in bunches, heads blown off, cut in two, every damned thing. And still they was always more men behind, coming out of the smoke like zombies.

•

Noise'll spook a man. It's the way it takes and shakes you like the whole world's flying apart. Once in Vietnam I was less than half a klick from a B-52 strike, and I thought my troopers were gone die of fright. But it was nothing like the sound that day in the place we called Thunder Valley.

•

Neither Top nor any of his men knew it, but the Chinese hordes were in the midst of a mortal miscalculation. The laminated maps on the wall behind Quinlan's desk showed how it happened.

The Chinese were pressing forward along a wide front. All the Allied reserves in the area had been brought forward in a desperate effort to slow the advance. But the Chinese assumed that the defenses in the narrows of Thunder Valley were shallow, stolen from other units and thrown into the breech. Despite the initial violence of the defenders' fire, they continued to believe that the valley was a weak point. They simply failed to imagine that a unit as large as the 3/11th could have moved as far and as fast as it did.

So when the Chinese hit the wall, they just kept beating on it, wave after wave. Sometimes they forced their way past the heavy weapons fire, and Payne saw their shapes emerging in numbers from the haze. Then the faces, the looks of terror when they first saw the extent of the American line. Some threw themselves into the crossfire. Others tried to turn and were cut down in shame.

And when the artillery drew down on the approaching phalanx, the sound echoed and grew until it seemed the cliffs themselves would shatter and bury the living and the dead. Payne and Flowers hugged the bottom of their holes, trapped inside a beating drum. Then the din would lift for a moment and they would rise again and take the enemy survivors one by one.

•

All of a sudden it stopped. Silence. Like you'll hear when you are dead.

I looked up, wiped the dirt out of my eyes. The wind was blowing back the smoke, and there were bodies everywhere, some of them not ten yards from our hole. I touched my shoulder, my face, my crotch.

It took a few minutes before I noticed that Jackson was doubled over like a baby. I grabbed him by the shoulders. His eyes were wide open. The helmet fell off his head.

I tried to call for a medic. But the noise had made my ears so I couldn't hardly hear my own voice.

I tried to get his rifle away from him, but he held it so tight I thought he might turn it on me. The only thing I could do was crawl out of the hole and go for help.

When I got back with the medic, Jackson hadn't moved. The medic gave him a shot that got rid of the shakes. He was trying to say something. I put my ear to his lips.

"The sound," I think he said. "The sound."

Then a shell casing fell from his mouth, and where it lay on the ground I could see he had bitten down so hard the end was crimped shut.

Don't let anybody tell you Jackson Payne cracked 'cause of fear of dying. When they got him to the aid station, they realized he had totally lost his hearing. That's what he was trying to tell me. Jackson thought he'd gone deaf.

2.

The preferred treatment for battle fatigue during the Korean War was not much different from the method used today. After an incident of nervous collapse, a man is to be evacuated no farther to the rear than necessary to stabilize his condition and put him in a position of reasonable security. If possible, he is to be kept at a battalion aid station with the other walking wounded from his unit. Only extreme cases are sent to evac hospitals.

Even in the hospital, every effort should be made to maintain a soldier's sense of unit affiliation. It is important to keep alive the expectation that he will return to the network of relationships he left, that he will be back on duty, in the line of fire, as soon as possible.

If you don't mind my saying so, doctor, it sounds cruel.

In some cases the patient is put to sleep for a few days to help him reintegrate and rebuild his strength. You said the field medic in this instance gave an initial dose of morphine. There are better choices, but this one was common at the time, since it was so ready to hand.

Once the pharmacological treatment is withdrawn, the man is put in an environment of counseling—often in groups—and subjected to renewed military discipline. He is given an ordinary work assignment, first on the ward and later beyond it. Everything is aimed at reestablishing the link to the situation from which he made his psychological flight. The patient, you see, has to deal with intense feelings of guilt for having abandoned his comrades. It is up to the medical staff to make him understand both that he has nothing to be ashamed of and that he has a responsibility as soon as possible to carry his weight again. So, as you can see, with respect to your subject, we seem to have done very nearly everything wrong.

After your telephone call I took the liberty of looking into the records. What I discovered was that within a matter of days after the engagement from which your man was evacuated his entire regiment was dismantled and its personnel reassigned to other units. This was done for the purpose of racial integration. The men were not moved in company-, platoon-, or even squad-sized blocs. They were scattered. So one of the critical elements in our usual treatment strategy was rendered unavailable. We could not maintain your subject's identification with his fighting unit because it was no longer there.

The attending physicians would properly have been hesitant to return him to the line, because if they had, he would have found himself among white strangers. Moreover, the medical corps was at the time under orders to be liberal in allowing black soldiers to return to the United States because it was assumed that new black replacements would more easily integrate than those who had been blooded with their own.

I can only say in defense of my colleagues that, whatever the consequences, their motives seem to have been benign.

•

Payne disembarked on a ship of strangers. They hailed from all parts of the country, all branches of the service, all levels of experience, from combat infantry to special services. So far as Quinlan could determine, Payne did not know a single soul.

According to the doctors with whom Quinlan spoke, his hearing probably returned slowly. He would have felt an initial surge of relief that it had returned at all. Then he would have compulsively tested his limits on the high and low ends of the spectrum the way he worried with his tongue the tender spots in his jaw. He would have paced the deck for hours on end, counting his steps, counting portholes, counting stars.

Payne bunked in the medical section among men who had lost hands and feet, limbs, eyes. He wished he had a fresh wound himself or that the red badge of his earlier suffering could somehow be renewed. Even the other head cases had it all over him. They were obviously twisted, dazed, seized by epic forces and thrown to the deck. Payne made a point of moving about in his shorts whenever possible, just so the pink, pale strokes of his scars would be seen.

He yearned to have an instrument to play over the vessel's churning wake. It wasn't only a matter of getting back his chops. He needed a horn to pull his head together, because you did not create music as much as music created you. Without an outlet, the droning monotony and crowded isolation of the sea voyage amplified Payne's feelings like a loudspeaker feeding back into a mic. If he was not a head case when he came aboard this vessel, he surely was when he left.

Like all returning casualties, Payne was offered the opportunity to go to a medical facility near his home. He turned it down. In later interviews, he had always said that this was because he'd heard that Bird was working on the West Coast, Miles as well, and nobody worth a shit was in Chicago anymore. But that did not ring true.

Then by chance Quinlan stumbled on something that filled in the picture. Early in his research he had put classified advertisements in all the jazz periodicals and the *New York Times Book Review* soliciting information about Payne for a "scholarly treatment of his life and art." What he got back, for the most part, was fan mail. He had almost given up finding anything of value when he came upon the letter from a man called Tony Lardener. It began typically, with an account of the correspondent's personal relationship with Payne's music over the years. Usually these tales led to an elaborate defense of some ultimate break with Payne when the music became too abstract and abrasive. There was always a sense of betrayal in these descriptions, as if the thrilling restlessness in Payne's explorations had taken him around a moral bend.

But Lardener quickly revealed just how personal his relationship to the music really was. He wrote that he had been with Jackson Payne in the psychiatric wing of a military hospital near San Diego. The letter did not say much from that point on. It centered on Lardener's difficulty in deciding to disclose this episode, so many years hidden.

"I must thank you, Mr. Quinlan," he wrote, "for giving me the opportunity for this modest act of valor."

Lardener lived in Portland, Oregon, and Quinlan flew in a half day early to give himself time to walk about and recall his student days at Reed College. The campus had changed very little over the years since he'd last been back for a reunion. He didn't even consider going to the latest one because he'd just separated from Donna, and he didn't want to have to explain the circumstances. Even now, he still saw things in relation to her: the hall where he'd taken her to see Charles Lloyd on their first date; the record store; the library where she did her Emily Dickinson and he his Roland Kirk. He stopped at the dining hall where they'd always had Sunday brunch. Outside on the green the music department had once mounted a performance of Stockhausen's *Anthems,* which was as close as he had ever come to experiencing the madness of war.

A taxi dropped him in front of a well-kempt frame house in a neighborhood students would never have reason to visit except perhaps to look for an upstairs room to rent. Lardener greeted him warmly at the door and introduced his wife. They both dressed as they probably did Sunday mornings for church. Quinlan took out his recorder and set it to the level of his own voice as she left them and closed the louvered doors on the bright, wickered room.

•

I guess I ought to start right out with why I was in the ward. Get that over with.

You don't have to if you don't want.

Even this many years after, I have a hard time dealing with my cowardice. No, don't stop me. Other men died fighting while I was shaking at the bottom of a hole. And when it was over they say I stripped off my clothes and rolled naked in the mud.

They took me to a MASH unit and doped me up. Whenever I came out of it, I carried on so much that they decided it was hopeless to think of sending me back to the lines.

I met Jackson Payne in the hospital in San Diego. He was not exactly what I needed, a regular hero with a couple of Hearts and a Bronze Star with V Device. Maybe he's screwed up, too, I said to myself, but at least he can wear his excuse on his chest.

I'd never been that close to a black man in my life, let alone one like him, his head shaved as clean as a basketball and a pair of arms that looked like they could snap me in two. So at first I kept my distance. But I couldn't help watching him, when I thought I could do it without him noticing.

I'd see him with his fingers along his buttons, head flung back. I'd see him on his knees, bowed down, chanting. It isn't Christian, I'd think. It isn't American.

Did he ever talk to you about meeting Muslims in Korea? I had no idea he had begun experimenting with their religion so young.

Like I said, I didn't get close enough for him to tell me anything. Then one day he got a pass to leave the hospital for an afternoon, and when he came back he had this funny-shaped suitcase, which he quickly shoved under the bed. I was afraid it might be a gun.

A few nights later I woke up and he was standing over me, blacker than a shadow. I was too scared to move.

"You were crying in your sleep," he said.

I guess maybe I apologized.

"I been there," he said.

"OK. Well, thanks then."

"You hear me talking to the Devil at night," he said, "you wake me up, too, OK?"

I turned away from him, but he touched my shoulder with one of those big hands of his. I flinched, but I was amazed how light it was.

"Here," he said. "I saved back a few of these."

He reached into the pocket of his robe and pulled out a handful of pills. I took a couple and squeezed them down. The rest I left in his hand.

"You got enough there to kill a bear," I said.

"These just tame him," he said.

I never did feel I could ask him why he was in the mental ward. Or even what was in that suitcase of his. Every once in a while, when we were shining up our low quarters, he would pull it out and dab a little polish on the outside. But he never, ever opened it up.

It was a nurse who finally got him to, one of the pretty ones, sweet but nosy, like a big sister. One evening when she came around with the pills and cups he was buffing up the case on his lap.

"Leaving us?" she said.

He put the case down and shoved it back under the bed with his heels.

"Infantry's always ready to saddle up," he said.

The nurse blushed, but I don't think he meant anything by it.

He took the little cup and slugged it back like he was throwing the contents down his throat and then gulped a mouthful of water. But I could see that, as usual, he had actually palmed the pills.

"Why don't you open up your hand and show me what you have," she said.

"You don't want to see this old hand," he said. "It's so big and ugly."

"Oh, but I do," she said. "The bigger the better."

I had never seen a white woman flirt so openly with a black man before. But apparently Jackson had, because it did not faze him.

"In this ward you must've seen everything," he said.

"I like knowing secrets," she said. "Like what you keep in that suitcase of yours."

I don't know what it did to Jackson, but the way she flipped her hair at that point sure got me going. Don't put that in your book, Mr. Quinlan. Mrs. Lardener, you know.

Suddenly Jackson reached under the bed and slid out the case. He lifted it to his lap and pulled off his dog tag chain, where he had the key.

She moved alongside him as he snapped the latch and opened the lid.

"Well, look at that," she said.

At this point half the ward was gathered around him. What they saw was a corroded old saxophone lying there on a red plush spread like a gnarly leg.

"Play it for me," the nurse said.

"Sorry," he said.

"I bet you're good."

"Not right in the head," he said.

four
off
the
bar

You're nasty, you're dirty,
Take it away.

"BUDDY BOLDEN'S BLUES,"
BY JELLY ROLL MORTON

1.

The story of Payne's second apprenticeship is well-known. In some respects Payne's experience of trying to reintegrate into civilian society could have been anyone's. Loneliness and disconnection, the shock of normalcy and the memory of the extreme—these are common in the literature of return. Payne never talked about nightmares, but it would have been a miracle if he didn't have them.

His Army separation money did not last long. He lost the deposit on several flats for blowing at all hours. Then he found a place that never slept. Nobody there minded when his scales and arpeggios rose over the hookers' cash-and-carry cries.

His tooth was still bothering him. He'd had it crowned at the hospital, but the job was done about as well as the one they did on his head. He had no way of knowing that a better dentist might have given him real relief, so he made an accommodation to the pain, which gave his bite on the reed its peculiar shape. He also found that it was responsive to anodynes. And so he ran up tabs at gin mills all over town, checking out the competition and sounding the numb harmonies at the bottom of a glass.

Los Angeles was another country. Nothing in Chicago had prepared him for the parching heat and dead air, the bleached colors. There was no grid, no center; it was all verge. The only organizing principle was exclusion, and you needed a celebrity map to tell you who belonged where.

The sound of California's jazz was as cool as the air was hot, the wrong climate all around. Cool was hollow. Cool was white. Yet the darker sounds had started to disappoint Payne, too. Everybody was still doing Parker's riffs, Dizzy's jokes. Whenever Payne felt himself imitating, he couldn't help remembering what he had done in the rectory of Ebenezer Baptist to earn the records he imitated from.

He worked himself up from #2-1/2 Rico reeds to #4s, trimming them with a knife to the proper density. Before long he was blowing on a 5-star medium Otto Link metal mouthpiece that he had to take on the right side to avoid a jolt as it touched the faulty crown. But the Link had the edge he wanted, the certainty of steel like the casing of a shell.

He built himself back on piano-book exercises and impossible Ravel runs. He found new fingerings that let him play faster. Ordinarily he spread the music out on his bed and sat on a straight-backed chair, the bell of his tenor muted by the mattress. But when he stood and blew free, the sound was nearly as wild as the one inside his head.

If it hadn't been for hunger and thirst, he might have worked longer in the woodshed. But there were only two things he knew how to do that could earn a man his rations, and one of them was a capital offense in the zone of peace. So he had to look for a street corner where he could go busking again.

In most locations there were too damned many people in cars and too few on foot. He wasn't used to the insults; in Chicago if they didn't like you, they just passed on by. At nightfall he would pick up his horn and carry it with him as he scouted new locations. If he had enough money, he would buy a bottle or two of cheap wine and bring it back to his flat. He could never afford to buy a woman. And no proper lady would even look at him in his olive drab T-shirts and Army-issue pants.

Then one of the girls in his building clued him in. The only place he had a chance of turning a decent buck was Hollywood, where the tourists were. It was a long walk, and the horn case blistered his hand. When he got there, he saw stretch limousines coming and going from the studio gates. Payne only had to stand on the corner with his hat on the ground to collect as much in an hour as he'd gotten elsewhere for playing all day. One man noticed his clothes and asked if he was a vet.

Payne earned a ten-spot for naming his unit and the places where he had fought.

That night on his way home he bought a decent meal and picked up a bottle of proper spirits. Then he negotiated a celebration with the girl who had given him a line on where the money was to be found. He played for her, and she swayed to the music and tried to sing. The next day he struck out again for Hollywood as soon as she left his bed.

The best location was near a studio tour gate. Across the street was a restaurant, a souvenir shop, and a beauty parlor that advertised the look of the stars. Payne had yet to see anyone famous, but there sure were enough people going in and out of the gate who looked like they wanted to be.

He set up against the high stucco wall of the studio about a half block down from the gate. His case lay open next to him with a dollar in silver inside to prime the pump. He let a reed soak in his mouth as he used his polishing rag to wipe dust and last night's prints from his horn. Then he set the reed and twisted the mouthpiece onto the neck. He did not need to tune the horn for solo work, but he blew a few notes anyway and fiddled with the placement of the metal sheath on the cork until it sounded right to his ear.

The sun was high, and he had to turn slightly to keep the reflection from the brass out of his eyes. He began with an up-tempo number, racing through the lovely circle-of-fifths changes of "All the Things You Are" to loosen up his instrument and, with any luck at all, attract a crowd. The studio tour gate provided a natural audience as people waited for the top of the hour to be led inside. The pickings were so good that Payne was surprised that he did not have any competition. Within a couple of choruses a dozen or more people had wandered over, and a fair number of them had dropped something in his case.

He went straight from the jump to a ballad, "September Song," which had worked so well with the lady the night before. Maybe in LA autumn seemed exotic. Nothing ever died here, did it? It just grew old and rich.

A small group gathered on the sidewalk near him. He made the horn wail for all things that end, putting a little extra into it, first just an obvious crescendo and then, in a way that surprised him, something of himself. It was the memory of wet, fallen leaves shining on the rocks at the Point and the shivering chill of the foxhole where he dreamed what it might feel like to be warm. Sweat ran down his face. He closed his eyes as he returned to the melody, concentrating now on making the phrasing perfect, hearing the gratifying response of coin clinking against coin.

When he opened his eyes again the group had moved away. As he let the frail note fade on a tightening vibrato he saw a policeman striding toward him from the direction of the studio gate. Payne took the mouthpiece from his lips and looked down at his case. In it was at least three and a half bucks beyond his seed money. He hoped the cop wouldn't make him move too far.

As he straightened up to receive the policeman eye to eye, the cop brushed past him to where his case lay on the concrete. There he stopped, gave it a kick, and sent the money scattering all over the pavement.

"Hey!" shouted Payne, kneeling down to trap the coins before they rolled into the sewer.

"Get up," said the cop. "Let's go."

Payne was reaching out to capture a quarter when the cop's boot slammed the coin flat on the pavement.

Then the cop seized his arm and moved him to the paddy wagon. Payne managed to cradle his saxophone as he went banging into the vehicle. The case came bouncing in after him, and not a cent along with it. As the wagon began to move, Payne wobbled to the long bench, rubbed his shoulder where it had hit the door. Then in the swaying compartment he put away his horn and rubbed with a wetted finger at a gouge in the leather of the case.

The first thing they did inside the jail was to grab the case away from him. Then they made him strip and submit to a mouth to asshole search. The smell in the big, dusky room was overpowering, a combination of shit and disinfectant. They sprayed him naked and then sprayed his clothes so they came back to him wet with stench.

"I supposed to put these back on?" he said.

" 'Less you want to go the way you are, boy," said a guard. "We got a few in here who'd like that."

After being fingerprinted, numbered, and photographed, Payne was put into a cold holding cell without any explanation of what was next. Every man with him was also black. Some were sweating for lack of the needle. Somebody asked Payne what he'd done.

"I was busking on my tenor. Copper tried to step on my hand."

One man sat in the corner tapping out silent rhythms on his knees. He must have scored before being busted, because he seemed farther outside than the simple paradiddle riffs might have suggested.

"You a lucky cat," the drummer finally said, raising his head without losing the beat.

"Could've crippled me up," said Payne.

"With horn players they usually go for the mouth."

•

Now I usually stay to myself in the slam, expecially when I'm only looking at short time. The rule is stay out of my shit and I won't dig in yours. You know what I'm saying? But this cherry said he was a tenor player. So I says to him, sit your ass down before one of the hard core over there takes a shine to it.

Then I offered him a kind of loan. When my old lady came in as a mule with something nice up her snatch, I put a deal to one of the screws—Payne's horn and my drumsticks for a half load of Mexico pure. It was kinda funny, selling the dope to get the instrument rather than the other way around.

County records verified that for thirty days Payne had three meals and plenty of time to settle into playing against a rhythm man again. Junior Leonard did not have a name, but he was good enough to hear something and build a structure around it. Payne heard something, too. It was the first time he had played with someone he couldn't easily leave behind, though he should have realized that a time would come when he would wish he had.

He was a little raggedy at first, but always working way out past himself. These steel bars do not a prison make. You know what I'm saying, Chuck? I used to tell him to lay back just a little, stay within himself. Nobody gone know the notes that are beyond you unless you reach for them and miss.

•

Payne wasn't sure he was ready to play the clubs. But when he came out of jail he was more vagrant than when he went in. The few things he owned besides his horn were being held by his last landlord. What was worse, he started having pain while urinating.

He had little choice but to follow Junior's lead and take the first job that came by, an R&B joint that had been stiffed by a booking agent and was desperate for anybody who could blow. The club owner made the deal as soon as he heard Payne do a couple choruses of a simple blues. It only took Junior a few hours to dig up a piano player.

"This guy's got a lot of Al Haig in him," Junior said.

When the time came, it turned out to be Haig and Haig. The man was so lit he could barely balance on the stool. As the crowd drifted in, Payne settled into a steady, three-chord rut. He even announced one of the tunes as "Ball and Chain," and Junior gave him a rim shot like he would for a lounge comic.

"I ain't gonna make it," Payne said after the first couple of numbers, "unless I get something to stop me needing to piss."

"Here," said Junior, turning his back to the crowd and holding out a bunch of pills.

"You're a regular pharmacy," Payne said.

•

Do I have to go through it all again? The pills definitely weren't the first the man ever took. He had that and plenty more in the Army. And as far as the other thing is concerned, how the fuck did I know he'd never done it before? Anyway, it wasn't me told Jackson he had to. That was up to the fat-assed Jew. I told him the afternoon we signed the gig, "You want to know whether my horn will dance, you go ask him."

But when it came time, the Jew said if Jackson wouldn't do what his customers wanted, we wouldn't get our pay.

"Climb up there, boy," he said.

Maybe I said something to Jackson, too. But I owed, man. Owed the piano and bass. Owed for the shit I gave Jackson to still the pain and for the shit I took myself. Owed for what I gave the screw to get Jackson his horn in the slam. So maybe I did suggest to him that he get up on the bar and wag his ass. Nobody said he had to like it. I didn't own the motherfucker. He could've split on me that very night. And he didn't have to come back the next night either. But he liked the dough as much as I did, liked getting mellow on whatever shit I brought, long as he could be steady in my face about what he had to do for it.

"Maybe we ought to put your traps up there on the bar some night," he said. "See how you like it."

"You the big motherfuck with the ax," I said. "You the star they want to see on high."

Sonofabitch never let me forget it.

"Junior," he'd say, "you never should've put my ass up on the bar."

Can you believe that shit? I don't know how many ladies he got by wagging his tail up there.

"Your ass," I'd say, "was one of your more interesting features, my friend."

•

At one time or another nearly every sax player who came up with the R&B bands had to do it. Walking the bar was a rite of passage.

Get that cat up here!

Lessee what he can do.

Nigger look like he can fly.

Some horn players claimed they didn't mind. It made you feel like a preacher in the pulpit, they said.

Down on earth the band hammered out the notes to a stripper's beat, the bitches touching his ankles, the men trying to get them hot under the counter.

Work it out, Rastus!

Make her beg fo' it.

Payne hated being seen the way they saw him up there. Even by his own band. He hated the women who came to him with hotel keys, though he often took them. Hated the whites who looked up at him and saw what they expected to see. *You know what the beat of that jungle music means? It's how the white man thinks of us.* On the bar he was back in the rectory, trading himself for the things of this world.

•

How am I supposed to remember what the joint looked like? It looked like every other gin mill I've ever been in.

Do you remember the owner's name?

He walked in the door right now I wouldn't know to say hello to him. Unless he was offering a gig. And even then I wouldn't make no arrangements for the tenor. At least I learned that much in this life.

That first night I wasn't at all sure what Jackson was gone do, even after he took the junk I gave him. The crowd started to get nasty. I'd seen riots that were more promising. Then all of a sudden I see Jackson looking down at his hands like they belonged to somebody else.

"What was in that shit, Wardell?" he says.

"Wardell's in another life, cap'n," I says. "I'm Junior. Your drum."

Then he got moving, but mighty slow. The junk I had would do that to you if you weren't used to it. A certain amount would put a horse to sleep. I think that's what they used it for.

Finally he's at the bar and some big arms haul him up. I get a rhythm started and the piano kicks in, doing his usual key. Jackson's up there looking over the room, which is getting rowdier by the second. But he's in no hurry. He looks up at the water spots on the ceiling, at the bar sign, at the funky old clock. The crowd is getting louder. One bitch even makes a move to climb up and motivate him, but her old man hauls her back and gives her a slap. It was ugly, Chuck. I'm thinking, he better start playing or either we best call the National Guard.

Then Jackson finally puts the horn in his mouth and gives it to them. I mean dirtier than I ever heard him play. You'd have to be dumb as a beer bottle not to realize what part of his body he was playing from. Eyes closed. Lungs heaving. Hips swinging. Six, seven choruses. Honking, moaning, stomping, the whole motherfucker. And when he was done and went onto his haunches to climb down, the hands of a half dozen ladies reached up, not to help him, but to cop a touch. It's a damned shame he had the drip so bad.

•

The owner held them over for two full weeks. They could have stayed longer, but by then the word was out and there were better offers—bigger rooms, stronger whiskey, and large enough draws to buy them a change of clothes and a decent meal every night. They dropped the hacks they had used on the piano and bass and replaced them with Wilson Graves and Al Sims. Thus constituted, they were the Southern Comforts, though not a one of them was born below East St. Louis, Illinois.

Quinlan owned several of the Southern Comfort 45s and had tapes of many of the rest. They were rare because they had all been cut on local race labels that came and went. Under the terms of Payne's will, they were not to be reissued, though a lawyer Quinlan had talked to said the provision would probably not be sustained if challenged.

Later in his career Payne never talked about his music of this period. But the scratchy old 45s were rich veins for Quinlan, taking him into aspects of Payne's music that later became blocked by complexity and revealing the earliest versions of Payne's distinctive sound. One day, listening by chance to bluegrass on the car radio, it

dawned on Quinlan that Payne must have learned his unique style of
attack from the harmonica, which he would have heard every night
at the county jail, some poor hustler blowing away the loneliness and
fear, the plaintive sound of it off in the distance, echoing on down the
tiers.

•

Payne stands atop the slick, glassy surface, mouthpiece clenched
between his aching jaws, blowing out the sin. The notes, they are
records and whiskey and pills, every currency he had ever been paid.
He looks down on the faces, witnesses to his passion. Good Friday at
Ebenezer Baptist comes back to him, with Rev. Corn taking the text
from a Catholic missal someone had given him, reading the part of
Jesus as the congregation read the part of the Jews.

"Kill him," they said in unison. "Kill him."

And he felt the sin of it coursing through his body as strong as the
throb of love.

The crowd shouts up at him where he hangs on a note.

"Play it," they cry.

"Blow that thing."

The bitches' faces rise toward him, shining with heat. His tongue
flutters on the sharp end of the reed, imitating every blues honker who
ever blew a note. And for a moment, in his anger, the shame is apart
from him, something written by others. *Kill him!*

The crowd noise rises. The Jew makes him do it. Rev. Corn leads
the congregation in the awful Easter words. Payne is imitating him, too.
Call and response. Strange how surely it comes out of the bell of his
horn. *Kill him!* And how the crowd loves him for it.

2.

It was one of those times you think you gone live forever. The money
was getting bigger and bigger. No more of that "Nigger, dance!" shit. It

was Mister Leonard to the club owners. Mister Payne will now walk the bar. We even had a white man as an agent.

Who was that?

Lanny Klein. A top guy at the time. Drove around in a white stretch Caddy like a pimp. Funny cat, man. Had plastic covers on the seats.

He handle R&B only or rock and roll as well?

Some of his bands were race, some weren't. He was willing to represent anything except for jazz. Art fart, he said. Who's gonna pay to hear you play shit they can't dance to? You don't give them what they want, one of my greasers will.

See, he knew Jackson was woodshedding wildman sounds in his free time and catching late sets when anybody came to town. We'd go to the jazz clubs looking like a million bucks, and the cats on the stand would be wearing funky old straw hats and seventy-five-cent ties. I told Lanny not to worry about Jackson, because he liked his bread. And I was right, too, until he went to see Bird.

Now you got to understand, at this point Charlie Parker wasn't booked into the best of joints. Shit in the gutters outside, little emeralds from broken wine bottles, scraps of shiny chrome somebody'd tore off the side of a car. I'd just got a new set of wheels myself, and I wasn't so hot for the idea of leaving it out there to be pulled apart, so I found a streetlight that was working and put it right there.

"Move it up a little, Junior," Jackson said.

"Do what?"

"Ain't good to do shit right in the light," he said.

I had a couple of bennies in my pocket, which I offered him. But you could take those in the middle of the street at high noon and nobody'd say boo.

"I'm talking real shit tonight, Junior," Jackson said.

"Since when you get into girl and boy?"

I'd been doing a little of the boy from time to time but just popping. That night all I had was some girl.

"I need something strong," Jackson said. "I'm gonna go in there and meet Bird."

Now a lot of people have said I was trying to hook him. And, sure, I was happy to turn him on. But I didn't push it on him. He came asking for it.

Did you have paraphernalia with you?

I didn't use a spike at the time. But I did carry a mirror.

"Don't sneeze now, motherfucker," I said.

Jackson watched me as I took out a blade and cut the shit into four even lines. Then he took the setup from me, and I pulled out a fiver, rolled it up and handed it to him for the virgin's honor of taking the first hit.

"Got anything bigger?" he said.

"The name of the president it comes through don't change the way the shit works," I said.

He balanced the mirror on his knee and pulled another bill out of his pocket. It was a fifty.

"Man's got to think large," he said.

He rolled the bill around his little finger, fast as a pro, leaned down and took the line in one long pull.

"You done this before," I said.

When we were through, Jackson licked the plate. Needed to numb his teeth, he said.

By the time we got in the club, we were flying. Expecially compared to the great man, all puffy and big-eyed, slouching in a chair while his piano carried the room.

Then all of a sudden, a couple of bars before the next chorus came around, he stood up from his chair and flipped the horn to his mouth and started to blow. I'd heard a lot of Bird on records, but that night the sound was hard, Chuck. And at the time every other cat seemed to be going soft. Parker himself had played with that white cat, Chet Baker, who always sounded like he had his feet up on the couch. But this Bird was different. You couldn't scratch his solo with a diamond ring.

We found a table. Jackson unrolled the bill we had used for horning and laid it out under the ashtray as earnest against the tab. I kidded the girl about whether it wasn't a little late to be buying a drink, and she said something about being on Whiskey Standard Time. From the look of the crowd, after-hours alcohol was the least of it. I was pretty sure I wasn't the only one with a bag of great getting-up morning in his pocket.

"Tell the Man that Jackson Payne here would like to sit in on tenor," I said.

"He know you, Mr. Payne?" she said, interested, like maybe she might like to know, too.

"He don't," I said, "but he will."

Now you probably heard a lot of stories about all the ways that Bird had of getting money. They said he'd even borrow a friend's horn and hock it to feed the monkey. But I had never heard about him or anybody else doing what he did that night.

The lady came back with our drinks and told us Bird was thinking about Jackson's request but wasn't sure.

"What's he want?" I said. "An audition?"

"He told me to tell you he wasn't feeling too well and maybe if he thought he'd start feeling better it would be different," the waitress said.

"Would $25 cure him?" Jackson said.

She said she'd see.

"You got any more of that good stuff?" he asks me when she is gone.

"It's the last I have."

"My teeth hurt, Junior," he says, "and I'm about to face the Man."

So I give it to him and he goes off to the can.

When he comes back and starts sucking on his reed, the girl picks up Bird's fee, and we know it's on. Under the table I take back from Jackson the crumbs he left in the glassine bag, and it looks to me like the cat has snorted enough he could've had all his teeth pulled.

Next thing I know he's up on the stand, waiting out Bird's solo. His hands are locked on the bell of his horn. His head is down, like he's praying. Serene, Chuck. That's what he was. If you didn't know, you'd never guess the cat had a nose full of spice.

Do you recall what tune Parker was blowing on?

Man don't forget a thing like that. It was "Koko."

It must have been something to hear Bird do that live.

Something and a half, Chuck. The "Cherokee" changes go by so fast. No white man gone catch *that* Indian. I started feeling sorry for Jackson up there. Bird didn't make it easy, either. He broke his solo right in the middle of a chorus. Most cats would've waited to jump aboard until the first bar came around again. But not Jackson. He comes flying in right behind Bird, seamless as if Bird himself had just taken it down an octave into the tenor range.

I've heard others do that.

OK. OK. There were plenty doing Parker riffs at that time. But I don't know anybody who would've tried what Jackson did next. He took the phrase Bird ended with and repeated it, three, four times over the chords going by so lickety split that you almost couldn't tell they didn't fit. Didn't but did, because pretty soon it was like a chant, adding a note or changing an accent every time it circled around again. The thing wound tighter and tighter until you knew it was gone pop.

And then it did. The riff became a rush. Flew right off the chart. It brought Bird himself out of his stupor, and the look on his face said, "Who the fuck *is* this cat?" Jackson answered by piling scales on top of scales until I couldn't tell what key he was playing in.

"Do it, Jackson," I shouted.

The man at the next table said, "That cat don't even know the tune."

I don't know if Jackson even heard the jeers, 'cause he was blowing thunder and lightning, flashing all over the place. Then all of a sudden Bird is up saying something in his ear. I'll tell you what I thought. I thought the quarter'd just run out in the juke.

But it wasn't ending. It was going higher. Bird was blowing along with Jackson now, feeding him things the piano and bass couldn't have found in a hundred years. It was a new language, Chuck. Bird and Jackson were the only two people who spoke it. African, I thought. They were talking like their granddaddies' granddaddies coming over on the boat.

Can you dig what I'm saying? I'm not just talking black. This was deeper. And when it was over, I won't say Bird had been cut, but he hadn't cut Jackson either. It was as if they had met across time, and Bird realized he was the ghost of Christmas past.

"What did the Man say to you up there?" I asked Jackson as he packed up his ax at the table.

"You kill me," Jackson said.

"The fuck did I do now?" I said.

"That's what Bird told me. 'You kill me, man.' "

•

Nothing killed Parker, of course, but Parker. As someone once wrote of another wracked soul, he died of everything. And as Parker's music entered the canon, so did his death. Too many became disciples, doing drugs in search of the sources of his sound and finding only the source of his silence.

Yet some did manage to survive somehow. Junior Leonard was one of them. He had started to get fidgety toward the end of the interview. Quinlan gave him twenty-five and watched him stuff the bills into his old jacket and limp outside into the chill.

Everyone had warned Quinlan that race would be insurmountable in writing his Jackson Payne. But as it turned out, race was only the beginning of it. There was also class and age and drugs and being wounded in a war. And even if you got through these, it didn't mean anyone would believe you had. Quinlan remembered the argument that had raged during his youth about whether whites and blacks really played jazz the same. The *Down Beat* blindfold tests became an experiment to test the proposition, but the results were always suspect. If somebody recognized the difference clean, it was said by egalitarians that he must have heard the recordings before. And if a black subject mistook white players for his own, the response of the race conscious accused the players of imitation. More of that Amos 'n' Andy shit.

Quinlan hurried through the hotel lobby and saw Junior Leonard climbing into a bus at the corner outside. He had to wave a twenty at the taxi driver to get him to follow because the bus route led straight to a place that Manhattan hacks did not care to go.

Keeping the tail proved easy in the choppy traffic. The taxi fell back then caught up again, accordion-wise, until from a half a block behind, Quinlan saw Junior alight.

The taxi pulled over beside a huge 1970s street mural that showed through the graffiti like pentimento. A group of boys was break dancing on the sidewalk, boom box blaring, all static and automatic drums.

Junior was only a block ahead and not moving fast. Before long a young man fell into step beside Quinlan.

"Shopping bro'?" he asked. He had on a shiny new Knicks jacket and a pair of hundred-dollar basketball shoes. "What I got'll make you feel fine."

"Going to meet a man," said Quinlan.

"He don't got nothing purer than this shit here," he said, patting his pocket.

Junior was still limping on ahead, and Quinlan kept his eye on him.

"Hard stuff?" Quinlan said.

"So hard it cracks."

"No thanks, then."

"Got nose candy, too."

Quinlan had to step briskly to close the gap with Junior and give himself some distance from the candyman, who quickly found another mark. When Junior slipped into a gangway between buildings, Quinlan crossed the street to a relatively comfortable vantage.

The man Junior met was nearer Quinlan's age than either Junior's or the candyman's. The business was accomplished quickly. When Junior came out of the shadows, Quinlan held to his side of the street and kept up with him until he finally turned in at a flat. With that Quinlan bolted across the street, car horns barking. Junior tried to close the door, but Quinlan was too strong for him, and they found themselves together in the vestibule.

"What is this?" Junior said.

"I want to see what you got."

Junior kept his hand in his pocket.

"I only got enough for me."

"Let me watch."

Junior pushed at the inner door. It didn't take much to get the lock to give way, and he led Quinlan up the stairs. The smell of urine in the dust made Quinlan want to gag.

"Did Jackson live this way?" he said. It was a smell Quinlan could use in the book, the way it made you want to stop drawing breath.

"All these holes are about the same," said Junior. "Except some are worse."

Junior reached the doorway on the second-floor landing and fumbled with its three locks. The sharp smell of the stairwell gave way to a more rounded stench inside Junior's single, bare room. The floor was littered with old copies of the *Racing Forum* and scratch sheets torn out of the *News*. The only sign of a musical life was a broken bass drum pedal in the corner.

Junior stripped off his old jacket and rolled up one sleeve on a gnarled, painful-looking arm. Then he went to the bed and drew from under it a candle, candle stand, and a blackened spoon.

"Can I see the drugs?" said Quinlan.

Junior handed the bag to him warily and watched, as if the thing were fine china and Quinlan a clumsy child. Quinlan sniffed at the bag.

"Cocaine?" he said.

"Smack," said Junior, setting up the candle on the end table and lighting it with a remarkably steady hand.

Quinlan opened the Baggie, and Junior rose off the bed to stop him. Quinlan put his back to Junior, wet his finger the way he saw TV narcs do.

"Hey man, careful," Junior said.

When Quinlan brought his finger up to his nose, he smelled a sweetness, like soap, and a hint of milk. As the finger touched his tongue, the taste was cold. He wanted no more of it, but by this time Junior desperately did.

Afterward what stayed with Quinlan most was the fear he felt as Junior cooked the heroin and drew it into a syringe. What if the police had followed them as he had followed Junior? As Junior shot up, a look of shock and relief came over his face. Payne had died doing this.

But then the needle was full of blood and Junior was lying easily back on the bed. The line between life and death had softened but held.

•

The night after his session with Bird, Payne showed up for the gig in a definite mood.

"You on something heavy tonight?" Junior asked.

"I'm 'bout as straight as your hair," Payne said.

The first tune was an easy, loping thing, but Payne played it differently, doing triplets on the quarter notes in odd, Monkish dissonance over the piano's simple blues chords. It was not eccentric enough to stir the crowd. But what the crowd couldn't notice was that Payne was playing runs that didn't fall naturally on the horn unless you had worked out the alternate fingerings and practiced them over and over to get the intonation right.

"Steady, Jackson," said Junior before they launched the next number.

With each tune Payne grew bolder, working himself into a kind of ecstasy as the crowd kept trying to pull him back. Later, when he recorded the tune he developed from his solo that night, the critics took the title to be a musical wordplay referring to its odd syncopation. He called it "Off the Bar."

"Get on up on there, Jackson!" the crowd shouted. "Get down!"

The tune was over now. The piano was idling around some

chords in B-flat, and Junior ticked the snare nervously as Payne picked the microphone off the stand. His fingers felt for the switch and threw it, producing a feedback squeal. When he first spoke, the stomping cheers of the crowd swallowed up the words. Then he tried again.

"I ain't gonna dance," he said.

The crowd looked around as if they hadn't understood.

"These feet stay on the ground," he said.

There were cries of encouragement, as if this were just a part of the act. But soon enough, as Payne stepped back from the mic and made no move toward the bar, the jeers began.

Junior was out from behind his traps now. When he reached the front he put his hand over the mic.

"What the fuck you doing, man?" he said.

•

That was the end of the set, the end of the gig. We were out on our ass and the man was promising we'd never work in LA again.

Wilson and Sims went off to see did anybody else need anybody. I found a gin mill.

What really brought me low was we could've played the Apollo. Bitches hanging off us. Money to sneeze. And then this fool had to get himself a dose of pride.

When I stumbled back to my apartment, who should I find waiting there but the very fool himself, just sitting on the stoop smoking a cigarette as if nothing had happened anywhere in the world.

"They're talking about you tonight," I said.

"Yeah?"

"Our ass is grass, my friend."

"Got us a new gig," he said. "At The Door."

"Get away from me, man."

"Not now, Junior. Ain't got time to get a new drummer. We start tomorrow night."

"You're a rotten motherfucker, doing that without telling me."

"Stick with me, Junior," he said.

At that point who else was I gone stick to but him?

3.

By the time they caught up with him, Wilson Graves already had another job. With a tenor, he said, who wasn't afraid of heights. It was this fortunate event that led Payne to seek out Showon Tucker, whom he had heard once in a piano bar.

Tucker was working on a fake ID, since he was not yet twenty-one, and looked more like a Golden Gloves fighter than a pianist. His head, squared off with a military burr, rested upon his shoulders with no discernible neck in between. His hands were thick and meaty, fit for making fists, and when he got going on the keyboard, you almost expected to see the piano bounce.

He lived with his mother in a neat little house miles from the centers of jazz. When Payne went out to see him, he found Tucker in the backyard weeding a flowerbed. The young man took him into a fastidious parlor, where a Stromberg-Carlson radio was tuned to a classical station. His mother entered as Payne was beginning to make his pitch.

"And what do you play, young man?" she asked, cooling herself with a folding paper fan.

"Tenor, ma'am."

"A singer then. Well, I'm sorry, but I'm sure Showon is not of a mind to make a career as an accompanist."

"Tenor saxophone."

The woman looked away.

"So it's race music," she said.

"He's offering a steady job, Ma," said Tucker, that soft, deep voice of his welling up as if from the earth.

"You won't lead him astray, will you, young man?" she said, her eyes still averted.

Payne gave Tucker a complicitous grin.

"That's not where I'm aiming to go," he said.

I had absolutely no time to rehearse with the group before we opened, so we didn't go beyond the standards. "On Green Dolphin Street," "Dancing in the Dark," "The Lady Is a Tramp." Stuff everybody did. From the start, though, Jackson liked to put tension in them. He'd call a ballad double-time, so none of our tired old tricks would work. Or he'd pick some godforsaken key that had us all struggling. You had to keep your ears open. He'd modulate in the strangest places, and if you weren't careful, you'd be playing in different keys without wanting to. And then he'd surprise you by saying, "Do some more of that."

Looking back on it, we were pretty raggedy. But the crowds were forgiving because of Jackson's gift. We got some reviews. Exciting new talent. Tropical heat wave in the land of the cool. That sort of thing. The club held us over. Pretty soon you start thinking you've got it made. But then the expectations rise. The crowd starts to notice when you're sloppy coming out of a solo, when you're falling back on lines they've heard before. Got to be sharks, Jackson said. Move forward or you die.

You must have been pretty fearless.

Thankfully, at eighteen I was so naive I didn't care.

After the first gig there was another. Then another. Offers to play out of town. I had an old brown suitcase that belonged to my mother. When I told her I'd be spending time on the road, she gave it to me, sighing that she wouldn't be needing it anymore.

Well, I kind of hate to put it this way, but she wasn't any lonelier than I was. We'd pull into town late in the day, have something to eat in a hash house, then play the job. Afterward I'd go back to the hotel room and try to get some sleep. But pretty soon the others would roll in with their newfound ladies, and then I'd hear every slap and moan through the wall.

This was before Vera?

She was the last person you'd ever think would fall for Jackson. First time I saw her was at The Door. I looked out at her face in the crowd and it was sweet as sugared coffee with cream. I thought, there's one I'd take home to Mama.

She had come in with an older couple. At first I'd figured them for her folks, but they turned out to be her aunt and uncle. Her own mama had just died. But she didn't look like she was in mourning. More like a flower that closes up at night.

As it turned out, Jackson had been watching her, too, and during the break he went to her table with a bottle of champagne. When we returned to the stand, Jackson brought her up to introduce her to us. Vera kind of slid back out of the light.

The next set, Jackson called the songs gentle. Afterward he asked Vera's aunt and uncle would they bring her again. They said they might. And that night, for the first time in a long while, Jackson went home alone.

•

Quinlan had seen photos of Vera from this period. She was as light-skinned as Payne was dark, thin and delicate, little more than a girl. It was easy to picture her in a hat and white gloves in the pews of the AME.

After graduating high school she had taken some secretarial courses. Then she got a job in an insurance office, though she probably didn't need it. The story was that her father provided a regular check. He was a mysterious figure, then and now. The assumption was that he was wealthy, married, and either white or Chinese. The latter would have explained the exotic look of Vera's eyes.

She must have heard Payne's music as many did at the time, both drawn to and frightened by it. In contrast to the baroque conventions of bebop, his sound cut through to the elemental. And yet it was not easy music to understand. The rushing surges had labyrinthine harmonic underpinnings. It took a lot of listening before one could begin to perceive the coherence. Some never did. They condemned Payne's approach as shapeless. This man, they said, was making war on song. But to others he was making wild, ecstatic love.

When he came to her table and introduced himself, she tried to concentrate on the coarseness of his language, his rough gestures, the crudity of his clothes. He did not seem well educated, let alone well bred. But when he brought out a cigarette and lighted the match with a flick of his big thumb, it was like a magician drawing fire from air.

The next night she went again, this time with a girlfriend that Quinlan was later able to find. According to her girlfriend, Vera told

herself she did not expect to stay. But the hostess at the front door recognized her the moment she walked in.

"Thank goodness you're here, honey," she said. "He's been driving us crazy looking for you."

Vera's girlfriend raised her eyebrows.

"Careful, girl," she said. "Sounds like the type who wants what
he wants."

The hostess seated them ringside and brought them a drink, then
she disappeared into the back. Vera tried to imagine what the room
would be like in the daylight, with sun streaming in the windows and
fresh air blowing through.

"You came."

His voice startled her. He had appeared from nowhere, like the
flame.

She introduced him to her girlfriend, Bessie Randolph.

"Vera told me all about you," said Bessie, giving him her hand,
which he took as stoutly as if it were a man's.

"She don't know much yet," Payne said.

"You might be surprised what a girl can tell," said Bessie, so sul-
try that Vera had to turn her head.

"I only spoke of the music," Vera assured him.

"If you know that," Payne said, "then you know it all."

"You didn't tell me he had such a sweet tongue," said Bessie.

"Oh, stop now," said Vera, flustered to hear Bessie talking the
way she herself would have if she hadn't felt the tug of her mother
holding her back.

"She don't bother me none, lady," said Payne. "I've heard it all
before."

Vera was truly sorry that he had. But not surprised. You could tell
from the way he played his horn that he had experience, and not all of it
good.

"Won't you sit down then?" she said. "Don't let Bessie sass you
away."

As soon as he was at their table, the hostess unbidden brought
him a drink in a tall glass. It was clear and bubbly. Vera's drink was
almost gone; she'd been sipping it steadily to keep her mouth from
going dry.

"Do you mind if I have another cocktail?" she asked. "Just a light one. I promise it won't put me to sleep."

As soon as she finished saying it, she felt foolish. He wasn't her guardian. He was a man, and she was behaving like a child.

"You'd better stay awake, lady," he said, " 'cause I have a surprise for you."

It thrilled her to think what it might be. Scared her, too. Surprises were things you did from right up close.

So she was grateful when Bessie stepped in. Where was he from? she asked. How long had he been in LA? Didn't he miss his kin?

Vera found herself drinking in his answers. He was so poor. So dark. But there was a spirituality in him that went deep, that she thought she could trust.

Too soon it was time for him to leave them. She stood up so quickly that she almost tipped over the little table. Foolish girl. She had let Bessie do all the testifying while she sat there struck dumb.

"I've enjoyed hearing you," she said.

He laughed.

What a stupid thing to say! Now he thought she was silly, that the drinks had gone to her head.

But that was not what his eyes told her when they finally met hers.

"Lady," he said, "you ain't heard nothing yet."

The other musicians emerged from the back and set up. The applause began when Payne stepped up to the stage. Vera clapped so hard her arms grew sore.

Payne looked at her as he approached the mic, and she could not help looking down.

"This is a new thing," he said softly. The audience settled down quickly. "I just wrote it today. I call it 'Vera.' "

She felt as though every eye in the place was on her. It made her wish she had two wings to hide her face. It made her want to cry out for joy.

•

Anyone even passingly familiar with Payne's work knows the tune. Its haunting, deeply felt ballad line made it a standard almost immediately. Payne himself recorded it several times and never seemed to tire of including it in his club sets. Quinlan hoped to find a place somewhere in his book to describe the evolution of Payne's approach to "Vera" over the years, because the song provided a measure of how far he had gone.

The composition itself was a significant moment in Payne's progress because "Vera" was the first piece he had built without a clear tonal center. What made it remarkable in contrast to classical works along the same lines was the way it created a deceptive sense of diatonic organization. Generally transcribed in C without any key changes, it moves so gracefully beyond the bonds of diatonic ordering that even a trained ear will often miss its lovely paradoxes on first hearing. You would have sworn it was rooted firmly in the harmonic earth until you analyzed it and realized that it was as restlessly chromatic as anything the late Romantics ever produced.

We know that Rev. Corn had introduced him to Wagner. But that brief encounter could not possibly explain the origin of Payne's musical idea for "Vera." To reach by study the technical understanding shown by this song, he would have had to work his way, score by score, through the masterpieces of the form. A more likely explanation was that Payne had discovered the idea anew from the material of his own chosen idiom. In one bold movement he drove jazz to the end of the diatonic idea. This was his first clear leap of genius, and the common explanation of his inspiration was love.

•

When Jackson first sat down with me at the piano and showed me the chords, I was just blown away. I'd never heard a progression quite like that. I had to write out the changes on a piece of paper to keep them straight.

Was that the night after he met her?

No it was maybe a month before. It was just the two of us fooling and he showed me how the song worked. Most tunes you can remember because at the bottom they have a pretty simple pattern. It's as obvious to a musician as a circle or a square. This one sounded as if it had that kind of pattern, but it didn't. The tune stayed with you, but the chords went in all directions. Even now, after playing it hundreds and hundreds of times, I'm still not sure I can tell you why it's so good.

Jackson took the band through it the first time the day after he met Vera. The rhythm was straightforward, so Junior's part came easily. Brother Al was a hell of a musician, but he was in a lot lower orbit than

Jackson was. So Jackson had him work in and around the II-V7-I of various keys. It wasn't right, but it was close enough. In fact it actually added another layer to the piece, with the piano moving in and out of contradiction with the bass.

That night when he announced that the new thing would be the opener, Brother Al said, "Oh, shit."

"Maybe we should start off with something a little surer," I said.

Jackson pointed at me with the crook of his horn.

"Just take it wherever it wants to go, Showon," he said. "I'll be there to bring it back."

Which is exactly what he did.

We played the song slow and sweet that night. Later, as you know, he sometimes did it very hard. There were a hundred variations. I used to call it the mood tune; we could always use it to find Jackson's head.

●

Nobody's ever wrote a song for me. But like I told Vera, Honey, don't be a fool. It's just like a mink or a bauble of gold. Don't you ever forget they want something back.

The girl wasn't listening, though. Not to me and not to all the things her mama's ghost must've been whispering inside her head. She was off in her own world. I knew what was going to happen next, and wasn't a damned thing I could do to stop it.

"We've got to get home," I said.

"You go, Bessie," Vera said.

"Tomorrow's a work day, girl."

"Tell them I felt something coming on," she said.

"Well, that wouldn't be a lie," I said.

You didn't have to be a doctor to see that.

4.

He stopped hanging around with the others after hours, and Vera started carrying herself with a bit more confidence. She may have felt in some small part responsible for the period of remarkable musical growth that began with their meeting. Showon Tucker said he could hear new elements slipping into Payne's solos nearly every night.

It was about this time that the quartet got its first recording date with a legitimate national label. Payne was already back on good paper with Lanny Klein after the embarrassment of his refusal to walk the bar. The Jackson Payne Quartet was hot. Its gigs paid more than the old ones did, and no matter what his feelings about jazz at the time, Klein could tell as well as any man the difference between an up elevator and a down.

One evening he appeared at the club with a portly fellow dressed all in black except for a canary-yellow handkerchief and tie. The man's expression hid in the folds of his cheeks so that when he smiled, it was like the mangled head of a screw. They sat at a good table near Vera's, and she heard them talking. The man in black praised Payne's chops. To Vera it was as if he were discussing a thoroughbred's teeth.

"I didn't like him," she said afterward.

"You're not supposed to," said Payne. "He's the bank."

When the man came again the next night, Klein finally brought the band down from the stage and introduced his guest: Sam Reiman of Groove Records. And he had an offer to make. Klein assured them that it was fairly standard. It gave Payne cash up front and each member of the band union scale at every date.

"Shouldn't they have a chance for something more, if they do really well?" asked Vera.

Reiman let a smile disfigure his face.

"I'm playing with other people's money here," he said. "If you sign the paper, you can have a little to play with, too."

You might have counted two beats, maybe three. That's all it took.

"We can dig it," said Leonard.

"I'm in," said Tucker, holding up his melody hand.

Sims touched it with his bow. Leonard raised a drumstick to the brotherhood of resin and oak.

Then Payne stepped up and added the decisive element of brass. He brought the bell of his instrument up from below, its circle trisected. With his mathematical bent, he would surely have appreciated the geometry.

Reiman clasped his hands over all of them.

"You're gonna be stars," he said.

They got happy that night, all of them together, including Vera. She was still sick at noon, and Leonard was a wreck. It took a little Benzedrine to do their gig that night.

·

We didn't see her again until the recording date. It was different at the club without her. We played with harder edges, you know? Sometimes a little crazy. So when she showed up at the studio, it was a relief.

I prayed that having her there would settle him down. I had never seen him wired so tight. He'd been giving us new tunes to rehearse then dropping them as soon as we got them down. He'd been riding Brother Al, making cracks about Junior. He even got in my face from time to time. I wondered whether he was using, but I had a hard time figuring her letting him. Funny the way you can sometimes completely misread a chart.

·

The studio was in a converted warehouse across town from the club, as dingy as anyplace they had ever worked together for pay. Sam Reiman was in the control booth behind a smudged window. What he said was not audible unless he hit the button on the console.

As the band set up in the dead space of the studio, the engineer came out from time to time to play around with the mics. Showon Tucker played a few runs to loosen his fingers. Junior Leonard thumped the pedal of the bass drum and hit a rim shot. Then a harder one. He could not get an echo. The room absorbed every stroke.

"It's like playing underwater, man," he said.

"Dig it," said the engineer. "Maybe we'll add a little reverb. When I get through you'll sound like fucking Krupa."

"How 'bout Art Blakey instead?"

"I've done them all. But don't think I'm going to mix it with the drums out front. It's the tenor Mr. Reiman wants to shine. Where is the great genius of the saxophone anyway? I need to get a level on him."

"In the lobby with his old lady," said Tucker.

"We go past three," said the soundman, "and the studio time comes out of your cut."

"The artist's life," said Tucker, rising from the bench on a bluesy little arpeggio.

Sims came in under it with a syncopated line and kept it up even when Tucker went to the door. As Tucker swung it open, street sounds flooded the dead space, the rush of tires on wet pavement, the squeal of brakes, a keening siren in the distance. You can still hear the sounds on the running tape.

Payne was standing by the water-streaked windows fingering the tenor. His back was toward Vera, so he did not see her shoot Tucker a glance. She did not look well. Maybe it was worry. But it looked like the effects of another hard night.

"They're all set," Tucker said.

"We aren't," said Payne.

"Just start with a standard," Tucker suggested. " 'The Lady Is a Tramp.' Something we know."

Payne went to his case and unsnapped the latches. The top fell back onto the linoleum. Under the bright, naked bulbs in the anteroom, the maroon plush inside the case showed the wear of the instrument. Payne reached down and picked up a sheaf of papers.

"Here," he said.

Tucker took the lead sheets from him and saw that the compositions, written in Payne's close, exacting hand, were all completely new.

"When did you do these?" Tucker asked. As he looked at the piano charts, he could not fix on the progressions. "You want us to sight read our way through our first recording date?"

"Forget it then," said Payne, popping the mouthpiece off the neck as if he were snapping the throat of a bird.

"What's this all about, Jackson?" said Tucker.

"Jazz," said Payne. "You know what that is, don't you? Something you ain't already done."

Tucker turned to Vera.

"He's fooling, right?" he said.

"He isn't," said Vera, and she did not even raise her sweet, blood-shot eyes.

"Well, then, you best come in and tell everyone, Jackson," Tucker said. "I wouldn't know what to say."

Payne laid down his horn and stepped into the studio. Tucker followed, but Vera stayed behind. She seemed to be on the verge of tears.

Tucker took the new charts to the piano and started picking out the chords.

"That's very nice," said a metallic voice over the speakers. Reiman sat in shadows so that all that showed was the glow of his high, balding forehead. His words seemed as distant as a voice from the moon.

"What's that piece you're playing?" said Sims.

"Jackson's got some brand-new tunes," said Tucker.

"We'll have to try them someday," said Leonard, nervously fiddling with his brushes, "when we got the time."

"What about now?" said Reiman from the darkness.

"The men say they ain't ready," said Payne, so loud it could have gotten through the glass.

"I thought you told me they could play," said Reiman.

Leonard slammed the sticks down across the snare.

"What is this shit?" he said. "What's wrong with the set we worked out?"

"You know what's wrong with it," said Payne.

"It was good enough the day before yesterday and the day before," said Leonard, "and the day before the day before that."

"It was dead, man," said Payne.

Tucker rose slightly off his bench and shifted the charts until he got the second one spread out across the top of the piano. The changes were odd but lovely. It was a ballad, and when he added the melody, it surprised him by falling easily under his hand.

"We can do this," he said.

"Shit," said Leonard.

Then Sims picked up on the chords, only stumbling at the bridge.

"Get your horn, Jackson," he said.

"Gone be sloppy as hell," said Leonard. But he was already working brushes on the snare.

Tucker and Sims were into it now, nice little exchanges passing between them like furtive encounters in the night. Payne laid the bass charts on Sims's music stand and then gave Leonard the rest of his.

"Let's try number three from the top," Payne said.

It was harder than the ballad—quicker and more abstract, the chords resolving against the way they drove. But there was definitely a logic to it. Tucker was first to find it. Then he showed the others.

Payne snapped his fingers to notch the tempo a little higher, turning to Leonard as he did.

"You out or in?" he said.

"Better get started," said the voice from the darkness.

"We gone blow it," said Leonard as he lifted the beat then steadied it up.

"We sure as hell gonna try," said Payne.

•

Legend has it that they did each tune in one take, starting with the title number, "High Wired": Showon racing through the exotic progressions as if he had been born to them, Junior laying down an unfailing beat, Brother Al filling in the pauses with a steady, swinging pulse at the bottom—and, of course, Jackson flying all the hell over the place.

It was the kind of moment that tests a biographer's character. The legend was so nice that he is tempted to take it uncritically. At the same time, if he finds contradiction, he is tempted again, this time to use fact to lay waste.

In reality, the session was anything but flawless. The original running tape is a clutter of fits and starts. On it, Jackson is not satisfied with anyone's work, beginning with his own. It is as if he has the sound in his head, like water in the ears, and he shakes and shakes, trying to get it out.

They held the studio four hours late the first day and still could not get a take of the ballad, "Blue Bottles," that suited Jackson. By the end of the first session he had everyone screaming at each other, even Vera, whose voice was painfully weary.

Pure spontaneity? At one point Jackson made Brother Al play a scale on each chord of "Complicity" and corrected his intonation like a teacher in a high-school band. Later Junior flung his sticks across the room when Jackson cut into his solo on "Junior's Got a Set" and accused him (accurately when you take the trouble to count it) of dropping a beat.

And yet, even though *High Wired* was not a perfect example of jazz's free genius, it was extraordinary. The compositions suggested the direction Jackson was going to head in for a number of years. The piano solos alone would have earned the album four stars if they had not been simply overwhelmed by Jackson's.

Both Showon and Junior recalled that no matter how enervated they were, once they listened to the playback, they realized what an amazing thing they had done. What they did not appreciate at the time, though, was how Jackson got them to do it. Freedom and control were not opposites. They were one.

five
that's
why
the
lady
is a
tramp

1.

Finding her was not easy. Quinlan was not the first to try. Rumor had it that she possessed homemade recordings of all of Jackson's early club dates. Explanations of her disappearance proliferated: She had died of an overdose the very same day as Payne. She had borne him a child, who was now recording for Blue Note under an assumed name. She had become a musician herself, living in Paris and singing club dates on several continents and seducing young stud tenors along the way.

It was easy enough to come up with certain official traces: the wedding license, the divorce decree, the record of arrest. To follow up on tips he traveled to Atlanta, to Las Vegas, to the south of France. For a time, Quinlan himself was among the missing. At one point, one of his sons fell seriously ill. His wife called his university colleagues, his agent, his neighbors. But he had stopped letting anyone know his where-abouts, so he did not find out about the problem for several weeks. By that time the boy's condition had stabilized enough so that all that was left for Quinlan to do was to send him a gift certificate to Toys 'R' Us and a card.

Despite all the chasing around, he got nowhere. He needed help, and not the kind found in the graduate assistant pool. So he got a line on a private investigator from a record producer who occasionally needed a professional to track down deadbeat talent. The name on the business card the producer handed him was Karim X. Hamed, and the insignia was a crescent and a sword.

His office was in one of those shabby historical buildings overlooking the El at the south end of the Loop. He shared the fifth floor with an electrolysis parlor and an outfit that somehow still made a business out of blocking hats. The door of Hamed's office was steel, with several locks. And under Hamed's name was a single word: "Inquiries."

The receptionist did not greet Quinlan as he entered, because at that very moment an elevated train passed by, shaking the place with a rattling din. Everything in the tiny outer office had an African theme. The colors were black, dark green, and blood red, like the flags you saw on the bumpers of cars on the Dan Ryan Expressway. On the wall behind the receptionist hung some kind of faux animal skin. On the other walls there were photos of warriors and game-filled plains. They looked as if they had been cut from *National Geographic*.

The receptionist was working on the *Trib* at her desk, using a large, lethal pair of shears to clip out ads. She was not an especially pretty woman, but he could not help noticing the tightness of her dress and the bright colors that descended into darkness at the neckline in a lovely curve.

"Mr. Hamed is expecting me."

She put down the scissors. "Usually they come in here holding their hats in front of them like I'm going to bite," she said.

"Maybe they're embarrassed," he said.

"I guess you're proud of what you got," she laughed over her bright red nails.

"Tell me about him," he said, nodding toward the inner door.

It never hurt to chitchat with the dean's secretary. Though she couldn't protect you, she might at least be able to put your telephone call through. But this was a little different. Most deans' secretaries were small, proper women who did not stray an inch out of the comfort zone.

"What do you want to know?" she said.

"The X in his name. It's Nation of Islam?"

"It stands for Xavier," she said. "He was raised by the nuns."

Her telephone buzzed. Another train passed. She waited for it, smoothing her hair at the earpiece, moistening her lips. When the noise subsided, she said, "He's ready for you now."

As he entered Hamed's office, the first thing Quinlan saw was the dreadlocks. Then the earring—a pirate loop that repeated the glint of his golden smile. The man rose to an imposing height at the desk, showing a red and green cummerbund against the black of his dinner jacket and the glaring, starched white of a gold-studded shirt.

"Don't mind my appearance," he said. "I have an affair to go to this evening."

"I'm Charles Quinlan."

"You may call me X if you like," the big man said. His grip was remarkably gentle for his size. "Shall we sit down?"

Quinlan settled himself across the desk, which did not seem very wide when Hamed stretched his arms out across it and folded his hands.

"You have a problem," Hamed said.

"I'm looking for a woman."

"Ah," said Hamed, bridging his big fingers into a spire. "Man's fate."

"Her name is Vera Bell. She used to be the girlfriend of Jackson Payne, the jazz musician. Maybe you have heard of him."

"Does she owe you something?"

A train came by again and raised a racket. The question lingered. Quinlan was going to try to answer it over the noise, but Hamed lifted one heavily ringed hand. The gesture was regal, from another time and place.

"My interest is solely biographical," Quinlan said after the noise subsided and the hand came down again. "I am researching a book on Payne's life and work. I need to talk to all the key people who are still alive. Vera vanished shortly after she left Payne in 1954."

"She has had a chance to go quite a distance," said Hamed.

"She only surfaced once," said Quinlan. "It was in California. An unpleasant affair. Drug related. She became quite revered in the musical community as a result of it. In such cases it is not uncommon, as you know, for police to offer an arrangement for information about others of greater prominence. It is less common for the police to be turned down. And when she came out of the experience, she apparently wanted to change herself."

"In my experience," said Hamed, "the self is not such an easy matter to change."

"Original sin," said Quinlan. "That must be the nun's contribution."

This stopped Hamed, made him smile.

"The girl told you about my initial," he said.

"Not before I asked."

"X can be made to stand for anything," Hamed said, drawing his hands together before him with the solemnity of an oath.

•

Showon Tucker described the basic shape of success in the white world this way: "You chase it and you chase it, and then they catch you." A band is drinking Thunderbird wine one day, Möet Chandon the next. There are more jobs than a man can handle, more interviews than are good for him. National tours, twenty-six cities, Tuesday through Sunday, six months on the road. After years of trying to get off dead center, suddenly it is a struggle to keep your feet.

Someone is always willing to buy another round. You tell the same stories over and over again. They become standards you are able to play inside out. And so you have to struggle to keep from becoming bored.

"Bored?" Junior Leonard growled. "I was having the time of my life. But there was never enough. You know what I'm saying? When you don't have it, just a little will make you high. But when you're holding, it takes more and more to get you off. Do you have a twenty I could borrow until next time?"

They did half a dozen recording sessions the first six months. Fresh material just kept coming out of Jackson's horn. As often as not, he did not even write the tunes down. He would arrive last at the studio, Vera in tow. He'd race each man through his part and then launch right into the take.

Once they got some new material down on wax, they would bring it out in the clubs, trying to stay ahead of the crowds, ahead of the clichés, ahead of habit. They played San Francisco, Kansas City, Philadelphia, Atlanta. At Newport they opened for the Basie band and got themselves an offer to share a date in Boston with Monk.

But they didn't play Chicago. Jackson would not listen to money arguments. And when he eventually did come around, he did not go to the highest bidder. He had Lanny book them into the South Side's legendary venue, the Sutherland Lounge.

Often they had back-to-back dates with no travel day in between. They would pack up Jackson's Buick after the last set, with the traps and bass along with the overflow luggage in the little trailer they pulled behind. They'd have one last drink, collect their money and shove off a few short hours before dawn. Jackson and Showon shared the driving. Junior and Brother Al nodded in the back and had to stop every once in a while to go into a gas station toilet and get straight.

Vera always rode up front no matter who was driving. The excuse was that she was navigating, though in fact much of the time there was some question whether she had any idea where she was. She was sick as they left St. Louis for Chicago after a two-night gig. Her skin had gone from coffee and cream to a shade of yellow nobody would ever have called high.

The length of Illinois was not as hard a push as some they had made. Still, Jackson was jumpy. He thrust the map over his shoulder to Showon and demanded to know whether they were lost. He complained about the state of the road, the weather, the sameness of the tiny farm towns they passed through in the rain.

"You acting like there's a man in Chicago you don't want to see," said Showon.

"He's dead," said Jackson.

"Who's that?" said Junior. "The man you used to be?"

•

We could've stayed anywhere. We could've put up in the Sherman House or the Stevens, with a full view of the lake. I'd been to Chicago before, and I said to myself, Junior, sun's gone shine on your back door someday. And then you gone do Chicago like it's meant to be done. Rise up in glory. Get your ass uptown. Cat bringing breakfast right into the room on a tray. White cat, maybe. Give him a big tip. But now when I finally got a chance to live out the dream, Jackson say we got to stay on the South Side. I'm not saying the joint was a slum. But it was down where the folks got off the City of New Orleans with their cardboard luggage and floppy-ass shoes.

•

The band arrived late, checked in at the Sutherland, and everyone tried to draw a little sleep from whatever elixir they had. Who had what, of course, was a key question. That and who was the mouth.

The first night the audience was huge. Payne's own people were there. Behind them were a couple of parties of guys who had played with Payne at one time or another. Payne made a point of buying them a round.

After the first set, the audience mobbed him. Junior always said one of the fans must have given him the Judas kiss. He remembered one guy in particular, who said he was a buddy from the war.

•

It was a hell of a night. Hell of a night. Seeing him come home like that in glory and me still jumping whenever a car backfired, like it was Joe Chink again.

I'd worn his albums down listening, but it wasn't nothing like seeing him up there in the flesh. Didn't look like the war had left a mark on him, until he began to play. Then he made that old horn moan. Not like a woman moans. Like something hurt inside.

When the set was over I asked him would he play "Taps" during the next set the way he did at Benning. He said he couldn't, because he wasn't there anymore.

•

Mama was so proud, even though it was a tavern. When you actually got inside, it wasn't so bad really. And you've got to remember that for the longest time we'd lost track of him. So when he showed up in Chicago, it was like Mama's prayers had been answered. She hauled us straight to Robert Hall to get new outfits. She even got the pastor to put a notice of the performance in the church bulletin.

The last thing we dreamed was that we would meet a lady. But that was surely what Vera Bell was. I liked her from the start, even if she did drink a little more than I like to see a woman do. She sure was good to Mama. Making certain she was seated comfortably in a spot where she could see.

Then Jackson played, and he made you want to shout Amen.

•

Charnette and the rest of the family were spared personal witness of his humiliation. After the last set, Payne put them in a taxi home.

The police came in from the back of the club. They had their guns drawn, the other members of the band in tow. Tucker said that even when the plainclothes detective spun Payne around and ordered him to assume the position, he looked as though he did not understand that the trouble was his.

Then they started patting him down and doing the same to Vera. He did not like to see another man's hands on her, and he tried to pull the gorilla off. The next instant his arms were wrenched behind him and his face slammed down on the cold, scarred wood of the bar.

"They're clean," said a voice.

"You ain't looked hard enough," said another. "Check that shit on the stage."

Hands propelled Payne forward.

"These come apart?" said a detective, his finger ticking against the head of the snare. "Sounds like there's something inside."

"It's supposed to sound that way," said Leonard.

But the detective wasn't listening. He nudged the drum with his hip.

"Open it," he said.

A pocketknife flashed and plunged. The snare head popped as it split.

"Nothing, sarge."

"Do the others."

"Hey, man," said Leonard, lurching against the restraining arms.

The knife flashed into the tom-toms and then the bass.

"They're empty."

"Check out that luggage over there." The sergeant pointed to Payne's case, but when the uniform tried the latch, it would not come open.

"In my pocket," said Payne. "The key."

The uniform reached in and found it, tossing it to the plainclothes sergeant, who did the honors.

"Bingo," he said as he popped it open.

There, laid out on the plush among the reeds, lubricant bottles and shining rags, were three glassine bags.

"Want to make a bet what this is?" the uniform said.

"It sure ain't sugar," said the first detective.

"Who you carrying for?" the sergeant demanded.

"Nobody," said Payne.

"You don't believe in sharing?"

"I don't know how the shit got there."

"Rastus," the cop said sweetly, "you had the fucking key."

By this time the papers had shown up. Leonard and Sims covered their faces with their hats. Payne looked into the lens.

"This guy any good, do you know?" asked one of the reporters.

"Beats the shit out of me," said the sergeant. "One thing I do know, though. Leroy here isn't too fucking smart."

They put Payne in cuffs and loaded him into a wagon. He watched as the steel door closed and then heard the bolt slide home. Vera was crying. Flashbulbs popped. He stood on his toes until his face was at the window. His fingers slipped between the bars and held on as the vehicle started up with a lurch. He remembered the Chinese POWs in Korea, the way they stood at the wire.

·

He wasn't holding for me. I think you ought to find that vet who had him cornered at the bar. Guy'll do a lot of stupid shit for a buddy.

Unless Jackson was using heavily himself.

What's the difference? He didn't go down. Shit just disappeared somewhere between the hotel and the cop house. Next morning, Jackson was free and clear with his picture in all the papers.

Bad publicity.

Turned out to be a damned shame we split town. I heard they had a turn-away crowd looking for us at the lounge.

·

It was a matter of faith to Quinlan that he could know from listening whether a man was strung out. So it bothered him that he was having so much trouble telling from the recordings of this period just when Jackson had gotten hooked. At no point was there a detectable fall-off of intensity, a diffusion of focus, a slip in precision or speed.

But from other evidence, Quinlan knew that there were times when Jackson came to a session so spaced out he nodded off during other men's solos. Then someone would shake him, he'd stir and be up and quoting from the riffs he'd slept through. It was as if the music came not from the higher centers of consciousness, but directly from his spine.

·

For several weeks Quinlan heard nothing from Hamed. Then one day he received a call from the receptionist, who told him to go to Washington, D.C.

When Quinlan emerged from the plane, he could not miss the detective. A silken handkerchief of black, red, and green punctuated

Hamed's white linen suit, and a pink Panama hat topped his dreadlocks. The man stood like a flowering tree.

Quinlan had not checked his bag, so they were able to go directly to a taxi. Hamed gave the driver the name of the hotel. Then he turned to Quinlan and grinned.

"I have taken the liberty of booking you a room adjoining mine, Sahib," he said in a mocking basso.

The taxi driver's eyes were in the rearview mirror. The name on the card was African.

"He means no insult," explained Quinlan.

In a lovely, Commonwealth accent, the taxi driver said, "Strange continent."

They crossed the river near the Lincoln Memorial and swung down the edge of the Mall.

"There are a few matters we need to go over," Hamed said. The taxi turned left before the Ellipse and got immediately caught in gridlock. The sun beat through the window, overwhelming the conditioned air. "She has immersed herself in the threatening element."

"She's down and out then."

"You will see," Hamed said.

The taxi rattled up to the Mayflower Hotel canopy. Quinlan pulled out his wallet, but Hamed pushed it down and gave the driver the exact fare and instructions to be back in one hour to earn an ample gratuity.

"There are always taxis," said the driver.

"To go where we will be going requires someone we can rely on to be there when we need him."

"There has been very much trouble," said the driver. "Perhaps you have heard about it. Men in fancy suits selling drugs in the neighborhoods. Other men shooting them down."

Hamed grinned.

"My brother here is a scholar," he said. "Aren't you, Mr. Charles."

In the lobby Hamed presented Quinlan with a room key. The room was a suite, its living room complete with a writing table and couch. Hamed went to a long, low cabinet, opened the door, and exposed a combination television and radio. When he turned it on, the jazz was unfamiliar but quite nice.

"They played some Payne last night," said Hamed. "It was not easy music to listen to. I found it very dark. Do you understand it?"

"I'm trying to."

"The lady is more like the light."

Quinlan went to the radio and turned it down, because trying to identify the horn player distracted him.

"They say she is part Chinese," Quinlan said.

"Are matters of blood so important to you?"

"We live in an imperfect world, Mr. Hamed."

"Under my glass, Sahib," he said, "it is a diamond."

•

The file Hamed handed Quinlan was thin. Vera's father's name was not listed on the birth certificate. But Hamed did find it in the record of her baptism: Thomas Woo. Hamed had also come up with several photos from her school years. She was hauntingly lovely in pinafores and Sunday school gloves.

Once Hamed had established the basics, he tried to reconstruct her movements after the time of Payne's arrest in Chicago. She apparently went straight back to where she had come from.

"Force a person out of his natural element however you will," said Hamed, "and he will still be who he is. This is the fundamental secret of my trade."

"Some learn to blow free," said Quinlan.

"And then surrender to addiction?"

"How bad did it get for her?"

"It is difficult to be precise about such things."

"She did get arrested," Quinlan said.

"Many do," said Hamed. He riffled through some papers in the file and withdrew several sheets. "As you can imagine," he went on, "the Man wanted to get at Payne and his friends through her. When she wouldn't give, they busted her and put the light in her eyes."

"Are we sure she didn't crack?" asked Quinlan.

"The cops asked for hard time for simple possession. That's what you do to somebody when you're very, very disappointed."

The next sheet Hamed handed him showed the verdict of not guilty. The cops had taken too many liberties for even a hanging judge to abide.

"Then she disappeared," said Hamed.

Through her acquaintances and the judicious use of some funds, Hamed picked her up again after she moved to Washington. She could

11 1

have lived on what her father had left her. And she also had occassional checks from Jackson Payne. But she ended up taking and holding a job.

"Sounds like she still had expensive habits," said Quinlan.

"As a great detective writer once observed, the basic curve in a person's life is regular." He drew a long, graceful line on the hotel note-pad. "Sometimes it will fly off the trajectory because of some superior force." He drew a tangent then brought the line back. "But then it will return. The man with a drunken mother runs away from home to marry a drunk. A woman who hates her father because he beat her finds an abusive man to love. All addiction is the same."

"She needed a job to get the money for dope," said Quinlan.

"She needed," said Hamed, "to give."

•

The taxi driver was back at the hotel right on schedule. Hamed gave him a piece of paper with the address. Within a short distance the bright, bland downtown offices gave way to blight. Interspersed among the run-down old buildings were newer, three-story, red-brick boxes characteristic of public housing everywhere. The stores all had steel gates pulled across the windows and doors, though most of the glass had long since been replaced with wood.

"A left up there at the light," said Hamed.

"I lived near here when I first arrived in your lovely country," said the driver. "Then I tired of gunfire. Sweet land of liberty."

Young men in tight, sleeveless shirts and baseball caps clustered around certain doors. Rap music from their boom boxes thudded into the street, numbing rhythms that even Miles had never been able to raise to art. Quinlan spotted a drug deal going down. There were some pretty fancy cars at the curb, the kind favored by commodities traders everywhere.

The driver pulled over a few doors past the last knot of kids.

"Wait for us," Hamed said, handing him a few bills on account. Then he led Quinlan to a door between two abandoned storefronts. It had been a long time since the locks provided any protection. Quinlan's foot crunched glass. He looked down and saw that it was a broken syringe. He felt a twinge in his heel, as if the needle might come right through.

They mounted the creaking steps. At the first landing the sound of a television came through the door, a baby crying, a woman shouting

angrily to shut up. The second landing was silent. Hamed knocked on
the scarred metal door to no avail.

"She's obviously not here," said Quinlan.

With that the door opened a crack. An eye fixed them.

"Yes?"

It was a frail voice, but not a frightened one. She would have been
forgiven if she had simply left them standing there.

"Friends of the church," said Hamed.

"Jesus save you then," said the voice in the door. The latch chain
rattled, the hinges creaked, and the door swung wide open in a dazzling
act of faith.

She was attractive and innocent-looking, just as she had been as a
child. This was not a junkie, and it was hard to believe she had ever
been.

"Won't you come in?" she said.

She wore a dark blue dress with a high starched collar and white
cotton again at the cuffs.

"Thank you, Sister," said Hamed.

She showed them to the couch and offered tea. The apartment
was immaculate, the parlor papered with a sweetheart rose pattern and
furnished with old, overstuffed pieces.

"You've come to me for help," she said as she placed the cups on
coasters before them.

"We have, Sister," said Hamed.

"God be praised," she said. "Is it both of you?"

"My friend . . . ," said Hamed.

She cut him off.

"Names are not necessary," she said. "Many of the men are wary
at first."

"I am Charles Quinlan."

"The Lord honors your courage, young man," she said, eyes cast
down. "Is your burden heavy?"

"He has an unusual habit, Sister," said Hamed. "Tell her about it,
Mr. Charles."

There was no weariness in Vera Bell's face as she raised it to him,
though she must have heard countless confessions, all of them just
about the same. Her warm, exotic eyes told him not to be afraid.

"Jackson Payne," he said.

She showed absolutely no response.

"You haven't had any of your tea," she said.

"I am researching his life," Quinlan said. He withdrew his wallet and took from it a business card. Then he leaned over the padded arm of the couch and lifted his briefcase to his lap. But before he could find the c.v., she gestured for him not to trouble himself.

"You are the first to discover my mission," she said.

"My mission is to prepare a definitive biography," he said. Then he took a sip of tea. His mouth was dry for fear of losing her. "People need models," he said. "They need stories to show the way."

"My story is too simple," she said. "I fell. Anything further would be excuse. Jackson did not fall. He threw himself."

"To understand him as a person is invaluable in understanding his music," said Quinlan.

For all he knew she might have grown to loathe the music, as many had.

"I would hate to see others follow him the way I did," she said.

"Jackson Payne looked for God," he said.

"That was later," she said. "You will have to find the women he was with at that time and discuss this interesting matter with them. You and your resourceful friend."

With that she stood and went to the door to show them out. He thanked her as the door closed behind them.

But to his surprise she called him the next morning. The Lord's purpose, she said, was clear.

"I was meant to find Jackson, and you were meant to find me."

2.

Sweet Jesus he was handsome. And glory to listen to. He took all my senses, Jackson did.

He had that effect on a lot of people.

The night I met him was the first time I'd ever been in a nightclub. I was just going through one of those changes in a woman's life: You become a schoolgirl. Then you're baptized in Christ. You take on a woman's body. Then you feel a woman's pain. My mother had died and I was on my own.

Did you think about what your mother would have said?

Oh, all the time. All the time. But I'll tell you what this headstrong girl thought to sass back: You did it, too, Mama. With the man who gave me his funny eyes.

I didn't care what anyone thought. Jackson filled that old house with music. He had an odd name for it. Woodshedding. Sometimes he'd stop and say, "You hear that, girl? Ain't nobody ever played those notes that way before." It made me feel so privileged.

Then at night we'd go to the club. He always had me seated at a front table where he could see me. I never thought I was much to look at, neither fish nor fowl. But when he'd play "Vera" it was like love late in the morning with the sun beaming through the shades.

But I wasn't used to musicians. They were awfully wild, all except sweet young Showon Tucker. There was just something about men who worked at night.

Bad influences?

I don't know who influenced who. Maybe I was jealous. The others in the band were with Jackson in ways I could never be.

We'd all get started at the club. Then we'd go back to the house and have some more. And the next day I'd wake up with sweet shame sour on my lips. And Jackson would make me drink a concoction of milk and scotch and the whites of eggs.

Forgive me, but it sounds to me like you were just tippling. Once in a while you'd get a hangover and you'd cure it with the hair of the dog.

The Devil doesn't make his bargain all at once. He haggles with you. Try this, he says. You can handle it. This will make you invisible, so no one will know.

Eventually she stopped going with him to the club, because at home she could have as much as she wanted without eyes on her, and have him all to herself as well. At this point he was writing strange new songs almost every day and sharing them only with her. This was flattering, but the thought of his performing them in public made her uneasy. They were too private, the notes coming in a rush. Lord, what would people think if they heard this? It was like inviting an audience into their bed.

That part of their life was thrilling beyond anything she had ever imagined. She felt emboldened to try things she had never dared. Pretty soon she was doing tea. She coughed but got enough down to discover the way it heightened flavors and physical pleasure and made even the most difficult of his music so accessible that she sometimes had to laugh for joy.

They say you did not look like yourself the morning of the first recording session.

I hadn't gotten close to hitting bottom yet, if that's what you mean. The trick the Devil plays on you is to make you think you have everything perfectly under control. I may have had a little hangover that morning, but that wasn't why I looked the way I did. You see, we'd had a fight.

•

She had made the mistake of offering a musical opinion. They were sitting across from one another at the kitchen table, the bottle between them, Benny Goodman on the radio live from somewhere or another, the glare of an overhead bulb. Payne was even more taciturn than usual, and she asked whether they were going to record the song he had written for her.

"They're all for you," he said, but he did not look up from his hands, which lay like dead weights on either side of his glass.

"That one is so beautiful," she said.

"I'll get your name in one of the titles. Don't worry about it."

His hands now were working open and closed before him on the table, all the tension in him pulling toward the fists.

"Are you OK, Jackson?" she said.

"Why shouldn't I be?"

His hand was around the bottle now, and it trembled as he poured a couple more fingers over ice. She put her hand out to steady him. He flinched at her touch.

"Standards," he said.

"You don't do them like anybody else, honey," she said.

She withdrew her hand. She did not know why he was doing this. The whole room was suddenly unsteady. She tried to calm it with another sip from her glass.

"I was only trying to say you could make it easier on yourself," she said.

"Listen to this shit," he said, waving his hand toward the radio where Goodman was playing over some obvious chords. "You'd like his dough, wouldn't you."

"Nobody's asking for anything, honey."

"You'd be willing for me to play shit like this to get it," he said.

"That's just not fair, Jackson," she said.

He stood up and gave the dial of the radio a violent twist. The knob came off in his hand, leaving the instrument tuned to some kind of saccharine swing.

"Here," she said. "I'll fix that."

She stumbled over the chair leg as she rose.

"Look at you," he said.

"Give me the knob, Jackson. I've done it before."

"Leave it. Leave the fucking thing alone."

"Play anything you want then," she said. "Get up on the bar and shake your tail. I'm not stopping you."

Afterward it was not even clear to her that he meant to strike her. She had lurched toward him, reaching for the knob he had in his hand just as he raised it to keep the thing away from her. She heard herself cry out as his knuckles struck her cheek, and then he bolted out of the room.

When he finally came home that night she was still awake, but she did not let on to him that she was, and he was in no condition to tell. The next morning she found him in the living room, his horn cradled against his shoulder like a sleeping bird. Music was spread out before him. A pencil lay on it, the dust of an eraser. He told her she'd better hurry up and get dressed or they'd be late.

•

He went out of his way to make it up to her. Even before the *High Wired* album came out, he was much better to live with. The woodshedding stopped. He had more time. They went to nice places, and he bought her fine things.

They were never happier. He had nothing but good things to say about Tucker and Leonard and Sims. He talked up Coltrane and Sonny Rollins, said Johnny Griffin of Chicago was starting to come on. Vera was thrilled at how comfortable it all seemed, how free. Then they went on the road.

•

Traveling with the band took some getting used to. The boys were always fooling around in the backseat, jostling, trading crude remarks. Lord, give me patience. And there was always something open in the car. It's a wonder we never got picked up.

In some ways Vera preferred the South. At least there you knew what to expect. There would always be room for them in a colored establishment, even if it was a fair distance to the hotel they were booked to play. In the North they slept where they worked, but they were often treated like the help. The worst of the places bedded the whole band in a common accommodation, which tested Vera's modesty and impaired everyone's sleep when Junior came lurching in before dawn and couldn't figure out which bed was his.

Was Jackson still happy on the road?

I wanted to believe he was. And that he loved me. At least second. Behind the horn. But I guess I was smart enough to know that he wasn't going to stay satisfied.

When did he start using heroin?

I can't tell you the date.

The others were first, though. Am I right about that? Junior and Al, I mean.

I've never talked about others. I never talked about Jackson before either. But nobody in this world can punish him anymore.

Then it's true that you refused to talk to the police when you were arrested in L.A.

The tea in his cup had grown cool, but he sipped it anyway. There had been a catch in his throat. She smiled.

You needn't be troubled. I've confessed a thousand times before. It's part of God's therapy, you know. Admitting what you've done.

I wouldn't go into it if I didn't think it was important.

God does forgive.

•

It didn't really matter who provided the drugs day by day. They were there all the time, like the air they breathed. Then, too, there was the grinding pace of the travel. The insults. The abusive club owners.

Are you going to try to list all the reasons they gave, Mr. Quinlan? Don't forget the culture of the music. I've heard that a lot. Charlie Parker and all the other role models. The search for the new inspiration every night. And, oh, of course, the terrible toothaches. There were so many, many reasons.

And you don't believe any of them.

The simple fact is that drugs were available. The first time, perhaps, you took them for a reason. Then you took them because you liked the feeling. I thought it was as close as I ever came to what Jackson felt when he played the horn. But finally the drugs themselves were the reason.

Had you ever toyed with drugs before?

Hadn't even dreamed of it.

You said the first time always had a reason. What was yours?

Does it really matter?

So much of this is beyond my own experience.

I wanted to be close to him. Just as you do.

I really can't go on.

Please.

Without using other names.

Junior has already talked to me. He makes no secret. I even watched him shoot up.

That must have been interesting for you.

•

Junior had disappeared for a couple hours before the set, and he returned with that numbed, sleepy look on his face. Then after the gig, he went into the bathroom with the shaving kit where he kept his works.

When he came out, Payne was stretched out in his T-shirt on one of the double beds. Vera sat at the rickety little desk. Sims and Tucker were gone.

"You gonna keep that all to yourself?" Payne said.

"All what, man?"

"I thought you were gonna nod right out on me on 'High Wired.' We were carrying you, man."

In fact, the whole chemistry of the band had been wrong.

"I'm lighter than air," said Leonard.

"Vera," said Payne. "You afraid of needles?"

"Just don't leave me behind," she said.

After the nausea, the sensation was as strong as any she had
known. She lay on the bed next to Payne. Even without touching, it felt
like making love.

How much was he doing by the time you hit Chicago?

That's the wrong question.

She abruptly took their teacups and returned them to the kitchen.
He heard her washing them, taking her time. When she returned, she
did not sit down.

I'm afraid I am getting awfully tired, she said.

•

The next day when Quinlan arrived, she sat him down on the
couch and began talking before he had a chance to set up his recorder.

. . . down on my knees and thanked the Lord you had come.
Because there was something I needed to get into the light. I had always
hidden it before. Even when I was breaking free of addiction. It shamed
me, Lord. Shamed me down to my very bones. You see, it wasn't Jackson who took me down. The dope he got caught with in Chicago, he
had gotten it for me.

I'll tell you how strong my need was. When he was sprung from
jail in Chicago, the first thing he did was to score for me again. That
was when he started using the needle regularly himself. Not before.

I've listened to the recordings from that period. I can't hear the
drugs.

Sometimes he'd be shaking so bad before a recording session that
I'd have to do a little myself to get steady and then do him. And afterward Mr. Reiman would come out of the booth grinning and tell Jackson they had another hit on their hands. All Jackson cared about was
getting his cut of the money. That's how he made the second contract,
the long one. We could have done a lot better if we'd been willing to
hold out. But at that point it would have been like trying to hold our
breath.

And then we went to New York.

•

If you were a musician with a habit, there was nowhere on earth
better than Harlem. They drove in at midday for a 9 p.m. gig. Vera did
the navigating. Junior and Al had nodded off in the backseat. All she
had was an old Texaco map of the Northeast. The bridges alone would
have been a mystery, even if she hadn't been wasted, the one-way

streets a nightmare maze of blocked hopes. At some points there did not seem to be any legal way to get from here to there.

"You got to learn to sight-read, woman," Payne snapped.

"I hate this place," she said.

"It don't appear to like you very much either."

She began to cry. The heat, the clamor, the horns blasting like the Basie brass. And then when they finally did find the address in Harlem, it was so squalid that she did not know whether it was meant as a place to live or to die.

"It was good enough for Prez," Payne said.

•

The one attraction it did offer me was a steady supply of junk. They might as well have listed it on room service.

It made me start to close up around myself at the very time Jackson's world was getting bigger. The men who came to sit in with him now were people we had only listened to on records before.

They say there was another woman.

I'm sure they do.

Are they wrong?

I'd become another woman.

Something must have happened between you.

Yes, I guess it must have.

Under the drugs she had deteriorated. Her breasts had gone slack. Her periods had become irregular. And yes, at the end the needle was a complete substitute for intimacy; for her there was nothing else.

Was the loss of interest mutual?

I really can't say what he was feeling.

You've been remarkably open, but something still seems hidden.

Do be careful when you leave. I see that your taxi has remained out front.

At some point I may need to sit down with you again.

By then perhaps I will have recovered.

•

Late that night in the hotel room—the mediocre new players on the radio distracting him like the buzzing of a fly—Quinlan had a hunch. The next morning he made his way to her building again, climbed the stairs, and knocked on the insufficient door.

"That didn't take long," she said.

"Something dawned on me," he said.

He was wearing a raincoat. She put it on a hanger and let it swing from a curtain rod over a radiator. Then, of course, came the tea. When the cups were full and the sugar stirred, she settled on the couch across from him, hands folded in the aspect of grace, if not of prayer.

Can we go back to Chicago?

Right now?

He made himself laugh. But they were about to move into something important, and he sensed that she knew it.

That's where I went off course yesterday. Pushing you to talk about New York when Chicago was the key.

It was a terrible place. I never want to see it again.

Her hands were no longer at rest. They tugged at one another, rubbing at the pain.

He did something to you in Chicago, didn't he.

He didn't hurt me any more than I hurt him.

He did hurt you though.

I don't even know who she was. You do have a knack for this, Mr. Quinlan. I have seen others with training not do half so well.

Jackson denied there was anybody, of course. But you would have expected that. He said he was gone so long because it took time in a new place to score the dope. But I knew. It was something I could smell.

This was the first time?

You've probably already spoken to a dozen of his women. Don't waste too much time on them. They will all say the same. Jackson was a cheating man. But before Chicago it was different. We were inseparable.

How did you find out?

I don't think that even you would have been able to recognize Jackson's deceit. He was a genius at it.

I'm sorry to put you through this.

She looked at Quinlan as if she had seen through to his truth, too.

I knew what Jackson had done, Mr. Quinlan, because I was told.

Somebody in a position to know.

Apparently.

One of the others in the band, then. Showon Tucker.

Well, perhaps you are not so perfect at this after all.

•

Vera was not yet sick, but she could feel it coming on, and Payne had been gone for hours. She lay on the bed with the rattling fan blowing across her and every lump in the mattress a glowing coal. She would not even have invited Leonard in if it hadn't been for her need.

"It's only me, baby," he said, grinning, as he opened the door.

"Kind of early in the day for you to be prowling," she said.

Her dress stuck to her skin, and Leonard had his eyes on the places where it did.

"It's never too early for a good thing, sugar," he said.

"You going to come in, or are you going to just stand there throwing off heat?"

She directed him to the desk chair. He straddled it and leaned back on his elbows on the desk. He did not bother to take off his hat.

"Your man's still gone?" he said.

"He's trying to get a fix for me. Maybe you have something'll help me keep 'til he comes home."

"He be fixing you all right, woman," Leonard said, laughing. "Oh, he fixing you real fine."

She stood up from the bed.

"Do you have some or not, Junior?" she said.

"Sure do take a long time for him to make a connection in this here city of sin," Leonard said. Then he whistled and shook his head. If he had been trying to get her to go to bed with him, he would not have gone about it by making her stomach turn. This he was doing for sport.

"Say what you're saying, Junior."

"I'm saying you ought to ask him who's the sweet thing he went off looking for."

Payne had taken a lot of time getting himself ready in the morning, but she thought it was only because he was home.

"You're just talking, Junior," she said. "You're not saying a thing."

But once he had put the thought in front of her, she could not leave it alone. She smelled it on Payne as soon as he returned.

The heroin he brought surprised her with its quantity. This stash could carry the whole band for a week. After she shot up, he locked the rest in his horn case. This she did not like at all, because it would keep her from forcing the matter of the other woman. Until they ran out, she would have to come to him again and again.

•

I did not accuse him of cheating on me until after the arrest. And then it was only because I was sure it was the woman who had set him up.

Not Junior?

I'm not saying he wasn't capable of it.

It took a while before you left him.

In New York I stole our stash and got on a westbound train.

Why then?

I had pretty much stopped going to the clubs. One night after he left I got to feeling a little off, so I went looking for a fix and found that he had taken everything with him.

When I got to the club the band was on a break. I found Showon at the bar, but nobody else was anywhere to be seen. I asked where Jackson was; he said he didn't know.

Showon was as bad at lying as Jackson was good. So I went up onto the stand and through the doorway at the back. It opened onto a hall that went past the kitchen and into the alley. Opposite the kitchen there was a doorway hung with a filthy old curtain. That was where I found him.

I don't think the woman even saw me, her head buried where it was. But Jackson did. He looked straight at me as I reached into the horn case and got what I came for. He just went right on with what he was doing. I stepped back and let the curtain fall.

six
my
funny
valentine

1.

One woman was never enough for Jackson, Showon said. He didn't have it in him to be true. But he'd play "Funny Valentine" like he loved each one of them from the bottom of his soul.

He must have felt something. To be able to play that way.

I used to tell him, you got to learn to do some things halfway. To you it's all dope.

How did he react to your anger?

He grooved on it.

•

To track down the other woman, Quinlan went to see Red Sloan. As it happened, Red had a pretty good gig, playing the Roost in the pickup band behind Ben Wheeler, who always drew a crowd. Wheeler had been on a roll since coming out of prison after something like thirty years, off and on. A lot of the fans, Quinlan supposed, were checking to see if he was nodding again. But if anything, he seemed to be on speed, steadily talking to his sidemen, snapping his fingers in the middle of a tune to get them at the tempo he wanted, berating the bass for walking off the beat.

At intermission Quinlan took Sloan next door to the Greek's all-night counter.

Did you see that motherfucker popping his fingers at me?

They had found an empty table in the corner. Sloan lifted two fingers to the waitress then leaned back and stretched his fingers out several octaves along the chrome edge of the table.

No wonder he was always in jail. It's like the motherfucker just begs you to rat on him.

I need some help again, Red.

I thought you came to hear me play.

Did you ever meet Vera Bell?

Jackson's traveling lady? May have shook her hand.

She told me he took up with another woman the time he came here and got arrested. I wondered whether it was Cassandra Butler.

Man does a lot of strange things when he wants to get laid. But no, it wasn't Cassandra he went to.

Who was it then?

> Heard it every way I turned.
> Couldn't miss the news.
> The man let everybody know
> He'd seen the bitch he burned.

Burned?

The one he left Cassandra for then went and knocked up.

The waitress came back to warm the cup and leave the check. She put it at Quinlan's place and stood there waiting until he paid.

I thought she was dead.

Who gave you that?

Charnette, I think it was.

The girl's family moved when she got out of the hospital. She didn't die. In fact, I used to see her every now and then when I was out to the West Side.

Why would Charnette lie to me?

Runs in the family.

•

He tried all the Sarah and S. Evanses listed in the book. Then he started on every Evans with a black address, no matter what the first name. Soon he had to turn to Hamed again.

"I'm looking for another woman," he said.

"You're insatiable," said Hamed. "I think you need someone with experience in the musical field."

"Who?"

"My assistant."

"Should I call him to book a time?"

"She is a modern woman. She will call you."

•

The voice on the phone identified herself as Lasheen Willis, and at first Quinlan thought it might be somebody who knew Payne. Then she told him to meet her at the County Building the next morning. Hamed, she said, had briefed her about the job.

He arrived early and was surprised to recognize her standing at the center of the high, smoke-darkened hallway, traffic parting around her. Though she was a smaller woman than she had seemed when he first met her at the receptionist's desk in Hamed's office, she was still imposing.

When Quinlan was a teenager the boys called such girls tough. Of course, he didn't know any quite like her, because back then his hometown was all white. But he was certain he would have wanted to. The tight, bone-colored dress against her deep brown skin. The look of her face, taken care of but not wholly tamed, her expression set in a street-wise frown. Very tough.

"Miss Willis."

"We might as well get going," she said, "and see where this leads."

She headed him first toward the registry of birth certificates. The man behind the desk was so overweight that it was impossible to tell whether he was young or old.

"What can I do you for, sweetheart?" he said as she lifted her hand to be engulfed in his.

"The usual. No known address. No mother's maiden name."

"You get the good ones, don't you, Lasheen. Somebody's runaway spouse?"

"A lost lady. That's all I know."

"Your friend here is?"

"He's the one wants to know," Lasheen said.

"Woman's white then?"

"Black."

His eye lifted to Quinlan.

"Another case of jungle fever," he said.

Lasheen laughed.

"You're bad," she said.

A number of other customers came in and queued up. The clerk paid them no heed as he left his post behind the counter and went into the file room.

"That was fast, Stanley," Lasheen said when he returned and handed her the traditional white on black copy of an original certificate of Sarah Evans, born three years after Payne and four blocks from the Ebenezer Baptist Church. "We'd better let you go. You got people."

Next she showed Quinlan how to check the marriage files and discovered that in 1959 Sarah Evans had wed one Willie Shaw. Then she called in a favor at public aid where Sarah Shaw née Evans was on the rolls for general assistance and, after Willie walked out on her, for ADC.

Lasheen followed the chain of documents as methodically as a scholar as it led to one of the more notorious South Side Chicago Housing Authority buildings. But she did not ask the hardest questions, such as why a man like Quinlan was so intent on finding a woman like Sarah Evans Shaw. Or how somebody who cheated so compulsively could be trusted when he played "My Funny Valentine."

"I need to visit her," Quinlan said. They stood under the arched ceiling of the lobby where they had started. Lasheen kept glancing past him. "But I don't want to go without Hamed. As you've probably noticed, I'm not a man of the world."

"I've seen worse," she said.

She looked at her watch and then looked around the lobby as if to see if anyone were watching them.

"Where are you parked?"

"Need a ride back to the office?"

"I blocked out the day for you," she said. "Let's finish the job."

•

He wished he had brought his tape recorder and didn't have to take her along to get it. But fortunately, the cleaning ladies had been through his apartment, so it was not as much a mess as it sometimes was. Lasheen was all eyes, checking out the pictures on the wall, lifting bowls off coffee tables and looking at the labels on the bottom. He wondered where she came from and whether it was close to where Sarah Evans and Jackson Payne did.

"Nice lay-me-down," she said.

"Pardon?"

"The apartment," she said.

"I'll be back in a second. My recorder is in my office."

When he started out down the hall, she followed. He opened the lock, which he had set to keep the cleaning crew from damaging the fragile ecology of his working space. The door swung open and he went inside, turning on only the lamp, which hung over his desk.

"Dear God," she said. "It's a shrine."

Quinlan had never really thought of it that way. It was simply a space that reflected what took place within it. The framed posters on the walls and the record jackets facing front on the bookshelves were to give him reference points when he needed to describe the pronounced line of Payne's brow or the damaged set of his jaw.

"This is really something," she said.

"I keep my material here," he said, "safe from intruding eyes."

She went to the bookshelf and picked up an album, *Third Floor Rear.* He disciplined himself against stopping her. But he could not take his eyes off the jacket as she turned it in her hands without regard to where her finger marks would go or whether the record inside was secure.

"We'd better get moving," he said.

"Nice equipment," she said, her finger ominously near the controls of one of the Nakamichi decks. "You must have a big collection of records somewhere."

"Yes, of course."

"Aren't you going to show me?"

To get her out of the office he said he would. This meant showing her his bedroom, but that was less intimate than the place she had just been.

"There," he said, pointing through the door to a wall of shelves that held yards and yards of records, tapes, and CDs.

"Look at that," she said.

When he turned to lead her back down the hall, she brushed past him into the bedroom.

"No rock and roll?" she said.

"I'm a musicologist, Lasheen," he said. It was the first time he had said her given name, and he felt faintly condescending pronouncing it aloud.

"Even a music professor has a childhood, doesn't he?" she said. "Songs he likes to remember dancing to? Slow ones where you got almost as close as a kiss."

"My ex-wife took all those," he said. "Fortunately, it freed up room."

"Where's the piano?" she said.

"She took that, too. Now I use an electric. I can take it out and put it away."

"I have a piano," she said.

"Really," he said. "Maybe we'd better go."

"First a phone book," she said. "It's getting kind of late. We could have tried downtown, but they always have pages ripped out. Makes me so angry, what people will do. . . . Both colors."

She let herself smile a little at his hesitation.

"White and Yellow Pages," she said.

The phone books were in the kitchen. Quinlan had a sinking feeling when she asked him for a soft drink and settled in. She slid the White Pages across the table to him, probably making a thousand tiny scratches in its surface, and told him to look for Sarah's married and maiden names and the married name of one of her daughters, which she had had the foresight to obtain from housing records. Meanwhile, she riffled through the front of the Yellow Pages and made a couple of notes.

"Nothing here," he said after a time.

"They sometimes don't want to be reached," she said.

"What did you find in the Yellow Pages?"

"I need to call my hairdresser," she said.

Her hair was long with highlights of auburn, but she had it pinned tight to her head.

"Your hair looks nice the way it is," he said.

•

Once they finally got in the car and headed south, Lasheen turned quiet. The all-news radio station's report of fires, political battles, and gunshots on the streets ran through the car like a rumor of war. As they left the Loop, she directed him to stick to the local lanes of the Dan

Ryan after they got through the narrows of Twenty-sixth Street. A short time later she poked him in the arm and ordered him to get off at the ballpark exit.

"Are you sure you know the way?" he asked.

"You'll want to lock your door," she said.

It wasn't long before she was swinging her head to read the street signs as they whipped past and then glancing down at a piece of paper in her lap.

"It's around here somewhere, I take it," he said.

They were passing along the east side of the long, ugly wall of high-rise projects that most people only saw from the west as they sped down the expressway. The barren, threatening spaces between the buildings looked as if nothing could ever grow there. One after another slablike building rose from the mud and broken asphalt. On the upper floors cage wire protected the walkways, presumably to keep people from throwing themselves or one another off.

"Do you have the address?" he asked.

"Do I look like a fool?" she snapped.

"I don't see any numbers on the buildings."

"Just keep going," she said, looking at the paper again.

They drove past burnt-out flats, taverns, storefront churches barred tight against the Devil or those he tormented on Earth.

"There," she said. "That's the one. See?"

It looked just like all the others. But he did not argue, because without her he would have been on his own.

"Park right here."

"What about the No Parking signs?" he said.

"Police aren't your problem here, honey," she said.

He pulled over and set the brake. She got a head start on him, and he had to run to catch her as she moved across the no-man's-land between the street and the nearest building's entryway. She did not pause until she got inside.

Crude symbols of evil covered every open space. The elevator, of course, was out of the question, even if it had been working. The door to the stairs had been removed and so had the lightbulbs inside. They had to climb in darkness.

She counted off each floor as they passed, and when she hit six, she announced, "This is it."

The corridor had a window on either end. Artists had taken magic marker to them, so they looked like stained-glass visions of Hell. Behind the closed doors televisions blared.

"I don't know which apartment is hers," said Lasheen. "We'll just have to try one and ask."

The door they chose was no more promising than any other. A stylized death's head marked its center and beneath it a large indentation as if it had recently been kicked in. Quinlan had to pound with the heel of his fist because of the noise inside.

When the door opened, in it stood a girl. She was no more than sixteen, belly out to here, a little one at her side. She wore an old, colorless housedress and had her hair up in a rag. A cigarette hung from her lips. In her hand was a can of malt liquor with a symbol of a bull on it.

"What you want?" she said.

Quinlan was about to begin explaining about Jackson Payne when Lasheen stepped forward.

"We're from downtown," she said. "We're looking for Sarah Shaw."

"I don't know shit," said the girl.

"Next time we could be looking for you, girl," snapped Lasheen, "if you don't mind that mouth."

"You ain't the cops."

"Try me and see," said Lasheen.

She pulled the cigarette off her lip and flicked it into the hallway. It rolled between Quinlan's feet.

"She just down and across the hall," pointed the girl. "There."

"You've been very kind," said Lasheen.

"Bitch," said the girl.

There wasn't much noise coming out of the apartment she had indicated. When Lasheen knocked, a man answered, but just barely. Through the crack he opened, Quinlan could see only a single eye. Then the door opened wider and the eye expanded into an overgrown boy. He was young enough to be a truant and about six-eight, or at least close enough to be worth any school's while to have him attend.

Lasheen used her downtown line on him, and it worked a little quicker than it had with the girl. He flung open the door, and they could see inside. A baby was asleep on a mattress that lay on the floor.

"We're looking for Sarah Shaw," said Quinlan.

"What's it about, Jimmy?" said a voice from inside.

"Your grandma, baby. Don't you worry none." Then in a whisper he added, "She got enough to worry about with her new kid."

"Yours?" said Lasheen.

Jimmy didn't miss a beat.

"That little runt? Shit, I ain't never even seen it before. I'm the uncle. Don't even live here. Don't let nobody tell you I do neither. I just now come by."

"Jimmy, you come back in here now," said the voice. "Get away from that door before somebody shoots you in your nappy head."

"Do you live in the building?" Lasheen asked.

"Who wants to know?"

Quinlan didn't understand why Lasheen was asking about babies and residency.

"We're only interested in Mrs. Shaw," he said. "When does she come home?"

"She be here tonight."

"Give her this card," Quinlan said, taking one out of his wallet. On the back he wrote, "I am seeking information on Jackson Payne. Will pay an interview fee."

"Jimmy!"

The voice preceded the girl, then she appeared. She was striking, or could have been.

"These folks want to talk to your grandma 'bout somebody named . . ." He looked at the card and took his time deciphering it. "Jackson Pine."

"She don't know nobody by that name," said Sarah's grand-daughter.

Was it only the power of suggestion that gave her the strong brow you could see on Payne's record jackets? For the first time in all the years of his fascination, he felt close to the actual physical presence of the man.

"Just give her the message for me, please," he said.

When the door closed, Lasheen did not tarry. She turned and headed straight to the stairway.

"Careful now," Quinlan said, hearing her steps bounding down.

"Careful is being gone," she said.

Back in the light again, she practically ran to the car, which in her heels was something to see.

He pulled away from the littered curb quickly, disregarded her directions, and took the first major cross street west. In less than a minute they were on an expressway entrance ramp, and when the traffic cleared, they shot north toward the skyline.

"I thought you knew the neighborhood," he said.

"You think we're all born in one of those places?"

Quinlan looked out at the clouds sweeping in from O'Hare, the sun dying behind them, the lights coming up on the buildings downtown.

"Why in the world did you lead me to believe you knew where you were going?" he asked. He didn't raise his voice. They were safe now, except for the sixteen-wheeler edging into their lane as they came through the big S-curve. "Look at this guy."

"I wanted to go with," she said.

•

Her apartment wasn't far north of the Loop. The street was run down at one end and renovated at the other. Some of the buildings down the way carried faded Eastern European signs. Makeshift Spanish marked a couple of going concerns. But the two-flats were promising. Hers was made of large stone blocks, and their sheer bulk made it seem as if it were part of a castle that had been cut up and moved.

"You can park right here," she said.

"Shall I walk you to the door?"

"It would make me feel so much more secure."

"Sorry."

"You can come in with me, though," she said. "I want to show you my piano. I don't often have an expert I can show off for."

Quinlan had found himself in this situation before. They would play "Moonlight Sonata" or, if they knew his interests, "The Entertainer" with a Liberace flourish. Worse, they would pound away at some wretchedly rich Brahms until it was almost too much to bear.

"I'm really not a critic," he said.

"The man upstairs is stone deaf," she said. "You can't believe how long it took to find a situation where I could play whenever I wanted. In this line of business, you work some very strange hours."

The inside of her apartment was put together with obvious care, but it had almost no character, as if it had come directly out of a photo in a catalog.

Everything, that is, except for the piano.

"That's quite an instrument," he said as he turned the corner and saw it.

"It's a Steinway concert grand."

"Overwhelming," he said.

Counting the bench, it stretched to within three feet of the opposite walls in the living room's longest dimension.

"It's too heavy for the floor," she said. "I had to pay to get it shored up."

She went to a cabinet and opened it on a row of bottles and cans.

"Look, do you need a drink?" she said.

"Are you going to have something?"

"Maybe after I play."

"Then I'll have a scotch and soda."

She made it quickly and then fetched ice for it from the kitchen.

"What are you going to perform for me?" he asked.

He hoped it would not be "Days of Wine and Roses" or the Beatles' "Yesterday."

She went to the piano and lifted its lid on the taller mast. Once she had gotten into position, she composed herself in silence. It was, he realized, the first time he had seen her truly motionless.

The piece was familiar. It came from *The Well-Tempered Clavier.* She did not play it brilliantly, but he was surprised she played it at all. It was not only technically difficult, but the story it told was subtle enough that performers often lost it in the flash of virtuosity. Lasheen knew better. There were moments when she had to fight her fingers, but she got through to the music.

"Brava!" he shouted the moment she lifted her fingertips from the keys. "That was lovely, Lasheen. I had no idea."

She went to the cabinet again and poured herself some straight cognac. When she sat down next to him, all the tension seemed to have lifted. She threw her feet up on the coffee table and flopped her free arm on the cushion.

"You must have studied for a long time," he said.

"My mama made me, until I was ready to make myself," she said. "It's a shame I'm not good enough."

"Oh, you are quite good," he said.

"Horowitz was good. Glenn Gould was good. Jackson Payne was good."

"So you know his music."

"I know what I am," she said, "and what I'm not."

She leaned forward and put her glass down on the table. Quinlan noticed that most of what she had poured was already gone.

"So what are you?" he said.

"You've got enough to worry about with Payne," she said. "From what I can hear, he's pretty difficult."

"Does his music speak to your experience?"

"What if I told you my experience was Bach and Mozart, just like yours?"

"Actually, mine was Louis Armstrong, Duke Ellington, and Charlie Parker. My father was avid. You saw some of his collection in my closet this afternoon."

"When I listen to his records I feel like Payne is all right there," she said, her hands before her, near her breasts.

"He makes you want to trust him," Quinlan said.

She turned her glass with graceful fingers.

"I was glad Hamed called," she said. "I thought I had probably scared you that first day in the office."

He hesitated to respond because she stirred a place in him that was not supposed to acknowledge fear. But then he realized that the thing that stirred him was not her boldness or any other obvious thing. It was subtle, and he could not be sure how much was taboo.

"I was a little put off," he said.

"I do that sometimes," she said. "Usually I want to."

Quinlan sipped his drink.

"I'm not sure what else I'll need from Hamed and you," he said. "Most of what I do, I do alone. But maybe we could go out to dinner. My way of thanking you. Unless you have other plans."

Lasheen stood up.

"I'd rather stay here," she said.

He rose, too, and took a step back from her.

"I understand," he said. "I didn't mean to be out of line."

"We could order something," she said. "I don't feel like cooking, do you?"

He took a long breath and let it out slowly.

"I feel like listening to you play some more," he said.

"I'll call first. Then if you insist," she said.

"Oh, I do."

2.

The pizza went dry in the oven by the time they got around to eating. First she played, this time risking some pieces she was still working on.

"I keep coming back to Bach," she said.

"He was an improviser, you know," he said. "A jazzman of his time."

"I can't imagine what it must have been like listening to him in person," she said.

"Play something else," he said. "Make it up."

"Oh, sure," she said.

She pulled out a yellow Schirmer's volume of Toccatas and Fugues and did the D-minor. The light over the music shone on her hair as, head down, she struck the first, haunted chords. The concert grand filled the room, as if it were a pipe organ.

He wasn't sure where her feeling for this music came from, but it was a place worth knowing. He watched her, with her head thrown back, the figures beneath her fingers growing into bold, resonating chords like the rising action of a story or desire. And when she was finished, he laughed and took her by the hand.

"Wonderful," he said.

"Do you really think so?" she said, perspiration shining on her high, dark forehead.

"I really do," he said, with an emphasis that kidded her just a little.

"I was afraid, you know."

She placed herself close to him.

"I find that hard to believe," he said.

"Afraid that you would think of me as crude," she said. "You know."

"Ah, but how you play. . . ."

She put her arms upon his shoulders and looked up at him and he did not look away.

"I wanted you to like it," she said.

He'd had to walk away from these situations any number of times. But it wasn't as if she were his student. Whoever she was.

When he did not move, she lay her head on his chest. His lips brushed her hair, which was wiry and sweet. Then she turned her face to him again and he kissed her.

•

At first he could not stop gazing at her, the strangeness of her skin, its texture, the varied shades in places that before he could only imagine. He felt the way he had the first time any woman had let him see her. It seemed an incredible and unrepayable gift. She made him use protection. Fortunately she was prepared, because he hadn't thought of such a thing for a long time.

It embarrassed him how much had been dammed up in him and how quickly it burst. But she did not leave him time to think about it. After a remarkably short break, she had him ready again, and this time it was better.

Afterward she wanted to eat, but he wanted to show her something on the piano.

"I thought you didn't play," she said.

"I'm a teacher," he said.

As he got dressed, she put on a robe and went to check on the condition of their meal.

"It's getting kind of old," she said.

"This won't take long," he said. "Do you know any music theory?"

"You mean harmony?"

"Think of playing sevenths and you have all you need to know about jazz."

He went to the piano and had her sit down next to him. For a moment she seemed like a pupil come to him to learn.

"You know the tune 'Autumn Leaves.' "

"Of course."

He played it slowly, showing her the chords on the bottom.

"And the theme from 'M*A*S*H,' " he said.

"Your man was in the Korean War, wasn't he?"

Quinlan played only the chords at first. Then he picked up the melody of "Autumn Leaves" and alternated phrases with "Theme from M*A*S*H."

"The two tunes couldn't be more different," he said, continuing to slip back and forth between them. "But the possibilities of melody over a given harmonic structure are endless. This is the secret of jazz. The melody line in jazz is related both to something in the original and to something unique in the individual playing it. Here, let me show you what I mean."

He played the basic chords again but this time put on top of it a little melody of his own.

"Now you try," he said. "I'll play the chords. You try the melody lines."

"I don't think I could," she said. "Really."

"Go ahead. Don't be afraid. It's you. I guarantee it."

She did make the attempt, just a few notes, picked from the centers of the chords.

"That's the idea," he said. "Now give it some more of yourself."

"Please," she said. "Let's eat now."

"I could put you in touch with an excellent teacher."

"After paying on the piano I don't have much left," she said.

•

When they had eaten, she threw the plates in the sink and reminded him she had work the next day. He did not even need to ask if she wanted him to stay. But when they went to bed, she was not ready to go again.

"You're as full of it as a boy," she said.

At dawn he awakened to see her preparing to leave for work as if he weren't even there.

"Be sure you set the lock," she said.

Quinlan eventually pulled himself out of bed in the silent flat and went into the bathroom, which was still moist from her shower. A pink plastic razor lay on the edge of the tub, but he wasn't about to use it. When he pulled on his pants and shirt he realized how silly it would look to wear a tie with the mashed up shirt that had at some point ended up under them on the bed. How in the world was he going to make room for this in his life?

Before he left the apartment, he got himself a glass of juice. Next to the telephone near the sink hung a bulletin board cluttered with cartoons, clippings, and notes. He glanced at them. She had a sense of humor that surprised him, running as it did to "Mr. Boffo" and David Letterman lists. He flipped up the notes to see what was pinned underneath. There were not too many phone numbers and none of them identified as belonging to men.

As he left, he glanced back at the piano and had a thought. He returned to the kitchen and took down a blank sheet from the pad on the bulletin board.

"This is for your first lessons. I will call Ned McBee today to tell him to get in touch with you. He's the best jazz instructor on the North Side. You'll enjoy working with him."

He was going to pin it up along with the check he wrote, but then he thought she might not see it, so he left it in the center of the table. Next he went to the piano and lifted the cover of the bench. Sure enough there was some blank staff paper. He took out a sheet. He did not have to refer to the keyboard very often to get the melody right. He used a few substitute chords he thought might pique her ear: Fm7/B♭m7/Em7 A7/A♭maj7. . . .

"Here's one to get started on," he wrote at the top. Below that, centered, he wrote the title with more than a little delight at what it suddenly had come to mean: "All the Things You Are."

•

When he returned to his apartment there was a message on his machine. He thought it might be from Lasheen, but it was not.

"My girl told me what you said and that there was money in it," the voice said, "but I never done nothing for money that wasn't right. If you just want me to talk about Jackson, well, I don't have nothing to apologize for. So if that's it, you can call me next door and tell me what kind of money you're talking about."

It turned out that she had put the message on the machine not too long after Lasheen and he had left the projects. When she didn't hear anything that night, she thought it had all been some kind of joke. He apologized. It did not take long to determine that a hundred dollars was more than adequate to continue the discussion.

Quinlan made the old public library building at Michigan and Randolph the rendezvous point. Unfortunately, it offered nowhere to talk. So when she found him in the lobby, he suggested they go to a cafeteria nearby.

"It do smell good in here," she said as they entered.

She was a short woman but not small. She carried her weight unbalanced, front and rear, which gave her walk a painful, twisted rhythm. The smile that had captivated Payne in the choir loft now lacked more than a few teeth.

"Pick something," Quinlan said, pointing to the long glass cases filled with croissants and muffins in dazzling variety.

"They all look so fine," she said.

They took their food upstairs and found a table in the corner where they would not be disturbed.

"This is just so I make sure I get what you say exactly right," he said as he set the tape machine down in the center of the table.

"You know it's gone take something more than a sweet roll to get me talking, mister," she said.

"Of course," he said and took out the five twenties he had gotten from the cash machine on the way downtown. "Here."

•

I was told by Jackson's sister that you had died.

Well, I can't get up and dance, but you can see for yourself somebody been talking trash.

Another story I heard was that you were pregnant by Jackson but miscarried.

My first died, all right, and it would've belonged to Jackson. That was a long time ago. I wasn't but a baby myself. I sure wasn't ready to have a child, and I guess Jackson wasn't either, 'cause he turned his back on me soon as he knowed.

Your family didn't want him with you, as I understand it.

Oh, that was just the Reverend stirring the pot. For a while there we was beautiful, him on the horn and me looking so fine. I loved him. But the baby scared him right off.

You must have been devastated.

I always figured Jackson would come back to me someday. So I wasn't at all surprised when one day he did.

How did he know where to find you? I bet Charnette told him you were dead just like she told me.

Old Charnette Payne ain't half as foxy as she thinks she is. I got his APO number from guys in the band.

So you stayed in touch all along.

Not nearly as regular as I wanted. But I told myself, honey, don't send to him 'til he sends you something back first. Man don't respect you if you're too easy. Sometimes months would go by. One time I got a letter said he'd been hurt and was in a hospital just like I'd been with our lost little child. Said he understood now how it must've been with me, all alone. Don't nobody care about the hurt you got, he said, 'cause everybody got his own hurt, too. Well, I felt so bad for him I got paper and pen and wrote him a letter telling him I could be good for him again, even better than before. I'd learned things. I don't want to shock you, but he wasn't the only man.

I don't shock easily.

It was a long time before I heard from him after that. He was back in the States, out West somewhere. Something had happened to him, but he didn't say what.

Do you still have any of those letters?

They're worth something, ain't they?

To me they are.

I'm afraid I got mad and burned them.

That's a pity.

Being mad came and went. Just like he did. The man would telephone me from all over the place. Long-distance operator asking after you like you was the most important somebody in the world. And then Jackson whispering, "I miss you, baby. I miss the milk chocolate, sugar, and spice."

At first I said, "Only thing you be thinking about is that licorice stick of yours, like you always do." But then he calls and calls and tells me how nobody ever love him like I do. Pretty soon a girl wants to believe. So when he finally says he's coming back to Chicago and needs to see me, what am I gone say but when?

Where did you meet?

Downtown. At the Stevens Hotel. For lunch. God, how they all
made way for him. And then afterward he says he has a room and
would I like to see the lake. Like I never seen it before. I'd seen everything he had to show me, but I still said yes, 'cause I wanted to see it
again.

Were you with him often after that?

For a little while. After he got rid of the bitch who got him busted.

It's funny, you know. She blames you for his arrest.

Me? Ain't that a comfort. I never so much as looked at the stuff.
And she says I got *him* in trouble?

*She thought you turned him in to the police because you were
jealous.*

That day he said all the things a girl wants to hear. Only thing I
was jealous of was the clock that said he got to go get ready to play.

Your daughter's child. I saw his features in her.

That was later. I was with him in New York and it happened
again. But this time he never come back to me once. He was into the
drugs pretty heavy, of course. I just didn't have any taste for it. But at
least I actually had his babies this time. Twins.

Are you sure they were his?

People said I couldn't prove it.

Which people?

The lawyers for the lady he was married to in the end. The one
with the Arab name. When he died I contacted his record company and
told them there was a child in case there was anything left over. They
referred me to the woman with the Arab name, and she sent me to her
lawyers, who just laughed in my face. They said I should go ahead and
try to prove it was his daughter, a woman like me. That's just what they
said. A woman like me. I might not be the best in the world, but I only
slept with one man at a time.

You said twins.

The boy, he was killed. Just like his daddy's daddy was. Maybe
his daddy, too, for all I know. There are all kinds of stories, you know.

Does your daughter know who her father is?

I brought home a tape of his once and put it on the box. She didn't
listen to more than a minute or two before she say, "What is this shit?"
and walks away. I can't say I blame her. He never once did right by her.
I'm just sorry she don't let herself love the music. They say it was

genius. And if it was, she got some of it inside her, running in her blood like notes from his horn.

•

Experts agree that the worst part of withdrawal is not the physical sensations, though they are strong enough that, like nausea, they drive out every other thought. The worst part is that the junkie knows exactly how to get relief. It is sometimes said that people use drugs to deliver themselves from the limitations of their lives. This is not precise. The primary reason they use drugs is to deliver themselves from the limits imposed by using drugs.

In New York Payne sampled all manner of chemicals. He was hooked, of course, long before he got the heroin habit. He was hooked on discovery, on release from the quotidian, on flying free. Whenever the stimulant was withdrawn, his brain demanded a substitute, any chemical that could attach itself to the jagged edges of normal life and produce the semblance of creative flow.

The solution to the aesthetic paradox of freedom and dependency is this: Art rewards its maker's obsessive works so fully that to the ruthless brain the product of genius and the opiate become functionally the same. And a maintenance dose is never enough. The brain demands its high. This explains why great minds so rarely are able to savor their triumphs. Instead, they relentlessly push the logic of their success until it no longer makes any sense at all.

•

At some point during this period, Payne came upon an obscure book called *A Thesaurus of Scales and Melodic Patterns* by Nicolas Slonimsky, which methodically categorized a wide array of combinations of notes. Payne systematically worked through the permutations, practicing them so much that friends thought he had gone mad.

John Stuart Mill once wrote: "I was seriously tormented by the thought of the exhaustibility of musical combinations. The octave consists only of five tones and two semitones, which can be put together in only a limited number of ways of which but a small proportion are beautiful: most of these, it seemed to me, must have been already discovered, and there could not be room for a long succession of Mozarts and Webers to strike out, as these have done, entirely new surpassing rich veins of musical beauty. This sort of anxiety may, perhaps, be thought to resemble that of the philosophers of Laputa, who feared lest the sun be burnt out."

The fears of John Stuart Mill are unjustified. There are 479,001,600 possible combinations of the 12 tones of the chromatic scale. With rhythmic variety added to the unbounded universe of melodic patterns, there is no likelihood that new music will die of internal starvation in the next 1,000 years. Slonimsky, *Thesaurus*.

The trouble was, most of those 479,001,600 combinations did not suit the ear, even under Jackson Payne's touch. But still he used them in solos and compositions, such as the one he called "The Standard Form of the American Popular Song," which proceeded formlessly from beginning to end. His improvisations beat against the limitations of melodic and harmonic convention. Then one day he vanished.

It wasn't until Tucker saw the item in the *Daily News* that he realized what had happened. The police were quoted prominently, because it was their duty to ensure that music in New York cabarets was made only by the pure of heart. To that end, they kept their lines open to Bellevue, where impurities often reached the surface, like rust, from below.

•

Quinlan waited several days, hoping Lasheen would return his calls. When she didn't, he tried her apartment at odd hours without success, speaking into the machine again and again with the eerie sense that she was sitting there like a cop on a wiretap, listening to his every awkward word. Finally he called at Hamed's during the day.

"Is this official?" she asked.

"I was concerned."

"About what exactly? The check or how I was doing on the homework you left for me?"

"I was afraid I'd done something wrong."

"Your performance was perfectly acceptable," she said. "The differences, I'm afraid, are a lot less important than men like to think."

seven
the standard form of the american popular song

Why, oh why do I love Paris?

"I LOVE PARIS,"
BY COLE PORTER

1.

The standard form of the American popular song is AABA. The theme is played twice to imprint it on the memory before the bridge briefly leads in another direction, then the song returns to the original melody. The best tunes make subtle variations as they repeat so that the repetitions both fulfill and violate expectations at the same time.

•

Quinlan was fortunate that Jackson had been brought to Bellevue, which took a certain pride in being an asylum to the arts. Over the years it had served an amazing array of poets, painters, playwrights, sculptors, musicians, and novelists of the first rank. He was able to locate a doctor who recalled Jackson's first visit. To his surprise, the doctor managed to summon up a good bit of the original file, which showed that an oral surgeon had removed the rotten roots of a tooth. It also indicated that Jackson had been treated repeatedly with electrical shock.

•

The theory, of course, was that what many of our patients needed was a way to reorganize the basic structure of their thought processes because they had developed habits of mind that were quite literally driving them mad. He assumed that the electric impulse would disrupt the diseased neural pathways the way an earthquake alters the path of a river.

Weren't you concerned about destroying the connections that let men like Payne create?

Perhaps we should have been. But in fact, we generally accomplished little or no lasting change, especially in highly creative individuals. You see, the mind of an artist embraces both the impulse to organize and to shatter. No matter how chaotic their personal lives and eccentric their mannerisms, great artists are in one sense meticulous. Yet at the same time their instincts resist the restraint this imposes on them. And it is when they reach a point of stability that they are most greatly compelled to break it down. This is why it is impossible for me to look at a Monet or listen to the "Pastorale" without being overwhelmed by fear.

•

Like all forms of communication, music consists of the interplay of patterns and violations of the pattern. Without order, sound is noise. But perfect order conveys no message, either. The C-major scale carries little musical information because everyone knows exactly where it leads. It is the unexpected that sings to us, the note out of the blue, F-sharp as the fourth of C. But the unexpected cannot exist independently of the expectations it frustrates. Freedom needs an underlying order for it to sing.

The clearest example of transcendence and the given is the tension between the diatonic harmonies that form the basis of all Western art music through the nineteenth century and the chromatic elements that slowly encroached. In the early days this was termed the conflict between harmony and invention.

Harmony binds the notes that follow; chromatic invention is the liberating knife. But the knife cuts deeply. There is no stopping point in the logic of the blade as it drives toward the absolute, which is entropy's mortal chill—the incommunicate, random whiteness of noise.

Looked at another way, harmony is reason, dissonance the spirit of passion. Diatonic structure sustains a person's sanity against the awful, chromatic knowledge of mortality. But only the chromatic can touch the unconscious and set loose its shattering creative forces.

And so the destructive repetitions of Jackson Payne's life relate directly to the musical liberation he was attempting to find on his instrument. No wonder he struggled to find elements of blackness to hang onto as he stripped the color from his sound, because only expectation and order can defeat whiteness, which is the color of death.

•

As a friend I am, of course, intrigued by these insights, Charles. But I'm not so sure other readers will be. I'd keep them to the bare minimum. If you must indulge, interlard them in the text, like a marbling of fat.

•

When they put the electricity through him, they said it was because the graph of his EEG was scattered. They wanted to shock it into a regularity that could sustain a normal life. The electroshocks came in furious white bursts. They set off lightning storms in his head, left the needles of the EEG quivering. The hope, of course, was that once everything settled down, Payne's mind would finally become harmonious.

•

Not long after the treatment, he was released. But he wasn't free. A narcotics crack-up leaves its mark on a man, and a carbon copy in the files of the police. The list of performers whose cabaret licenses had been suspended at one time or another turned out to be an all-star band. And as for comedians, to flip through the names would lead one to think the police could not take a joke.

Fortunately for a biographer, the city exercised its dictatorial power slowly, with an elaborate display of paper procedure. Fortunately for jazz, too, because upon his release from Bellevue, Payne joined the hottest group in New York, the Damon Reed Sextet, and had time to produce some of the finest recordings in the jazz discography.

•

"I didn't know you'd take it wrong when I wanted to pay for a music lesson, Lasheen."

"I bet you always leave the maids in the hotel a great big tip."

"Look, I've never tried to get close to a person like you before. Cut me some slack. It takes time."

"Did I forget to thank you?"

"I only wanted you to learn a little jazz so I could know you better. The way I know Jackson Payne."

•

Damon Reed had been one of the bebop originals as a teenager, playing alongside Charlie Parker and Bud Powell and competing strongly with Dizzy and Miles. Since then he had always gone his own way, a loner, just like Payne.

In his latest group Reed had that garrulous old belly John "Tall" Dawson on alto, Pete Williams on bass, Smash Stevens on drums, and Homer Thornton on piano. He had just dumped Billy Coburn, his tenor, because he felt the man had too much wind. Everyone knew he was ready to throw Thornton over the side, too, as soon as somebody else came along.

The first night Payne and Tucker joined him on the stand at the Village Vanguard, Reed called tunes off his latest album, which had only been out for a few weeks. He assumed that Payne and Tucker had heard it, which fortunately they had. But since they had not studied it with the idea of public performance, they played with extraordinary looseness that Tucker said approached the permissive quality of Payne's later experiments.

The next day the reviews were unanimous that in his travail Payne had found something altogether new. The Vanguard booked up solid for the week and bumped Lee Morgan so it could extend the run.

Less than two weeks after Payne's discharge from the hospital, the Damon Reed Sextet was in the studio cutting an album. Even people who became disgusted with Reed's later excesses have to acknowledge that his work with Payne and Tucker was magnificent. Many of the tunes Payne is now remembered for he owes to Damon Reed. And the competitive interplay between the two men was remarkable. They went at it as if somebody were giving a prize.

> *Say what? Why you blowing hoodoo?*
> Do what? Do anything you want me to do.
> *You what? I can sure God do what you do.*
> Ain't God. More like some kind of voodoo.

They stole quotes from each other, bewitched them, then twisted the whole thing until it was under some kind of a pentatonic spell.

The first recording took the simple title *Sextet*. Reed's producer, Sam Cameron, was confident that everybody would know to whom this referred. And he was right. The record was a huge success. Meanwhile

Cameron pushed Reed to expand the group's repertoire so that he could do one more quick studio date and then a live shot. It was as if he knew the group burned too brilliantly to last.

•

Tell me about Sam Cameron, Damon.

He's a motherfucker.

I mean his technique. How he operated.

What does it take, man? You only got to hire the hall.

And yet you kept going back to him.

I've had a lot of bad habits in my life.

It seemed to a lot of people kind of strange. Your teaming up with this smooth, Ivy League lawyer from old New York money.

You don't know shit, you know?

That's why I'm asking.

You come in here and say these things. What kind of way is that to do me?

You know I respect you. You've read what I've written.

It ain't what you wrote. It's who you are. All you white cats are the same.

I'm sorry. I didn't think I was talking about race.

Skin is sound, man. You don't have to say a fucking thing.

And yet you've had whites in your group. Your lead guitar today. What's his name?

I forget.

And then there was Saul Arkin and all those arrangements he did for you, the years you stuck with Cameron.

I kept the same cleaning lady, too. And she wasn't half the motherfucker you motherfuckers are.

•

The Regency Club was Cameron's choice. Quinlan was happy to agree to the location because of the edge of menace he felt going in. The Regency at least had a respectable reputation. U.S. Senators and university presidents had belonged to it over the years, their names etched in brass by the front door. Quinlan looked over the list of rogues and reformers as he waited for Cameron. Then a man at the front desk directed him to the game room off the Grill, where men could speak freely, whatever the game.

Cameron was well into his sixties. His face seemed dangerously flushed. Squash, he said, unfolding his handkerchief to wipe his fore-head of sweat and then folding it back neatly on the creases. Forgive me. My opponent would not go quietly to his rest.

They settled opposite one another across a nicely inlaid table with a few noticeable scars. To get them started Quinlan put the nar-cotics allegation in the mouth of gossip.

It's what you hear all over.

You aren't dealing with some ignorant street person now, Mr. Quinlan. I do not know who else you have talked to who repeated this slander to you. But I mean to impress you with this one thing. I will protect my reputation, as I always have.

I have no desire to expose you to any difficulty, Mr. Cameron. These are simply things I have been told. And I am not the only one who has heard them. These things are said in the open.

If they light on the page, I will smash them.

As I told you on the phone, I am not interested in you directly. But I think you can help me understand why Payne went back on the needle.

You come to me about a notorious addict and you have the temerity to accuse me of procuring him drugs. Jackson Payne was an overrated player throughout his career. Dying before everyone realized it was the best thing that could have happened to the man.

There are many, many people who disagree with you about that.

Find me a shred of evidence beyond the envious, vindictive charges of utter failures with nothing left to lose.

Jackson Payne was clean when he left Bellevue. That much is clear from the medical records. Not long afterward he was back on the junk as heavily as before. I am only trying to establish the circum-stances. And whatever you did or didn't do, you were there.

He was a junkie. Those were the circumstances. He wanted the needle the way a baby wants the tit.

Was he using when he recorded with Damon Reed?

You will never hear me utter a word against Damon Reed. And if you write anything that suggests otherwise, you will learn just where I got my reputation as an unpleasant man.

All I'm asking is whether, when you produced those records, you had any reason to think he was using again.

Was I supposed to check his forearms? The insides of his knees? I had no relationship with him whatsoever. Damon wanted him for some reason, him and that self-righteous piano player he dragged along with him. Damon had his impulses and usually I let him indulge them. Even when it meant I had to be in proximity to losers like Jackson Payne.

•

After our first studio date there was another. Then another. Cameron kept Jackson and Damon happy with whatever they had an appetite for. We must have cut eight sides in a month and a half. Damon was writing good charts. They gave Jackson just enough structure to blow his new, outside sound. Damon often let Jackson play fifteen or twenty minutes at a stretch, then cut off Tall Dawson after a chorus or two.

The crowds lined up for an hour to get into any club we played. This went on for more than a month. Then one night Damon arrived with some pretty little thing at his elbow, cute as the light. Jackson wasn't many minutes behind. But his eyes were so glazy it was a wonder he could thread the doorframe or find the right end of the Kool. He struggled with the latch of his horn case and bobbled as he took off his old gray straw hat.

"You're fucked up," Damon said, right in his face.

Jackson smiled gratefully and just said, "Yeah."

"Look at me when I'm talking to you!" Damon shouted.

"Are you my mama?" Jackson said.

"Your mama puke to see you. You're a motherfucking mess."

Jackson turned to Damon's lady and bowed, stiffly, over his hat.

"Welcome, darling," he said.

Then he leaned toward a mirror and turned the collar of his wrinkled, plaid shirt down over his tie where it had been sticking up like a wing.

"There," he said.

"There nothing," said Damon. "You're fucked up. Starting with your sound."

Jackson was pretty mellow, but when Damon started talking down what he did on his horn, that was hard no matter how much he'd put into his arm.

"All those fucking notes," Reed said, turning to Tall Dawson. "Man can't even decide which ones to play. Scales. Fucking scales. Up and down. Up and down. Like some kid when his mama makes him. You call that jazz? Sounds to me like you got nothing to say."

Jackson put the horn back in the case, more gently than I would have expected, then lifted the strap from around his neck.

"Man don't have nothing to say now either," Reed said. Dawson moved closer to him and laughed.

"All I got to say, Damon, is I'm gone."

I still don't know for sure whether Damon had advance warning that the next week the city was going to move against Jackson's cabaret card. Maybe he had gotten tight with the authorities. I've seen men on the needle do a whole lot worse.

•

Despite all the money that had come Payne's way lately, he did not have enough left to hire a competent lawyer. And after months of bureaucratic delay, the review board suddenly moved in jump time. Within a week and a half Payne had lost permission to earn his livelihood in the City of New York.

This left few options. He could stay in New York and live on studio gigs, but commercial work called for a sound a whole lot less personal than his. He did not feel fit to go on the road again. So he was ready when somebody said the magic word.

•

Paris? What did we know about Paris? Jackson had heard Dexter Gordon jiving about it one night like it was some kind of hipster heaven. Money, adoring audiences, white chicks at the snap of a finger, and drugs straight from the laboratories of Marseille. We were such fools we didn't even know we needed passports until we tried to book passage over.

"They understand you over there?" Jackson asked Dexter. "It's all different sounds, isn't it?"

Dexter got that smile of his that made you think he was about to put his hand in your pocket.

"They understand you a whole lot better than you do," he said.

2.

Abandoning the United States for Europe confers upon a jazz musician no particular distinction. "I Love Paris" is a tune anybody can play. But for a young man of the mid-century whose only experience abroad was in a rifle company, the trip did not seem like a cliché.

Word of Payne's exile had preceded him, so work was his to turn down. The gig he selected was in a joint whose name he could dig in any language, Les Bleues. It wasn't much more than a cellar located on a blind alley. But it came with a bass and drum, which was convenient, since in the beginning Payne had no idea where to look for sidemen of his own. Part of the arrangement was that he was expected to accommodate any visiting musician who happened to come through. One night it would be a Bohemian violinist who also sang scat. Another they'd have to play host to a whole Spanish brass section or a chorus of Swedish reeds. Payne picked up little things from each of them—national harmonies, folkish riffs, gypsy runs you couldn't find in Slonimsky.

Most of the borrowing, of course, went the other way. Europe received black performers the way it had received American Indians brought back on explorers' ships. They embodied Rousseauian innocence, aflame with eros and authenticity. Any one of the amateur philosophers who bought the players drinks between sets could expound upon these virtues. And then the American object of flattery would look at the young, perfumed mouth from which it came and grunt something presumed to be profound.

•

Once we got the gig at Les Bleues, we moved into a *pensione* Henri Arnault recommended. We called it the Roost. Every room had a bureau, a squeaky bed you could hear jingling whenever a man got lucky, a pole in the corner where you could hang your clothes, and a little table where Madame Sueratte kept a water pitcher filled to quench a junkie's thirst. The bathrooms were communal, and they stunk like they belonged outdoors. We shared a kitchen, too, which did not smell much better, and sometimes we all ate bouillabaisse or bourguignon out of a single bowl.

From time to time the Roost got a little wild. One afternoon I was up in my room trying to sleep when all of a sudden I heard a shot. When I ran into the hall, Jackson was already there. Zeke Leyden, the trumpeter from the Irish side of Boston, was sitting in a chair, his feet propped up on a window ledge, a pistol between his knees, aiming at a guy on top of a roof a few doors away. The guy didn't seem to be able to hear the noise. But there in the hallway the sound of the pistol took your breath away.

"The fuck you doing, Zeke?" Jackson said.

When Zeke turned, the pistol swung around until it was pointing right at Jackson's gut. Jackson reached out his hand. Zeke did not move. He just sat there staring. Then Jackson yanked the pistol away from him.

"You can't just shoot at a man like that, Zeke," I said.

"He don't have nothing to worry about," Zeke said. "I'm a lousy shot."

•

Quinlan was lucky to find Rufus Rand, a vibes player who had worked with Payne in Paris. He was one of those who never really came home. But when Dave Sullivan died on the West Coast, Rand flew in to play the wake and Quinlan tracked him down.

He wore a straw hat you could find in any haberdashery on the South Side of Chicago, a natty sport coat, and a pair of two-toned wingtips you didn't see much anymore. Somebody said he must have kept them on trees, taking them out only to put old friends away.

Did you have a line on Jackson Payne when he came to Paris?

Just what people were saying. The cat'd got busted in New York and had to leave the land of the free. I was playing a regular gig in a dive in Montparnasse. Chickies all over. Can you dig it? *Mademoiselle, la belle.* The lovely ladies of *La France.*

You were playing with Dave Sullivan?

The late one, the great one. Cat never did the bad shit, and here he is, stone dead, and I'm still on fire. Crazy, man.

I always thought he was a good, clean player.

You could eat off his chords. But what the hell would anybody want to do that for? This music is about getting laid. In fact, I think Jackson hired me to keep him honest about that. I'd get into an R&B groove, dig? And pretty soon he'd be wailing like he was back on Forty-seventh Street at the Get Me High Lounge.

There aren't many recordings from that period.

Course Showon could do blues as well as the next man. But it was always like he was embarrassed. You dig? Like a cat trying to pass.

I guess that made me the nappy-headed cousin who shows up at the rent party eating watermelon and spitting seeds on the rug. One night Showon got so upset he walked out.

That isn't like Showon.

Somebody was buying, and Jackson had some jump powder that we started snorting even before the first set. Showon always looked down his nose whenever he saw another man putting some fun up his. But I don't care what Showon tells you, the crowd loved it when Jackson jumped up on the bar.

He must have been at the end of his string.

I think he may have met Brigitte that night.

•

In those days there weren't nearly as many African nationals in Paris, with their brightly colored pillbox hats and street-corner ebony. The few with native wares to sell gravitated toward the jazz joints. When a band was hot, the street sellers did a swift business in phallic statues and doe-eyed tribal masks. It did not take them long to discover Jackson Payne.

The band had to run the gauntlet every night between the Africans' rickety tables through the thick smell of food from the braziers.

"What is that shit they eat?" asked Rufus Rand.

"Whatever it is, it goes straight to the bitches' butts," said Billy Hughes, who at that point was the drummer.

"These people are righteous and clean," said Payne, nodding to an elder who had raised his hand, spread-fingered in greeting. "That's what they are."

"Clean, shit," said Rand. "You can smell them around a corner."

"Ain't no worse than a Frenchman," said Hughes.

"You're a little ripe yourself, Rufus," said Tucker.

It was not too long afterwards that Payne took Tucker to see the neighborhood where the Africans lived. He led the way to a mosque, but they did not go inside because he said they were not ready. So they stood outside listening to the eerie, plaintive, ancient call and response.

But Middle Eastern was not the only new influence in Payne's life. Brigitte was the first Frenchwoman Payne had given more than passing attention. She was as beautiful as a statue and as cold. Pictures of the two of them began appearing in magazines. In *Paris Match* they captured the French fancy for antithesis—fierce and fragile, elemental and sublime, black and transparent white. You may remember that in *Life* they had a somewhat different effect.

•

One night it was well past showtime and Jackson hadn't shown up at the club. We were about to start without him, when in he stumbles like a bum begging change. I mean he looked like he'd pulled his suit out of the Seine and wadded it up under his head overnight to dry.

Brigitte wasn't with him. He started calling hard blues and playing like the Devil. He didn't walk the bar, but he was all over the place. Back then I didn't know what it looked like when a man took C on top of horse, but now I'm pretty sure that was what it was.

Then halfway through the set, here comes Brigitte. With her she's got one of the ragheads from outside. He's kind of propping her up by the elbow because she's not very steady on her pins. Not so sweet to look at either, with one eye covered with some kind of bandage and the other all swollen up red.

I don't know what the tourists thought. Maybe that this was what they did in Paris—guys with striped shirts and kerchiefs throwing ladies in black stockings around the barroom floor.

We were coming to the last chorus of this D-minor thing we'd been jamming on. Showon was so far into the piano I don't think he even noticed her standing at the back of the room in a tight white dress that showed off her bruises and everything else she had.

The next thing we knew Jackson was calling another tune. It was not one I had played with him before. But I knew it. Everyone did.

So that's how we ended the set. With "Vera." Jackson took the solo slow and sobbing, for ten or fifteen choruses, before he finally let it go.

And when he was done, he walked through the room and took her by the hand. Nobody got up to avoid the second cover, I'll tell you that. He headed her back up front so everybody could see his handiwork, just as they had heard his song of love. If the tourists wondered which one was the real Jackson Payne, I sure as hell wasn't going to try to tell them.

Good thing, too, because I would have been wrong. The last thing I would have said was that this was a man who was about to get religion. But he did. Got it but good.

•

Even for me it got to be a little much. The sermons. The lectures about abstinence. He started wearing this knitted cap that one of the Africans gave him, like a desert priest. And pretty soon he was hassling Henri Arnault about serving liquor at Les Bleues. He regaled the poor man with stories of the oasis of Mohammed, the polluting of the spring of the spirit. Henri was used to his talent having some pretty eccentric ideas, but this was a new one. "Jacque-son," he said one night, "liquor *is* Les Bleues."

Then came the night when Payne put his act onstage.

The evening had begun normally enough. The band performed a rather restrained first set. By the break the audience began to overflow the little tables. Henri bustled around, happily keeping everyone's glass full. He always enjoyed the music more when it was accompanied by the brushstroke rustle of paper money and the tambourine jingle of coins.

Many in the club were from a tour group, folks from Davenport or Toledo, perhaps, trying to get the most out of Paris. Their enthusiasm was genuine, if not informed. At the break the band members gave desultory little bows and hustled off the stand.

This left Payne up front looking over the crowd, a little dazed. But as far as the Davenporters were concerned, it was just too much light in his eyes. What was his name again, dear?

He unsnapped his horn from its strap and laid it lengthwise on the piano bench then returned to the microphone and twisted its neck upward off its stand. The crowd hushed until the only sound was from the carillon of bottles and glasses in back. Is he a singer, too, hon?

Welcome to my parlor, he said.

The crowd shook off its anticipation and easily laughed.

I see you are enjoying yourselves. Visitors to Paris?

Mais oui! The voice was Midwestern. Payne had been hearing it all his life.

You're going to find a lot of things that will tempt you here.

Tell us where!

A man shouted it, since in such matters all men are men of the world.

In the back of the room Henri was looking up nervously toward the stand. The break was when the audience was supposed to think about its thirst.

I want you to give Henri Arnault a hand, folks. Back there by the bar counting the money that used to be yours.

The applause was no more than polite, unsure of the sarcasm, a modulation that caught them by surprise.

Now, I'm not going to judge this man, brothers and sisters. For who am I to cast a stone?

The sign outside says Jackson Payne.

I am a sinner!

There was a nervous silence as he paused for the amen they were not socialized to give.

But God is good, brothers and sisters. God is good because if we listen, He will tell us the way.

Henri looked grievously pained.

He'll tell us to avoid the sins of the body and the awful sins of the mind. For the eyes, they tempt us with all the lovely evils of the world.

Bring on the girls!

The laughter was sparse and uncomfortable. But nobody was leaving. He held them the way he did on the horn.

And the smells, brothers and sisters. Sweet spices and vapors come to you, aromas that go to your head. Perfume on a woman's breast. The dark scent between her legs.

Legs that were shifting under the tables now, nylons hissing, chairs scraping, the women whispering to their men that maybe it was time to get back to the hotel because tomorrow was the Louvre. But the husbands were in no hurry. Payne had touched a memory, the way an odor can.

You've also got to mind what you hear, brothers and sisters. The songs that excite you, the lyrics that draw you on.

He picked up his tenor and blew a gospel riff. Then he did a little flutter and took it down a whole-tone scale. The effect was haunting. And at the bottom he hit a dark note that was an apparition.

The drink in your hands, brothers and sisters, it is poison.

I need another.

This time he blew the scale ascending. Again and again, each time reaching higher like a widening gyre.

Drink will make you crazy. Drink will cut you down.

Again the strange, chantlike scale, over and over, each time a little different, each time the same.

God is good. Allah be praised. God is good.

The notes seemed to circle when he returned to them. Around and around.

Oh, sweet Allah of my soul!

•

Henri was more generous than an American owner would have been: two weeks notice to give the band a chance to find a new gig.

"It isn't what you've been playing," Arnault said. "I would go to hear it, even with the sermon in the middle. But then I would go somewhere else to drink."

Tucker was worried. This was more than just Payne's new obsession with the Africans' God. Brigitte had begun wearing scarves, and it could have been to cover marks.

Then one day suddenly Payne was back among them at the Roost, gear and all. He did not say why or how it had happened, but she never came around again. And without her, he dove headlong back into the life he had preached against.

•

I couldn't do anything to bring him out of the spin. Sometimes he'd disappear and we'd blow a gig completely. Nobody wanted us as a trio, so I would try to rustle up a horn and fake a set of Payne, a tribute, like he was already dead.

Then Jackson would show up with Zeke and a bunch of the others, and they couldn't even say where they had been. Or else he'd just walk out of the night into whatever club we were supposed to be playing, raggedy as a wino in that beaten up old overcoat of his. Pretty soon my resources started to get pretty thin. Everything I'd laid by went into his arm one way or another—except the open plane tickets home. I hid those, because I was afraid I was going to have to take him back in a pauper's box.

•

The cat was basically tapped out. I never saw any man take his habit back so far so fast. Me, I'd been chipping right along, but I'd never wanted him to see it, for fear he'd give me a dose of Muslim. But when the white bitch left him and he fell in with Zeke, I figured, what the hell, it don't look like he'll be preaching anymore.

•

He was hurting. Every muscle in him seemed to be making a fist. His last fix had barely reached him, and then there was something in it that made him sick.

He had heaved his guts out in the Roost's communal toilet with a couple other cats banging on the door because they were also sick. It was lucky they heard him in there so at least they knew he'd taken the bad shit, too.

Looking at their ashen faces as he left the toilet, he realized now was no time to talk to them about going out and scoring some more. So he went back to his room and lay down on his bed and counted the cracks in the ceiling. One. Two. One two three four.

When he finally got up again, his muscles were aching like a fever. Except that aspirin wouldn't touch it. There was only one way to get well, and he didn't have any money left.

"Just until Saturday night," he pleaded with Tucker.

"Call another tune, Jackson. That one's gotten cold."

"I need it, man."

"Something that will please the piano. You know. Nice changes. Nothing too fast, 'cause I'm kind of tired, listening to you fools puking all afternoon."

"I'm sick, man."

" 'What Can I Say, Dear, after I Say I'm Sorry?' "

"You owe me," said Jackson.

"Without you, none of this would be possible." Tucker's hand swept from one corner of the room to another, the water-spotted wallpaper, the rickety furniture, the sagging old bed.

"Just enough to get me over."

"You speak a little French? *Un peu?* Then I'm sure you'll understand this expression: Not a *sou.*"

The wind was raw in Payne's face as he left the Roost and made his way up the narrow street. The air held an edge of rain. It was coming down weather, like a bad case of the shakes.

He walked with the shuffling gait of an old man, barely able to keep his legs under him when the pavement seemed to tilt like the floor in a funhouse, trying to slide him off.

When he reached the door of the pawnshop, he had to seize the burglar bars to steady himself. Through the glass he could see no one. The doorknob rattled in his fist but did not turn.

"Open up!" he shouted.

A chill went through him as he gripped the cold metal, and the rain kept coming down.

"You're in there, motherfucker!" he screamed.

The man may not have understood a single word of Payne's language, but the sound of Payne's voice drew him like an ancient curse. He appeared from whatever he had been doing in the back, padding along in carpet slippers, eyes cast down as if he were cringing before the lash.

"Come on. Come on," said Payne.

The key the pawnbroker drew from his pocket was as large as a penitent's cross, and he fumbled with it before he managed to disengage the deadbolt and swing the door open so Payne could wobble past him, shaking from the rain.

"Took your sweet-ass time," Payne mumbled. "Back there counting your money?"

"*Quel avez-vous?*" said the pawnbroker.

"I'll *avez* your ass someday, my friend," said Payne, lifting the heavy wool coat from his shoulders as the stooped gray figure moved behind the counter. Once he had something solid between them, the pawnbroker stood straighter, framed by the high, orphan shelves.

Payne slung his coat over the counter and tapped his fingers on it.

"*Qu'est-ce que c'est?*" said the pawnbroker.

"What does it look like, fool?" He rubbed his fingers deep into the weave and then rubbed them together in one symbol that had escaped the sundering of Babel.

The pawnbroker pulled from beneath his shirt a chain that held the key to the lockbox. A thief would have to cut off the man's head to get it away from him because the end of the chain was firmly attached to a choker around his neck.

"Wonder you don't hang that sucker from your dick," said Payne. "Come on. Come on."

The man carefully counted out a small stack of francs and pushed it across the counter. Payne did not even check to see how many there were. The amount did not matter. He just needed something to show.

"You're a Jew prince," he said.

The pawnbroker grunted at the one word that was universal. He offered Payne the door, slamming it behind him. Payne had to hunch against the rain like a man cast into a storm.

When he got back to the Roost, he hid in his room counting and recounting the bills, trying to bring the chills under control. Chills looked like withdrawal, and nobody would let a junkie in a panic cow for them, even if he was able to show them a roll of bills as big as his fist. Every user knew that a pusher would calibrate price to the level of the customer's need.

Finally Payne settled down and went to Tucker, this time to borrow his peacoat. He told Tucker how slowly the pawnbroker moved, how he had told the man he should keep his key tied to his dick.

"Pawn this and I'll chop off yours," said Tucker as he reached over and tossed to Payne the heavy blue wool mass. The force of it almost knocked Payne down.

"I owe you," he said.

"Yeah."

"Really, man."

The other cats had gathered in Zeke Leyden's room to do a little reefer to carry them through the long afternoon.

"Time for a run," Payne said.

"I just got over the last shit you got," said Rufus Rand.

"That was from another guy. Not my regular candyman."

"You ain't got any money left," said Leyden.

Payne reached into his pants and pulled out the francs he had carefully rolled around some strips cut from newspapers to give the roll heft. The pawnbroker dealt in such heartbreakingly small sums that there was only one bill of decent denomination to put on top.

"Wella, wella," said Zeke.

"Musta sold half his blood," said Rufus.

Payne drew himself as tall as he could.

"Don't you worry how I came by it," he said.

"Maybe one of those ragheads gave it to him for the love of Allah," said Zeke's Boston friend, Ivan Dunne.

"God is good," sang Rand. "Ain't He, Jackson."

"You don't want any shit," said Payne, "it's fine with me."

The bluff was better than the plan he had for explaining how he had lost their stake. That was one part hope cut with nine parts need.

"I'm in," said Leyden, throwing a flutter of bills on the table. To Payne it looked like only enough for one good hit.

"Stay away from the rotten meat this time," said Dunne, pitching in his ante under Leyden's counting-house eye.

"Some cats never learn," said Rand, adding his capital to the venture.

The others in the room were in, too. Even though the total was not enough to make for a decent skim, the cash in his hands thrilled Payne. A charge leaped from his fingers to his belly, the way it did when he found a woman or something new on the horn.

"Don't let anybody take it off you," Zeke warned. "Maybe you better carry this." Leyden pushed his pistol across the table where the money had lain.

"That thing scares me," Payne said, knowing that Leyden had meant it to.

Payne went again to the pawnbroker's. The man asked no questions when Payne put down the ticket and redemption sum. The premium cut into the other men's ante by only a few francs, but it was the crossing of a line.

The rest of the money went to his connection, who did not inquire why Payne had two coats now. The price of the drug was high. Even if Payne didn't take something for himself out of what he purchased, there would not be nearly enough to satisfy everyone. But he did not haggle. There was plenty.

He hurried to Les Bleues and used the key he had conned from a pale girl who worked behind the bar. The chairs were not up on the tables. That only happened in joints they cleaned every night. Here the tables barely got a swipe of the greasy cloth across their faces, like the gypsy urchins on the corners.

He had not been back to the club since Henri let him go. It was preternaturally silent, broken only by the snags of his own labored breath.

•

Quinlan breathed easily. On the machine was Payne's tune "The Pawnbroker's Revenge." In this recording Payne was so tapped out that it seemed to come straight out of that Paris night. Listening, Quinlan met Payne in the empty club, watched him pull out the spoon and take into it a couple of drops from the faucet behind the bar. Then he put the spoon carefully down on a table and pulled a matchbook from his pants pocket. The striking surface mushed the head off. He threw the mess onto the floor and kicked at it, just short of panic, until he saw the jar of kitchen matches sitting at the far end of the bar. He retrieved several and hurriedly struck one to light a candle.

The powder in its translucent packet was amber in the dim, flickering glow. He gently tapped the right amount into the bead of water then boiled it over the flame until the solids disappeared. It was strange how steady his hands became as he filled the syringe. Then came the struggle to reach a vein. He held the syringe in his mouth at the plunger end. It was as hard against his teeth as the shell casing or the metal mouthpiece of his horn. He was working a spot behind his left knee these days, so he hiked his pant leg and rolled it tightly to his thigh, twisting it like a tourniquet until a throbbing spot presented itself.

The needle slipped in. He pushed the plunger down in a single, swift movement and held it that way for a few moments before letting the syringe fill back up with blood to dissolve whatever precious residue remained. The needle dangled from his leg as he sat back and waited for the rush that would bring the numbers to an end.

He had been generous with himself in his plenty. The heroin surge was as engulfing as love, as thrilling as battle, as sure as a magical chorus on the horn.

Quinlan sat back in his chair before the computer screen and stared at the lines that had come to him so easily. Did Payne nod off in the hush of satisfaction? Oh, but the cats would be looking for him. And so when his eyes opened upon the guttering candle, he retrieved the needle, which had slipped from his flesh, leaving a penline of blood. He rinsed it out before putting the works into the pocket of his coat, which he hid along with his stash behind some crates of wine in a remote storeroom. Then he went to the mirror behind the bar and switched on the light. He was a mess.

He had never even reached the connection. A gang of Paris thugs had attacked him, left him lying in an alley. It was a wonder he did not freeze to death. I should have taken that gun of yours, Zeke. They had my sorry ass.

How could they be angry with a man so cast down? They probably wouldn't trust him again for a while, two strikes against him now, but he would worry about that when his supply ran out, and by then there would be more money from somewhere, because there always was.

He closed his eyes again and rehearsed his lines. Should have taken your advice, Zeke. Man's got to protect himself, 'cause there's folks out there'd do anything for a fix. Lots of bad ones, Zeke. Take a black man down. Yeah, that riff would get them. You and me, Zeke. Those fucking Frogs.

•

Yeah, I was there when Zeke found the leader of the band. He'd cut himself and smeared himself with blood to make it look like he'd been mugged. But if he had been, they'd given him a dose of painkiller first.

Looking back, do you wish you'd stepped in and helped him?
I lost a steady job, if that's what you mean.

•

It might have been minutes or an hour, the dope still working, slowing down his reaction when he realized that Leyden stood over him with a pistol pointed at his belly, finger fluttering on the trigger like he was doing a trill.

"You copped!" he shouted.

Payne lowered his eyes to the floor so the pistol wouldn't take his voice.

"They beat me, Zeke," he said. "I'm hurting. They beat me 'til I couldn't move no more."

Leyden lunged forward, grabbed Payne by the hair, and jerked his head back so sharply that Payne felt his spine give a crack. Suddenly he was staring at the ceiling, and he closed his eyes.

Fingers clawed them open. Zeke's face pushed down toward his, the foul breath enveloping him.

"Look at those eyes!" Zeke said to others Payne could not see. "Wide as a fucking whore."

"It was the beating," Payne wept. "Can't even focus right. I didn't cop, man. I'm hurting. Can't you see?"

He tried to point to the blood, but a blow caught him short. It was not a bullet. That much he understood as soon as the stroke was delivered. He felt the pain, but he heard no report. Only a ripping. And maybe that was not a sound at all but a feeling, the slash of sharp metal across his neck.

"Let's kill the motherfucker."

It was Ivan Dunne's voice, as offhanded as if he were calling something everybody had played a thousand times.

"Get up!" shouted Zeke.

Bleeding from beneath the eye, with the pistol jabbing painfully into the notch at the base of his skull, Payne did not see much chance but to do what he was told and die. Die with a week's stash unused. For a moment he thought telling them where it was might save him. But then, if they didn't kill him, he'd be in the same shape he was in before.

Suddenly he saw his only friend coming through the door. That was when the second blow fell. It was as heavy as a hammer, the butt of the gun against the back of his head. It doubled him over but did not knock him unconscious.

"Your buddy stole from us," Leyden said.

"He steals from everybody," said Tucker. "Stole my coat. The one there on the chair."

"You better come along with us, then," said Leyden.

•

Zeke was capable of anything. He would not have had a moment's hesitation about silencing Jackson forever, even if he thought Jackson were Hawk and Prez and Dexter and Trane all wrapped into one.

"How much did he take from you?" I asked.

We were in an alley a few blocks from the club now, and I was freezing my ass off. I could have killed Jackson myself. Rufus was holding my coat like he had a mortgage on it. I took out my wallet and gave Zeke what he said Jackson was into them for.

"Now he's my problem," I said.

"Give him the coat," said Zeke. Rand handed it to me and I put it on.

But Zeke was still holding the gun on Jackson. I went forward to take possession of the prisoner. Zeke waved me away.

"Turn around, Payne," he said.

Jackson didn't want to do it. He was shaking. Zeke seized him by the shoulder and spun him. In one motion he flipped the pistol so he was holding it by the barrel. And as Jackson came face to face with him, he smashed the butt flat into Jackson's mouth.

**eight
stuck
in a
groove**

You give a kid your best . . .

"DAT DERE,"
BY BOBBY TIMMONS AND
OSCAR BROWN, JR.

1.

Tucker packed up early and picked up Payne at the hospital, where the doctors had removed several broken teeth, repaired his lip with sutures, and then wired shut his jaw to let the fractures heal.

On the way to the airport Payne mumbled to the taxi driver to pull over near the Eiffel Tower.

"Give me a couple of francs," Payne said to Tucker through clenched teeth.

Tucker gave him the coins then watched him cross the wide expanse and disappear into the crowd. When he returned, he had a small red balloon on a string.

"You can't get high on helium," Tucker said.

Next, Payne insisted on stopping at the club. He disappeared into the basement with the balloon and returned empty-handed.

"Are you ready now?" Tucker asked.

"Where do they check you?" Payne said.

"Check?"

"Look through your shit looking for your shit," said Payne.

"At customs in New York. When we change planes. What are you carrying?"

"You don't want to know. Or where."

•

1 7 7

Jackson nodded off almost as soon as we got in the air, so I didn't have to keep him company. I couldn't sleep myself for thinking of him there, broken, tapped out, with his stash stuffed up his ass like a Thanksgiving bird.

We cleared customs in New York without a hitch. And when we got to L.A., Jackson stopped at a men's room. He laid his horn down on a washbowl and started to unzip the case.

"Careful," I said, interposing myself between him and the shoe shine man. At that point another cat came in the door. The next thing I knew Jackson was holding a fresh shirt, smoothing out the wrinkles with his hand against his front.

"You don't smell too good either, my friend," he said.

All my stuff was in the bags, so I just washed my face while Jackson gave himself the next best thing to a bath to get ready to greet my mother.

The first few days in her house, Jackson worked his magic. He made her love him. It was as simple as that. All you had to do was to look at her.

He had a good mother, too, you know.

Part of it was that she knew what he had achieved. She had all our albums, and one night she showed me a manila envelope full of old clippings that mentioned Jackson or me. One day I found the two of them listening to our records. It was clear from the lack of scratches that they hadn't been out of the jackets very much.

"You got to kind of lay back and let it flow over you, Mrs. T," he said through the clench of his wired jaws. "It's like being with someone you adore."

"Oh, Jackson," she said, "that's for girls. It's been a long time since I had those feelings."

It was the first time I'd ever thought about her having them at all.

How long did this go on?

Until she found him out. The way they always did.

Usually he waited until she left the house. But this time he cooked up while she was in the kitchen working on dinner. He was bent over when she appeared. He stood up, a needle hanging out of that chicken leg of his. She threw him out that very afternoon.

Did you know when he started selling?

Only because he was hitting me up less.

Did you ever confront him?
I guess you've never been around an addict.
I feel as if I have.
You can't get anywhere with junkies by rubbing their noses in it.
They get kind of used to the stink.

•

Even after the wires finally came off, Payne still drank his meals.
Money came in from dealing. If he needed to give the drugs a reason,
his struggle to get back on the horn was all the excuse any man could
want. It was ten times more painful to clamp his mouth to the metal
now than it had ever been with the broken tooth. Even a doctor might
have prescribed some dope under these circumstances. His fractured
jaw was a clawing animal whenever he bit down. It tore its way upward,
engulfing his head, and downward along his spine so that at times he
thought the pain would take the legs out from under him.

At first he could not even recover his basic tone. The only sound
he could achieve was pinched, constricted, like the parts of his anatomy
that produced it. Even his fingers refused to cooperate. The most ordinary scales tripped him up and left his forearms and shoulders aching,
as if he had been lifting weights instead of simply trying to direct a thin
column of air.

It was humiliating to struggle with simple exercises. But eventually the damage began to yield to the miracle of his obsession. Every
moment he wasn't hustling, he was out at the end of a long pier at
oceanside, alone with the gulls, running up and down the scales, doing
Slonimsky patterns to the unfathomable rhythms of the waves.

•

Sure, I remember Jackson Payne. I'd listened to him for years,
then one day, bingo, I bust him.

He's got about a quarter k of heroin on him. This isn't just to heat
him up on his horn. So I bring him straight downtown and explain to
the living legend the facts of his life as I see them.

This is no stupid guy now. You ever talk to him? You don't have to
sing the tune twice.

"Forget it," he says. "They'll ice me."

I have to laugh 'cause colored guys usually don't get the Outfit
lingo right. But this one's got an ear.

Retired police detective Frank Riordan was a big man with pure white hair, translucent skin and a rosy glow that suggested he liked a little stimulant. His home was in what in Chicago would have been a bungalow but which in L.A. had a mission look. He said that when he was a kid he had played the piano. If he'd had the stuff for jazz, he would've liked to have been a player. But not to live the life of players like Payne.

"We lose a lot of dopers between here and the Q," I tell Payne. "More the first couple weeks there."

"I didn't tell you nothing," Payne says, as if there was an official transcript.

"I can make sure the bad guys don't find out you been here," I tell him.

"This cat," he says, "he knows."

He was talking about a man they called *El Leopardo*.

Mexican?

He was as Anglo as you are, my friend. He just didn't want anybody to know.

I tell Jackson, "OK then. I'll just go ahead and book you a room at the Q. Guys there are very understanding. Especially when you're going cold turkey and can't protect your face, let alone your ass."

At this point Payne makes the proper medical judgment and decides to play along.

Why didn't they kill him?

I'll get to that. But first I got to tell you who he gave us, 'cause this is a good one.

They say he gave you Johnny Dill. They say Getz.

Eventually he introduced us to so many players we called him Symphony Sid.

Why did you target musicians?

'Cause they were there, angel.

The detective's expression was beatific. It made Quinlan uncomfortable to be face-to-face with someone more relentless than he was.

Did you have a special squad?

Just me and my partner Scali, and he's dead.

Did he listen to jazz, too?

I'm afraid he didn't get much beyond Tony Bennett and the Hollywood Bowl.

Did you ever hear the album Bennett did with Bill Evans?
I came that close to busting Evans once.

•

The deal was simple. Payne had to take himself back into the clubs and keep his eyes open. His first foray was at a Del Dewar gig. Dewar turned out to have some pretty sweet shit with him, and Payne got a very good high. It did not bother him that he was playing the snitch, because it was Del's last night in town. By the time Payne woke up and reported to Riordan, the man was long gone.

Riordan and Scali had an interest in club owners, too. Some of them paid their talent through the jazz equivalent of a company store. When the two detectives raided the Half Note on Payne's tip and found junk in Ted Paxon's safe, it put a scare into everybody. They started paying the talent in cash, and the cats who got it flocked to Payne.

In the beginning Payne only gave the police second-rate names. He offered up the cats who played pickup for cats who played pickup for the cats from out of town. But as time went by, this was not enough.

"A junkie's a junkie," Payne said, "no matter how bad he plays."

"You ever heard of a role model?" Riordan said. "If I could've put Bird away maybe you'd be playing today instead of flushing your gifts down the can."

"You right down there with me," Payne said.

"Give us names, angel," said Scali. "It's names or the people who'll whack you. Think about it."

"Damon Reed," said Payne.

"There's one," Scali said.

•

Reed's advance billing was lavish, and the first-night crowd went way beyond the usual critics and hangers-on. Payne quietly slipped into a place at the bar.

Reed was struggling with the local piano. The bass seemed to be looking for somebody to give him the beat rather than taking responsibility for it himself.

"We're going to attempt an original," Reed announced. "I recorded this a few years back. Maybe some of you remember it. It's called 'Stuck in a Groove.' "

Applause went through the room like a scatter of paper. Payne took the rest of his drink and stepped forward toward the stand and into the verge of light.

"I know that tune," he said.

Reed shaded his eyes against the glare.

"I thought you were dead," he said.

"I got my ax," said Payne.

"Jackson Payne, ladies and gentlemen," Reed said, "Jackson Payne back from the grave."

As Payne mounted the stage, Reed began snapping his fingers in a punishing tempo.

"One. Two. One two three four."

Payne was right there with him. They started tight, doing wild intervals, whipped back and forth like a cocaine high. Just to keep it interesting, Payne threw in a little something extra here and there.

The first solo was Reed's, full of muscle flexing, showy leaps, breathtaking bursts of speed, as if he needed to prove something.

While Reed played, Payne remembered to the tips of his fingers the shape of the chord changes, sheets of notes in glittering curves as bright and transparent as blown glass. His solo on the recording of this tune he had made with Reed had been played and replayed so often on the radio that it had become as fixed now as the melody itself. This was what everyone expected, so he went somewhere else entirely.

He began slowly, half-time, building on whole tones. The piano couldn't seem to hear it. Payne wished he had Tucker behind him. But he could do it without a piano. He could do it against the piano. He could do it into the fury of a gale.

He took this idea, raised it a level, then in case anybody thought he started slow because he didn't have it anymore, he doubled and redoubled the tempo, making the figures spin into mantras, scale upon scale like ladders to the sky. These were the things he had been doing at oceanside. The changes did not matter anymore. They were the flattened features of the earth, and he was soaring above the wind.

Reed had to do something to answer. He waved the rhythm section into another chorus, picking up on Payne's original motive and carrying it in a different direction, following the contours of the terrain at a dangerous rate of speed.

The pure liberty of Payne's blowing fascinated him, but he was not ready for it. He kept slipping back into basic changes. Still, the audience dug it. People were on their feet after his second solo and they stayed there when Payne came in for another turn.

This time he was brief, just four bars. He was not speaking of the sacred now. The sound was angry. The subject was what had passed between him and Reed in New York. His saxophone barked and shouted. It was an assault.

Reed tried to get a conversation going, but Payne took his horn out of his mouth and turned his back on the trumpeter like a matador shaming a bull. The crowd burst into wild applause. The band may still have been playing, but the song was over.

The critics were divided. The *Los Angeles Times* man called the set Reed played with Payne "the voice of jazz to come." But the man from the *Herald* wrote that Jackson Payne should have stayed in hibernation. "His tone has become harsh and raspy," he wrote. "His attitude is as surly and immature as the punks coming up behind him half his age. It is a pity, because this man used to be able to sing."

Reed didn't need to wait for the reviews to tell him what he had heard. As soon as they came off the stand, he told Payne he wanted him back.

"I'll hang around for the second set if you want," Payne said. "After that, I've got things to do."

When Reed left him in his little dressing room to go to the bathroom, Payne took care of one of them. He pulled a small bag of heroin from his pocket and stuffed it into Reed's raincoat.

As he went back onstage, he saw Riordan at a table and gave him a nod. The detective relaxed in his chair and got ready to enjoy the rest of the show.

•

We busted Damon Reed outside the club. The courts weren't as screwed up in those days, so we weren't afraid to pat him down. Jackson was clean, of course, but we pulled him and the bass player in, too, just for show.

Reed was the picture of wounded innocence. They always are.

"I find out who did this," he said to Jackson, straining against Scali's arm around his neck, "I'll get you."

Can you remember the music they played that night? I would have given anything to be there.

I recall thinking how screwy it was that we were busting Reed, since Payne was the one who played like an advertisement for coke. The man had so much in him, he sounded like he might play three notes off a single reed.

He could do it, you know. Play chords, I mean.

No shit.

He had a technique that split a tone. Then he'd hum the fifth or seventh. I didn't realize he was doing it so soon.

Riordan tipped the rest of his beer from the bottle into the glass with the festive holly fronds.

Payne went free without even going before a judge. If you did a lab test on his pockets you probably would have found enough to presume an intent to sell. But he'd done his job. The word on the street was that Jackson Payne was back. And we knew his ass was ours.

He didn't take any steady engagements at first. He just floated. Had a gig pretty nearly every night. Got a good buck, too, though not nearly what he was getting from hustling. We protected him, of course, because he was providing us with a steady supply of what we wanted, too.

Did it ever bother him?

I look like a father confessor?

In fact, to Quinlan he did—the same weary self-righteousness, the same red-faced glaze.

These were his people he was turning in.

Let me put it this way: Jackson did not think highly of the way most of them played.

You talked music with him?

One of the job's little compensations.

How about being found out? That must have bothered him. Everywhere he showed up, somebody went down.

Riordan replenished his glass. Quinlan couldn't see where he kept the bottles, which he brought up from beside him, each one full.

Give us a little credit, angel. We didn't let him become a one-man panic. And don't underestimate how good a snitch he was. I've seen twenty-year cons who couldn't put on the act the way he could.

But there was only so far you could go busting talent. Know what I mean? We nailed a lot of names, but pretty soon he was offering up some pretty cheap shit again—tinkle-tinkle piano players who played for second-rate singers, guys from the rhythm section nobody ever heard of. And the more we busted, the duller the music got. So at some point Scali and me decided it was time to twist Jackson around from where the dope was going toward where it was coming from.

•

"Didn't I do everything you asked? Why you want to do me like this?" Payne's big hands clutched the front end of the table. "I gave you Stan Howell," he said. "I gave you Treat Maxwell. I gave you Damon fucking Reed."

"There was a lot of talk on the street about how close you were to Reed," said Scali, who always went at his fingernails with a little penknife when he was bored.

"Reed's a miserable motherfucker," said Payne. "But the others . . ."

"They're the salt of the earth," Scali said.

Payne slumped back into the hard chair in the interrogation room.

"I'll give you anybody you want," he said. "But I won't do the Leopard."

"Have we ever left you hanging, angel?"

A tremble came over Payne as if he'd had a bad dose.

"I'd rather be in stir with the fairies," he said. "Maybe I could keep them off me. But the Leopard will have my ass for sure."

"Just try to get near enough to him that you can see how he works," Riordan said.

"I'll do hard time first," said Payne.

Riordan stood up and opened the door of the interrogation cell.

"Go ahead, Jackson," he said. "But it isn't just you. You've got to think of your son."

•

When Sarah Shaw had said she had lost her boy, Quinlan had never connected it with Payne. But young Jay Shaw turned out to have been a musician, too—a sixteen-year-old dropout playing electric bass in several of the shifting, nameless rock 'n' roll bands that played the pickup bars. His mother had kept the identity of his real daddy from him until one day she caught him with some drug paraphernalia. Then in a panic she used Payne's troubles to try to scare the young man straight. This man was your daddy, she said. Now look at him. The picture came from the *Defender,* taken by somebody at the hospital in France.

Unfortunately, young Shaw sought out his father's records and listened to them high. He would have been more at home with the sounds Payne had made from atop the bar, but the aura was irresistible. So one day Jay left home, went west, and showed up at the club where his father was playing.

"You're not my son," Payne said.

"My mama say I am," said Jay.

"Next she'll be after you for food money, Jackson," somebody said.

"No woman alive," Payne said, "gonna get into my pocket through my dick."

"Is that any way to talk in front of your child?" one of the musicians said.

Payne turned to Jay. "Go home to mama, boy," he said.

"She was called Sarah Evans," said Jay.

Payne took him by the arm and pulled him to the side.

"Who sent you?" he said.

"She didn't want me to come. She said you was a mess. But I'm a musician like you. Maybe someday you and me we could play."

"What's your instrument?"

"Electric bass."

"I don't play with nobody who plugs into the wall."

But gradually Payne yielded. He even went to hear Jay play one night. He saw absolutely no gift. The young man was all habit. Payne felt a pang he had never felt before.

•

We played hardball with him. Sure. He should have expected that when he got in the game. Maybe he'd had it too easy up 'til then.

He was an infantryman in Korea.

Like I always said to Scali, the guy's Jack Armstrong. He's Captain America. Red, white, and blue. You believe that, you'd've liked his son.

I just meant he hadn't been a stranger to tough spots.

He didn't want us anywhere near the kid. That was absolute. The lad was using as heavy as his old man, but he was off-limits. Payne was still dealing, of course. Pretty good amounts, too. Enough to cover his needs and the kid's without even touching the dough he made on the horn. I used to say to him, "What are you whining about, Jackson? You're a provider."

Trouble was, he wasn't providing us much.

"They're holding me away from the Leopard," he said. "They must know something."

But we knew better, because the dope kept coming to him. Then all of a sudden Jackson falls off the face of the earth.

I go out to the club where he's been playing, and they don't have any idea what happened to him. I go to his pad, and it's empty. I ask around about the kid, and find out he's gone, too. I got to tell you, angel, it surprised me.

You had gotten a line on Jay, hadn't you.

You're a smart guy, professor.

You had started working him. It's one thing that would have set him off.

Had a man on him. But just watching. We never once even spoke to the lad. All I can figure is that Jackson heard about it and freaked.

But what about El Leopardo?

You finish the movie. What do you think he did when his gopher ran for a hole?

I wouldn't put it past Jackson to have walked off with the dealer's stash. He was not a guy who learned a lesson.

Let me give you a little hint. I heard on the street that the Leopard was acting perfectly cool.

So you figured Jackson had moved toward him, not away.

Good, Angel. That turns out to be pretty much the way it went down. Jackson hears about the tail on Jay, runs to the Leopard and says what we'd been telling him to: I want more. I want it so bad that, here, take my horn. I'm sick of having to play it.

The Leopard, he can see he's got a guy of better than average intelligence in front of him. For a junkie he's a guy of substance, too, a guy some people respect. So the Leopard says, go to Tijuana and see this man. He'll tell you how to get shit past the gate.

And that's how Payne gets onto the fast track to disaster. See, among other things, a lot of the Leopard's other guys start wondering why Payne gets a break while they're still out there busting their balls. Nobody likes to see another loser get ahead.

2.

When Payne went cross-border he took the young man. The detectives watched them in action there several times. Payne made it easy. In Tijuana he had a hotel, a bar, a couple of whores. This was his circle, and he stayed within it.

The pistol the Leopard provided felt good in Payne's pocket. But carrying the little case full of the Leopard's money made him feel like a clarinet player, and the only one of those he could listen to was Jimmy Giuffre.

Down the street from the Madrid Hotel, where Payne and his son always stayed, was a sex joint. An old man slept on the floor by the front door and flipped on the flickering sign of twisted neon tubing whenever a patron roused him. After letting the customers in he would awaken the girls, who danced until somebody got interested. Payne visited there frequently with Jay.

Meetings with the supplier always went down the same. Runners would appear in a car that looked as though it had come through the Dust Bowl. Then a few minutes later a second car would arrive, a late-model stretch limousine with white walls and black windows, clean as a hearse.

This always followed by a day Payne's receipt of instructions, which came to him at the Madrid. Sometimes he had been there only a day or two before he got the word, which disappointed him because there were certain girls he and Jay did not grow tired of quickly. One of them had a face that reminded him of Jay's mother when she was in the choir. He liked to lie on his back and let her work on him. Jay liked her, too, though what he did with her sometimes got a little rough.

•

Oh, they had a fine old time in TJ, even though I wouldn't have touched those women with the end of a billy club. Needless to say, we took steps not to let him see us. Not that he was careful. After all, he let Digger Morton and Petey LaPaz get behind him. Luckily, Scali and me saw them coming a mile off. You couldn't miss Digger. He had a face on him as long as a gravestone and about as lively. They said you could crack him in the nuts with a two-by-four and he wouldn't blink.

"How's it going?" Digger said to Jackson.

"The Leopard ain't gonna like this," said Jackson.

"He ain't gone know."

They pushed him off the trail and into the bushes where nobody but the shitbirds would see them. And the shitbirds wouldn't mind because he was about to be prepared for their evening meal. He tried to resist, but it didn't do much good.

So Scali and I popped out of nowhere behind our guns. This show of force for some reason failed to impress the two assailants. Digger dropped to one knee and brought a pistol up into a brace. I was ready to take him down, but I didn't have to because somehow in the confusion Jackson had gotten LaPaz's piece from him and—bang! bang!—the shitbirds had twice the lunch they were counting on.

"Drop it, Jackson," I said.

He didn't fight that. When he recognized us, you'd've thought we were kin.

"You got trouble, angel. The *federales* take a dim view of guys blowing away other guys without notifying them in advance."

"My son," Jackson said. "We got nowhere to go."

We didn't even need to mention what the Leopard was going to think about his wasting two of the boys. There was only one window of opportunity.

"You're going to have to go down, Jackson," I said.

"Not in Mexico. Not my boy."

"What'll you give us?"

"What do you want?"

"You know. But first you got to pick up the shipment."

So we drag the stiffs into the weeds, and Scali and I back way off. There's not a lot of time to spare, 'cause here comes a beater with the supplier's muscle. The Chicanos climb out and sniff the air like they can smell what had happened. Jackson shows them the pistol and fires it at one of the shitbirds. They laugh and shoot a couple of shitbirds themselves. Then the supplier himself rolls up and they do the deal.

We had to really move to get to the Leopard before the bodies turned up. We carried the drugs across the border ourselves so Payne didn't blow the crossing. We had to let father and son get happy, of course, to dampen down temptation, and even then it wasn't easy to get them to part with the stash.

"You're looking at hard time, angel," I said when Payne met us on the other side and asked for another taste. "You bring in the Leopard, and I'm still gonna have to put you away, or else they'll take you out for sure. So you better get used to doing without. That's what hard means."

The equipment we had him wear when the time came wasn't as miniaturized as it is now. You had to dress a guy carefully. Once we got everything set, he put the call. Some guy answers, and Jackson says he needs to talk to the Man. The guy says you're shitting me. Jackson says it's important. The guy says Jackson ain't as important as he thinks he is. Jackson says we'll see about that. The guy says wait.

Then the Man himself comes on and Jackson asks is there anybody listening. The Man says nobody listens in on him. Jackson looks over at me with my earphones on like a producer in the booth. Jackson says that's good 'cause you got trouble with somebody. The Man says really.

"There were intruders out at the drop site," Jackson says. "They almost got what they were looking for."

"Who were these individuals?" says the Leopard.

"You know them," Jackson answers. "Like I said, we better talk. Face-to-face."

Jackson lets the Leopard name the place and time, which is smart. He balks a little then goes along, which is smarter still. The Leopard is a guy who can't believe in anything he doesn't have to force.

"I want you to be alone, too," the Leopard says.

"You got it."

"Leave that idiot kid."

"He doesn't know a thing about this," Jackson says, which isn't half as smart as it needs to be.

•

The arrest itself was uneventful. It took place in a supermarket parking lot. The body mic worked intermittently. The Leopard didn't come alone. But the uniforms did a good job handling his backups. There was no shooting. *El Leopardo* said nothing. For verisimilitude the detectives handled Payne roughly enough that in the mug shot he had a puffed-up eye.

They did not go light on him afterward, either. The charge was a major felony. Payne copped a plea. The arrangement sent him away, and not among friends. But at least young Jay had gotten off clean. Payne had given him a plane ticket back to Chicago and left him in the hands of the detectives who were to see him safely out of town.

They did not tell Payne that they had lost him until Payne was in San Quentin, and by then he already knew.

•

Jazz Confidential: There have been a lot of stories about how you landed in jail.

Jackson Payne: Only one way that ever happens. The man comes up and says, "Surprise! You're on *Candid Camera.*"

Jazz Confidential: There were a lot of guys who were saying you weren't going to make it to San Quentin alive.

JP: I never testified against anybody. Could've cut my sentence in half if I did.

Jazz Confidential: Still, you had to be afraid.

JP: In the county jail they put me in a cell with this muscle beach cat who thought he could scare my habit away. I talked to the guard. I was lucky. He just laughed.

When my number came up to be transported, the photographers were outside to get a picture of me being loaded into the funny bus in irons. The guards pushed me in front of the cameras, and I couldn't even raise my hands to hide my face. Sweat was running down my nose. Flashbulbs popped. I shuffled as fast as I could go. Ladies and gentlemen, Jackson Payne.

Then at Quentin the bus pulls up inside the gate. We stumble out, guys with shotguns all around us, steady yelling at us like drill sergeants. I got in line and hung my head.

Then, sure enough, the guard at the front yells, "Which one of you dumb f***s is Jackson Payne?"

I wondered, What the f*** did I do?

"Right here," I said.

"You the hot tenor from L.A.?" the guard said.

I didn't know the right answer, so I took a guess.

"Played a little."

"Come with me."

All I could think was how fast the Leopard moved.

•

As they walked him through the corridors, he saw a lot of places to die. Those four square feet behind the stairs provided just enough space to fit a man and the shiv that had been slipped between his ribs. That corner of the exercise area of C block, partially obscured from the view of the rifle-bearing guards on the catwalk, could neatly accommodate a man and his fate. And the shower offered unspeakable privacy. He was certain there was a contract out on him. Every shadow was mortal. Every face a killer's.

"This way," said the guard. "They're waiting."

Finally they stopped at a doorway in the subterranean maze.

Like all the others, the door was made of painted steel. The knob rattled as the guard took hold of it and pushed. Payne instinctively pulled back. The light was as bright as judgment, and for a moment it blinded him.

•

How did you let Jay get away from you?

He wasn't our prisoner. We kept our word. We gave him a safe place and put men on it. He sneaked off the second night his father was in the county slam.

Bored? Scared?

He was a junkie, angel. They're all twelve years old.

•

The door swung open slowly. Something glinted. Payne flinched. Then he saw that no one had a gun or a knife. They had musical instruments.

They sat in the traditional flat-fronted line, saxes ahead, brass and rhythm behind. His eyes got used to the glare sparkling off the polished bells of the horns. There was Art Pepper, looking disgusted. There was Coot Collins. Roy Samson on piano. Del Dewar. Some were serving time on busts he had arranged.

"Fellas," said the guard, "meet Jackson Payne."

•

Two days later he learned about Jay. It was Pepper who told him. Pepper liked doing that kind of thing.

"You heard they popped that kid you were hanging out with," he said.

"Jay? He's back with his mother."

"Mother of all mothers," Pepper said. "Guy like the Leopard gets busted, somebody's got to take the fall."

They had found Jay in the trunk of a Buick. The young man couldn't even die original. Two shotgun wounds, heart and head.

•

JP: Somebody in the back blew a little riff. The drummer hit a rim shot then rolled the bass.

Pepper says, "Word is, you lost your chops."

"Over the rainbow, Art," I said. "Wish again."

The band went "Oooo." And I knew it was gonna be all right.

Jazz Confidential: They say some blamed you for being in prison.

JP: Where'd you get that? We were brothers, man. As long as we stayed in line the screws treated us good. Tailored us uniforms. Put us on a tier where everybody played the right sh*t on the radio. If you were a player, you could put up curtains, give yourself some space.

Jazz Confidential: Were you able to stay straight?

JP: The dope was better than it was on the outside. Felt like I could've played four notes at a time.

•

He was in the middle of going through the Xeroxes of the magazine interview when Donna called, wanting to know if he was going to take his turn with the boys.

"Maybe when my schedule settles down," he said.

"What about my plans?"

"They're called visitation rights, not duties," he said.

"I'll tell them you said that."

"It'd be easier for both of us if you found yourself a man."

There was some decent music going behind her. But even when she fell silent, he could not tell who it was.

"I hear you found a woman," she said.

"Who told you that?"

"She did. She sounded black. Was she good, Charles? The way they are in the songs?"

"Give the boys my love."

•

The arrangements at the federal penitentiary at Marion, Illinois, moved more quickly than Quinlan had anticipated. But compared with Marion, San Quentin was a summer camp. Coot Collins had earned a place among the hard cases, not because of his crimes on the outside, which amounted to no more than the usual record of possession, sale, and petty theft, but rather because of what he had done in stir. As a younger man, when others like Jackson were taking it all out on their horns, he looked to other means. He used his charms to lure young guards into conversation. After a while, the guards would let down their defenses and come right up to the bars. Then Collins would reward them with a slash to the throat or a homemade blade in the gut. It was as if he were daring authorities to execute him. But his timing was poor. The Supreme Court had put capital punishment on hold.

•

I was mad at everybody. Couldn't even remember the smell of fresh cold cream on the slide or what it was like to have the mouthpiece settle against my lip. I got a little crazy. But look what cats were doing on the outside.

Most of them who played angry were black.

Hey, there were things that pissed me off, too.

This observation set him off on a long monologue, which was clearly a solo he'd played many times. A square of thick, scratched glass separated him from Quinlan. To talk, they had to use the telephones, and this gave the conversation a heavy reverb.

I'm here to learn about Jackson Payne.

Jackson and me, we was tight. Ask anybody. He said he wanted to use me when I came out. But when the time came, he was dead.

You still playing?

Lost it.

The dope?

The dope is something a man can count on. Don't have to be with somebody as good on the horn as Jackson to feel it. You can do it with any ignorant motherfucker in a shooting gallery or all by your lonesome in a toilet somewhere.

Collins's ghostly pale arms were a sideshow—tattoos on every surface, some intricate, some homemade. He could have given the needle to the plump, peekaboo bottom of a nude standing on a streamer that said "Nancy." Or he could have made a variety of eagles, leopards, and snakes very mellow. For old time's sake, he could even have shot up at any of a dozen spots etched with the name of a prison the dope had taken him to.

You were both using, right? He's been quoted as saying that a line of supply came with being in the band.

It wasn't anything anybody came right out and made official. You had to buy the shit.

The money come from outside?

Some cats got it that way. Others had sources inside who'd deliver for them if they had something to deliver in return.

Playing for them?

Collins's hard old face lit up ugly.

Shit.

What are you saying?

You figure it out.

Help me, Coot.

There's only so many things a man's got to offer after they take everything away.

Are you saying some of you sold yourselves?

Collins opened his mouth in a gaping, cavernous look of feigned shock. Then, through the scratched glass, it collapsed like something had shattered it, and he broke into a sucking, toothless laugh.

You're something else, man. Who you been listening to, Lawrence Welk?

You're not saying you did this, are you?

There was always somebody who dug a horn player. It's all in the chops.

I guess I have to say I doubt it, Coot. At least about Jackson.

Well you can doubt anything you please. Just so you understand that you don't know shit. And never will unless you find your sweet ass on this side of the glass.

Some things had happened to Payne a long time before.

The things that happen to cats, they're all pretty much the same.

He would have died first.

He did that later.

•

The routine was numbing. Every morning the din woke him even before the screws came through banging their sticks against the bars. The noise echoed against the walls of stone and steel, no windows to see the dawn, only the voices of the radios announcing it before inmates' voices shouted to turn the motherfucker down. A man could not sleep with all that banging around in his head.

So he swung his legs over the edge of the bunk, retrieved his works from behind the toilet where the pipe went through the wall. He kept his shit there only for the sake of form. The screws did not shake him down for it. Payne had power behind him.

It did not take long to cook up and get well. Then morning rose on the horizon, a warm heroin sun.

He didn't do enough to get him high, but it did take his appetite. He went anyway to the cavernous room where they served breakfast and got a cup of coffee with a lot of sugar. Three other horns lounged at a table in back, but Payne did not go to it. On the opposite side of the room the Mustapha sat with his lieutenants. An empty table stood next to them. That was where Payne knew he'd better go.

He made no greeting, got no acknowledgment. The lieutenants gave him a look, but no more than that. They would have been happy to kill him if their job had not been to keep him safe.

He was a trophy. The Mustapha did not come to him often, just enough to mark his territory. He used others to get his daily satisfaction, taking nearly anyone he wanted. From Payne he mainly wanted respect.

Payne really did not understand what would be expected of him when the Mustapha first offered help. But then the collar went around his neck, and the choke chain pulled tight.

After that, when the Mustapha summoned him to his cell, Payne went. The man's inventory stood in neat piles—cigarettes, toilet paper rolls, bars of soap. A sign facing out into the tier warned, "Nothing you can see in this space is worth dying for." Inside, dozens of pictures torn from girlie magazines hung on the wall. Payne often found himself gazing up and counting them, then having to close his eyes.

For days afterward, snatches of Coleman Hawkins kept coming into his playing, along with some punishing riffs nobody could place. Payne did not tell anyone why he was quoting Sousa's *"El Capitán."*

•

The routine was comforting. The music awakened him before the guards came, so he was ready for the clank of their truncheons against the bars. Once he was up, other habits carried him: the fix, the march to breakfast, the practice sessions.

The others in the band warned him to stay away from the Muslims, but he paid this no mind. It wasn't like he was signing on to their creed. He couldn't, so long as he liked his dope.

•

Those Muslim cats were weird, man. All that white devil shit. I think Jackson admired the way they carried themselves, straight as preachers. Straighter, he always said. I told him to stay away from them, because whatever color God and the Devil were, the Man was surely white.

•

The routine was tolerable. Every morning the din woke him up even before the screws came through banging their sticks against the bars, but he had a way of dealing with such distractions. There was always enough to let him take off any edge. In this sense, inside and outside were one. He played his horn, and by playing it, got what he needed in order to play some more.

•

"Why are you asking *me*?" Lasheen said.

"I need advice, that's all. I just can't believe Payne would have submitted himself."

"Despite appearances, I've never been a Muslim or to prison. Please say it wouldn't have changed anything if you had known."

"It's just that I'm having trouble sorting this out."

"The question is why you think it would be easier for me."

•

The routine, usually so comfortable, now drove him crazy. Every day he rose early, had his morning fix of coffee, and then got down to work. Before him was the previous day's effort, which he read and had to put aside. It was never right. Each successive improvisation built on the same thin structure of fact. But it was impossible to say this one is more clearly right than that.

In the end Quinlan had to set aside the issue. Without more evidence, he was not prepared to assert that Payne had a second homosexual experience. Instead he stuck to the facts: the return of the habit, the musical evolution as Payne worked on his chops. There was no recorded evidence of the work of the San Quentin All Stars during this period. But by comparing the pirate tapes of Payne's last performances in L.A. with what he produced just after his parole, you could hear starkly how trouble had taken root in his sound.

He used as much volume as he could and gave it a gnarled edge. It was as if he was no longer content with merely musical effects. He wanted to cause physical discomfort. One critic who went to hear Payne not long after his release told a story of seeing another member of the audience, as Payne's solo lashed into its second half hour, begin slowly to bang his forehead against the table. The critic wrote that as far as he was concerned, both the solo and the response to it were perfectly valid.

3.

I know what happened when Jackson went to prison, Sarah.

She took a bite of bread and chewed it a little too carefully, then worked it down with sweet soda.

So you heard about Jay.

She did not stop eating.

I knew you'd find out. You or that girl. I guess I could've just told you. Or told her when she called. But all this time Jay has rested pretty much in peace.

She called you? When was this?

Asking what did you ask. What did I think.

Think of me?

She's a black lady, isn't she.

If I didn't need to understand this terrible thing, I would never have troubled you again.

I told her you were as polite as a choirboy, but you definitely
knew what song you wanted to sing.

Jay was your daughter's twin?

You could ask Lasheen to check the birth certificates at South
Shore Hospital if you don't believe me. That's your black lady friend's
name, isn't it? She said you met when you hired her boss to do some
detective work. If her boss was here I'd tell him, that lady's got a future,
'cause she do know how to get a body to talk.

The story they tell is that Jay learned from you who his father was.

Jay's biggest ideas were about how to get through the day. He
made it up as he went, just like his father did.

When he left did you try to find out where he went?

I didn't have anybody like that pretty young black lady of yours to
help. I told her, Girl, this man of yours has a thing. And it's all he really
cares about. If you can help him with it, then you're gone be all right.
You can't and it's goodbye Lasheen, no matter what he tells you now.

When Sarah Shaw laughed, it was like Saturday night before
trouble breaks out.

*Your son apparently led Jackson to believe he wanted to share the
music.*

Jay could sweet-talk you. They were father and son that way, too.
I suppose he could have just said he wanted dope. It wouldn't have been
hard to sell Jackson on the need for that.

Did Jackson say anything about it after?

There weren't any more envelopes from him. Nothing. It was just
as well. If he'd ever come sniffing around again, I'd've had to lock my
daughter away.

•

When he finally caught up with her, Lasheen turned the phone
over to the answering service and put a Back Soon sign on the office
door. She was wearing an outfit of red and black, and the way it hung on
her, it might have been a flag of battle. She led him to a place where he
hoped they could talk peace.

"This isn't business," he said.

"I thought everything was."

"You could have at least let me try to explain," he said.

"Nobody's stopping you," she said.

"I like you," he said.

"That's all?" she said. "You weren't so speechless at my place the other night."

"You called my ex-wife, Lasheen. You called Sarah Shaw asking after me. God knows who all."

Quinlan looked away from her toward a stranger across the room who was not looking back.

"I never said a love supreme," he said. "Not even love at all. Not yet. Just like. Trying to find out how much. We never should have moved so fast. It's not so easy, even when nothing stands between. Nothing artificial, I mean. Nothing you didn't make."

"You have trouble with women, don't you," she said.

He breathed out. That at least sounded a little better, since it was only about gender. And that was older than Cain.

•

Now that he had the story of Payne's son, Quinlan no longer had to puzzle over the rapid changes Payne went through after his release from San Quentin. Nor did he attribute them, as so many others had, solely to the brutality of his prison experience. Grief takes many forms, and one of them is the loss of self.

Payne did not take a new name, as others were doing at the time, but he altered his sound so profoundly that he might as well have.

"Listen to this. Hear the bass? Pure junk. Dum-dum-dum-dum. You can hear the same dreck behind any crummy three-chord band to this day. And there it is behind Jackson Payne. His son could probably have played better. Where did he get this guy?"

"Is that a professional opinion?"

"After a little wine I lose all self-restraint."

"And so here you are."

"I guess I am."

"I hope so," said Lasheen as she poured him another glass and sweetened hers just a touch.

"Here. Listen. Can you hear the way he's forcing the anger? You're too young to remember, but everybody was doing some of that back in the early '70s."

"Sounds awful."

"At the time they said it was authentic," he said.

"So is what the cat leaves behind. What were you like then?"

She had changed out of the battle flag and into a flowing wrapper that came to a rest around her in ways that attracted the eye. And she did not seem to mind where his eye lighted. For a moment he thought he smelled incense in the air, but it was probably only the herb soap she had in her shower. She was so young that she probably thought of incense as second-hand smoke.

"I was as foolish as everybody else," he said.

"Hard to believe."

"I wore some very colorful shirts."

He had pictures, though he would have been embarrassed to show them, faded Polaroids showing long, stringy hair, tie-dyed T-shirts, hip-hugger bell-bottoms.

Donna had found him this way, she a sophomore, he a senior. From the start she was the teacher in the relationship. He wondered where she had gotten all the experience, but he did not dare ask. It was probably no wonder that they eventually stopped pleasing one another once they were married, she because she had so much to compare him with, and he because he felt he should. During his first junior faculty appointment, they had their first son. The campus environment was, to say the least, open to suggestion. And so when one of them started talking about experimenting, the other was quick to assent.

He took up with students from time to time, but never let it last. Meantime, Donna drifted into a pattern of somewhat longer attachments, steady enough that when their second son came, he knew exactly whose eyes and coloring to look for, though this proved frustrating, since the other man's were actually fairly close to his own.

When people looked back upon those years with nostalgia, Quinlan wondered what they were thinking about. He remembered the war and the fear of getting swept up in it, the giddy enthusiasms that often ended in tragedy, the loss of intimacy that the love generation brought on itself. He had thought of setting a match to those Polaroids a hundred times.

The guitars were wailing behind Payne's solo, as if they were trying to drown him out.

"It wasn't a good time, Lasheen," he said. "Don't let anyone tell you otherwise."

She stood and poured him the last of the wine. The wrapper moved as if there were a gentle wind.

"Should I open another?" she asked.

"Not for me," he laughed.

"It's early," she said. "You're not a short-ball hitter, are you?"

"I guess you'll have to be the judge of that," he said, with a good deal more confidence than he felt. "Wait. There's something coming up here, I think. I haven't played these cuts for a long time. Yes. It's almost there. Yes . . . Yes . . . No. Another few bars."

Payne was blowing full bore over the clamor of a synthesizer set to strings and brass and the din of amplified drums. His tone was almost unbearably extreme.

"Listen. Listen. It's coming now. Listen."

All of a sudden the tone broke, as if Payne's reed had split. But no, it was something else. Quinlan leaned into the sound.

"That's the first recorded example of him getting two notes at once. He had been practicing it for quite a while, and apparently he had done it in clubs a few times, but never with the tape running."

"No wonder," she said.

"Do you know how much control it takes?" The tone broke in two again, this time sustained. "See? He put it right where he wanted to."

"I really don't see the point," she said.

4.

Payne changed direction so often during the period following his release from prison that, if jazz did offer privileged access to an artist's inner being, the only conclusion one could draw was that he must have been in a highly dissociative state. Sometimes he appeared onstage with his face painted with vivid, warlike slash marks. Sometimes he wore a tribal necklace of bones. He always entered to the clang and gurgle of guitar and synthesizer, a kitschy ruffle and flourish. A cartoon chieftain, he was as cocky as a man walking the bar.

The cognoscenti divided over whether he still set the musical standard or whether he had become a clown. Where was jazz heading? To the stage of Bleecker Street West, sharing the billing with the Handlers of the Corpse? Some critics, of course, were willing to consider anything. Since the point was freedom, anything that was possible was good. But those who believed in privileged access found this new Payne almost unbearably sad.

"Have you ever actually listened to Frank Zappa, Mr. Quinlan?"

"Not since Moon Unit won my heart with 'Valley Girls.' "

"Seriously. There's something there."

"He rips dolls apart, doesn't he?"

"That's Alice Cooper. Definitely retro."

"This would be retro to when exactly?"

"I was only a little kid."

All of Quinlan's students were, and more so every year. And when Quinlan tried to teach them what was good and what was not, the students called it cultural hegemonism, a product of the Western white male, even if he was speaking up for the work of black musicians and found himself with a black woman in his life.

"That just proves the point."

"Which point was that?"

"Don't tell me the woman I see you with is on an equal footing."

"It's none of your business, really."

"It's as much my business as Jackson Payne is yours."

•

Why did you stick with him after he got out of prison, Showon?

I ask myself that sometimes. On one of the old album jackets, I swear to God, I look like the Mad Hatter. Like the guy said in the song: It ain't me, babe. What's he now? A mayor?

And the trumpeter. Shane Smith.

He sure was pretty, though, wasn't he? White cat who brought the kittens around.

So for Jackson it was just money and girls.

Not always. There were nights when it didn't matter that the crowd didn't care if we knew the chords or that the drummer banged away like a carpenter. Because sometimes Jackson and I got something going, just the two of us, and it was New York all over again. It was "High Wired." Except bolder. He'd play those split tones, and it made my hair straighten, like the first time I saw Miles and Trane. In those

solos you could hear all the things that had happened to him, and most
of what was to come.

I've heard recordings.

There's a lot more out there that you haven't heard.

*Maybe someday I can play you some of what I have from this
period, see if you can identify any of it more precisely than I've been
able to.*

I don't think I could take it.

Tucker shifted on the bench enough to reach the keyboard. He
touched a couple of chords. Quinlan looked at his hands to see if he
could recognize the voicings, but Tucker was there and then he was gone.

You've never played in that style since.

Like Jackson always said, even Bach couldn't talk backward.
Which was funny, because sometimes Jackson would actually put one
of his pieces in a mirror and try to do it that way.

Why did he do that?

Maybe just to see if he could.

But there had to be some kind of authenticity.

When he came out of prison there were things he needed to get
out of his system. His son's death obviously did something to him. I
think he must have wanted to make something out of the kind of music
Jay did.

Did he know where it was taking him?

He wasn't ready for love yet, if that's what you mean. Let alone
for God. He'd just gotten into costume.

Did he ever find peace?

If he did, it was a transition.

And you?

When we were rocking together and all the kids' faces melted
away, I loved it. I really did.

•

Believe it, man. Like, I was playing with Jackson Payne and
Showon Tucker, and I had to poke myself and say, This isn't a contact
high. You're not hallucinating. This is real.

I was still a kid. Hardly any experience. Then I run into Shane
Smith. The trumpet? Went on to play in the Slick Red Stone? I'd played
with him before in Stuffed Heads, you know, before Jimmy Borne

died? And he says he just got this totally wired job. And I should take a look because he didn't think they had a bass.

The place they had the audition is like a little bungalow. I go, Shit. What's this? Grandma's house?

Probably the one Showon Tucker inherited from his mother.

Jackson is over there on a bunch of pillows like a sultan, smoking a joint and not even asking did anyone else want a hit. I go, Another hotshot leader thinks he's Jim Morrison or something. So I just got my shit together and set up.

"Do you play lots of notes on that bass?" Jackson says.

"As many as it takes," I say, you know, cocky-like, the way you are before you know shit.

"I play most of the notes in this band," he says, blowing a mouthful of smoke my way.

"You the man that signs the check," I say.

That kind of sucks him back up.

"Don't talk black, boy," he says. "It makes you sound ignorant. And I don't want no ignorant white boys in this band."

"Black don't sound ignorant to me," I say.

At that he kind of rears up on his pillows.

"It does when you don't know how," he says. Then he lets out this big old laugh. "You do it to get chicks, I bet."

"Any way I can."

"White meat only?"

That threw me again. Like, I don't have any clue where this is going? So I just go, "I believe in equal opportunity."

He lays back and I think maybe I got it right. But then he gets this tightness in his eyes?

"Do you want to get close to me, boy?" he asks.

He's got his arm thrown up on the back of the pillows, and I can see the hair up under there.

"I usually hang back," I say. "Give the lead man some distance."

He laughs again. Like real deep this time, the way he sometimes blew his horn.

"I hate motherfuckers who try to get close," he says. "Now play me something."

So I ask him what would he like to hear.

"You can play a motherfucking march for all I care," he says. Like I was supposed to know the bass line.

So I just say, "Groovy," and he gets that look again.

"Where I come from that's a word for fags," he says. "You a fag, boy?"

I didn't answer. I just gave him a blues riff, plain and simple.

He let me do a chorus and a half before he came in. Out of the corner of my eye I saw him bring his horn to his lips. But I figured he would wait until the start of the next chorus like anybody else. It was a real surprise when all of a sudden I felt him. Like, there he was.

And the first note, I go, What? Doesn't he know the key? Because I was in F, and he was somewhere four or five flats to the right of that. I didn't know what to do but to barrel on.

Then he stops.

Just stops cold.

And I know I'm fucked.

His eyes are closed. The tenor is still in his mouth, like he's sucking on it.

Three beats after I've given everything up for lost, he comes in again. I mean this guy plays the rests. Like, makes them sing? I wish I could've once in my life done a line as sweet as he did silence.

It was Miles who played the rests. With Jackson he was just stopping to think.

Well, like it really like floored me. I was expecting fuck-you blues, but he was in a real different groove and I started grooving on it, too. Then right in the middle of a line he stops again and goes, "Cunt!"

I thought for a second he meant me.

But then he wipes his reed on his sleeve, sucks it a little, then blows the last note over again. I don't know what he got on it that he didn't the first time, but he seemed to like this one a little better. Then he takes the horn out of his mouth slowly and eases it down onto the strap.

"Don't even know which way's up, do you, boy?" he says.

"I did like you told me."

"You always gonna jump where somebody tells you to?"

"When he's right I will."

"Then you better get your white ass out of here," he says and takes one of those long rests I told you about. I hear it there, beating like your heart? " 'Cause I don't want you wearing that cheap shit tonight on the stand. Here." He pulls out a C-note. "You got to look sharp. Get you something silk and pretty or they gonna think we scared to let a white boy look fine."

•

Later Payne took on another white musician, a drummer named Ben Dayton who didn't have an idea in his head but loud. They recorded tunes by Jimi Hendrix, the Stones, Marvin Gaye. Their new agent, Sol Hampson, even got them to cover a song by the Supremes. Some A&R thought the title might just be funky enough to go gold.

"Funky?" said Tucker.

"Like, wild, you know?" said the A&R man. He said it with his hands, as if a dove flew up between them.

Hampson did not have much of an ear for jazz. But he did have an instinct for marketing to the herd. His one guiding principle was this: You either had to be just like everybody else or so entirely different that they all had to be like you.

•

Purists complain that the rock labels fuzzed Payne up with reverb and other electronic effects. And it was true that you never really believed these sounds existed out in the world. Even so, you could not miss Jackson's. You were afraid to get too close to the speaker for fear it might make you bleed.

Payne and Smith often did battle on the stand. Sometimes this would eat up one whole side of a record. It was Joe Louis versus the Great White Hope, except that the Brown Bomber at least had the mercy to dispatch his opponents quickly and cleanly. Preserved on vinyl, these sides made Quinlan uncomfortable even today. At times he felt he could actually hear the meth kicking in.

Of course, by that time you didn't have to be a musician to do the drug scene. Everybody seemed to be on something; what it was depended on personality type. Speed, acid, heroin. Blood, bile, phlegm. Even perfectly proper ladies popped amyl nitrate in the midst of the act of love.

•

One night Jackson asked us all to dinner at Zack's for Ribs. We didn't know what to expect. In the back was a room you could separate from the rest with a folding vinyl door. Whenever it was closed we figured there was something going on that we shouldn't see. This was where Zack directed us that night.

Jackson arrived with a bottle in a sack, which he put down in front of him on the long table. He lifted it out of the paper bag until we saw that it was very fine whiskey, which he poured. No matter how fucked up he looked, he didn't spill a drop. When he'd taken care of everybody, he stood behind his chair and raised high his glass to each one of us in turn.

"One of you is going to rat," he said. And then he drank.

Nobody else did.

"You're crazy, Jackson," somebody said.

"Far fucking out."

Jackson sat back down, easy as you please, and held his glass up to the light.

"Who the fuck you talking about?" Shane demanded.

Jackson laid his hands down flat on the cloth. Like he was going to float the table right up beneath his palms.

"The one I'm talking about," he said, "he already knows."

He was looking straight at Shane. But he never said. He just called for dinner, poured the whiskey, and pretty soon we were all feeling pretty fine. Then Sol Hampson took over.

He passed around a chart that showed week by week what we were able to get in bookings. The numbers were going down. So was the line on a chart that showed our airplay.

"Gentlemen," he said, "you are no longer hot."

Jackson was just sitting back like it was about somebody else's band.

"You aren't hot," the agent said, "because you aren't doing anything new."

Then Jackson rose up in his chair and spoke.

"Dayton," he said, "you're out."

Dayton looked at me. Then he looked at Shane. He didn't even try to look at Showon, because I guess he knew what he'd see.

"I've been playing my ass off," Dayton said.

"Showon," said Jackson, "find me a real drummer."

It was pretty late to come up with somebody off the *Downbeat* Critics Poll, but Showon didn't argue.

"This sucks, man," said Dayton, then he turned and left.

It wasn't long before Jackson poured the last of the whiskey, paid the check, and led us across the street to a shoe repair where he stood us all to a shine.

•

The trouble, of course, wasn't Dayton. The biggest problem in Jackson's band was Jackson. Falseness had come into everything he played. The recorded evidence was irrefutable. Payne did not believe in anything he was doing anymore.

•

They were back from San Francisco, working a tired booking at the Heads Up, a raunchy rock house that had until recently specialized in exotic dancers. The band had set up on one side of the stage. The Crystal Shards, dispirited by the overdose death of its lead singer, slouched on the other.

Payne showed up a step ahead of the police. Afterward some people who witnessed it said it almost seemed as though Payne had been hurrying to make an appointment, which was strange, since he did not usually concern himself very much with the scheduled starting times of his sets.

The raid went down with all the common elements. The harsh commands. The rough shoves when a man did not move as fast as the police thought he should. The humiliating public search in places meant to be dark.

Except that this time Payne was clean.

"Don't tell me you're not a user, sweetheart," said one of the attending vice officers.

"I didn't say a thing," said Payne.

The bass and the new drummer were arrested, though all they had was an evening's worth of grass. Tucker, of course, was always sober, so he was able to stand the frisk. Shane Smith did, too.

"Near miss," he said after.

"It's over," said Payne.

"They didn't take you down," said Smith. "You were wrong about that."

"Didn't take you down, either."

"So what?"

"You were carrying," said Payne.

"What?"

"I put it in your horn case," said Payne. "They gave you a pass."

nine
the
kensington
sessions

You won't see your homeland
'Cept through me.

"THE OLD COUNTRY,"
BY NAT ADDERLEY AND
CURTIS R. LEWIS

1.

After he changed the band, something started happening. And not just in the music.

Did you know why?

Not at first, because none of us could take seriously any woman he wasn't sleeping with.

But Taiana fooled them all. Showon recalled her striking figure, her long legs emerging from tight sheath skirts, her tall, stately profile, like something you'd see in the window of a store. It was hard to locate her by accent or manner or hue. Her voice had small turns and lifts from somewhere you've never been. Her features were exotic, too, almost Semitic, like someone risen from the desert.

What do you know about her?

She was a tune you'd heard but couldn't place. Not a show tune. Certainly not the blues. That hair of hers, as jet as a sister's, but wavy in a way you knew didn't come out of a bottle. She wasn't jazz, that's for sure.

I've seen the pictures.

The pictures lie. Jackson always had them light her funny. Or else he'd have them angle her out behind the veil of a curtain like a Bedouin queen. She was beautiful in a way, but it was beauty like a Monk tune. All corners and edges.

I never thought I'd catch you speaking of anyone to rival Vera Bell.

Showon put down his coffee cup and wiped his lips.

Vera doesn't figure into this.

But Taiana was like Vera, wasn't she? Someone you could feel for?

We were older by then, all of us. It wasn't the same.

She didn't stay with Jackson at night?

You didn't even really think about it. That was the kind of woman she was.

•

The music that has survived from the period after Payne went back to an acoustic band is clearly transitional. In some ways it was a throwback to Payne at his most strung-out. He took on players from the older ranks, moved out of the big, young rooms and back into the basements where he had begun. He also got out of his deal with his agent, who was more than willing once he heard the new band.

There always seemed to be something physically wrong with Payne: stomach cramps, runny nose, hacking cough, aches, and other complaints. Perhaps this explains the group's looseness. Before, he had always exacted a discipline, even from the young inadequates. Now he barely insisted on a consistent tempo.

As he rationed his drugs more tightly, Payne often lacked the wherewithal to finish a solo. His tone would waver down to a whisper and then gutter out. Several critics accused him of recording drugged, not realizing that his faltering technique was, like a spiking fever, the first step of the cure.

Taiana was a big part of it. Whether she was born Islamic or had converted, she had a stringency that was good for him.

•

I saw a lot of bums come through my club, and some had names as big as Jackson Payne's. But I never saw a man lift himself right in front of my eyes the way he did.

A man can only play on hop so long before it comes out the horn. I'm talking about forgetting who he is, let alone where. Did you ever hear the recording where Chet Baker loses the words on "Every Time We Say Good-bye"? It was one of his signature tunes, for Christsake. He must've sung it ten thousand times. But there he was, in the middle of nowhere, humming something to try to get over until he figured out what the fuck he was doing. Made you want to cry a little. Say goodbye, Chet.

Payne was like that. He'd come in looking like hell and play a set that would make you want to call an ambulance.

But then something happened.

"I want you to give Showon a two-week booking with the trio after I leave," he said.

"Where do you think you're going?" I said.

"To a prison you check yourself into," he said, "to get out of the prison you've built."

•

He took the sleeper for privacy as much as for rest, but as soon as the train began to roll, a radio began to blare and did not abate. The Jefferson Airplane, Crosby Stills Nash & Young, Cream. He had shared billings with some of them.

"There are some things," he wrote to Showon that first day, "you shouldn't have to listen to even through a wall."

The train was a children's express. Within a few minutes of their departure, the car reeked of marijuana, and when Payne passed the porter, the man gave him a wink.

The kids wore thrift-shop clothes and carried their things in backpacks festooned with the symbols of Eastern faiths whose harsh, abstemious discipline was obviously not their principal appeal. By contrast, Payne must have seemed absolutely buttoned down. He had gotten rid of the dashikis and robes. Now he wore a linen suit, white-on-white shirt, and bright silk tie that Taiana had bought him.

That evening in the dining car a few of the kids recognized him, and later a delegation found the courage to knock on his door.

He opened it expecting the porter, but instead he found three giggling girls barely out of high school and a young man of uncertain years.

"Hi," said the tallest girl.

She had on a long, shapeless paisley dress and some kind of combat boots. The top of the dress was cut low enough to show that she had curves.

"You're somebody," she declared.

"Everybody is," he said.

That set everyone aflutter, and Payne could not help noticing the way the loose fabric suggested the shape and free motion of what was hidden.

"I mean like really somebody," she said.

Behind, her sisters struck poses. The skinny one in a flowered hat and lacy halter looked soulfully past him out the window into the darkness. The plump one in jeans and work shirt placed her hand on a generous hip like someone off a Motown album cover.

"You should have seen the cat with them," he wrote Tucker. "I don't know which one of the chicks he was doing, but I could tell he wasn't too sure who she'd be doing next."

The girls all came on to Payne, of course, when he finally revealed who he was. The girl in the lacy halter put her arm around him and whispered in his ear.

"You'd do that?" Payne said out loud, looking straight at the guy.

"Just to get started," said the girl, her breathiness boiling into a marijuana laugh.

"There's isn't room here for everybody," Payne said, nodding toward the young man.

"It's a long ride," said the one with the curves.

"Here to forever," said the plump one.

"You pick then," the one with the curves said to Payne.

All three of them started to vamp. It was kind of funny. White chicks didn't know how to do it right.

"Him," Payne said.

"You're shitting me," said the stud.

"Far out," said the one in the hat. "I didn't think black dudes were that way."

"Let's get out of here," said the stud.

"He didn't mean anything," the plump girl told him. She seemed relieved not to have to complete the game against the other two. "Like, he's just got his thing, you know?"

"Too bad," said the one with curves. "I was getting kind of interested in that thing."

"Sorry," said Payne.

"Maybe the right one would get you interested in the things she had, too."

"It's been tried," Payne said. And he must have known it would be tried again.

•

Did he truly say that?
Not in so many words.
Then what, exactly.
Are you my priest?
They're going to be laying for you, Charles. They aren't going to like it that you've appropriated this man and then taken liberties.
Did you ever hear the quote from the great physicist? He said there are many more things you can know than can be proved.
You're taking a lot on faith. And, given what you are, a lot of people aren't going to have much faith in you.

•

He had nodded off when a knock on the door brought him back up again, like a soap bubble bursting and nothing is there. He looked around confused, pulled a shallow breath. The knock came again. He sat up and leaned over until he reached the knob.

"Hi, again," said the one with the curves.

With the door open, she flooded the room with an incense scent. There was musk beneath it. He could smell that, too.

"I was sleeping."

"Can I come in?"

She slid past him, sat down on the bed, lifted her heavy, fabric purse to her lap and began rooting around in it. As she did, her breasts fell under his eyes, creamy in the dim amber incandescence of the chamber light, cradled so loosely that he thought he could see the first shadow of her nipples where the cloth of her peasant dress enfolded them.

"You ever do acid before?" she asked.

"I'm a jazz musician," he said. "I've tried everything twice."

"Really?"

"The third time it's a cliché."

He hated to admit how old fashioned his tastes had been. The kids were ready to experiment with anything. Mushrooms. Aerosols. The fumes of paint.

"There it is," she said, then lifted a little square of foil from her purse. When she unwrapped it, two pieces of paper stuck together fell into her hand. She had the long fingers of a piano player, with nails bitten down to the quick. They said LSD showed you the face of God. Anybody'd be nervous after that. "Think you can handle it?"

"Don't be fucking with me," he said.

He did not lash out, but she was obviously the kind of woman who had been around the kind of men who did. She moved up closer and took his arm, cushioning it against her soft breast.

"I can't promise not to fuck with you," she said, "but I guarantee you'll like it."

The train swayed dully through the darkness. The letters to Taiana and Showon rested in his horn case.

"You aren't really gay," she said, carefully separating the two pieces of blotter paper. Her breath smelled of wine and eggs. He was surprised by the clarity of his senses. Each thing was separate: sight, smell, and sound. Los Angeles was there, and he was here. Kensington was to come.

"You ever heard me play?" he said.

"Sure," she said. "My parents had all your records. That's how I knew you were lying. Your music used to get me so hot."

Her words were beginning to have a similar effect on him.

"This paper soaks up the acid," she said. "You suck on it."

She placed the gray square in his pink open palm.

"Ever do a Benzedrine inhaler?"

"Acid is better," she said.

"Benzedrine gets you up," he said. "This shit, doesn't it knock you down? I thought you said you wanted to fuck with me."

"I want to fuck with your mind first," she said.

•

The manner of Jackson Payne's death to the contrary notwithstanding, the believers insisted that as soon as he met Taiana he had a spiritual awakening that was akin to being born again. A few critics had suggested chemical origins for some of his revelations, which was hardly a radical proposition, given the times. But they were shouted down.

Nevertheless, Payne described his "trip" in the liner notes to *The Kensington Sessions*. Any moderately close reading of the text suggests, in both style and content, its true import.

"Trip of a lifetime. Lifeline. Lines of time. Explosions of color, black and white, two sides of the same mountain, shadow and sun, shadows on the Moon."

That sort of thing was common then. The liner notes consisted of a thousand words of it, taken from a document five times longer. Quinlan had dutifully copied out the original, which he had found in the archives of Columbia Records. A lot of it must have come from the girl, in whose hand it was written, because phrases like "mindscapes on the rails" and "rainbow-flecked dreams" just were not the sort of thing that even chemicals could induce in Jackson's mind.

•

The acid came on slowly. It was very different from mainlining. You weren't sure you were going until you got there. It was something like pot, but it took you farther. You didn't really feel anything happening and then it was like a sweet, easy groove or touching somebody slowly all over.

His eyes fixed on her breasts, which rolled with the movement of the train until he was floating on ocean waves. The rhythm lulled him, led him to the sea. Did they know about this shit at Kensington?

The girl was into even deeper waters. Her head lay back and swayed from side to side. It could have been ecstasy, or it could have been pain. He could not tell the difference and wondered whether he ever really had known.

"Hey," he said. "You're getting way ahead of me, girl."

"I know where I'm going," she said. "Want to come?"

"You ain't been there with anybody like me before," he said.

Soon he saw her beckoning from across a barren plain, growing more distant by the moment. The waves had parched to sand. In the liner notes he referred to Badlands. He had definitely been there before.

He reached across and touched her. Out of nowhere he told her how the noise of battle had once stolen the music away. She cradled his head upon her chest and told him that she was against the war. He told about being arrested, being set up, the beatings. But he did not mention the preacher or how he had survived in prison. And he did not tell her what had happened to his son. Wasn't this shit supposed to take all that away? Suddenly, out the train window he saw Jay's black body bag spread out before him, just beyond his reach.

He cried out. The porter came, his head filling the little compartment like a balloon. When he saw the girl there, he smiled and left.

The girl held Payne, then began to work on him. She had been here before and knew how to take him higher. He felt the prickly hair of her legs around his middle as she rode him, smelled the sweet, scented hair under her arms. This moved him, the way a man can be moved by the things of the earth.

"Earth and fire," she said.

He left it in the liner notes, as if these were the source of all wonder in the world. And maybe they were. For what else was there but matter and energy, the one the stuff of creation, the other the spirit of music and of God.

When they finished they dressed and he led her to the rear car beyond the other passengers. There he took out his horn and played.

It was like being at the Point again. His fingers felt huge on the keys. The sound was swollen, too. It poured out around them as if something had burst.

"Out of sight," said the girl.

"I've been looking for something new," he said.

He blew a few angular notes, a rapid and oddly intervaled run.

"Wow," she said.

"Sometimes it's been circles."

The pattern he blew was not as intricate as he got into when he gave the thing time to build over Showon's comping. But it was clean.

Then something came out of his horn like a big dog's bark.

"What was that?" she said.

He did it again, a rude statement you only made to frighten or to hurt.

"I really fucked up here," he said.

"You been tripping, love," she said.

"That's what I said."

"Fucked up how?"

"You got about a year?"

•

Nearly all of our walk-in residents come to us on the remorse of one final fling. Our records show that your subject tested positive upon admittance. And he reported a recent ingestion of LSD. The initial screening showed him mildly depressed. There had been some sort of sexual encounter. Nothing our screening psychologists felt concern about.

Do your records say with whom?

The sexual matter? This isn't anything we would find particularly interesting, unless there were legal issues that needed to be pursued. In this case it appeared to be a consensual act between adults, so we left it at that.

But you must be concerned about knowing where they've been. And when they are lying.

This, of course, is a challenge.

You should have had him play.

•

"You were really into a mantra," the girl said as they listened to the rhythm of the wheels on the rails. "It was like a prayer. No, wait. It was more like making it. The way it went over and over the same spot until something started to come inside."

"I got to get clean," he said. "That's all it was."

2.

The professionals at Kensington did not believe in depth psychology. Like all bureaucracies, this one reduced its subject matter to the fewest possible dimensions: stimulus and response. And it seemed to work. Within a few weeks Payne had gotten past the crisis stage and begun settling into sobriety for the first time in years. He seemed to respond well to the later stages of therapy, too, and in October of 1974 he emerged with a perfectly clean blood test and just enough cash to get him back to Los Angeles by train. Instead, he traveled north to New York City, where his certificate from Kensington was enough to get him back his cabaret card.

•

I'd moved to New York not long after I stopped representing Jackson. When I finally heard from him again, I was working out of a milk-glass office over a peep show off Broadway. Doing OK, you know? Semi-retired. The shit kids wanted to hear had gone way past me.

He just showed up one day?

Straight out of the blue. That's somebody's title, isn't it? How many cats who couldn't remember when they last *been* straight have used that word to name a tune? Sometimes we'd sit around in the booth and dream the titles up. Cat would jam for seven minutes nine seconds in the key of G, and somebody'd say, "Jam for Gene." Then the talent would wake up and ask me, "Who's Gene?" The fuck do I know, kid.

What did Jackson say?

He wanted work.

I said, "You got to have a card, Jackie."

"I'm certified Grade A," he said, "by the New York PD."

Lanny, I say to myself, what do you need an old doper for? Tell him you're doing children's music now. Tell him you're looking to bring Rosie Clooney onto the comeback trail. Tell him any ofay thing at all.

So of course I said, "What kind of gig are you looking for?"

"I want to do an album."

"What century did you do the last one again?"

"This one's going to be different," he says. "Something absolutely new."

Like I never heard that before.

"The A&R men today, they're just kids," I said. "Everything's new to them."

"Get me a gig," he says, "and bring him there."

"Bring who?"

"A guy who can make his name giving me back mine."

•

You could've blown me over when I heard Lanny Klein had put the word out on the street looking for me to do a job with Jackson Payne. I went to the club Jackson was playing. Right away I realized the thing he was doing was way beyond me. It didn't even have a name yet. It was freer than harmolodics. Freer than Trane. Freer than anybody. Against the chords, against the rhythm, against the whole fucking room. I could barely stand to listen to it.

Then I saw Lanny over at a table with some kid had to be from one of the record companies. Where'd they get these sweets? I picked up my drink and went over to pay my respects.

"Lanny," I said, like it'd just been a week instead of ten long years, "where you been keeping yourself?"

"What're you drinking, Junior?" Lanny said. "Funny you should stop by tonight. I've been thinking about you. This is the thing I was telling you about, Jim. Jim's from Columbia, Junior. So don't be talking Blue Note here."

I'd never seen Lanny so nervous before.

•

Lanny called me, too. Wanted me to get on the first train east.

"It's a comeback, Showon," he said. "The Original Jackson Payne Quartet. Brand new together again."

"Even if it kills him," I said.

•

When he came to the table, Jackson made like he didn't even know who I was.

"I've been talking to Jim and Junior about putting the Quartet back together again," Lanny said.

"That won't work," said Jackson.

"That shit you're playing now," I said, "it's like blowing into a hole."

I saw Lanny waving at me to shut up.

"What've you been doing lately, Junior?" Jackson asked.

"This and that," I said.

"I ain't heard a thing for years."

"I wasn't the one they all said was gone be somebody someday," I said.

"Did you explain what I have in mind?" Jackson asked Lanny, like I wasn't even there.

"That," Lanny said, "is for somewhere down the road."

"Talk to me," said the A&R man. I couldn't make out his sound. The accent came from nowhere, like an announcer on TV.

"I want it solo," said Jackson. "Absolutely pure."

•

I always tell youngsters who want to go into the representation game that every client they'll ever have will assume they can sell themselves better than you can. Jackson was no exception. I said, Jackson, your reputation isn't good enough to peddle a cold drink in the park on a hot day.

Then wouldn't you know it? Columbia bought his solo idea.

The man made an offer right there at the table. I could have shot him. I tell all the A&R men, Let me make my living, and I'll help you make yours. We cut the deals away from the talent.

"You don't take a shit in the living room," I told him after. "You don't make a contract at the table."

"What *is* your role exactly, Lanny?" he said.

•

Hence the origin of the famous *Kensington Sessions* album and of the relationship between Jackson and Columbia that for the first time in his life made Payne financially secure on the basis of his best rather than his worst.

As it turned out, the deal worked well for Columbia, too. The rumor mill began grinding out word of the album even before Payne signed the papers. Club owners came to Lanny Klein for bookings. For the debut he settled on the Black Rose, which attracted a hard-core crowd that might be able to sit through a whole set of solo horn. The club had an inner courtyard that opened up in good weather and accommodated maybe ten tables of four.

"I want to play under the stars again," said Payne.

"He's going to be hot," Klein assured the owner.

The owner looked up to the sky.

"As long as it doesn't fucking rain."

•

Randy Sons, *Village Voice:*

Jackson Payne must have been doing some serious woodshedding since his last recording. Some say it was at Kensington. Some say L.A. But from the sound of him today, he's been to the mountain and met someone there.

Playing on a pawnshop horn his agent got him when he hit New York City flat broke, Payne circled all the ambiguities of the human soul Tuesday night at the Black Rose.

•

You can see Lanny Klein's handiwork in the lie about where Payne got his tenor. It worked exactly as intended, except that the writer left out Klein's name.

"Jackson was furious," Klein recalled. "I told him it wasn't any worse than all the bullshit he'd laid down over the years. But he said this was different; it soiled his horn. Like he never had."

•

Roger Coles, *Downbeat:*

The most remarkable thing about Payne's new groove was that he got there, given where he's been. The man was so fresh from a stay at Kensington that he had to borrow money from his agent to buy a second-hand horn.

You can be sure that that old instrument had never before produced the kind of things it did at the Black Rose. No horn had.

Jackson Payne has led the way before, and he has paid a price for it. This time he's again heading into some pretty scary territory, which may be why he's going it alone.

It is more than music he's after. It is some sort of Higher Truth. We can't quite see it yet. But we'll follow him if we can.

•

That was *Downbeat's* first reference to Payne since he left for Paris, except for a listing near the bottom of the annual readers' poll when the recordings with Damon Reed were reissued in a boxed set. Though the magazine did not usually give numerical ratings to live per-formances reviewed in the "Caught" column, this one carried a simple headline, "Five Stars."

What was it that captured everyone's imagination? Without diminishing the magnitude of Payne's achievement, one must recog-nize that he made his reappearance at a time of parching drought. Play-ers were either cloying away for listeners' affection or getting in their face with non-negotiable demands. Many had taken, as Payne had at one time, the worst of rock and fused it with the least of jazz. What Payne played at the Black Rose was a masterpiece of introspection, a chant, a dervish, a yelp of joy.

"We are not much for the wisdom of the East," wrote *The New Yorker* in the "Talk of the Town," "at least the East beyond the river. But the other night a little west of that at the Black Rose on Amsterdam Avenue we came across a man with a horn who seemed to go outside the known universe into some sweet, sweet beyond."

•

It was magic. Everybody wanted a piece of him. Even *Vogue* called and asked could he model some kind of crazy print robe. He wouldn't do it. Didn't like the material or something. Or was it the materialism? He was talking an awful lot of shit in those days.

What kind of talk?

Cosmic this. Universal that. Look, I told him, I don't give a shit *what* church you go to, any more than you ever cared about mine. *Mazel tov.*

"We are all one," he said.

"Gotcha covered. It's all right by me if you become a fucking swami."

You know, sometimes I wanted to believe him. All one, instead of the old grab and get. Then I'd catch myself and have a drink.

•

Columbia hired an artist who had done some of the Beatles' concepts to do Payne's jacket design. And he immediately seized on the thing Payne had written with the girl on the train.

Bad poetry, excellent music, and psychedelic art propelled *The Kensington Sessions* onto the pop charts. The fact that nobody had quite figured out what Payne was up to only increased the appeal. When Miles started insulting him, Payne's triumph was complete.

Pulling out the recording today produces some very mixed reactions. On the album cover Day-Glo circles wound in a long progression across an oil-on-water swirl like a serpent in a comic book. In each circle rested a letter in irregular type, and these came together to form the title. Payne's name rose like puffs from the caterpillar's hookah. The artwork is a product of that unique moment when severe substance abuse became a form of kitsch.

3.

Somebody along the way told Quinlan that Taiana's name in an Arabic dialect meant "mirage." Later he decided that the story probably started with one of Payne's nighttime friends, as apt as it might have been if it had been so.

The click of her phone falling back onto the receiver did not deter him, nor did her door failing to open. He sent letters, which never received acknowledgment. He dispatched emissaries—an A&R man who had worked with her on a retrospective, one of Jackson's admirers who had for a time become virtually part of the family. But it was no use.

Eventually he called Lasheen and asked whether she could meet him in San Francisco.

"I'm not a traveling companion," she said.

"I'm not traveling," he said. "I'm staying put."

"So I've noticed."

"I hoped you would."

"I've been too busy to think about it," she said.

"There's a lady I'm trying to get to. I think you can help me," he said. "I've already talked to Hamed."

"You didn't dare."

"He said I'd better talk to you."

"Smart man."

"So?"

She was silent for so long that he began to think they had been cut off.

"Should I count on it?" he said. "I mean on you."

"You do want what you want, don't you," she said.

The weather out of Chicago did not cooperate, so Quinlan had to wait for more than an hour at the gate. When the plane finally did roll up, Lasheen was among the last ones out.

She did not see him at first. She stopped, realized she was holding up the line, stepped aside. Her eye went right over him in the crowd. She seemed overwhelmed, which was a side of her he had not seen before or imagined, though while they were apart he had imagined her in almost every position.

"Lasheen!" he called. Several people turned at the curiosity of the name.

As they reached the baggage claim her suitcase hit the carousel with a thump. When he lifted it off, he had to use both hands.

"What have you got in here?" he said.

"I didn't know how long you wanted to keep me," she said.

For some reason that sent a nice little tingle through him.

"I'll keep you as long as you want to be kept," he said.

"We'll see about that."

In the rented car she fooled with the radio as they drove among the wet, brown hills toward the city.

"What's good here?" she asked.

"Seafood. Sourdough."

"I mean radio."

The traffic had gotten tricky on the way out of the airport, so he could not look to get her expression.

"Pretty much anything you have a taste for," he said.

"Jazz?"

"That's the first button," he said. "The second is more up your alley."

She backed into it, punching buttons he quite obviously had not programmed. They brought on somebody else's selections—blue guitars, saccharine voices over strings, some kind of sports talk. When she reached the classical station it was doing a Mahler. She barely paused before going to the jazz.

"Gerry Mulligan," he said after the first few notes. " 'Walkin' Shoes' from his tentette album of the same name. That's young Chet Baker on trumpet and Bud Shank on alto. It was recorded in L.A. in 1953."

"I could have gotten who was playing baritone sax," she said.

"You've been listening?" he said.

"I finally took a couple of lessons," she said. "It isn't easy getting the chords. But there's definitely something there."

"Maybe someday you'll be able to show me."

"Something that needs to be said."

•

This cat really wanted to get in the sister's pants. Paid her all the way from Chicago. Don't let him kid you, he's no different than me. And Junior can tell you a thing or two about the things lonely cats will do.

•

He said she was a woman I'd introduce my mother to. So I said, Let's meet her. Well, she may be a little coarse. But I think she's the genuine article, even though she's too brightly wrapped.

•

Don't be a fool.
Man only thinks about his tool.
Don't know her and don't know you.
But some things you know
Just 'cause they're true.

•

The G is grand and gaudy; the G is for the girl.
Tell it, brother.
And C is Charles, all concerned and correct.
But don't be deceived, brothers and sisters. There's no cur more cursed than C.
Amen.

•

Quinlan opened his eyes, and she was there on a chair next to the bed, watching him.

"You slept hard," she said.

"I had a dream," he said.

"About me?" she said.

"In a sense. People were trading fours about my intentions."

"Those were pretty hard to miss an hour ago."

He turned a half turn away as he got dressed.

"Some of them didn't give me much credit."

"Black or white?"

"All black," he said.

"Usually it's somebody's mother. Wondering what you have against your own kind."

"Was your mother like that?"

"Is."

"She knows about me?"

"I tell her everything," Lasheen said.

"So there's a lot stacked against me."

"Join the club."

He found his shirt. It was not too wrinkled, and the tie was still buttoned in the collar.

"Let's just do room service," she said.

"This is why we never seem to go out on the town," he said.

"You dog."

"And here it is your first time. . . ."

She grinned. "Sweetness," she said, dark as he'd ever heard her, "I be saving it all fo' you."

"First time you've been in San Francisco. We ought to at least take a walk."

"You know, baby," she purred. "I'll do anything you want me to."

She got up and went to her bags, from which she drew a sweater and jeans. Then she took out a cosmetics case and went to work at the mirror. As part of their preparations, he had taken a cloth and softly washed the makeup off so there would be nothing between them but the lovely smooth surface, like a polished maroon stone.

It did not take long before she was ready to meet the world, though he half expected to be challenged when they reached the lobby. How obvious he must have seemed to everyone. A man of a certain age. Of a certain everything.

"I left my heart . . . ," Lasheen sang as they stepped out onto the hilly street.

"You've been listening to Tony Bennett, too?" he laughed.

"I wasn't sure he was acceptable, but a nice man at Rose Records said he was."

"There was a time when I thought he was just a tux with shiny elbows. Then I opened my ears."

"What did you hear, baby? Tell Lasheen the truth."

"A guy giving it a lot," he said.

"He reminds me of you," she said, back off the street again now.

"Tony Bennett?"

"The way he strains," she said, "and the way the strain is sweet."

They ended up walking quite a distance, despite the steepness of some of the grades.

"What is it you want me to do with Payne's wife?" she asked.

"I can't seem to get close to her," he said. "Maybe you can. Use your music. She's affiliated with a conservatory."

"Does she know I'm working for you?"

"You're a student," he said. "You've become obsessed with Payne's music. She'll have seen that before. You need to know everything. Like a jealous lover."

"Or a professor."

"I'll give you a list of people," he said. "I've talked to most of them. And I've transcribed most of the sessions. You can read them to prepare."

"Obsessed," she said.

"Yes," he said. "That's the effect you want to convey."

•

Charles was always obtuse. Well, he's found himself a trophy now. He's a little ahead of himself, don't you think? Aren't you supposed to do something first and then get the bimbo as a prize?

•

It's that old black magic, all right. And as pale as this man is, it ain't a spell he knows very well.

•

It's been this way since the days of slaves.
Color is how a man behaves.

•

The flimsy curtain in the high hotel window was red with dusk. She lay back insouciantly on the bed. She had been out all day.

"You showed her one of my articles?"

"I did."

"And she read it?"

"She did."

"What did she say?"

Lasheen pulled herself up and leaned into her reply.

"What a man," she said.

Quinlan waited, but there wasn't any more. Lasheen slowly eased herself back.

"That's what you want us to say, isn't it?" she said. "What every man wants to hear." She was laughing now. "You're so serious, Charles. Learn to kick back and enjoy it a little. Let's celebrate. She saw that you were respectful of the music. I told her you were very open-minded. Which was right, wasn't it?"

Quinlan nodded.

"A complete democrat," he said.

"The people's choice. Come let us reason together," she said. "Or is it the other way around?"

"And she bought it?"

"I had a really good talk with her," Lasheen said.

"About what?"

"Men with a mission," she said. "We hit it right off."

4.

Quinlan stopped when he saw the wreath and lights.

"Are you sure you spoke to the right person?" he said.

Lasheen led him up the steps, tapped the doorknocker, and lifted herself to her toes to look through the windows above it. Then she knocked again.

The elegant woman who opened the door was dressed all in white, as she was in the photo on the cover of Payne's album *African Gods.* She could have passed for Iris, messenger of all the colors on earth.

"Please come in," she said.

She hung their coats in a closet just inside the door then led them down a short hall. It opened onto a strikingly decorated living room, which used the symmetries and repetitions of the Mideast style to make it appear much larger than it was. Pillows on the deep red and blue carpet softened the effect, suggesting something of an oasis.

Then there was the Christmas tree. It stood in the corner opposite the doorway, hung with a hundred identical silver stars that glittered in the sunlight. Under the tree lay brightly wrapped packages arranged in perfect, pyramidal piles.

"Kafi is coming home from college soon," Taiana said.

"You never told me where," Lasheen said.

"Eastman," Taiana said.

"Still playing tenor?" Quinlan asked.

"Among other things," said Taiana. "He also writes and conducts. The force of his father's records sometimes pulls him, but more often these days it pushes him to try something else."

"Like Charlie Parker pushed your husband," Quinlan said.

"Yes, I suppose," she said. "But at least Bird wasn't Jackson's father."

The way she took the question emboldened Quinlan.

"Excuse me for asking, Mrs. Payne," he asked, "but did you raise your son Christian? I mean the tree and everything."

"I raised him as Jackson would have," she said, "without distinctions."

Then she took Lasheen into a warm, familiar smile.

•

Her parents had come to the United States from West Africa before she was born, her father an ambassador and a member of one of his country's wealthiest clans. She was born in Washington, D.C., educated in an integrated school there, then at Howard University, where she took a four-year course of study from her classmates in being black.

As a child I breathed in music like the scent of a garden. It was all around me, the chantsongs of my father's homeland, and also his later love, American jazz. He himself played piano a little. The embassy had a big old grand in the formal living room. When we arrived it was decades out of tune. Getting it into shape was one of his first official acts. He used to sit at it for hours, trying to improvise over the chords of simple show tunes or playing along with a record on the Zenith console. And I loved to listen.

Did he ever play music from his country?

Sometimes on national days he would have a group of native musicians. Then he and mother would sing. It was haunting.

Often I wanted to go back there with them and become part of it. But I never really could, you know. By the time they had to return, I was in college, and I stayed behind. But I did wear the clothes my mother sent me. Folk dresses in the beautiful colors of the African earth. Of course, at that time this didn't exactly set me apart. Everybody had some kind of costume. And also grand ideas about Africa. So sometimes I would affect what I thought of as the right accent, faintly British colonial, you know, with a patois. People who heard me probably thought I was poking fun at the West Indians. Actually, I just wanted to fool people into thinking I was real.

Real.

Somebody from somewhere.

You were an American citizen, no?

Everyone born here is a citizen. This country is very odd in the way it denies the importance of accidents of birth and then makes such an important thing turn upon one of them. But I do not mean to seem ungrateful. It is just that I did not feel wholly a part of this country.

Of course, my classmates at Howard didn't either, whether they came from Mississippi or Prince Georges County, Maryland, Harlem, or Evanston, Illinois.

I can identify with that, Lasheen said.

You are and you aren't. Want to be and don't.

Was this the way Jackson seemed to you, too? Tugged by an Africa he had never seen?

I'm afraid it was a bit more complicated than that.

Tell him, sister, said Lasheen.

It was awfully hard not to be caught up in the romance of the times. This was after college, now. All those things that had happened down South. God, didn't that seem like another world? But even as it began to change, we started to think it could never be as good as something all our own.

Did you ever manage to make the journey back?

I didn't have to. I learned from Jackson what I am and what that means.

To be African?

To be American. Just like you.

•

She did not meet Jackson Payne by chance. On the radio one night she heard something that made her stop what she was doing, drop the dish towel to the counter and listen. A friend who was visiting from the East came into the kitchen and began to say something, but Taiana hushed her. The music came to her deeply, sounding of home.

"That's Jackson Payne, girl," said her friend. "He's playing somewhere. Look in the papers."

You weren't supposed to go to bars, were you?

It did feel a little like sin.

You should've talked to me, said Lasheen.

I wasn't worldly like you. Islam protects its women.

You ought to meet my boss, Hamed, said Lasheen. He was raised by the nuns.

You didn't tell me about him before.

I was afraid you would think I was making him up, said Lasheen.

He is a little out of the ordinary.

I seem to be drawn to them, said Lasheen.

•

Taiana had grown up on abstinence. She was uncomfortable to see what people wore on the beaches, the working clothes that showed legs high up the thighs. When she arrived at the Krazy Kat, where Payne was playing, the women around her had plunging necklines, glazed expressions, slightly open lips. The atmosphere was like smoke in her eyes.

When my parents died, it shocked me to my roots. But even then I was not really following all the tenets. I wore my long black sheath dress buttoned to the chin, but it was so tight that if one of the mullahs from home had seen me, he would have had me whipped.

Maybe that was what made it so thrilling to be there. I was Muslim enough to believe that all good and evil is predetermined. And they were both powerfully present that night.

Could you tell which was which? Lasheen asked.

I could not get really near him the way he was at first. I had to use Islam on him, like a sorceress with an ancient spell.

Do you know any? Lasheen had a smile of complicity.

If anyone could draw wisdom out of me, it was Jackson. He pulled me back to all sorts of things I'd never known.

•

He played far from the top of his form that night. Yet she heard echoes of the soul of this man, and it shone. So she was not deterred that he looked so wasted, that he sweat with the least exertion, that his hands shook as he lifted a glass to his lips. He was obviously not well in spirit, but his music showed that he yearned to be.

No, she did not know much about him at the beginning. She was ignorant of the weakness he had in and for the flesh. The bell of his saxophone moved in tight spirals as he played, a pattern of departure and return. She followed him away and back, away and back again, and it left her breathless to have gone so far. As she sat there brushing away the glances of other men, she sought his out.

Did you go to him after, or did you let him come to you?

That is a man's question. Not that I didn't think of it. I knew what men expected when a woman approached them. But by the time the performance was over, it didn't matter. We were going to meet. I did not care how.

Atta girl, said Lasheen.

Every other woman who looked at me must have known.

I do not know what moved me to give him money the night we first met. I never gave him money again, though he tried to get me to. But at that moment, when he first asked me for it, I was afraid to refuse.

Did he want anything more from you that night? Lasheen asked.

•

"You still here?" he said as he emerged, with such a disappointingly small buzz that did not make anything disappear.

"I said I would be," she said.

It annoyed him.

"What's your name anyway?"

"I'm not ready for that yet," she said.

"You gave me money, baby."

"Money I can always get more of."

Payne now had a good look at her from head to foot.

"What will it take to get your number?" he asked.

"You can pay me back. That would be a beginning."

"Is that all?"

"No," she said.

"Motherfucker owes me Friday," Payne said.

"You can stop using words like that," she said.

Payne laughed.

"You got to play your own sound," he said.

"I will not stay in the presence of people who shame themselves," she said.

The shape before him was very nice as she rose tall on her heels.

"Shit," he said.

She turned and he followed her legs with his eyes.

"Wait, sister," he said. "Say I watched my tongue. What could we do then?"

"We could talk," she said.

•

You must have known right away the power you had.

Actually I was afraid that he would just go out of my life. But I also had this feeling that if it was so sure to me, it had to be sure to him, too.

Did he show any hesitation?

He met my conditions. If he hadn't, I don't know what I would have done. Dignified language. Dignified setting. And no sweet talk. No Hey, baby, you don't know what you been missing all your life. Because, of course, I didn't. And I was not even thinking of sleeping with him.

Oh yes you were, said Lasheen.

Quinlan nearly jumped in to apologize. But then he heard Taiana laugh.

Maybe unconsciously.

Baby, you'd been missing it, said Lasheen, full of the street. Missing it even if you didn't know what it was 'til you saw him and suddenly knew what you never had.

Maybe.

We've all been there, honey, said Lasheen.

In a way, I guess I had made up my mind as soon as I saw him play. But it wasn't the man. It was what I heard crying out. Haven't you ever met a man you had to work on before he was ready for you?

Only the one I work for, said Lasheen.

They both were looking at Quinlan.

She's talking about Hamed.

Of course she is.

•

Before the next set he did join her at her table, all eyes upon them as she ordered two glasses of something soft.

"That's some weak shit," he said.

She stood.

"I mean weak stuff," he said. "This is going to take some time."

"It's my religion," she said.

"I been to church," he said.

"I think you have."

"But now my faith runs more to scotch and milk," he said.

The waiter brought the soft drinks to the table. She lifted hers to her lips.

"Islam forbids," she said.

"You don't look the part," he said. "Muslim women I've known all been plain."

"You're thinking of Americans," she said.

"That's who we are."

She shook her head.

"I am African," she said.

"I can tell where things come from by the sound," he said.

"Like a blind man," she interrupted.

"I hear what I hear," he said.

"I am not in the habit of having to prove anything to anyone," she said.

"Then you're a pretty lucky b—." He caught himself in time. "A lucky broad." He really felt the need for a drink or something stronger, to get them loose, because right now they were both tuned a couple of steps too far up the scale. "A man got to prove himself every day of the f— filthy year."

She sipped her soda.

"A man only has to prove what he doubts," she said.

He wolfed down his drink and then rose up with more steadiness than he had expected. He wasn't sure whether he liked that or not.

"You proved something to me before," she said.

"I'll get you your money back," he said.

"I mean when you played," she said. "You proved that you believed it. Every note."

"Sometimes you do."

"That's why I wanted more," she said.

"You look like a broad who gets her way," he said.

"There's another word," she said.

"Shit," he said and turned and walked away.

•

I was taught that God would select my mate. And that God spoke through my father. His death left me spinstered and spiritually alone. I flirted with the Nation of Islam, but I hadn't had enough experience with white people to make me think they are devils.

Give it time, said Lasheen.

My mind had been opened, but opened like a wound. At Howard I studied philosophy and went to Christian churches with friends. I practiced the faith after a fashion but did not believe in the one true way. In my darker moments I wasn't sure there was any way at all.

I thought the death of your parents drove you toward Islam.

What to eat. What not to drink. How to hold back from a man. But I could not be a believer. Because I was not pure.

Payne complained that you were.

That's because I knew with him I had to be.

•

She presented him a figure of serenity and self-control. When he tried his usual approaches, she either laughed him off or added new phrases to the forbidden list.

"The bitch is froze," he told Showon Tucker.

"But she isn't going away," said Tucker.

"Ain't that some shit?"

•

One night he showed up at my apartment. Until then I wasn't sure he even knew where it was. When the buzzer squawked and I heard who it was on the speaker, my first thought was, He's come to pay me back.

Silly girl, said Lasheen.

"It's your mystery man," he said.

Oh, boy, said Lasheen.

You're right. He could be a prize sometimes.

"I didn't ask you to come here," I said.

"Maybe you just didn't know how much it shows," he said.

The trouble was, I thought it probably did, so I said, "I know what I want and what I don't. And I do not entertain gentlemen callers in my home."

"Maybe I'm not feeling very much like a gentleman," he said.

"Jackson," I said, "you know what I think about that."

The speaker clicked a couple of times, and I thought I had chased him off, but then it clicked again.

"Woman," he said, "I don't know how you can be so different from every other I've ever known."

"I don't want to be like them," I said. "None of them lasted."

That stopped him, but not for long.

"To last," he said, "you got to start."

"And to start," I said, "*you've* got to stop."

It must have seemed to him like Zen.

"No fat-butted broad's gonna tell me what to do," he said.

"I wouldn't think of trying," I said.

How foolish you get. I went straight to a mirror to be sure I hadn't grown big in the rear. I even started doing exercises. But I knew that he would come back. And before long he did.

"I can't do this thing by myself," he said. "It's stronger than anything."

"God is stronger," I said, and I hoped to God it was true.

"He's a long way off," Jackson said.

"You've been trying to reach Him," I said. "I can hear."

"There's a program in Kensington, Kentucky," he said. "I've known a lot of cats who've gone there. But most of them come back still wanting to cop."

"Cop?"

"Score. Uh, get high again."

"You won't."

"I don't know."

"You won't be alone," I said. And then to be sure he understood I made it as clear as I dared. "You'll have me."

At this point I started practicing Islam again more seriously. A lot of things began to come back, comforting things. I started to wear even more modest clothes—long, loose dresses, eventually even a scarf to cover my head.

My new appearance did not seem to dampen his enthusiasm. In fact, the more I withdrew from view, the more attention he paid. He had already started to back off drugs and whiskey. And he stopped smoking in my presence, though I knew he would scoot away during Showon's solos and have a puff.

It's a wonder I ever got past the smell of him, smoke and whiskey and cologne over sweat. I guess my eye and ear overcame my nose and throat. The Koran does not have much to say about such priorities. It simply warns that all the senses are media of both temptation and delight.

Did you talk to him often about religion?

In the beginning very rarely. Once in a while I would bring the subject up. Jackson felt he was very far from attaining the spiritual connection he yearned for.

I confess that I was a little concerned about his interest in the local Muslims. I didn't want Jackson to cut off all his hair and wear a tiny bow tie on a white shirt. That wasn't Islam. It was America. Islam was the side of me that *wasn't* America. But eventually Jackson made me understand how both sides fit. I've never met a more American man in all my life.

You said something like that before.

"Listen close to what I play," he said. "It's all in there. Everything I ever heard. From Bach to the barwalkers. That's America, lady. That's jazz."

And yet he was always trying to get past the influences, to be utterly original.

He used to say, "Lady, you ever watch a dog fight? The mongrels usually win."

"Then nothing is pure," I said.

"Pure everything," he said, "is the purest you can be."

And I thought to myself, I could be American that way.

Did you tell him so?

I used to say that God wants every person to surrender to the divine plan.

That's different.

Very. And he knew it. But I was working on him. Just the way he was working on me.

"That divine plan of yours is trouble," he said. "I'd want to break free."

"You cannot, of course," I said.

"This God a white man?" he said.

"He is the color of all colors."

"He into diatonic harmony?"

"I'm afraid I don't know what that is," I said.

The European system of structuring the movement of chords.

That's what he said. But he called them white man's chords.

"When a group is playing," he said, "everybody has his own thing. Nobody tells anybody what to say. But there is a plan: that's the tune, the harmony. Everybody gets to play whatever they please within that, and if they want, to go outside. You are free, lady. Even when you choose to stay within the lines."

"Pure everything," I said. "Like the image of God."

"Like black is the color of all colors," he said.

He sounds more political than others describe him.

He could put together things that fought one another in the rest of us. He said that everybody was at home in America because nobody was. Each one of us is out there every day creating himself for the crowd. The ones that start out knowing who they are, they are just repeating what they've been told. But you don't have to accept that. In America all they give you is the chords.

He was a long way from the neighborhood by then, said Lasheen.

He had it in him, though. Don't forget, he was still putting it into his arm several times a day. "The trouble," he said, "is that you get to liking the thing that holds you in." I could tell that he was scared.

Scared of Kensington?

They say that Alexander the Great wept when he realized he had no more worlds to conquer. I think Jackson knew he was getting near the edge of pure everything. And that beyond it there was nothing else.

Pure everything was what? America? God?

Oh, please, said Lasheen. Sometimes you just got to say, "Amen."

Amen. I must have said it to myself a thousand times when he was getting ready to leave. Amen. Amen. Amen.

But you knew Jackson would cheat, said Lasheen.

I had seen the way his eye wandered. I asked one day, "Do they have women at Kensington?"

"I'll be too sick to think about it," he said.

"You aren't too sick now."

"I'll be thinking about that reward you promised," he said.

"The real reward is being clean," I said.

"Yeah," he said. "That, too."

So it wasn't a complete surprise when you heard he had been with a girl on the train.

I had talked to him on the phone.

"I'm all alone, baby," he had said.

You should've said, "You better be," said Lasheen.

I was weak to his weakness. I could hear it in his voice.

Did you hate her?

That's not who you hate, said Lasheen.

I pictured her. There were thousands like her in those days, wandering around sampling everything on the shelves.

Did he ever hit you? asked Lasheen.

You don't have to answer that.

It's all right. We're pretty much at an end for now.

I hope you will let us come back to the happier parts sometime.

They don't have to hit you to hurt you, said Lasheen.

They can do it on a telephone from thousands of miles away.

So you did hate him, said Lasheen.

I couldn't help it.

But you forgave him.

I did.

Why? asked Lasheen.

Because of everything I'd heard.

Were you sure you wanted to marry him? asked Lasheen.

No more than before, but no less.

You're stronger than I am, said Lasheen.

Don't be so sure of that.

I'd like to hear about the wedding, said Lasheen.

I actually have a leatherette album of pictures. Would you like to see it?

ten
celestial
faith

Say a prayer for the Preacher...

"THE PREACHER,"
BY HORACE SILVER

1.

Somewhere down in that smoggy, patchwork valley, she was waiting for him, knowing he had not been true. The plane banked out over the water, so low that he could see the waves. He had to tell her everything, say this was what he had done and would never do again. I am a drug addict and an alcoholic. They told you always to start there. Every day, one at a time.

The moment they met at the gate he said, "You know what I did."

"Tell me," she said.

"I was untrue."

"I was afraid you would be."

"But now I am otherwise. I want you to marry me," he said.

And to his astonishment, she simply said, "Of course."

•

The historical irony of jazz is that it developed its freedom out of the experience of people who were given none. Louis and Jelly Roll and King Oliver were among the Founding Fathers. Even now there is no greater showplace of democracy than a good group in a groove.

E pluribus unum, out of many one. This is the challenge. It is not easy to play together in a regime of free choice. The many assert themselves, each with his own conception and sound. Without some kind of magic, the result would be cacophony. And the magic is the players'

free and mutual agreement to unity. But oneness, too, has its risk. For at
its extreme it requires the submersion of the voice, the loss of the self.

Jazz is synthesis. It takes everything in. Certainly it has had its
nationalisms over the years. But then somebody like Jackson Payne
comes along and sweeps aside all distinctions and makes himself a
multitude, a messiah, even a martyr in the end.

•

The last phase of his musical exploration can be said to have
begun with the song entitled "The Bluest I" on the album entitled *Autobiography*. So wrenching were its cries that many people at first
thought it told Payne's own life story. But in fact it drew its rhythms
directly from a famous passage from *The Autobiography of Malcolm X*.

> . . . I have eaten from the same plate, drunk from the
> same glass, and slept in the same bed . . . —while praying
> to the *same* God—with fellow Muslims whose eyes were
> the bluest of blue, whose hair was the blondest of blond,
> and whose skin was the whitest of white. . . .
>
> . . . Perhaps if white Americans could accept the
> Oneness of God, then perhaps, too, they could accept *in
> reality* the Oneness of Man.

Payne had done pieces without a tonal center before. But in songs
like "Vera," "Green Streak," and "Stony," he had always created the
illusion of it. And the more he had strayed from clear harmonic structures, the more he had built upon a strong, rhythmic pulse. "The Bluest I" broke all these moorings. The piece was ten minutes of rubato. Its
mood came not from the pulpit but from the minaret. The broken intervals of the East mixed with the proximate grace notes of the blues.

No matter how many times one heard it, "The Bluest I" was
always startling. What carried it was pure voice. The words spoke of
eyes of the bluest blue, and yet the sound was as dark as memory, as
eerie and enveloping as déjà vu.

•

Was he deeply into Islam when he wrote "The Bluest I"?

I knew you would ask about that piece. It worried me when he
first played it. So personal, so exclusionary. The first time I heard it, I
did not know the reference.

Most people did not.

Then he showed me Malcolm X's text. The words were all-embracing, but the music curled in upon itself so much that I could hardly find any way to enter.

You had been married how long at that point?

We had already moved to San Francisco. But don't get me wrong. We were fine. Better than fine. God is good.

At first it's always Paradise, said Lasheen.

Muslims are not confused about physical love the way Christians are. Pleasure is simply a reward for virtue.

I wish somebody had taught that to the nuns, said Lasheen.

You never told me you went to Catholic school.

You never asked, said Lasheen.

I guess you are going to have to expand her education.

Yes, Charles, said Lasheen. Loosen me up.

The two women seemed delighted to see him ill at ease.

Charles sometimes seems a little disconnected, said Lasheen. We have drunk from the same glass, slept in the same bed, but the differences are there.

I'm a little worried we're losing our focus here.

Of course you are, said Lasheen.

When we studied the Koran together, Jackson became fascinated with the *jinns.* You probably know them as genies, bare-chested figures in cartoons wearing turbans and vests. But true *jinns* are not creatures of humor. *Jinns* can take very nearly any form. But mainly they are fire. This was what captured Jackson's imagination. As temporary as the wind it drew into itself, it had the power both to warm and to destroy.

"I am not the flame," he said. "But the flame speaks through me."

I'm not sure I follow.

You had to be as totally immersed as he was. You had to do your cleansing. You had to pray five times a day. You had to hear him worrying about whether the *jinns* who spoke through him were good or evil, whether his verses were Satanic or pure. Then the things he said began to make some sense.

•

He made prayers on his horn, circular breathing turning them into one continuous rush. He felt as if he were finally approaching the source of what had been lashing at him all his life. It had been there in the night sky filled with rain, in the sound of the waves. It did not take him to a place with coordinates and contours: mountains, sea, or plain. This was more like a field of energy.

Nor did he reach this state by simply lifting his horn to his lips and blowing a shapely pattern of notes. He had to get beyond the changes. By letting go of all order, he could shake loose of himself and seek Truth in the gathering gyres of sound. Behind him, the drums were aleatory, the bass a measureless drone. He would start with a four- or five-note theme. Sometimes it was one he had practiced. Sometimes it simply leaped to consciousness the moment that metal touched his lips. He would repeat it over and over until it began to suggest some direction, the way a divining rod suggests the presence of water.

His practice sessions often drove Taiana out of the house. She would take Kali to a friend's place or on some long excursion in the stroller. And when she returned she would find him still spinning through the same notes, like a dog turning at the farthest end of his chain.

As Payne reached the limits of endurance, he sometimes came upon the most exquisite sights. He saw a glowing sphere turning, like a bright crystal in the sun. He saw vapors twirl and leap, the limbs of beckoning *houris*. He met his mother, his stepfather, the men who died near him in the war. They spoke to him, and the words came out of his horn.

On the rare occasions when he was able to attain this level, for a few moments he felt close to pure. But then he would lose it in shame and spend fruitless hours trying to find it again.

"If only God could take me while I was playing it right," he said.

"Don't be foolish," said Taiana. "You aren't going anywhere without me."

No matter how fast he whirled, he still trailed remnants of the old self, like smoke.

She would never forget him working on the exercises that led to *Celestial Faith*. For hours he would play an eight-note theme, never varying it. Sometimes he would make a mistake and then repeat it over and over, not to correct it, but as if to inflict it upon himself like the merciless judgment of God.

It did not seem to concern him that his horn spoke a language no one else could understand. He was off in a place all his own. He kept a notebook full of strange geometric figures and columns of numbers, like some kind of code for what he had seen. In it she found clippings from *Muhammad Speaks.*

"Have you been talking to the Fruit of Islam?" she said.

"They show up backstage."

"You don't need to belong to anything, Jackson," she said.

"I need to belong to God."

"But you don't need an introduction," she said.

•

He was finally drug-free. He had a beautiful, loving wife. His music seemed transcendent. Why was his spirit still not at rest?

Something remained beyond him, and he did not know how to reach for it except to raise the level of intensity to the point where everything finally converged. As he did, it seemed not a Song of Creation so much as of the unvariegated energy from which Creation came.

•

Jamie Karlson, *Village Voice:*

Have you listened to Jackson Payne lately? Can you without holding your ears and letting out an Edvard Munch scream? Payne has become a pious bore. I suppose we're expected to greet this desert mysticism with awe. But to me, it's less a call from beyond than the sound of a dentist's drill.

Salvatore Tratiano, *Downbeat:*

Here's the thing. I know that I will be told by the free thinkers that I've sold out, but this stuff Jackson Payne is doing just doesn't make it. Make what? Hate to say it guys, but I guess I mean it doesn't make sense.

Komeni Jabahir, *Amsterdam News:*

The reaction to Payne's latest recording tells us almost as much as he does on his horn. It tells us that some people aren't ever going to understand.

Daniel McLaughlin, *TriQuarterly:*

It is difficult, but so was Beethoven. Payne has traveled somewhere; he is the eye in Plato's cave.

SJ in *National Review:*

When I went to see him for the interview, he told me that I had caught him levitating. The whole time I was with him I do not think he once touched the ground.

Prof. Jonathan Klein, in the *New York Times:*

The trouble with this sort of thing, of course, is conceptual. Music works as one discovers a pattern and then takes exquisite delight in the subtle violation of it. But if no expectations are created, there is no possibility of joy.

In Jackson Payne's most recent work we begin nowhere and end nowhere. It celebrates randomness. I do not say this to disparage the technical accomplishment, which seems to me to be prodigious. No other tenor saxophonist I know, except perhaps the late John Coltrane, has had Payne's sheer power and skill. But as someone said of a virtuoso piece by Paganini, it might be good, if someone would set it to music.

2.

I don't want you to think I was paranoid, but it worried me how easy it was for anyone to get to him.

Did he think he was being followed?

He said the scales had fallen from his eyes and now he saw clearly the faces of men. Showon Tucker was the one who explained to me to whom those faces may have belonged.

Did he tell you Jackson sent the man called the Leopard to jail?

It made me crazy proud. Where did this man come from?

People like that generally have no origin. They like to give the impression of materializing out of thin air like a jinn. The police say he had been a sailor in the merchant marine. Started smuggling small amounts from Asia and moved up from there.

White?

Yes.

Mafia?

He certainly knew them to say hello.

Poor Jackson.

There were the police to contend with, too. They were all over him.

Perhaps I am naive, but I never thought the police were implicated in his death. This other man, though, I think he is the one.

Perhaps.

Am I foolish?

It is a mystery.

●

Showon was working a club called The Alhambra not far away. This gave Quinlan a good excuse to take Lasheen out. The woman at the door gave her the eye and then turned it on Quinlan. The hostess was dressed in flimsy purple pantaloons and a gauzy top that showed through to her curves when the light was right.

"You've been here before," she said.

"Yes."

"Alone?"

"Thank you for remembering," he said.

"Got lucky tonight, I see," she said.

"Meet my associate," he said.

"You can have him if you want, honey," Lasheen said. "I'm just his business partner."

Since Payne's death Showon had returned to the standards. As his "Foggy Day" came to an end upon a lovely and unexpected chord, Quinlan moved Lasheen around to the side wall beside some of the tables. Behind them curved a Disneyesque sultan's arch.

The crowd gave Tucker a nice tribute and he bowed to the keys like an acolyte. Then he spotted Quinlan.

"Haven't seen you lately," he said.

"I've been distracted," said Quinlan. "Have you met my associate, Lasheen?"

"Distraction's my business," she said.

•

Taiana had *Transcendence* playing when they arrived. It was odd hearing it at such low volume in the background, because the penultimate recording Jackson made with Showon fairly shrieked for attention.

I hope you don't mind. Sometimes it helps bring him back to me. That's a gift, said Lasheen.

It was as though he was calling the world to prayer.

He would look as if he could see through you into the center of things. Oh, listen. Don't you like this part? Yes. Sometimes he let you see it, too. When I told him I was pregnant, I had never seen such joy.

He must have been afraid, too. He must have thought about Jay.

The record ended. She stood and put on another. It was *Godsounds,* the next session after *Transcendence.* Not every critic agreed, by any means, but Quinlan felt it marked a step back, and he was sure Jackson must have thought so, too, because after it was issued, he broke up the band.

Why did he get rid of Showon Tucker?

I was very pregnant. The doctors ordered me to stay in bed for the last two months. So I didn't know much of anything that was going on outside these four walls.

And where was Jackson?

He tried to dote on me. It was really very cute. He would come in and play. I have to admit, he was a little unreliable when it came to meals.

He played Transcendence*?* Godsounds*?*

Beautiful children's things. Lullabies, play songs. I loved to listen to them. It was his way of giving the baby a name.

Did he ever record any of them? They say you have quite a cache of recordings. They could help fill in the history.

And what does history think it would find there?

It would hope for a revelation, a side of him previously unknown. Lullabies and nursery rhymes, for example.

What would history make of such a thing?

People would love to have more of his sensitive side, said Lasheen. At least the women would. Didn't you?

I'm not a good measure. I adored him.

If you have recordings of the songs to Kali, they would do a lot to humanize Jackson.

He would have found that very funny. Humanize. As if it were some kind of chemical treatment you give a car. They call sometimes, the young people who worship him. Or Kali will bring somebody home from school, and we'll have to devote the dinner hour to questions much like yours. They all hope to find the real person behind the music. But you don't need those recordings to tell you that he was just a man.

She paused, arranged the things on the coffee table, did not look up.

Look, I'm sorry we got off in this direction. It is all quite pointless really. There are no tapes of the lullabies. They were totally private. Remember, he was a man who became uncomfortable when I played any of the things he did record.

I bet he didn't really mind, said Lasheen. I've never known a man who didn't want a woman to want to sneak a peak.

Sometimes I thought that if he could have done it, he would have wiped out everything he'd ever created.

But he did want a baby.

The idea was very new to him. But the day after we brought Kali home he came into my room and said, "Resurrection Morning."

From the song of the same name.

Yes.

That one was hardly a lullaby.

I understood about new beginnings and what they meant to him. Maybe he wasn't strictly Islam, but he improvised a faith, and it was beautiful.

"Resurrection Morning" on Godsounds *was the last recording he made with Showon Tucker.*

Unfortunately, fresh musicians couldn't free him any more than the baby or I could. Jackson worked hard with his new group. He wouldn't return until it was time for me to feed Kali. Even then he wouldn't really be there. He would sleep for a while and then call the band together to rehearse again.

He always came home?

Jackson loved to play for Kali. And Kali would always settle when he heard his father on the horn. I tried records, but that never worked. It had to be Jackson in person.

About this time, he had to start going on the road a little again. He had always had offers, but with the new band he felt he had to get around some. There were trips to New York and Boston and Montreal. Even a trip down South.

Were you worried?

I was about the last one.

But otherwise?

You have a hard time believing that I trusted him.

Other people did and shouldn't have.

I would have heard something in the music.

A lot of folks tell me I'm crazy when I say that.

Women?

And men.

Perhaps they have never really listened.

•

Payne had been playing for more than a month with Fazir Flynn, True Daniels, Szabo Walsh, and Rashan Roboleaux before Tucker went to hear the group. When Payne arrived on the stand and saw Tucker in the crowd, he gave him a nod.

The club piano was not in good shape. Payne had a hard time tuning to it.

"God is good," he finally said into the microphone. The crowd took it as a benediction and murmured something back.

As the band arranged itself to begin the long, one-tune set that had become its signature, Payne noticed one of his shadows at a table toward the rear. There was one of them at the club every night.

"Allah will protect," Payne said. The congregation stirred.

"One. Two. One two three four." His fingers snapped off the backbeat, the way God meant man to count.

Sometimes he took solos thirty or forty minutes at a stretch. Since he used circular breathing, they often seemed without beginning or end. There were always a few in the crowd who leaned forward and watched his fingers, as if these would provide the cipher's key. Showon Tucker was one. Taiana another. The shadow sat back in his chair gazing at his own reflection in the bar mirror.

•

A waitress in an Arabian Nights costume brought drinks. Lasheen had cognac, Quinlan scotch. Tucker stuck with soda water and lime.

Did he play well that night, Showon?

You've heard the recordings. You tell me.

•

The sense of playing as individuals was first to vanish. The band and the crowd became singularities, with Payne between them, driving and being driven by both. The reed in his mouth was no longer separate from him. It connected him to the drum strokes, to the slamming piano chords. His fingers moved as if a force went through him like an electric shock.

Next vanished the sense of place. His vision clouded. Sounds came to him distinct, each upon a separate azimuth, crystalline and complete, like rays of light. This was the way the world began and ended, awakened by angels, burned.

•

He was just in way too deep for me.

Or too high.

Yeah, maybe that, too.

Icarus and Daedalus.

Speak English to the man, said Lasheen.

•

Then it all came to an end in one, great, crashing collapse. Payne was blowing a split tone. Flynn was in another key. Cymbals flashed. Walsh pounded away. The bass droned at the bottom, more felt than heard. Then everything stopped, and Payne stood there like a man touched by lightning, bearing its inscrutable mark.

•

Why was his music failing him?

For him everything was music. God was music. But so was the junk. The women. The lies he told.

He drew you into all of it, like a whirlpool. Just the way he has drawn you.

Tell me about it, honey, said Lasheen.

eleven
sweet
thing

Ah, yes, I was wrong.
Again I was wrong.

"LUSH LIFE,"
    BY BILLY STRAYHORN

1.

European art music took centuries to evolve from the tempered scale and diatonic order through chromaticism and back to postmodernism, which uses earlier forms without believing in them. Jazz went through the same trajectory of revolution and reaction in less than one hundred years.

This pattern is similar to what one finds in the sweep of history and the well-known creative destruction of economic cycles. Things advance, not like an arrow, but like a great turning wheel.

A line of development begins with infinite promise. It proceeds by following its own logic, until at some point it exhausts itself. Then the only option is return. But one must not consider this failure, because the journey back will be informed by all the knowledge previously gained. Listen, for example, to the New Orleans renaissance of the 1990s. It rediscovered the simultaneous group improvisation of the turn-of-the-century street bands, but with all the harmonic innovation of the twentieth century now in play.

The moment of turning, though—toward revolution or away from it—is always troubled. Lives have been staked on the continuity of the prevailing idea, and it is never shattered without a mortal struggle. No wonder that at such times it seems as if history itself has a terrible compulsion to repeat.

•

Had it grown cold between you?

Since the baby. I'm told it often does.

I'm sorry to have to ask.

He was looking for something.

The question I'd have, said Lasheen, wouldn't have been what he was looking for. It would have been who.

He was deeply frustrated. That much is clear. He wasn't achieving the spiritual deliverance he sought.

So did he see God or didn't he? said Lasheen. Or are we talking about some pretty little girl?

Lasheen.

It wasn't like you think. But it did seem that whenever things got nice and settled, it was like a fire in Jackson's veins.

So the baby came. You started to feel content. And he started pulling away from you.

He said he needed to find the way of purity. I said, "Am I impure?"

Good for you, honey, said Lasheen.

"You're becoming like a Sufi," I said. "They don't amount to anything in this world."

"Maybe they know something about the next," he said.

I bet you were sleeping apart, said Lasheen.

Quinlan tried to catch her eye but could not.

I think you may judge him too harshly.

I agree.

You're the one writing the book, said Lasheen.

I'm afraid I've made us seem more distant than we were. But I did worry sometimes.

Taiana hesitated, straightened the things on the coffee table again.

What is it, Taiana?

I did more than worry. Before God, I did more.

One day Kali was playing at a neighbor's, and on an impulse I followed Jackson when he left the house. His first stop was a little café a few blocks from here. It wasn't much more than a counter and a couple old tables, but people there knew him and let him be.

I saw him sitting in the window as I passed by across the street. It wasn't easy finding a place to secret myself.

Lasheen could have helped you there.

I don't know whether I would have been willing to put anyone so pretty in his path. Anyway, it was a long time ago. You were only a child.

A very stealthy child.

You don't know, said Lasheen. Not even the first thing.

The trouble was that the neighborhood was so deserted that I was conspicuous no matter where I stood. In my Islamic clothes I must have looked to people like somebody waiting for a camel.

It was only a few minutes before I saw the girl. She crossed over, pok-poking along in her clogs. When she went into the café, I worked up my courage and walked past again. As I did, I saw what I was afraid I would. There she was in the window, sitting across from him. It obviously wasn't the first time.

Suddenly, all I could think of was Kali. A chill ran through me, as if something terrible had happened to him. Then I realized that in the café it just had.

I ran back to the apartment. Kali wasn't there. I panicked. I had already dialed the police when I remembered that I had taken him next door. I felt so foolish that I broke down and cried.

In the country of my parents, all a man had to do to leave his wife was to say the words "I divorce you" three times and it was done. Women lived like Scheherazade.

One more place to stay away from, said Lasheen.

At least in Islam there is no opprobrium attached to being divorced. In fact, honor is accorded to a man who takes such a woman in.

You've got to watch out for the ones who like it on the rebound, said Lasheen.

But I could not imagine having anyone but Jackson.

You really had a case, sister, said Lasheen.

•

She could not help herself. She had to go back. When she got there, the young woman seemed to be explaining something, and Payne wasn't liking it. He put his hands to his ears.

Hateful thoughts brought Taiana's hands to her own head. God, it is terrible the way You made this man. Terrible what You inflicted on him and had him inflict on others. It had been vanity to believe that she could change what God had wrought.

She turned away from the window and set off toward home again. As she reached the corner, a man appeared in front of her so abruptly that they almost collided.

"Sorry, sister," the man said. He had a smug little smile that looked familiar.

"You almost ran me down," she said.

"You were the only one running, girl," he said.

She turned away and started on, but she had seen that face before. A Don't Walk sign blinked, and it came to her. An album cover. Leaden sky, towering buildings, stoplight. New York City. Two men walking against the light, Jackson and Damon Reed.

He was much younger then, but he had the same smirk. An angry scar now slashed across his cheek, so his good looks were even more demonic. It was a face any woman would recall.

She slowed to a stop on the hot street. It could not have been a coincidence that brought him here. Taiana turned, and as she did, she saw Reed duck into the café.

When she got back to her observation post, Reed was standing next to where the woman sat, his arm around her. The young woman had one hand on Payne's where they knotted together on the table. The other lay on Reed's hand at her shoulder. From Payne's expression the circuit this completed was for him entirely negative, pole repelling pole.

Suddenly he rose and moved out of view. The girl slumped. As he burst out of the café, Taiana retreated as far into the shadow as she could, pressing against the hard metal of a security door, its locks like daggers at her back.

He turned abruptly toward home, and the only way she could get there before him was through the alleys. A cat leaped off a garbage can and chased after something skittering along the ground. She felt as if she were going into the valley of death.

God is good, she breathed to herself.

The buildings loomed over her, cutting off the hazy sky. Up the way, the alley took a corner. She had never been in this place before, and she prayed that she would not hit a dead end.

To her gratitude, after the corner the alley opened out into the light. At the sidewalk, she looked left in the direction he would be coming from. The street was empty. He might have gotten ahead of her, but she doubted it. He did not move very fast.

She turned to the right and took the back way to her home. When she reached it, she raced inside to the bathroom, where she took off her things, turned on the shower, and got in. She let the water pour over her head and down her body, but she did not permit herself to indulge the feeling. Quickly she shut off the tap, dried herself, and put on a dumpy terrycloth robe. In the mirror she looked to herself a picture of a wife who has let herself go.

Hurrying back downstairs, she parted the drapes to see how much time she had to compose herself. There was no sign of him yet on the street.

"Jackson," she called. The house was silent except for the drip of the shower.

At dusk there was still no sign of him. The club was dark Monday nights, but she called anyway, in case he had decided to rehearse the band. She let the phone ring and ring. As it did, she heard the familiar rattle of the front door.

"I needed to straighten something out," he said.

He moved past her and into the kitchen and got a drink of water. Then he went to play his horn.

•

That night was the first time he played the past. Ballads. Songs he had written and forsaken years before. Some had become so familiar that they weren't even his anymore.

I got his dinner ready and held it warming while I listened. Lord, how it frightened me, those songs from before I knew him, so warm under his fingers again.

Did he tell you about the woman in the café?

The other musicians said she was the daughter of someone he had known back in Chicago. He had kind of taken her under his wing.

I bet he did, said Lasheen.

There was nothing furtive about it. Jackson introduced her to everyone in the band. They said he was trying to protect her. You see, along the way she had managed to pick up Damon Reed.

Did you ever actually meet Reed?

Once, at a club. He had the girl with him. Jackson was very cold.

Reed isn't a man anybody would warm up to.

I felt so sorry for the girl. I don't know whether she was drunk or what, but she hung off him like an ornament. And he appeared to like it that way. Do you know what happened to her?

Quinlan looked at Lasheen.

Do we?

Do we want to? said Lasheen.

Seems pertinent.

You're the doctor, said Lasheen.

•

Reed was not hard to find. He was no longer a tough stud with an attitude. His lip had grown tired on the trumpet's mouthpiece and tiresome off. Pretty soon he was doing nothing but quoting himself.

Lasheen was not interested in going back East just to help interview him. So while she pursued leads in San Francisco, Quinlan took the red-eye.

At the recording studio a young assistant producer rested his head back against the wall in the hallway, talking on the pay phone to somebody about rights. Quinlan introduced himself and his purpose, and the young man opened the control-room door and nodded him inside, all the while keeping up his end on the phone. The sound equipment was surprisingly high-tech for a space so dingy.

The engineer had an ashtray precariously balanced against two of the dials on the tilting master console, which freed both his hands to work at the controls.

"Tommy, give me a little more of the ta-ta-ta," the producer said. "Very bright. This is happy talk we're talking. Couldn't you tell by the housewives' faces?"

On the other side of the glass, the musicians looked distracted, and Reed seemed to be in pain.

"Looked like they need a good fucking," said a voice from the band.

The producer's finger crunched the intercom button like it was something alive.

"I should inform you, gentlemen," he said, "that I've got you individually miked so I can isolate the origin of any wise-ass remark."

"You got a warrant?" said a gravelly voice on the speaker.

"I got your money in my pocket, Damon, is what I got," said the producer. "Now give me that ta-ta-ta, bright as a silver dollar."

"Ta-ta-ta," the trombonist sang, racy as hell.

"Make it clean," said the producer. "This shit is soap."

"Clean like a shirt right out the box," said the trombone.

"Like a lady who's too good for you," said the piano.

"No," said the producer. "Like the shine on a fucking floor. We're ready. Let's roll."

At this, the alto snapped off the tempo just like it was going to swing.

But, of course, it did not. And in less than a minute it was over.

"Beautiful, beautiful," said the producer. "Who says you guys are all bums?"

Quinlan left the booth and pushed through the heavy, padded studio door. Reed was on the other side, wiping down his horn.

"Got a minute?" said Quinlan.

"You got a smoke?" said Reed.

"Sorry."

"Where do I know you from?"

"I talked to you once about Jackson Payne."

He picked up his case.

"Buy you a drink?" said Quinlan.

Reed looked at his watch.

"I got a little time," he said.

•

Maybe Jackson was off the needle. Maybe he wasn't. But that shit he was playing? I told him maybe he should just fucking die. I didn't think the motherfucker would up and do it, though. Cracks me fucking up. Cat was always getting his ideas from me.

The question is the woman.

I'd been fucking her for months. Before she went to him and he got her that job at the club. Then she finally tells him about her and me, and he freaks. I'm not fucking kidding. She was a real piece.

How did you find her?

I heard from Junior Leonard in New York that the bitch had started hanging in the clubs.

What was her connection to him?

You know Junior. You couldn't depend on him.

Junior introduced you?

It wasn't a debutante ball. He just brought her around.

He knew she meant something to Jackson.

Motherfucker had a real hard-on for that cat. Almost as big as mine.

What was it he was trying to do?

Junior brought her to the joint where my band was booked, and I started playing hot. Real hot. Bitches can't get enough of that shit.

Kismet.

Who the fuck recorded that anyway?

So you hit it off with her right away.

I told my cocksucker to book me out West. He was white, so they didn't fuck around with him. Set us up at the Fairmont. Big suite with a grand piano.

She wanted to go to the clubs, but I wouldn't let her. Bitch had a stubborn streak, just like old bigheaded Jackson did. She was afraid to go see him at first. But after I worked her awhile, she did like I told her to. Didn't leave a mark on her either.

·

"Damon, I'm bored."

"Shut your face."

He thrust the bright tongue of his tie through the loop then pulled it tight over the collar tab of his two-tone shirt. Turning slightly to get the full effect of the jut of the knot, he checked out the other elements: tailored suit, fresh haircut and manicure, gold rings. He hardly paid a glance over his shoulder at the woman on the bed.

She hadn't even bothered to dress. She still had on the teddy he had put her in for play.

He looked at his gold watch, which glinted beneath his cuff like a grin.

"Where the fuck is the cocksucker, anyway?" he demanded.

She wanted to answer, of course, just as she wanted to respond to all his requirements, but she did not know how.

"I should get dressed," she said.

"Go ahead," he said, "or either give him a cheap thrill."

She flopped back against the pillow and pulled the sheet over her breast.

"When can I come with you?" she said.

"I don't have time for this shit, baby. I got my mind on what I'm gone say on the horn."

"Say it to me," she said.

"I'm fucking the craziest bitch in the world," he sang, sharp and angular as an old, loopy bebop riff. "Maybe you can get the cocksucker to take you to see old bigheaded Jackson. He's playing against me across town."

"And say what to him?" she said.

" 'Hello,' " he said.

"Then?"

" 'You sound real nice, Jackson,' " he said, mimicking her sweetness. " 'You look good, too, so black and strong.' All the sick shit you said to me."

"Damon."

"And then strut your stuff for him. Show him what you got."

Looking in the mirror, he brushed invisible contaminants from his lapel. When he turned, she was at the edge of the bed, her face in the corner.

"Why do you want me to tell him about us?" she asked.

"You been to college," he said. "You tell me."

"Because you know the man," she repeated.

"There you go, bitch," he said.

She breathed and took a drink from the glass beside her. It wasn't much, mostly the meltdown of the ice.

"I'm afraid of what he'll think of me," she said.

Reed turned and reached out with both hands to lift her from the bed as a gentleman would.

"We were partners, Jackson and me," he said. "We did the good thing. He's gone think if somebody got to be fucking you, it might as well be me."

•

That very night the bitch put on the nicest dress I bought for her and went to the club Old Bighead was working. When I got back from my last set she couldn't stop talking about him. How different we were, him all fire and me so nice and tight.

I asked her which she dug. She answered right, so I let it pass. Then I had the cocksucker produce some shit. I wasn't doing anything but a little C when I met her, and she didn't even smoke. But the C worked a miracle. C can make you a lot better in the sack, you know. Old Bighead would've been proud of her, putting away the shit like she did. Pretty soon she's begging for it.

What was she to him? I still don't get it.

Michelle Bell. Don't that name mean anything to you?

Tell me.

You're a simple shit, aren't you. Motherfucker was her father, fool.

2.

Before Jackson Payne, when they talked about jazz geniuses, they meant players who pushed rhythm or harmony beyond anything that had been done before. After him, they wondered whether genius had anywhere left to go.

At some point he had to return to the Slonimsky thesaurus. What he discovered was that even 479,001,600 combinations of notes were not nearly enough.

•

One has to conclude that in his final musical phase, Jackson Payne was a towering failure. He pursued his end so furiously that it left him with nothing more to say.

•

Jackson Payne was the last towering colossus of jazz. Listening to his late works is like being in touch with an element as pure and reactive as free oxygen.

•

One has to conclude that Payne in his final musical phase was toweringly possessed. He reached for the voice of the deity upon his tongue, and from the sound it must have been a terrible God, indeed.

•

It is a towering romantic fallacy to think that jazz gives privileged access to a player's being. How can a deceptive, manipulative man make music that seems to have the clarity of the greatest truth? The same way a man with palsy can do precise work with his hands. A bad man can do beautiful music because the ability does not extend beyond the task.

•

One night after the last set Payne drove out to the ocean. The waves rose on the wind. At one time he had felt he could reach across the waters, but now they seemed deep and wide. He uncased his horn and found a place on a rock just above the splash of the waves. Squarely into the wind he blew, his jaw growing stiff on the hard metal bit, his fingers cramping on the keys. He played for hours that way, sometimes not even able to hear his own wild, headlong rush of notes.

God did not speak to him.

God was inscrutable, drawing him forward.

God was the whiteness of the waves.

And Payne was blown like sand.

But do not despair.

Tell it, brother.

In the valley of the shadows, there you will find the light.

Amen.

When the wind howls and the thunder cracks, do not fear.

Mercy, Lord, it's cold.

For God will always find the pure of heart.

Lord a mercy.

Amen.

Speak to me.

Speak to me.

Speak to me.

Please, Lord, speak the word!

He wailed and sweat. He prayed to the God of his youth and the God of the East. He spoke to Anyone who would listen, but he heard no answer in the wind.

•

Back in the club, he mounted an assault set after set. But he could not break free. Something held him like a leg iron, like a hand upon his thigh.

One night he blew so hard he burst a vessel in his mouth. The people in the front row found their tablecloths suddenly spotted with blood. After closing time, the waiters discovered that they had cut off pieces and taken them home.

•

When they told Jackson, he was like, "Are these people spooky or what?"

Roboleaux told him it was voodoo. I said it was because of the magic numbers he was always talking about. Numbers touched by God. A sharp second, a fourth, a sixth, a flatted ninth. Or something rising by twos, whole steps all the way from bottom to top. Sometimes he would tell you what he was doing. Sometimes he just said, "One. Two. One two three four."

Did you see anything in his behavior that worried you?

I'm not one of them that thinks he offed himself. He loved that baby of his. And his old lady, too.

Did he ever talk about his daughter?

They say Damon got her using.

Would Jackson have known?

We could tell it bothered him.

From the music.

I'm lost, man.

You heard it there.

Heard?

About Damon Reed. His daughter. In the music.

I heard the notes he played.

But what did they say?

A toot diddle ah da toot.

Help me a little here, Szabo.

They said, "This is an A-flat. This here is a B-minor seventh."

Sometimes it's hard, I admit. Especially given race and every-thing else. But you were very, very close to him.

I don't know what you're talking about. You ask me, you're crazy to write a book. Play something on the piano, man. Call it by his name.

That's what I'm saying. Music makes connections you can't make any other way.

Black key. White key. You learned to transpose anything into any-thing else. That's the way it was on the stand, even if it wasn't anywhere else. To a man's ax, he's just his fingertips, lips, and tongue, and last time I looked, everybody is pretty much the same color there.

•

When Quinlan got back to San Francisco and told Lasheen what he had learned about Payne's daughter, she did not show any surprise.

"Taiana already told you, didn't she," he said.

"We only talked about you," said Lasheen. "She's worried you're losing sight of what matters."

The television was on, its sound muted. She had apparently been watching one of those prime-time soap operas. His eye was drawn to a woman in a satin nightgown.

"The music," Lasheen said.

"Yes, well, I've been having a slight problem with that."

A bare arm slithered silently across a pair of bare shoulders. The mouth whispered something close to an ear. Even if the sound had been on, it would not have been right to hear.

"She asked me how deeply I was involved with you," Lasheen said.

"Just so she didn't say we weren't welcome."

"I told her we had our moments," said Lasheen.

"Is this one of them?"

"I don't know yet," she said.

But before the moment could arrive, Taiana came knocking at their door. Quinlan looked through the peephole then let her in.

"I guess you wanted to continue the interesting talk you had with Lasheen," he said.

Taiana gave Lasheen a look that left him out.

He put the tape Walsh had given him into the machine and turned it on. The frenzied saxophone made up in intensity for what the little speaker lacked in fidelity. Payne would make a couple of tight circles and then wheel off on a tangent, only to return in the end. AABA. Behind him Walsh hit anvil chords over and over while Daniels and Flynn and Roboleaux fluttered dazedly in place.

"Do you recognize this performance?" he said. With the tape recorder occupied, he wasn't able to record her answers this time. But if he was right about how she would respond, he was pretty sure he'd be able to remember.

"I'm not very good at that sort of thing," she said.

"You were there the night this tape was made," he said.

"I'm sorry," she said.

The straight back of the chair made her posture prim. He could see that she was uncomfortable. He let her stay that way.

"I was especially wondering if you'd seen Jackson's daughter there," he said.

"So you've discovered that," said Taiana.

"What kind of expression he had on his face as he looked out at her in the audience. What each of you would have been thinking at that moment."

"You are a long way from music," she said. The tenor was high up into overtones. Jackson was straining so hard it was like electricity straight into a nerve. "At that point I didn't yet know it was his daughter."

"Apparently everyone else did," he said.

"Oh, I heard many things," she said. "But he denied it. He told me she was the daughter of a very old friend. Someone he wanted to help get away from Damon Reed."

"Daughter of a lady friend?"

"He didn't say."

"And you didn't ask," he said.

"I don't know why this makes any difference to you."

"I want to try to understand why Jackson thought he had to lie," he said.

Lasheen had gone over to Taiana and laid her hand on her shoulder. In the mirror it was quite a natural gesture, though from the front it appeared that Lasheen was awkward about how close she should get.

"It was the only time he deceived me after coming back from Kensington," said Taiana.

"We've all been there," said Lasheen.

"But I had it wrong," Taiana said. "I thought she was someone he'd been with before. Maybe even the girl on the train."

The recording had reached such a level of intensity that it made the cheap little speaker buzz.

"Why do you think he was holding back?"

"Part of him felt weak and wrong," she said.

Quinlan turned off the tape in the middle of a long, punishing run.

"If I had been you," Quinlan said, "this music wouldn't have made me worried about what he was doing with another woman. It would have made me worried about what he was doing to himself."

•

"I can't move it no more, baby," Jackson said. "It's a thousand-pound stone." She was afraid even to touch his hand for fear it would burn them both. "That God of yours ain't left me a way."

She tried to tell him he must be thinking of some other God.

"Milk and honey," she said. "These He gives us."

"I can't taste anything anymore," he said. "It's beyond nothing, baby. It's the thing that eats nothing up."

•

Jackson Payne was hardly the first twentieth-century figure to endure the burdens of *Weltschmerz*. His project had been to reduce the architectural elements of his music so completely that he could express himself unmediated, directly from his soul. It was not an uncommon conceit at the time. The novelist stripped narrative of everything that had moored it to the mundane and produced work that nobody but he could ever hope to understand. The painter created canvases as aleatory as drop cloths. Poets became so personal that they spoke in empty confession booths.

These were not happy people. They were lashed by a logic that drove them to absurdity. They flayed away like ascetics, enduring any ordeal in order to reach the perfect Truth. But in the end they found only the zero that is the beginning and the end and is unbearably cold.

•

"Don't you see? The music was the *jinn*," Taiana said. "Now please turn it back on."

Quinlan did as she asked. The sound came on in the middle of a slashing phrase.

"They all come and want me to tell them about his genius," she said. "I ought to play this for them and say, 'This is what I lost, and how I lost it.'

"Then toward the very end sometimes he would put a recording on the turntable and play his part note for note. It was haunting, as if he were lost and trying to retrace his steps. What I heard made me want to cry."

•

Jackson enjoyed having Michelle near. He could see the resemblance—more to Vera than to him, a hint of Asia halved again with African blood. And yes, there was a little of himself, too, just as he had seen in Jay.

But she was entirely different than his son had been. She told him about the college she had gone to, the honors, her senior thesis, the things she had written about him. She had come to his music before ever learning what he was to her. A roommate had introduced her to the albums of the quartet with Showon Tucker and Junior Leonard and Al Sims.

"They're so damned old," he said.

Michelle had come home from school one vacation with a stack of his recordings and begun to play them in her room.

"It really bothered mother," she said. "At first, I thought it was because some of the songs, well, they are a little raw, and she is pretty straight-laced. Was she that way back then?"

"She was lovely," he said, "just like you."

During the following weeks of Michelle's vacation, mother and daughter struggled over everything. Vera did not acknowledge that there was anything to this but the avoidance of temptation, a perennial theme. And Michelle was too annoyed to care.

She had a summer job at a local field house, teaching little children to play soccer and softball. The first morning she appeared at the breakfast table in her program T-shirt and shorts, her mother told her to go back and cover herself.

"The best defense against temptation," Vera said, "is the good Lord's shame."

All summer it was like that. So Michelle would sulk in her room with a book of Langston Hughes or James Baldwin and not think for a moment that the records she played behind her reading were the cause of it all.

·

Michelle told you this, Showon?

She needed somebody to talk to. Sometimes the three of us spent time together. Down by the ocean. Or at some little restaurant far away.

·

"One day I was especially miserable," she said. "I put on 'The Bluest I.' It spoke to me, lifted me up. You did. Like you knew what I was going through."

"We knew your mother at a very different time," said Showon.

"Suddenly she walked in," said Michelle.

"What are you doing, girl?" she demanded.

"Nothing," I said.

"Well, that man's not going to do anything for you either, any more than he's done for anybody else in his life."

"She got that right," Payne said.

"It makes me feel better, Ma," Michelle said, "just listening."

"I don't want that music in my house," Vera said.

"But why?"

"Just turn it off and put those records away or I'll have to take the lot of them from you and throw them right in the trash."

As Michelle told the story, Tucker could not help hearing Vera Bell herself.

"I did as she asked, but it tore me up," Michelle said. "I felt like I was losing you both."

"You'd never had me," said Jackson. "I wasn't there."

"I turned my back so she wouldn't see my tears, then I slowly stacked the albums on the floor near my bed. There were quite a lot of them, and I had to clear a space in the closet so I wouldn't have to see you looking at me from the covers all the time. I heard her leave as I was putting them in just the right order. One. Two. Three. Then she returned and I heard the record player click and you were back, too. It was something I'd never heard before, but I knew it was you."

"There are some here you probably don't have," Vera said, handing over a stack of albums.

"Where did you get these?"

The empty album cover carried the title *High Wired*.

"She put on that old thing?" said Payne.

"Sweetheart," Vera said, "I've had these forever. Since we were together."

"Together?" said Michelle.

"Your very own mother with Jackson Payne," Vera said with a proud, embarrassed smile. "I didn't think I would ever be able to bring myself to tell you. But when I heard you playing those records, I was afraid some malicious mouth had already spoken."

"Spoken what, Mama?"

"Told you that Jackson Payne was your Daddy, Sweet Thing. We were together when he made that album. It lasted more than a year. Then I got pregnant and things became impossible between us, so I left."

"He *was* playing for me, then."

"I wish I could tell you that he was," said Vera.

"Do you still see him?" Michelle asked.

"Oh, heavens no," said Vera. "I don't even know where he is. But I hear him. I still hear him, just as you do. I buy every record, even when what he's doing leaves me totally lost."

Payne touched his hand to his temple and then moved it down to his sore, old jaw.

"She always did like the tried and true," he said.

"She told me the things you did together," Michelle said. "She talked about the trouble, too."

"I been punished for that pretty good," Payne said.

•

Damon Reed laughed at the last remark when she repeated it to him. Now he was the punitive instrument, and it was time to make another move.

•

She wasn't at the café when Payne arrived. He took the booth by the window and looked across the street to the wall of dingy buildings, some boarded up, all emblazoned with graffiti.

When he bit into his sweet roll, the sugar howled on his teeth. It was his last vice and he indulged in it, amazed at how much pleasure you could get from the rush of simple sugar and caffeine when otherwise your system was clean. As a junkie you craved it, but it did not satisfy. Clean, it hit you like the exquisite surprise of making love straight.

"Hello, Daddy."

Suddenly she was there before him, as if he had just awakened. He pulled back from the word she used. Hard to get any distance when they thought of you that way. Hard not to hurt them.

"You snuck up on me," he said.

She gave him a little kiss next to his lips and hugged him half turned aside. He liked the modesty, prayed that it would hold.

"What do you see way out there in the place you go to, Daddy?" she said. "I hated to bring you back."

He looked at her arms, which were only exposed to just above the wrists.

"It's lots of things," he said. "Mostly I see myself. I may be ugly as sin, but when you're with me, I'm like a brand-new song."

"All my girlfriends were in love with you, you know."

"That was before the mess caught up with me." He reached across the table and gently touched her smooth cheek. "Don't ever let life get hold of you, Sweet Thing, the way it got hold of me."

She let his fingers rest there a moment. But it was as if she were counting the measure, and then she pulled away. He let his hand drop to the table, hoping she would pick it up. She did not.

"I've got news that makes me very happy, Daddy," she said, the paper napkin twisted in her hand until it looked like a pastry swirl.

"Johnny," he called out. "What's wrong with you? Don't you see that the lady here wants something in her cup? Maybe a little something to eat, too."

"I'll have one of those Bismarks," she said. "And maybe some of that candy."

She could not help but see the way her father looked at her.

The counterman came with the roll and the candy. She chose a piece of candy first and sucked on it. Then she took one of Payne's hands in hers.

"We're getting married, Daddy," she said.

His hands tightened. Then he touched her third finger, which was bare.

"We didn't even think of a ring yet," she said. "You know how musicians are."

That tightened him more.

"It's so amazing, really," she said. "First, that I even met Damon. Then to fall in love and come out here and find you, and you are more than I had ever hoped a daddy to be."

"He hasn't played shit for years," Payne said.

That sent a cloud across her, but only for a moment.

"He knows that," she said, lowering her eyes. Then she looked up again proud. "He says that with me he will get it all back again. My dream is that at the wedding you two will play together."

"He only wants to hurt you," Payne said, "and that way to hurt me."

"That's just not so, Daddy," she said. "You should hear the wonderful things he says about you."

"That I'm a motherfucker," said Payne. "It's the only word he knows."

"He admires your music."

"This has nothing to do with music," Payne said.

He felt as if he had been stripped and sprayed and thrown into a cell, where he was helpless to protect what he loved.

"He'll be here in a little bit, Daddy," she said. "He wanted to tell you himself, the old-fashioned way. But I asked him to let me do it alone."

"You need him to give permission?" Payne said. "What else has he been doing to you?"

That brought out something hard in her for the first time.

"Nothing I can't handle," she said.

He hated to see it. But at the same time, he hoped maybe it was solid enough to stand up against Reed.

She abruptly stood at her place.

"He's going to be here in a minute. We can do this with you or without you."

"So that's the way this plays," said Payne.

"I'd hate to lose you."

"My God, girl," he said. "Don't you see? You're losing you."

He looked at her silent, immobile face, and for a moment it was Vera before him again—hurt and stubborn and beautiful. He reached out to touch her hand again, but she pulled it back.

Just then he heard the little bell above the door sound and saw Reed pushing through the door beneath it.

"Here he is," she said.

Payne did not stand.

Reed said, "Looking kinda weary, old man."

He gave Michelle a hard little kiss on the lips, showing off a bit of tongue as he did. Then she sat down at the table again, with Reed standing behind her.

"I guess she told you the news," said Reed. He put his hand on Michelle's shoulder and worked his fingers down to just above her breast. The gesture was gentle enough in itself, but it carried with it a sense of ownership and the potential for force.

"I know why you're doing this," Payne said.

"I think she's just too damned pretty," Reed said, "to have sprung from your ugly black dick."

The fingers dug in a little deeper.

"If you think I did you," Payne said, "take it out on me."

Reed smiled the smile he'd smiled on the cover of *The Warlock*.

"Daddy," Michelle said.

It cut him to hear her plead. Vera had never pleaded.

"It's between Damon and me, Sweet Thing," he said. "None of this is about you."

"He respects you, Daddy. Don't you, baby?"

"You're the one," Reed said. He let his hand drop from her shoulder and then with the slightest upward motion levitated her from her seat. "You're definitely the one."

•

The motherfucker kept watching my hand, and I kept moving it on down. Slow as shit, you know, so he'd think I was going to feel her up right there in front of him. Man finally realized he should never have fucked with Damon. Because a motherfucker do that, I take it all away from him. I'd even take his sound, but it got so foul I didn't want it stinking up my place.

3.

A clear critical separation must be made between the moral evaluation of an artist's life and the aesthetic evaluation of the way he transmutes his experience into art. The former inquiry may use tools common to all ethical situations since the artist, in this sense, is no different from you or I. But aesthetically he operates in a world apart. Genius does not excuse what he does, but neither does conventional morality fit the creative act. A saint may produce execrable poetry; many have. A thoroughly troubled soul may sing to Heaven of glory beyond the brilliance of gold. As a great piano player once said, "Ugly music's the only thing God don't forgive."

·

"So what's your pleasure tonight?" said the man at the door of the club where Payne went looking for Michelle. He had a cloud of frizzy hair and a face of pink. His clothes—a gaudy orange shirt and red tie—made him look like a sunset.

"That's some other guy," said Payne.

"You don't look so good," said the sunset man. "Like you need something, you know what I mean?"

"You and me got nothing to talk about," said Payne.

It would be sweet revenge for them to get him to put the needle in his arm again. Oh, yes. The Leopard would see the justice of that. And it had this much to commend it even to Payne, the unblessed relief it would bring.

"I'll tell you what they're saying," said the sunset man.

"They don't even know the scales," said Payne.

"They say you burned Damon Reed. Set him up holding what he was always careful to hide. So now he takes your daughter as repayment for the time he did. Are they right, Jackson?"

"That's nobody's business," said Payne.

"They say they've seen her beg Damon for it," said the sunset man over the icy glissandos of the electric guitar and the brushes whispering an open secret on the snare. "They say he's got her trained to do anything he says with whoever he says to do it for. If you'd ask him, maybe he'd have her do you, too."

Payne reached and grabbed the man's shirt. But the man slapped his hand away, which stung Payne back to himself.

"Just tell me where she is," Payne said.

"Gone," said the sunset man.

"Where?"

The sunset man started to recede. This time Payne got flesh as well as cloth. He had more strength than he thought he did, and he held on.

"The Leopard is in this, isn't he," said Payne.

"I don't know anybody by that name," said the man.

"Then what do you know?" said Payne.

"Reed took her to Chicago," said the sunset man. "Left today. He was walking tall. She was on a leash."

"Where in Chicago?"

"The fuck do I know?" said the sunset man. "Chicago's a big place."

"What does the Leopard want from me?" asked Payne.

His hand loosened, and the sunset man eased back a step.

"I meet somebody calling himself that," he said, "I'll be sure to ask."

•

The vast majority of narcotics addicts return to their habit periodically, even if they do manage to break free of it for long stretches of time. This happens across all social classes. The successful physician is as likely to lapse as the streetcorner pimp. The commodities broker may drive a Ferrari, and the ghetto junkie may have to walk, but they both move in the same direction, lemmings to the sea.

The cerebral stimulus provided by the chemicals offers only part of the explanation for this tropism. One must also consider the psychodynamics. Scoring drugs becomes itself an organizing principle, part of a surrogate achievement structure. It becomes an end in itself.

Freedom and constraint.

I would never equate drugs with freedom. But the illusion of it, perhaps.

Wanting to break loose, but not wanting.

The pain is psychologically ambiguous, too. As others have noted, one flaw in the behaviorist model is that it does not recognize individuality in the interpretation of what is reward and what is punishment. In many addicts, drugs seem to meet a deep appetite both when they are administered and when they are withheld. The rush is false but intensely satisfying. The pain of withdrawal is real and in its own way satisfying as well. On the one side the need, on the other the just desserts.

•

Lasheen had parted with him at the airport. It had been a mercy to separate, because now they were talking past one another all the time.

"Look at that old man with that young girl," he had said at the ticket counter.

"Maybe they think the same about us," she said.

"Think what?"

"Different. Better off separate."

"I don't care what they think," he said. "I really don't."

"You. You. You. You and Jackson Payne."

•

After Michelle left, Jackson went and got himself a whole new group. I can't even remember all their names. The piano, though, was Billy Hunter. I'd admired some things he did. I don't like to say so, but it was kind of eerie because sometimes he was more like me than I was anymore. The minute I heard Jackson had hired him, I knew something was wrong.

•

Jackson Payne is back, and if my senses don't deceive me, he has finally come to his. His Tuesday night opening at the Black Beret introduced an all-new quartet and a set of brand new compositions. But the style, though sophisticated still, was the one that had won him his largest following. No longer did Payne seem intent on driving all but the most fanatical away.

•

. . . Buzz Street is all atwitter about the comeback of jazzman *Jackson Payne*. Some say he never left. The universe, maybe, but a lot of old friends thought he had gotten lost in space. Now he's back on terra firma, and Daze Records is silent about rumored plans for a new five-record deal because he isn't their kind of bomb thrower anymore.

•

This, of course, was before Archie Shepp found the spirituals, before Miles went back to Gil Evans and the blues as his lip started to fail.

Today, of course, the assumption is that if he had lived, Payne would have led the way into something totally new. As with most such Messianic faiths, this one was not amenable to proof or disproof.

•

No, he didn't consult me. He's an artist. They're all goddamned artists. All of a sudden he opens at the Beret with a bunch of cats I've never heard of before. "Lanny," he says, "I got a new sound." Like it's a new tie.

Didn't he even talk to you about it?

What am I? Just an agent. So I get to wait with the rest of the crowd to see what the hell he means. Is it gonna be the polka? Will he be doing Mozart? Brubeck's Greatest Hits? What?

I got to tell you, though. Frankly, I liked what I heard. He seemed more inside himself. Less of that Allah business that always made me a little nervous as a Jew.

I started thinking, maybe a nice background of strings. Then he springs it on me: He doesn't plan to record.

"I want to keep it pure," he said.

"That's a sin," I said.

•

Sure I went to hear him. As soon as the reviews came out. It was hard, but I did.

What did you think?

The sound came way up from the bottom, like it used to. But he cut off the top. He did not reach. On the tune he called "Michelle," he used devices he'd used back when we first did "Vera." He still blew chords, but it was only to make the horn weep. It made me want to weep, too, because I knew what he was saying.

Knew?

Kindertotenlieder. He was grieving. You know the sound I mean.

After the set I went backstage and found him sitting on a garbage can out in the alley.

"I envied Billy Hunter," I said. "I liked what you two did together."

"He isn't as good as you," he said.

When I said goodbye, I didn't know it would be the last time. But something was wrong. That's what he was saying. Wrong but beautiful. Do you know what I mean?

4.

I knew you would be back.

Funny. It kind of surprised me.

Something about the way we left it.

You weren't completely forthcoming.

I needed to get away from you.

You aren't the first woman who has felt that way.

Oh, I think you're being a little hard on yourself.

Do you want to tell me about Michelle?

Damon Reed must have done unspeakable things. May God have pity on him. I will not let you go away thinking the person you have heard about was my daughter. My daughter was a beautiful, gifted, gentle child.

They do say beautiful.

Do they talk about honors at Cornell? Offers from graduate schools? The grace of her dancing? I bet you didn't even know about the dancing, did you. She was good enough to have gone onstage. I swear she was. If she hadn't met him on the way.

Had you ever told Jackson about her?

Would you have?

For me nothing like this has ever come up.

Well, then you are fortunate in the woman who left you. But I left still wanting him. And believing perhaps that in his better moments he wanted me, too.

After everything that had happened?

Even when he lied, there was still something true. As if he really wanted it to be. Sometimes when he played it was as if he were painting a picture he wanted us to walk into—and clear out of this world.

But for the baby's sake I had to leave him. Leave and disappear. I figured that if I gave it enough time, I would not be able to go back to him even if temptation got the better of me, because he would have moved on. I imagine he forgot long before I thought he did.

I'm not so sure.

That's kind of you to say.

I don't think he ever forgot. And when he met Michelle, found out who she was, it all came back. Were you addicted at the time you left him?

Oh, yes.

Was she?

Thank the Lord, she was not. We did not understand these things as fully then as we do now. But I had sense enough to change my ways. Michelle was born just fine.

The police did talk to you, though.

Yes.

Before or after she was born?

Both. They wanted names.

You must have paid a terrible price.

They didn't make the arrest properly. So even though I wouldn't help them, the public defender got me off. After that I stayed clean. With the good Lord's help, I stayed clean. God bless Rev. David Brown, who took me in and gave me his hand to comfort me. God bless the leaders of the Sodality at the Faith Mt. Hope Church, who stayed with me during the worst. I have been trying to repay these gifts of theirs ever since.

The baby had no ill effects?

Vera stood and went for tea. She poured steadily, and he sat back watching her.

Michelle had definitely had a taste of it when she was inside me. There's no doubt about that. How much this had to do with what happened later nobody really can say.

Men who were walking evidence of the consequences had been in our house every day of her childhood for prayer and counseling, and yet she did not heed. She returned to me as bad as the worst of them, with eyes that would not focus and a thirst nothing could quench. She had put on a cute little dress and had her hair done all nice, but all I could think of was what did she do to get the money for all that.

You knew immediately.

Until then she had never given me a moment without pride, but yes, I knew. Even the way she tried to put herself back together again. I guess I saw myself in that.

If you'd like to stop for a moment.

She heard jazz music first through her dancing. She loved the moves, though to me they always seemed suggestive. I surely would not have liked to see her dancing to one of her father's songs.

Then one day you heard her playing his records.

I won't tell you the hurt and pride.

Pride?

She had so many questions. It didn't take long before I regretted answering them, because soon she announced she was going to put off grad school so she could go to New York.

"It's a hurtful place," I said.

"You went," she said.

"And I learned."

"Learning's something everybody's got to do," she said.

I had raised her strictly. But I'd never tried to take the stubborn out of her, because stubborn is what saves you. So when she decided, she decided. All I could do was pray.

Did you know Damon Reed before?

I had the records he had made with Jackson. So when she told me, I got them out and listened.

What did you hear?

I imagined somebody in a black cape.

"Oh, Sweet Thing," I said, "please don't make the mistakes I did."

"You came out fine," she said.

"You don't know how bad it was."

"How bad could it have been?" she said. "You had me."

What could an old church lady do to argue with someone who had practiced in classrooms so much?

Were you concerned that she would eventually find Jackson?

As soon as she went to New York, she started using his name. It didn't get her dancing jobs, but it brought her to the attention of this man, Reed. I can just see them all sizing her up through the smoke, what features she got from him, what flaws they could exploit.

When she called and told me about Reed, it was not a good conversation. I was harsh. But I didn't know what to do. Then the call was over and she was gone.

At first I prayed that she would call again. Then I prayed that the police wouldn't. I was so afraid. Eventually, I called people in New York I thought might remember me. They were the ones who told me where she had gone.

Did they say anything about drugs?

No. And I did not ask.

But you knew as soon as she walked back in your door.

"You're like the men I minister to," I told her. "I can minister to you, too. But only if you are willing."

All she said was did I have twenty dollars until next week. And I guess the worst part was hearing Jackson's voice in hers.

She did not stay with me that first time. She had to fall farther. Reed had dropped her in Chicago, but there was always someone ready to pick somebody like her up. It grieved me to think who.

Do you know where she went after visiting you?

Back to Chicago. To get dancing jobs, she said.

Jackson went there at about the same time. Did she ever say she connected with him again?

This time Vera did not pour tea. Her hands fluttered with a napkin in her lap, which was where she held her eyes.

I can't talk about that.

There are so many different things that might have happened. I need someone who can help me sort them out.

When you have spent as much of your life as I have trying to stand up against just one of them, you come to understand what a frail thing knowledge can be.

Please help me.

I don't think I can.

Where is Michelle now?

It would not be good for her to relive it all again.

I could find her if I needed to.

She has a new life.

I found you.

Vera stood and went to the door, but before she opened it to show him out, she stopped and moved to the window. The lace curtain framed her in a light so delicate you would never have guessed what was on the other side of the pane.

You wouldn't do this to her.

It is not easy to find someone when they don't want to be found. Remember the man I was here with before? I also use a woman, who has been quite successful. But it intrudes. And in the end nobody is happy.

Michelle hit bottom. Then she picked herself back up. And now nobody knows.

Did he see her in Chicago?

Jackson?

Did he talk to you about her?

When Michelle went off to Chicago I was so afraid. I got his number through the operator. When I called, a woman answered. I had seen her picture and read something, so I was surprised. I had always thought of Muslims as being standoffish. She was the one who told me that he had also disappeared. We had a long talk. She was worried, too.

•

He went to work in his studio on the old sounds, things he remembered, things that were gone. He rediscovered moments of ambiguity where a forgiving God could hide. No matter where he started, something drew him. He could not let it alone.

Between pieces he heard Taiana puttering around in the next room, and it broke his concentration. He went back to basic changes and began to build outward again. As the stroller rattled down the hall, he kept on blowing. Then the door shut like a bomb from the bass drum. He blew for a few minutes more just to be sure she was clear.

At the window he watched them go around the corner. Then he put down his horn and went into their bedroom. The suitcase was in the closet behind his clothes. She would only find it missing when, awakening in the morning without him, she thought to look.

He gathered his clothes by the handful and stuffed them into the bag until it was almost full. On top he folded a couple of jackets and pairs of pants. It snapped closed easily under his weight.

To cover his absence, he had told her he was going to be rehearsing that afternoon. He locked the door behind him, hailed a taxi, and set off.

The club owner was always in his office upstairs after lunch, doing whatever it was that club owners did.

"She finally throw your ass out?" he said when Payne appeared in the doorway with his bag.

"I got to take a trip, Sy," he said. "Right after the first set."

"You're kidding me," said the owner. "I was going to extend you."

"I'll book with you again as soon as I come home," Payne said.

"You're probably going to the Vanguard. Am I right? They hear about something, they want it right now."

"I'm going to Chicago," Payne said. "I may play and I may not."

"Don't shit me, chum."

"Personal business," said Payne.

"A la-la lady?" said the owner.

"I need to leave my things here until the show."

"Take them downstairs. Stay there if you want. Practice. Here, take the key."

"Thanks."

"Just tell that agent of yours we got a handshake deal," the club owner said.

But he did not hold out his hand. He never did.

When Payne let himself into the basement club, the air felt different than it did at night. No smoke. No man and woman smells. But a thin, crooking finger of alcohol beckoned. It reminded him of being alone in another place long ago.

The club actually looked nothing like Les Bleues. It had a false ceiling of tile that had only begun to yellow and a floor covered with something that showed the sweeping curves of the mop. Still they were both holes in the earth where he ran for sanctuary.

He took out his horn and put it together, wetting the reed in his mouth as he did. It was newly trimmed, and it tasted of the hard-grained plant from which it came. Sometimes he liked to take a new one barely damp and work the sharp corners of sound until they began to soften, the way you might work a woman until she came around.

No. That was from another time. He might be deceiving and deserting Taiana, but it was not forever and not for the old reason.

He fixed the reed to the mouthpiece and played a warm, generous sound. It was like Michelle calling out to him. From afar, but from inside him, too. Calling in his own tormented voice.

He had a hard time continuing to play, because with the club empty, the sound came back directly from the walls. He could not bear to hear her speak as he had spoken, as his son had spoken, as everyone who has ever been enslaved has spoken. So he bent the song to prayer.

Deliver me beyond this empty room, this body, this soul. Deliver me from this city, this nation, this universe. Deliver me beyond the knowledge of the void.

This was not a prayer like the ones with which he had tried to touch the God of Islam, not a whirling circle of fire. It was gentler, supplicant, and he did not know what faith it came from.

First a triplet.

Lord, heal me.

Then steady quarter and eighth notes, straight and strong.

Power me to do what I must.

And to avoid, this once, what he mustn't.

I've been a sinner. In my very heart and soul. I repent.

Bursting out now, wild sixteenth notes running over and over again like something dammed up had broken.

I don't know who You want me to be.

I don't know who You want me to be.

I don't know who You want me to be.

And had not known since he learned he could manipulate anything, even music, to his sinful ends. Sin had always driven him. Sin in every note on the horn. Long quarter notes, wavering at the end, as if unsure.

Lord, I submit to You. Show me how I can save her. Don't let me lose this child, too.

Sweat ran down his back. His fingers were wet on the keys. There was blood on the mouthpiece. It blew out through the open octave key and lightly speckled the brass.

twelve
taps

Dear lovely Death,
Change is thy other name.

LANGSTON HUGHES

1.

The expressway from O'Hare was crowded. In the distance Payne
could see tall new buildings on the lakefront beyond the aging neighborhoods through which they passed. But they were not the landmarks
he used to navigate by—the Board of Trade, Tribune Tower, the Union
Carbide. Many were without ornament, as if they had been looted.

"Are the clubs still on Rush Street?" Payne asked.

"Looking for action?" said the driver. "Tell you what. I'll go in by
the back door. That way you'll see the places where the fishing's best.
Meter'll be about the same."

They took the next exit and made their way into an industrial
area. Up ahead a rusty old bridge spanned the river and beyond it a line
of ramshackle warehouses. Farther on stood a cluster of taller red brick
structures that looked as though they must have been apartment houses.

"Cabrini," said the driver.

"That's new," said Payne.

"It was a thousand years ago," said the driver. "Now it's the old-
est place in the world."

Not a soul was out strolling, even though the sun was high
and the air crisp and clean. The only people he saw skirted the pe-
riphery. Or if they did have to plunge into the interior, they did so at an
anxious trot.

Within a few blocks the setting changed so abruptly that it might have been a back lot at a movie studio, where a Western town backed up on a vampire's castle next to Main Street. The buildings were of the same vintage as the one he grew up in. But these had aged differently, getting richer with time.

"Just up ahead we get into nighttown," said the driver.

Payne did not seriously expect to see her on the street, but still he studied each young woman they passed.

"Some lookers, eh, Boss?" said the driver.

•

I'm sure he did not find her immediately. Michelle hated admitting it to me, but she was selling herself awfully cheap.

"I've been there," I told her.

"Hooking?" she said.

"Feeling as low as scum," I said.

"With my father?"

"And just after."

"I'm sorry," she said.

"There's plenty of sorry to go around," I said.

•

Another taxi, another day. Cruising, cruising.

"Here," he said, shaking the driver's shoulder. "Pull over."

"You can do a whole lot better than that," the driver said.

"She's the one I want."

The driver cut sharply to the right, leading a horn ensemble in the process. Payne pulled himself out of the taxi and carried himself across the street to where she stood with a man at least his age.

She saw him first and for an instant looked as though she would run. The john ducked his head and turned down the sidewalk. Michelle started to follow him, but Payne caught her by the arm.

"Come with me," he said.

He did not want to be rough with her, but he knew what it might take. At a certain point there is no easy way.

Her face was so thick with makeup that she looked like she was trying to be somebody else. She dressed just like some of the women he had seen near Cabrini. He took off his coat and wrapped it around her. She put up a little struggle, but nothing he couldn't handle.

"A pretty girl is like a melody," said the driver as Payne got her into the cab.

"Fuck you," said Michelle.

"Just take us to the hotel," said Payne.

Michelle shivered on the seat beside him, her face toward the glass. He put his arm across her shoulders.

"You need, don't you, Sweet Thing," he said. "You got any?"

She shook her head.

"You know anyplace I can go?" Payne asked the driver.

"That's where I draw the line," the driver said.

Payne touched Michelle's hand, covering it completely with his own.

•

Was that why he went right out and scored?

Michelle told me that as soon as she got into the room, she started climbing the walls. Have you ever been addicted?

People say to my work.

If you have the hunger, you'll do anything.

Are you going to have to write about this? Please think of her children.

I've gotten this far. Others will too.

I'm not sure their hunger would be as great as yours.

•

He had no connections anymore. He was jumpy, and he recognized the symptoms.

She sat on the edge of the bed farthest from him, her hands pulling on the spread, worrying the points and hollows of her face. She tried to light a cigarette, struggled, would not let him help. When she finally got it going, it fell to the floor.

"Hold one hand with the other, Sweet Thing," he said, handing her an ashtray. "Don't burn us down."

The smell of the smoke went into him sharply. In the clubs the nicotine had never called to him quite the way it did in this tiny, closed room. He went to the window and opened it. The gauzy curtains billowed out like a ghostly woman with child.

He did not know what to do but call information and check some names from the past. That was how he found Red Sloan.

•

Don't hear boo fo' years and years,
And then I get the call.
You think he's thinking of me?
Just needs some shit is all.

Did you take care of him?
"I thought I heard you'd kicked," I says.
And he says, "You hear a lot of things."
"I heard the Muslims wanted to make you a poster boy. Get you one of them nice bow ties and everything?"
"When we gonna do this thing, Red?"
"Promise me you'll wear the tie," I says.
Did he say anything about his daughter?
First I even heard he had one was from you.
She was an addict.

Sad song to sing.
Don't want your kid
Doin' the lines
You used to did.

•

When Damon brought her to Chicago, he called me.
"Junior," he said. "You should've seen Jackson when he heard who I was fucking."
"Somebody said you were getting married."
"Shit," he says. "I'm gone throw that muzzy bitch out. Maybe you want her. If you keep her in shit, she'll do anything you want."
Did you feel any sense of obligation?
Damon got what he wanted.
Have you seen her since?
I don't even know if she's alive.
She is.
Don't tell me where.
I was kind of hoping you knew.
Funny. The other day Damon asked the same thing.

•

I agreed to meet him at Ming's. He said he'd be there right away.

Who was playing that night?

I look like a playbill? I got there and took a table in back. When he got good and ready, he showed.

I'm not saying I hadn't gotten older myself, but it knocked me out, the age I saw in him. Fat. Stoop shouldered. I don't think anybody would have noticed him on the street.

"Been a while," I says.

"You playing?"

"I play here. I play there."

"Heard anybody good?"

"Nobody in a long time," I says.

He sat down real heavy and checked out the room.

"You got the shit?" he asks.

"I been playing pretty good," I says. "Maybe you'll come sit in sometime."

"Sure. Sure," he says, but he didn't even ask where. He just pushed a bunch of bills my way.

I counted them out slow.

"Where is it?" he says. I thought he was gone jitter right out the chair.

"You ought to look out where you wave your money, Dad." Then I pushed the table back against him, pinning him so he couldn't move.

"Don't do this to me, Red," he says. "What do you want from me?"

"Here," I said and tossed the package out in full view. It was wrapped in a *Sun-Times*. What did I want from him.

> He had to ask.
> He didn't know.
> Respect was what I came for,
> Not to tell him so.

·

With the package in his pocket, he felt as though anyone on the street might come up and take it away. He walked as fast as his stiff legs would carry him until he found a jitney. Then he realized he didn't know whether she was carrying her works. So he had the driver drop

him off on State where there was a pharmacy he knew. At first he panicked because there was a young man at the counter. But then he saw a
much older man doing bookkeeping at a desk behind the shelves.

"Brother Bones," Payne said.

"Who is it, son?" said the man.

The young man at the counter looked and said, "Excuse me?"

"Friend of your old man," Payne said.

"I think it's another musician, Dad."

"It's Jackson, Clifford," Payne yelled. "Jackson Payne."

The older man rose from his desk, steadied himself, and moved
forward toward the counter with one hand sliding along the shelf.

"You staying out of trouble?" he said.

"Up 'til now," said Payne.

"Go ahead, son," said the pharmacist. "You can take your break."

"Dad," said the young man.

"It's all right," the pharmacist said. "I know the man."

Payne had played with Clifford Gray's band when he was in high
school. Gray had done various clubs on weekends while studying to be
a pharmacist. He had become well known to all traveling players, even
though he usually told them no.

"What's the occasion, Jackson?" the old man said.

"The works is all," Payne said. "I got the rest."

The old man padded back among the shelves and opened a
drawer.

"I thought I read something about you getting religion," he said.
"I didn't believe it."

"It's for a woman," Payne said.

"Like the last time?" the pharmacist said.

"You still remember that?"

"The heat was on for a month after," said the pharmacist.

"Hell," said Payne. "You never would sell."

"You must've been nuts for this woman."

"It's a story."

"Well, I don't suppose you have the time," said the pharmacist.
"Here. This is a needle somebody turned in. They used it to give shots
to their dog. I'll sterilize it, if you care."

"You have anything that will help a body get off the junk?" Payne
said.

The pharmacist reached around and took something from the shelf, then tossed it to Payne. Aspirin.

"Works as well as anything else," the pharmacist said.

•

She didn't know where he got the drugs, of course. But after she had her fix and was able to sleep, she woke up to find he had gone out and bought new clothes for her. Nice clothes, she told me. Things a body could wear to church.

I'm not sure I could have brought myself to maintain her. The very thought of the needle going into her is like a lance piercing my flesh.

•

In front of the pharmacy he hailed another jitney heading back to the Loop. Just to be careful, he had the driver leave him off at Marshall Field's, where he went down to the basement then back up and out the alleyway, so he could see if anybody was following. Simply holding the heroin made him feel alive.

Back at the hotel, she must have been standing at the door, because she threw it open the moment he knocked.

"You startled me, Sweet Thing," he said.

She was in very bad shape, so he did not make any pretense of conversation. He simply sat down next to her on the bed and, with steady fingers, prepared the hypodermic.

It came back to him like one of the standards. He lit a candle he'd picked up at Field's and unscrewed the cap of the aspirin bottle, pried out the paper insert with a pocketknife and made sure there were no remnants. She turned off the overhead light as he pulled out the folded newspaper with the cellophane bag inside. Red had put a lot more paper on it than was necessary, which made the package at the center seem pathetically small. But if it didn't turn out to be dried milk or baking soda, it was enough to last until he got another idea.

He tipped some of the powder into the lid then felt the weight of it on his fingers. He had tweezers from Clifford, and he used them to steady the lid.

"OK," he said. "Let's cook."

"Be careful, Daddy," she said in a frightened voice he had never heard before.

The smell came up to him as he heated the heroin. The flame

shuddered, a spirit surrendering, a *jinn*. It was a subtle smell, hot as metal in the sun, waxen as church. He breathed it in. When the heroin was ready, he drew it up into the syringe and handed it to her. She had already prepared herself to receive it, lifting her leg. The fabric pulled back so immodestly that he had to look away. She was quick about it. He felt her lay back against the bedstead. He turned and saw the needle still inside her, now filled with her blood.

He reached down, pushed the plunger until the glass was clear again, and then withdrew the needle. She did not so much as move, though he knew that sometimes you wanted to stay connected, did not want the needle ever to come out.

"There," he said.

She let go a sigh so erotic that it made him pull back. But it meant nothing. He put his hand behind her head and lowered her to the pillow, then he covered her bare legs.

•

It only took a few days of maintaining her before he began to run short. Her habit was rich. She told me that she offered to help get the money, but he wouldn't hear of it.

"I got to go it alone, Sweet Thing," he told her. "You never know who you're gonna meet."

She had no idea who he meant.

Do you?

I have my suspicions.

Who?

I've heard Jackson had enemies.

That he did.

•

The Leopard's men discovered him once he showed himself. It would not have taken much detective work to find the club where he was sitting in.

•

We've heard a lot about Jackson Payne over the years (though he hasn't played this city since the legendary drug bust). We've heard Payne angry. We've heard him spaced. But we've never heard him the way we did Tuesday night.

Opening at the House of Jive with what amounted

to a pickup band of local talent, he was doing things so remarkable that you would have thought he had been playing with them all his life.

Gone were the cosmic, high-energy waves of sound that marked his latest recordings. Gone the restless searching. This was a man who has found something. It was beautiful, like a monument to an ancient wrong.

•

His solos had shortened. He no longer had to try path after path, attempting to exhaust the possibilities each night. Now he knew exactly where he was going. Everyone who heard these performances commented on their profound sense of order. Quinlan would have given anything to have heard just one set.

•

Payne never saw any of the old Chicago crowd in the audience. The next best thing to being invisible was for everyone else to be. Then the Leopard's men appeared.

They stopped him in the kitchen coming off the stand. He hadn't known the Leopard's reach extended into the Midwest.

"I heard this town belongs to somebody," Payne said to the pair of thick necks as the rest of the band wisely moved on.

"He lets us use it when we have to," said the uglier one.

"What does the Leopard want from me?"

The ugly one did the talking.

"He just said to say hello."

"Tell him thanks," said Payne.

"He heard about your daughter. Where is she again?"

"Around somewhere. You know how they are."

"It's a problem, what can happen to your kid."

The steamy heat of the kitchen made him weary. The saxophone grew heavy around his neck.

"We could help you cop," the uglier one said.

"Thanks," said Payne. "But I'm OK."

•

What were the Leopard's men doing, Red?
Ask them.
Do you know their names?

Forget it. Everybody's dead. Or is going to get that way.

Vera Bell thinks they did Jackson.

Then have her call the police.

•

When Quinlan got Lasheen's message to call, he immediately rang her at the office. Another woman answered and said that Lasheen didn't work there anymore.

"Where did she go?" Quinlan asked.

"I'm not allowed to give information out," the woman said.

He called Lasheen's home and got the machine. The message was new, but there was nothing unusual until the end. After the niceties, the recording paused and then said, "If this is Charles, I have received a package for you from our acquaintance in San Francisco. Give me an address to send it to."

He left his phone and room number as well as the hotel address. Then he said, "Call me if you have a chance. I think we need to talk."

•

Payne secured an advance from the club manager and approached Red Sloan, to no avail.

> You're in a different league now,
> A long way from old Red.
> I may not be too fancy,
> But I sure don't want to be dead.

So Payne went home empty-handed, and she was spooky when she realized he did not have the goods.

"You probably been eating out of my bowl," she said.

"Trust me, Sweet Thing."

"Is that what you told my mother?"

It wasn't the worst he'd ever heard from a woman he had let down.

•

The package was at the front desk the next morning when Quinlan returned from a short session with Vera Bell. Taiana had stuffed the FedEx container with a generous amount of bubble plastic to cushion the contents. When he got through it, he found several cassette boxes the color of the one-way glass on stretch limousines. The tapes inside were of the grade Quinlan used for making listening copies of his most precious records. None bore any label. He picked up one and slipped it into the portable. Then he swung his feet up onto the covers and switched the machine on.

The track cut in smack in the middle of something. The horn leaped back and forth over strange, repulsive intervals, seemingly without aim. This was very different from even the most difficult of Payne's performances. Those were raw enough. But this seemed as jagged and irregular as broken glass.

What punishment Payne inflicted on himself, taking his horn over a rebarbative section ten, twenty times until it was perfect, then moving it up a half step, then another until he had it in every key.

After three-quarters of an hour of this Quinlan switched off the tape. Even in silence the sound stayed in his head like a migraine. He picked up the telephone and dialed. It rang three times on the other end, and he expected to hear the machine kicking in. But it didn't. Five, six, seven. He held the line. Finally on the tenth she picked up the phone.

"Thank you for the tapes," he said.

"So she was able to find you."

"I made it easy," he said. "She's been avoiding me for some reason."

"It is complicated I think," said Taiana.

"I didn't know what to make of what I heard," he said. "It was Slonimsky, wasn't it."

"You didn't start with that one, did you?" she said.

"I never quite realized what it must have been like for you to have to listen," Quinlan said.

He snapped the tape out of the machine and turned it over in his fingers. It captured only an hour and a half of a session that might have gone on five. And there might have been seven of them that week alone.

"I didn't expect you to actually listen to it all," she said.

"When was it made?"

"I really don't know," she said. "In the months before he went to Chicago he was only playing the old things and new things like them. The others I sent are from that period. You'll hear one tune that is especially wrenching. Later I was told he called it 'Sweet Thing.' "

•

This must have been the sound of his Chicago performances. Quinlan could hear echoes all the way back to Payne's origins. He played some solos unaccompanied again, the way he did on *The Kensington Sessions*. When Sonny did that, it returned him to the street corner. But Payne brought to it everything he had ever known. It was like what people say happens when a man is drowning.

•

I guess I been everywhere and back again, Sweet Thing. And for a while there I thought there was nowhere else for me to go. But then I found out: What I was looking for, I had. Where I wanted to be, I was.

You know about the natural scale before they tempered it, don't you? B-flat and A-sharp aren't the same. Billie Holiday used to sing the difference and find a whole story there. Well, I think there's languages that nobody has ever spoke. And one is right here on my tongue. So please, Sweet Thing, listen to what I'm trying to say.

•

Jazz is about feelings, emotions in the moment. It comes up from the deepest self, not as memory so much as memory made new. Now Quinlan understood why Jackson had gone back to the beginning and practiced all the old songs. He had to do that in order to bring them back changed. The sound he got at the end was not a return to the life he had lived but rather the profoundest statement of who he had become.

•

He had bought baking soda to stretch the dope to get her through, but now he couldn't cut the heroin any further. As it was, it barely kept Michelle from crawling out of her skin.

"I got a man tonight," he promised. "Then you'll be fine as wine."

"I've heard that one before," she said.

"Here," he said, giving her the syringe. "Take the last of it. That'll hold you. Watch some television. I got a bottle of gin."

"That doesn't help."

"Don't you think I know that, Sweetness?" he said.

"You better know somebody," she said.

But as he looked at her getting ready to shoot up just below the fringe of her dirty slip, he knew nothing.

"I've got to go, baby," he said as the dope kicked in.

"Mama said you would."

•

On the B side, the mood was different, more angular. It reminded Quinlan of the tunes Payne had written when he was playing with Damon Reed. Except that now the spirit was repudiation. He was a preacher in the pulpit raining down judgment against the very ecstasy he summoned up.

•

When I am working on a dependency case, I can usually tell when he is in trouble. He starts getting down on himself. Or either he's the greatest ex-addict in the history of the twelve steps. Whichever way, it means he's not sure of himself anymore. And when that happens, it's only a matter of time.

The man you are interested in was known to have purchased drugs near the time of his death, is that right? But he might have been buying them solely for his addicted daughter. Does that about sum it up?

Yes.

Well, I would say that was possible, but unlikely. Is that him you are playing?

It's a practice session. He usually played with a group.

He was very accomplished, wasn't he.

He was very everything.

•

When he called, it bothered me—the way he sounded, I mean. So calm. He asked me not to call Leticia, which I wouldn't have anyway, because I know what she would have said.

We talked. He wanted to know about Sarah Evans. He told me not to come to the club that night. Afterward, I wished I had gone anyway. Not that it would have changed anything. But at least I would have seen him.

And heard him play.

And had him touch me one last time.

•

The third cassette was the most extraordinary. A deep, renewed blues element predominated. "Sweet Thing" was like some of the tunes he wrote around the time she was born. And yet it was as contemporary as anything anyone was doing today. Lilting and innocent, it was blue the way the sky is blue, without a cloud.

•

I can't really help it people come here like it's Graceland. I don't advertise my club as the last place Jackson Payne played. Look, I've known all the beautiful dead ones over the years. Bird and Lester. I had Lee Morgan and Booker Little right here on this stage. Tina Brooks. Chet. Dicky Twardzik. Hell, I knew Chet when he was still as pretty as the chicks he brought in with him. And Twardzik's pal, Serge Chaloff. Serge Jagoff I called him. So don't give me anything about what Jackson Payne did or didn't do here that night, because I couldn't have stopped any of them if I tried.

Was Payne trouble?

Not at all. As punctual as the alderman's bagman. Don't write that. The alderman is a personal friend of mine.

The fact is, I never saw Jackson take even a taste of anything. So I wonder, Why is he talking to the heavy hitters? I see them with him in the kitchen and I think, All I need is the mayor and the superintendent of police to make a royal flush.

•

At first Quinlan did not even recognize the plaintive notes on the final tape for what they were. Maybe it was because Payne played them as three equal quarter notes, steady as a metronome, the last rising to a perfect fourth. It could have been the start of one of his modal tunes. Or even a Slonimsky. But then the pattern went on, slightly syncopated, and Quinlan leaned forward, because now he knew what it was.

Day is done. The sound was everything Wardell Flowers had said it had been. Simple, unadorned. Tones held just an instant beyond themselves and then released, the force of it rising where you expected it to fall. *Gone the sun.* Genius makes everything its own, whether it is a sophisticated harmonic substitution or a tune written for a piece of valveless brass. *God is nigh.*

•

The heavies showed up every night to see him. What do you want from me? I try to stay out of people's way, OK? I try to make a place where cats can play. And if the cats play dirty, well that's their problem, not mine.

One night we were full and I had to put them at the bar. But they were good about it. They really were. Don't believe everything you see in the movies.

Whether he bought from them, I don't know. That would have come later. And not here on the premises. That's one thing I do not allow. Later a guy told me he saw Jackson walking down the street with them, but I don't know that. People see all kinds of things. It's not worth getting in a jam over, I'll tell you that much.

The Leopard's long gone.

Yeah, and so is Jackson.

The police called it an overdose.

Jackson Payne or John Doe, to them he was just another dead male Negro junkie. So they didn't ask much, and I didn't tell. Detective Sgt. Rock came by inquiring, of course. Look, sergeant, I run a clean joint here. It's a damn shame when the colored boys come in and make a mess of things, I said, so the detective would put a checkmark in the box that says, "OK guy," and then get out of my life. Which is what he did.

•

The coroner's records were dog-eared. A lot of people had apparently gone to them before Quinlan. If the deputies had given the matter a tenth as much attention as it deserved, maybe some of the mystery would have been resolved. But there was no record that a tox screen had been done for drugs, let alone a test on the charred things they had found in the room. The ash could have held arsenic or flame accelerant for all any official seemed to have cared.

•

She has condemned herself every day for having run away that night. She has looked deep inside herself. But it was just as simple as this: The hunger grew greater than the love. So she went to the street. And after she was finished, she had the presence of mind to return. But by then it was too late.

So that's the story she tells.

You should be ashamed of yourself.

Like you said, my hunger is great, too.

•

Nothing felt right. Not going up to them in the bar. Not taking them up on their offer. Not leaving with them, full of false cheer. Not waiting while they made a call or getting into their car without so much as a glance around to see if anyone was following. Not the trip south to the dingy three-flat or the scene inside with the little kids underfoot and the man with the shoulder holster.

"Go ahead," they said, "taste it."

•

Of course they killed him. You can't imagine how ruthless these people were. For them killing Jay wouldn't have been nearly enough.

But why would they have waited so long, Showon?

For a way they could get to him. Michelle finally provided it.

How did they actually do it?

Use your imagination. I'm sure they used theirs.

•

The night was hot and the bag grew warm against his thigh. He worried that his sweat would get through somehow and damage the goods. When he put his hand in his pocket, the plastic was like a sheaf of dead skin.

It had taken all the money he had, but they assured him it was worth the price. He wondered how much he should cut it so as not to get her in deeper. He would have to keep it away from her or she might hurt herself trying to get the buzz he'd been denying her. She always watched his every move when he was doing the preparations, sometimes mirroring the movements with her own hands the way you might move your lips to the words of a song.

In the elevator his hand pressed down on the package, which doubled back over his fingers. He let it loose for fear of breaking it.

At their door he knocked softly and said his name. When you get as strung out as she was, everything is frightening. You had one kind of nerves when you were carrying, another when you were without.

"I'm coming in, Sweet Thing," he whispered.

There was no sound through the heavy wood. He lifted his eye to the peephole, but it was like looking into the wrong end of a telescope. All he could tell was that the lights were on. She might be sleeping. That would be good. When you slept it was better, except for the dreaming. He took the key from his other pocket and put it into the lock.

•

So we're pretty sure he made a purchase that night?

You asking me, Dad?

Just what people said after.

They say he took too much.

They say where he got it?

You know where.

But how could he overdose? He knew this stuff as well as he knew the C-major scale.

Unless he wanted to.

Or they did it to him.

•

He looked in the bathroom, then for any kind of note. There was none.

He sat down heavily in the chair, head in hands, and began to weep.

He heard something outside the door.

He sprung up. She had come back. Probably high, but that was all right.

He opened the door wide to greet her, and there they were.

"Hello, again," the Leopard's man said. "There was one thing we forgot."

•

I don't think they would have done it with drugs, angel. Too gentle. Back here in L.A. the Leopard's guys used to like to beat people to death with baseball bats.

•

She is a good woman. You must understand that. After he died, she pulled herself together. Now she has a husband and two lovely children. Our granddaughters, Jackson's and mine. I told her she didn't need to talk to you, but I'm afraid she thinks she has some responsibility.

Michelle, come on out now.

The young woman appeared in the kitchen door where her mother had so often emerged with nervous pots of tea. She was tall and dressed for success. Jackson's features were in her, and the hardness of life had brought them out.

•

Maybe the girl did it. You ever think of that, Dad? To get the shit he had bought.

He bought it for her.

Maybe she wanted it all. Maybe she wanted his money, too. Did the coppers find either drugs or cash in the room?

Everything was pretty badly burned up.

Course if they had found it, they would have pocketed it anyway. Then cleared the case as a bum getting too happy.

Do you know something, Red?

Me? I only know the melody and the chords.

•

I can't tell you how Daddy impressed me. From the very first. You've seen him. You know what I mean.

I never did, actually, except on film.

He had a bearing. A wisdom that you couldn't penetrate, that could stand up to anything. I guess I tested that.

It wasn't the only test.

I know all about the life he led.

When you first met him, he had hit a difficult period. He felt as though his music had come to nothing. He didn't know how to revive it. With you things started happening for him again.

All I saw was strength. And the incredible energy he invested in his performances. It was beyond anything I had dreamed.

But you left him to go to Chicago with Damon Reed.

Yes, I did. Mine was the opposite of wisdom. And then I was alone.

But he found me again somehow. All of a sudden he just appeared on the street and said to me, "This mess is over. You're coming with me."

Were you with someone?

No. Just a man.

I mean did you have somebody behind you?

I promised myself a long time ago that I wouldn't implicate any-one else, even Damon. The problem and the responsibility were mine.

Was it someone you knew from before?

Daddy swept me off the street, even though I struggled against him. He cleaned me up, fed me, got me looking decent again. He even went out and bought me drugs. But he would not let me have as much as I wanted.

Wasn't he afraid he would lose you again?

He was looking for the smallest dose that would hold me.

But you demanded more.

Sometimes I made such a fuss it's a wonder the hotel didn't throw us both out on the street.

How did he react?

He'd just fall silent. I'd be going on and on and then I'd realize that it was like screaming at a stone.

That's the way he was, all right, said Vera. He could turn off so. But I think usually it was music. That's the place he went.

He never lectured me, never did anything but build me up. But I knew he had gotten himself off the habit. So he had to be thinking, What's wrong with her that she can't?

He didn't use while you were together.

My God, no.

But he always kept it with him.

To keep it away from me.

Maybe so he could have a little without you knowing.

Never.

How can you be sure?

Because it would have been so much easier for me if he had. And I can't help thinking how he was all right when I met him and then he was dead.

You didn't do that, Sweet Thing, said Vera.

And I'm trying to figure out who did.

I was scared to death of coming off the needle. I knew that was where he was trying to head me.

Why didn't you just leave him?

He was taking care of me. I always needed somebody to do that.

But you couldn't have kept it going indefinitely. You knew something was going to have to change.

I was only thinking from shot to shot. And I didn't trust him nearly enough.

You barely knew him, Sweet Thing, Vera said.

I'm not as bad about it as I used to be, but I have to be honest. It wasn't Daddy who walked out on me. No, Mama, really. I have thought about it a lot. I was sure he would come back empty-handed. To trick me into going cold turkey. So I dug out my old clothes and got myself up as cheap as I could. Then I called a man I used to know. And when Daddy came back and did not find me there, it happened.

The question is how and why.

•

It was not really a surprise to him that she was gone. The surprise was that she had stayed as long as she had.

Now she was out on the street, vulnerable to whatever anybody had in mind for him. If he had been able to find her, the Leopard's men could, too. And would. Just as Damon Reed did.

The new clothes he had gotten her were all still in the closet. Only the awful outfit she had been wearing when he found her was missing.

His mind kept coming back to what she was probably doing at that moment, and with whom. He lay down on the bed and tried to close his eyes, but that only turned him over to the clamor of the dark. His thoughts did not come to him in words. It was more like the howling harmonic buzz of the reed or the crash of waves. Fear was only one of the sounds, but it was the strongest. Fear for what would become of her. Fear of what he had in his pocket. The thought of it igniting his veins. Giving shape to a new thought, how to defeat the drug with the drug.

He found himself sweating in the cool, muggy air. As he struggled, he rolled from side to side to find some position to settle in, but of course he knew there was no respite. One. Two. One two three four. The reed in his mind threw off a high, thrashing frenzy of notes, but they did not alleviate the feeling, did not even express it whole.

Nothing had ever brought him transcendence. Not all the practice. Not family. Not love, which he always managed to damage. Not religion. Not drugs. And the new sound he had been working on, even its promise now seemed doomed. Whenever he thought he had found peace, it turned out to be like every other melody he'd ever made. Pretty soon it was like copying off Rev. Corn's records, and he needed to destroy it and find something true.

But he had never lied to Michelle. She was the one thing he had kept himself pure for. And now she was back on the street. Because she was not ready to free herself. There was only one line left for him to play.

But would the devil *jinns* be waiting? He shuddered at the thought that he might receive what he deserved. Would he see Jay?

He threw himself to his other shoulder to try to spin away from Jay's face, the voice hissing through the reed. Tonight, during his solo on "Sweet Thing," he had found himself wandering into the vernacular he had used in the days he spent with the boy, the awful fusion of senti-mentality and fire.

Fusion. Things coming together. Authenticity and deceit. Life and death. Final things. He lit a candle. The *jinn* whispered, "Go ahead." Because everything was one in the end.

This was the only way. Yield. Submit to the glowing element. Frighten her awake. Be the light. He would be the example that would save her. He would give the Leopard the vengeance he wanted, so his men would not have to do it through her. He could not reverse the fact that he had not been there for her all along. But at least for once he could do something to protect a child of his.

He pulled himself upright, like a man in a hospice. The air from the vent blew the sweat cold on his back, and he shivered. There was only one thing that would surely warm him like the joy of music or the surging pulse of love. It always did.

•

No. No. He did not want the high. You must not believe that.

It is your story. I just want to understand.

He hated what he had to do. He was making an example of him-self for me. And to be so all alone, to find the courage. I'm sure that was why they found his horn next to him. It helped him through.

•

He took out his saxophone and put it together. The reed was still damp, and he tried it for a note or two just to make sure it was playable, though he did not intend to play. Then he went to the bathroom and checked his hiding place behind the pipes. She had not found the syringe. Providence.

He pulled the limp bag from his pocket and weighed it in his hand. They had given him much more than enough to render a lethal dose. He found the blackened spoon in his horn case and took it out. With the syringe, he drew water from the glass, then lit the candle, slipped off his belt, tied off his arm, and laid the horn gently lengthwise against the pillow next to him. In the spoon he mixed a large quantity of the heroin with water, and the dust magically transformed itself into elixir. He could taste the aroma of it.

He pulled the liquid into the barrel of the syringe. Then he took the rest of the dust back into the bathroom and tilted it into the toilet. He

flushed it as it dissolved then ran water into the bag to make sure there
was absolutely none left in case she returned.

Back on the bed he lifted the syringe upright with both hands,
like a preacher, and pressed the rubber bulb expertly until it expelled a
single drop. It was easy to find a vein. Time had healed him, at least to
the depth of vessel and bone.

When the needle touched the flesh above his pulse, he paused,
leaned back next to his horn, and only then broke the skin and sent the
needle home. As he did, he heard something, a sound beyond the
waves, a new sound that spoke to him like the voice of God.

·

No.
The effect would have been the effect. It is chemical.
He was stronger than the chemical. What he did, he hated. It was
all for me.

·

His arm fell sideways as the heroin coursed through him. His
hand struck the candle next to the bed, which tipped and fell onto the
rumpled sheet. He did not notice because by now he was hearing whatever it is that one can never come back to express. The flame slipped
gently along a seam then spread downward and out. Gold and yellow.
And as blue as a song. The flame leaped up and touched his sleeve. It
flickered and flashed. The *jinns* swayed above him and winked and
hissed.

2.

On the videotape, the band was playing very tight. But the drummer
that night was a stand-in, and if you watch very closely you can see
Jackson throw him a look.

Quinlan aimed his remote at the VCR and rewound the tape a few
seconds so he could catch the gesture again. When he froze it on the

screen, it was priceless. If he could capture the frame with enough reso-
lution, he could use the image as the cover of his book. Horn in his
mouth, eyes swung left, Jackson flared as bright as a match. But it was
not just the passion. There were hundreds of photos of Payne that
showed that. What made this image unique was that he had someone
else in his gaze. And on the drummer's face was a look that you could
have found on any disciple in the audience, on any woman with ideas,
on Quinlan too as he watched.

"Pretty intense," the woman said. "You're going to have to tell
me more about him."

Quinlan touched her hand where it had found his knee, and it was
remarkably soft for something that looked as perfect as porcelain.

"Don't get me started," he said.

He had met her at a party for new faculty. She was not in the
music school. And it flattered him that she seemed to want to make conversation easy for him, young as she was. She could have talked spe-
cialties with any tenured man in the room.

"I'm in no hurry," she said. "Unless you are."

Though she came out of a different discipline, that simply meant
another kind of hermeneutics. They talked about his book. Her mono-
graph on Berryman, who was a drunk. She had different theories
about that than he did, but that was what made for exciting, scholarly
intercourse.

•

I think it was Stravinsky who said, "Art dies of freedom and
thrives on constraint." Try to keep that in mind, Richard. Your book
threatens to become diffuse. I had something of the same problem with
my Mahler. All those chaste lovers. The sister. Then that vixen Alma.
What a piece of creation she was. But eventually I brought it back to the
music. Yes. Make the life serve the music and you will have a book with
form. Music is never as messy as people are.

•

Talk to my lawyer. You best be aware, I am going to protect my
family's rights.

I received his letter, Leticia. That's why I called.

I have nothing to say.

I talked to Charnette. Did she tell you?

She knows how I feel.

I'm trying to be sensitive to everyone's needs and still be true to the facts.

Here's a fact for you. It is hard to be a black man in this world today.

It would have been hard to be the kind of man Jackson was under any conditions.

What do you mean "the kind"?

If I'd said black, you and I would have been saying the very same thing.

No, we wouldn't.

•

You have probably been expecting this letter for a long time. I have hesitated to write it. I cannot tell you how deep my gratitude runs for all you have done to make my work possible. I was especially moved by the tapes you sent. They have proven invaluable and have revealed things I could have known in no other way.

I believe anybody who heard this music would under-stand the true passion of Jackson's final days the way you and I do. In their own way, these sessions show a deeper spirituality than any of the more overt works.

I want to try to persuade you to let these recordings be brought out. I know you may think it a betrayal for me even to be asking. But I pray that you hear me out. I would not take this course if I did not think it was in your best interest and the best interest of Jackson's memory.

I would be glad to help facilitate the release. I could place the recordings in skilled and trusted hands. I would, of course, accept nothing for this except the satisfaction of having advanced the understanding of this great man's legacy.

May I suggest that I arrange a time to return to San Francisco at your convenience so we could discuss my pro-posal? I will telephone you within the week.

In the meantime, you might want to be thinking of the two principal options. I know of several excellent archival companies that do exquisite work with treasures such as these. On the other hand, any of the larger firms would also leap at the chance, which would bring more exposure and consequently more value to you and your son. Either way I am sure the work could be accomplished relatively expeditiously. It could even be timed to coincide with publication, if you agreed. Of course, I will take my every cue from you.

By the way, Lasheen sends her regards. She has left her former employer and gone off on her own. She says our project gave her the confidence. Rest assured that she continues to perform miracles in discovering men's secrets. Until we talk, I remain

> Yours truly,
> Charles

•

Your book ever come out? I been asking and asking, but the VA nurses don't know shit. I thought maybe I missed it. And I been thinking about Jackson a lot since they told me I got a spot on my lung.

What come to me is maybe it took everything that happened to make Jackson as good as he was. But then it gone and killed him.

Put this in your book, and it'll be my gravestone words. Wardell Flowers, he was part of what made Jackson Payne. And when I go, I want them to play me "Taps" on the tenor horn.

•

"I think something is happening, Charles."
"I'm too old for you."
"Do you hear me complaining?"
"Maybe it's just because I haven't been very successful."
"Everyone has had a first marriage."
"Afterward either."
"Nobody now?"
"Not really. It hasn't worked out."
"To my good fortune."
"You're pretty aggressive, aren't you."
"The very Wife of Bath."

•

When I heard there was a substantial unreleased cache of Jackson Payne material, I did not dare to imagine that it could be as important as the Dean Benedetti recordings of Charlie Parker, but it turns out that

this is ten times more significant. These final examples of Jackson
Payne at last complete him. There may be those who regret that in the
end Payne pulled back off the limbs to reexamine the roots. But this
was an authentic artistic decision, and it was as valid as any other risk
he had taken.

•

What can you say about genius? He had it to the very end. Are
you looking for a title? I'd call it "The Best of Jackson Payne."

•

Washington has been good. I'm working with a group of talented
youngsters at Howard. They call me professor, like the piano player in a
cathouse. The real news, though, is Vera. Isn't she something? Thank
you so very much for leading me to her. You know me. I never would
have lifted a finger.

•

"You've got somebody else, haven't you."
"What are you talking about?"
"The white girl."
"It's just somebody from the university."
"She stays pretty late for just somebody."
"Have you been following me?"
"It wasn't going to work anyway, honey. Too much between us,
and not enough."

•

I don't know what to tell you, man. I got the recording you sent,
and when I heard "Taps" I knew I could die happy, 'cause he was
playin' it for me.

•

I wasn't sure I'd be able to find you again, Junior.
Guess we're just two lucky cats.
*There are a few loose ends. About the last time he went back to
Chicago.*
What do I know about that?
They say you were there.
Who does?
People who know.
They don't know shit.
Did you know she was there, too?

I'm lost. Who we talking about now?

Michelle. Did you find her for him?

Who says that?

One black hooker in a big city. And it only took him a couple of days.

Sometimes a man can help another man get what he wants.

Were you her pimp?

Get out of here, man, talking shit like that.

You've got nothing to lose.

You gone protect me, music man?

She came to you after Damon threw her out, didn't she.

What did she tell you?

She wouldn't talk about anybody but Jackson.

Don't bullshit me. Once a whore, always a whore.

Here's how I'm going to write it. Damon broke her spirits, then you stepped in to make use of her body. She was hooked, and you were connected. You used her to set Jackson up.

He set himself up. I knew he would. If he got near the shit again, I knew he couldn't pass it by.

You were talking to the Leopard's men.

I'm going to tell you about that? Come on. You don't know any of this shit.

It's like he whispered in my ear, Junior. Listen to him, and he'll tell you everything you need to know.

You ain't the first cat thought Jackson was talking straight to him on the horn. Some of them was black and should've known. But he was good. Sometimes the shit he did even fooled himself.

So you go tell all the white folks about this poor black boy who had more to say than he could handle. Make them feel so bad about him they'll feel better about themselves. Put me in there, too. Maybe it'll get me a gig.

But you never knew Jackson and never could. 'Cause he's the only one who could have told you. And that sweet never blew the truth once in his whole damned life.

ACKNOWLEDGMENTS

A number of people have helped me with this novel. Composer and bandleader William Russo gave me excellent technical advice, as did jazz critics Doug Ramsey and Larry Kart. Peter Walker, a colleague and skilled pianist, also worked with me on the musical elements. Howard Reich, Fred Hunter, and Ruthellyn Musil were also kind enough to look at the manuscript.

I want to thank Victoria Wilson of Alfred A. Knopf for her smart, persistent editing. As a former editor, I appreciate her skills immensely. Special thanks go to Gail Hochman, my literary agent, for all her encouragement and wise advice and for having confidence in my work.

And to my family—Alyce, Tim, and Kate—I owe more than gratitude. They remain the heart of everything.

ABOUT THE AUTHOR

Correspondent, lawyer, music critic, and editor,
Jack Fuller served as a combat correspondent for
the Vietnam bureau of Stars and Stripes *and wrote*
reviews of jazz for The Chicago Tribune. *His books*
include News Values: Ideas for an Information Age,
and six novels: Our Fathers' Shadows, Mass, Legend's End, Convergence, Fragments, *and* The Best
of Jackson Payne. *Winner of a Pulitzer Prize for ed-*
itorial writing, he is currently president of Tribune
Publishing.

Phoenix Fiction titles from Chicago

Ivo Andrić: *The Bridge on the Drina*
Jurek Becker: *Bronstein's Children*
Thomas Bernhard: *Concrete, Correction, Extinction, Gargoyles, The Lime Works, The Loser, Old Masters, Wittgenstein's Nephew, Woodcutters, Yes*
Arthur A. Cohen: *Acts of Theft, A Hero in His Time, In the Days of Simon Stern*
Jean Dutourd: *A Dog's Head*
Wayne Fields: *The Past Leads a Life of Its Own*
Bruce Jay Friedman: *A Mother's Kisses*
Jack Fuller: *Convergence, Fragments, The Best of Jackson Payne*
Randall Jarrell: *Pictures from an Institution*
Margaret Laurence: *A Bird in the House, The Diviners, The Fire-Dwellers, A Jest of God, The Stone Angel*
André Malraux: *The Conquerors, The Walnut Tree of Altenberg*
Dalene Matthee: *Fiela's Child*
R. K. Narayan: *The Bachelor of Arts, The Dark Room, The English Teacher, The Financial Expert, Mr. Sampath—The Printer of Malgudi, Swami and Friends, Waiting for Mahatma*
Morris Philipson: *A Man in Charge, Secret Understandings, Somebody Else's Life, The Wallpaper Fox*
Anthony Powell: *A Dance to the Music of Time* (in four *Movements* with three novels in each volume)
Peter Schneider: *Couplings, The Wall Jumper*
Paul Scott: *The Raj Quartet* (in four volumes: *The Jewel in the Crown, The Day of the Scorpion, The Tower of Silence, A Division of the Spoils*), *Staying On*
Irwin Shaw: *Short Stories: Five Decades, The Young Lions*
George Steiner: *The Portage of San Cristóbal of A. H.*
Richard Stern: *A Father's Words, Golk*
Stephen Vizinczey: *An Innocent Millionaire, In Praise of Older Women*
Anthony Winkler: *The Painted Canoe*
Christa Wolf: Accident: *A Day's News*
Marguerite Yourcenar: *A Coin in Nine Hands, Fires, Two Lives and a Dream*